BANG
BANG
TALES

For my wife

ISBN: 9781798249291

Editor: Mark Burstein
Cover and interior design: Iain R. Morris

The stories, names, characters, and incidents portrayed in this work are fictitious.

Lots of writers dream of publishing a novel: I'd like to thank the team at Cameron + Company for turning the dream into a reality. Special thanks goes to my editor, Mark Burstein, who was enthusiastic for this most unorthodox project. A good editor is the unseen hand that fortifies a manuscript and creates an illusion so that the author appears far better on the printed page than they really are. My thanks go to Mark and his unparalleled abilities: The world need never know that I can't spell and that all my best ideas are borrowed from William Shakespeare.

I also want to thank Iain R. Morris, my art director, who designed and laid out the book and also created the unique graphic for the cover. I asked him for a distinctive image: something simple but aesthetically pleasing that would resonate visually and reproduce well. He gave me the smoking finger. I told him that regarding it was like meeting my wife for the first time: That's it—I can stop looking now.

I also want to thank both these fine gentlemen for their commitment to this book, especially as neither have a background in shooting or blood sports. As a writer, we work in solitary confinement, creating for years in a vacuum. We're never even really sure we've got anything until we finally show it. The fact that these two old pros shared a conviction in the manuscript really bolstered my confidence.

Finally, I'd like to thank Chris Gruener, publisher of Cameron + Company, for taking this project seriously and then deploying such exceptional talent to the cause.

BANG BANG

Clark Stoneridge

TALES

3 novellas

CONTENTS

I
THE HAS-BEEN

Pete Geiger sat up in bed, swung his feet on to the painted concrete floor and turned off the alarm: seven-thirty. He put the coffee on to brew on the old-fashioned hotplate and the coil hummed a glowing orange. He ran his hands through his full head of salt-and-pepper hair and surveyed the damage: four doubles. *That's normal*, he thought. Everyone has two or three on a Friday night. Four was fine. He was fine. He screwed the cap back on the bottle of Jack Daniel's and marked the level with a grease pencil.

He returned the bottle to the closet shelf and removed six shotguns in soft cases, laying them on the bed. Pete pulled each one out and examined it. Six guns, none of which he owned— not much profit in that. They were all consignments, and his cut would depend on the price he was able to fetch. The 1100 and Beretta 391 were worth next to nothing. The 101 was okay. The K-32 was a less desirable 28-inch, 4-barrel set, but it was clean. Perazzi was the gun to have at the club and even this early clapped-out Ithaca gun might find a buyer.

The Midas might be his salvation. A good Belgian Midas Grade was valuable, and this was a good one: thirty-inch barrels, ventilated narrow rib, square knob, long tang, fixed choke at Modified and Full. Engraving was by Andre Watrin—14⅝ inches to a rock-hard, Pachmayr pad. He fingered the relief engraving and gold inlays, and mounted on the full-length mirror in the corner. Good dimensions. He dry-fired the trigger, gently thumped the butt pad on the floor to reset the second and then dry-fired it. He lowered the gun and regarded himself in the mirror. His pot belly protruded grotesquely from his boxer shorts. *To the right person this was a $10,000 shotgun*, he thought as he slapped his midriff. It was just a question of finding the right person.

It didn't matter how he added it up, he still wouldn't be in the clear even if he sold every gun. He pulled a battered metal airline case from under the bed, laid it on the dresser and opened it. Gold stitching against a blue velvet background inside the case read PETE GEIGER, 1994 WORLD CHAMPION OLYMPIC TRENCH, 1996 OLYMPIC INDIVIDUAL SILVER MEDALIST, ATLANTA. He contemplated the object at hand, a Beretta SO-4 bunker-trap gun, and made up his mind.

He navigated his way out of his room and through the men's locker room to the workshop. A full set of golf clubs waiting to be regripped lay beside the tennis racquet stringer. Pete laid the opened gun with its receiver on its side on the workbench and backed the screw out of the pistol grip with an electric drill. The coin bounced off the concrete floor with a hollow, metallic clank, and he flat-footed it in his bare feet to keep it from getting away. *This was all that remained*, he thought, picking it up: the only constant throughout his shooting career. It had been mounted to every competition gun he'd ever shot. Back when Pete was a child, the Indian-head nickel had been plugged by a .22 round from a long-forgotten showman at a now defunct gun club that overlooked the Sound's craggy shores. A newspaper photo at the time showed Pete holding the gift while the showman shook his hand. Later, Pete re-flattened the coin with a hammer and drilled out the center to accept a setscrew. This plugged nickel was all he had left, all he had to show for a life lived badly: a touchstone reminder of who he'd once been—now a worthless souvenir to anyone but him.

He drove his decrepit four-door Volkswagen Rabbit along the golf cart path in direct violation of Little Kill Country Club policy. This was by far the most direct route from the men's locker room to the gun clubhouse and the ground was frozen solid, so there was no chance of turf damage. Pete also didn't want to drive past the main entrance, where an early-rising member might see him and want to talk.

Lou was smoking a cigarette and reading the *Post* in his idling car when he arrived. "Luigi, *paisan!*" Pete called lamely, thumping the roof of the car twice. Lou was a stout, big-barreled little man of forty-five, who had a square head and a dark shaggy mane of hair that he'd been cutting himself for the last ten years using an attachment on the end of his vacuum cleaner. Lou was the grill-man at a local steakhouse. He got out of the car and crushed out his smoke.

"Jets got it all this year," he said, grabbing two guns out of the trunk of Pete's car.

"Sure, Lou."

"Defense, offense: that new quarterback . . ."

Pete unlocked the clubhouse door. "Want to start the fire?"

Slowly the log cabin gun clubhouse came to life. The fieldstone fireplace warmed the room, and a pewter coffee service and a platter of donuts and bagels were sent up from the main dining room. Pete tidied the gun-cleaning table and looked up at the plaques. Every championship at trap, skeet, sub-gauge, five-stand, the Member-Member, and especially the Member-Guest were all painted in gold leaf on these varnished wood plaques that dated back to 1946. Pete turned to his own name posted for the 1985 Member-Guest. He was a senior in high school at the time and he had accepted the invitation only two days before the event when the member an old friend of Pete's father, discovered his guest had to withdraw for sudden, and ultimately fatal, health reasons. It was the biggest weekend of Pete's life up to that point. A prestigious championship at the most exclusive country club in the area, combined with the gentlemen's Calcutta, also made it by far the biggest payday of his burgeoning shooting career. Afterwards, he always thought that that was the weekend that he ceased to be an amateur.

Little Kill is known primarily for golf. Like all good area clubs, it boasts a stately clubhouse—whitewashed brick Federal. The food and drink are first rate, as well as the comprehensive selection of court games, which include the only regulation royal court tennis in the County. The Little Kill Creek bisects the golf course, and can flow a muddy trickle or a raging torrent depending on the season.

The club is a haven of wealth and privilege, a place where nice people from good backgrounds mix and mingle. It is a place where a shallow, spoiled princess can wed her dimwitted, handsome prince and marry their fortunes together.

The gun club at Little Kill has always operated in the gray area of the law. In a community that doesn't permit the discharge of a firearm within town limits, this gun club was quietly grandfathered. Every few years, a homeowner neighboring club property commences legal action to have the gun club cease operations. Invariably the lawsuits go nowhere, and the shotgun games continue to be played over the same hallowed grounds.

The shooting facilities are simple but exceptional for a country club. Two skeet fields are the original footprint. The low-house on field one doubles as the high-house on two. The three blockhouses are in excellent repair and state-of-the-art traps are rebuilt every third year. Field one also hosts a sixteen-yard-trap. Field two uses the stark drop-off beyond skeet station eight to great effect by incorporating an additional eight traps, allowing it to serve as a five-stand. Trap field two is unique in that it has cement handicap markers back to the twenty-seven-yard line and the trap house rises from a valley floor, making it seem like the block house hovers in space. This trap can also operate on fast-wobble, meaning the hard-right and left angles are more extreme than on conventional trap, and the variation in height and added target speed makes a round of wobble trap one of the club's most challenging games. Trap field two is also home to the club's second five-stand, and is universally regarded as the longer and more difficult of the two.

At nine-thirty sharp the gun clubhouse door opened and the club shotgun chairman, Douglas McCashin, walked in—half an hour early as usual. He was surly and wiry and hard. He stood ramrod straight, had angry gray eyes and wore an ancient shooting vest with USMA, WEST POINT, NY embroidered across the back. He also wore a wool Little Kill club cap over his flattop crew cut and Hy-Wyd glasses with blinders at the temples.

"I'll win the Member-Guest with this gun," he said matter-of-factly, and held out his autoloader like a soldier at *present-arms*, waiting for Pete's inspection. Pete took the gun. "That limey just turned me some offset chokes. Now I can change my point of impact by rechoking: I don't have to switch guns for trap!"

The autoloader had a synthetic thumbhole stock with an adjustable comb cheek piece made of carbon fiber mounted to titanium hardware. The barrel sported a custom, extra-high rib that stood a good two inches above the barrel. The action bolt was jeweled alloy. The trigger group was heavily customized, and its safety had been removed. "Everyone will be shooting one of these in a couple of years," McCashin added smugly.

Pete mounted the gun, but the adjustable Morgan pad had so much twist it was very awkward. He dry-fired the trigger. "That trigger's not right," he said.

"The hell it is—I ground it myself," McCashin snorted.

"Can't be more than two pounds. It's too light. You're going to maim someone with that."

McCashin became belligerent. "That trigger's set at exactly two-and-a-half pounds—check it yourself if you don't believe me!"

Pete put the trigger-pull scale on the gun and pulled the spring until the hammer dropped. The meter read two-and-a-half pounds exactly. "There's a reason why no reputable gunsmith will set a trigger lighter than three pounds, especially on an autoloader. When the trigger falls out of tune, the risk is too great of the gun misfiring when you close the bolt."

"That's just a lot of insurance-liability pants-wetting. I take this gun to pieces every time I shoot it. It won't misfire on me—because I'll make the adjustment before it does."

"Alright, Mr. McCashin. The first time that gun misfires, you're giving the trigger group to me and starting over from scratch," Pete demanded.

"Think you're dealing with a six-year-old, Geiger? Going to take my toy away?! Fine: First misfire and it's yours." Pete handed the gun back to a red-faced McCashin, who muttered, "World Champion—World Champion Jackass!"

Of all the members at Little Kill, Douglas McCashin was Pete's worst nightmare. Truthfully, he was nearly everyone's worst nightmare. He was a West Point teetotaler who'd served multiple tours on active duty in Vietnam. He'd led men in combat and been good at it. The only reason he ever left the service was that the war was winding down and he wasn't interested in a peacetime military. After returning stateside, he made a six-month study of how to make a fortune and concluded auto sales would get him what he wanted fastest. He went to work selling used cars—jalopies—and perfected the *hard sell*. After a year, he sold new vehicles, and after six months of that, he knew he was ready to make his big move.

In the early 1970s, the Japanese were a laughingstock in the U.S. car market. They specialized in reliable, inexpensive, efficient cars and mini-trucks, but gas was cheap and Americans wanted to drive the grandest status symbols their wallets would allow. Some of the dealer bias was profit driven—little cars mean slim margins, but much of it was pure discrimination. There were still a lot of WWII vets walking around who remembered the bloody Asian campaigns like they were yesterday, and they'd be damned if they'd export one red cent back into the pockets of the enemy.

Douglas McCashin had been a child during WWII and certainly hated the Japanese, but he knew a good product when he saw one. He'd experienced the phenomenon of the Volkswagen Beetle up close by selling them and that car, with all its quirks and personality, practically sold itself. After just one sit-down, the executives of the Japanese motorcycle-cum-car manufacturer had a new regional dealer. Within eighteen months, the first gasoline embargo paralyzed the nation, and suddenly everyone wanted a fuel-efficient car. Douglas McCashin had a sales lot full of the best small cars on the planet. He was a millionaire by his thirty-fifth birthday and a member of the Little Kill Country Club by his thirty-sixth.

Through the gun clubhouse's bay window, Pete could see

McCashin setting up at the patterning plate. It was obvious he was antsy and wanted to get started. Pete stepped out onto the porch. "Ten o'clock and not a minute sooner, Mr. McCashin," he called out.

McCashin glared up at the Pete, the veins in his neck bulging in anger. He pointed to the watch on his wrist. "That's an atomic watch! If your clock says I'm early, it's wrong."

"Ten o'clock!" Pete reiterated before he stepped back inside and standing there, staring out the bay window, was McCashin's son-in-law, Alexander Vanderstein. Blond and balding, doughy, with fair skin and baby-blue eyes, what most distinguished Alex Vanderstein at Little Kill was that he was one of only five Jewish members in the club; the other four were all his immediate family. Alex was married to McCashin's daughter, Candy.

"He seems in fine form this morning," Alex lamented. Pete rolled his eyes. "Can I interest you in a little five-stand, Mr. Vanderstein? I could probably sneak you out before he even notices."

"I think it'll be easier on all of us if I just shoot with him," came the reply.

There is a precept in certain circles that when a woman "marries up," she's simply negotiated the shrewdest deal possible for a chance at the good life. When a man is perceived to have done the same, there is a corner of society in which he will be roundly despised for the rest of his life. Maybe no one ever mentions it directly, but his shame is always there, hovering about him like a spectral apparition and languishing on the tip of every tongue, like a mouthful of pennies waiting to be spit out.

The name Vanderstein brought to mind nobility, privilege and public service. Relatives have included a secretary of state, a Supreme Court justice and the current ambassador to Belgium. Alex was a thirty-four-year-old, Jewish blue-blood from a legendary banking family that had barely made it out of Austria in 1935. His parents were in the process of depleting the last dregs of an already diluted fortune. Someday Alex would inherit what remained, but his lifestyle of signing his father's initials to a country-club chit as a mere afterthought ended unceremoniously the day he finally passed the state bar. Mom and Dad took up residence in Bermuda, and Little Kill was suddenly off-limits. For the first time in his life he was expected to live on what he earned. Sure, there was a modest trust income, but not nearly enough to fill the shortfall of a meager assistant district attorney's salary. What he needed was an alternative source of income, and he found it in Candy McCashin.

Old names tend to be attracted symbiotically to new money, especially when the old name happens to be broke. Any future for Alex in government or politics would require resources. Candice "Candy" McCashin Vanderstein was thirty, beautiful, bright, athletic, wild, spoiled and had a history of substance abuse that predated junior high school. She'd already been married once when Alex took up with her. Candy was dark-haired, with olive skin, brown eyes, a pert bosom and an ass that had literally caused a fatal midtown traffic accident. She rode two horses every morning, drove her convertible like a maniac, smoked Dunhill Reds which she contemptuously ripped the filters off, never wore panties and enjoyed having sex—frequently. She had an edginess to her and exuded the vibe that she'd screw you at the drop of a hat if she had the mind to. Alex met her fresh off a stint in rehab; she was still going by her most recent married name. By the time he figured out she was Douglas McCashin's daughter, the deed had been done—in the men's locker room sauna, in the back of the car, on the ninth fairway and in the swimming pool. Sobriety made her sexually insatiable, and the word around the club that summer was Alex Vanderstein had bitten off more than he could chew.

Marriage to Candy was a package deal: to keep her living in the style to which she'd grown accustomed and fulfill his newfound financial obligations, Alex would leave the law and sell cars for Douglas. McCashin would show him the ropes and, in time, the quiet introspective young man was expected to develop into a dynamic salesman.

"I want to show you this," Pete said to Alex, pulling the SO-4 out of its gun sleeve. "It's handmade. Thirty-inch, thin-wall chokes and perfect triggers."

Alex picked up the gun and awkwardly mounted it like he was holding a shoulder-fired missile. "It's a true side-lock." Alex nodded obliviously. "I can give you a deal on it."

Alex brought the gun down off his shoulder. "But it's not . . . Tonto?" he asked.

"No. Tonto's got the coin screwed to the grip, and that's one gun I'll never sell. No sir. This was just a gun I picked up for my wife."

"Really, you'd think a Russian shooter would have shot something . . . uh, Soviet?"

"She did for years, but never liked them. As soon as that wall came down, they all switched. They'd been importing Western guns in the white and stamping them EAST GERMANY for years anyway.

"I had my heart set on a Perazzi," Alex said, regarding the gun's modest engraving.

"Good gun—no doubt. But every rack in the County is full of them. Everyone's different of course, but I never wanted to shoot the same thing as everybody else. I always wanted to be different."

Douglas McCashin came into the gun clubhouse. "Trying to skin my son-in-law, Geiger?" he demanded.

"Pete's just showing me a gun, Mr. McCashin," Alex replied.

"You just watch yourself, Vanderstein. You're dealing with an operator here and, frankly, you don't have the sense not to come up with four retreads and a cracked block."

Pete turned wryly to McCashin. "I'm paid to take abuse, Mr. McCashin—that comes with the job—but I'd appreciate it if you wouldn't call me a crook to my face."

"Alright then," McCashin added. "I'll call you a quitter—suits you even better!"

"Think of your job," Alex said to Pete under his breath. "He's really not worth it."

"I could chastise you all day about winners and losers, Geiger. I'm a winner—have been all my life and I'll go to the grave as one. But you, you're not even a loser: You're a quitter, and a quitter is the most useless thing on God's green earth. Wouldn't have them in combat with me—undermine a unit's ability to wage war. Christ, Geiger, you could still be winning Olympic medals. You could probably own that FITASC championship if you cared to, but instead you're a caddie: Seven months out of the year you're a glorified caddie. You wipe down my clubs and scrape the goose shit out of my spikes—a grown man doing a job every high school kid outgrows. It's just a damned waste!" McCashin reached for his wallet, pulled out a wad of hundred-dollar notes and slammed them on the table with a flatted palm. "You broke? That's twenty-five hundred! Instead of fleecing my idiot son-in-law, that's yours if you can beat me. One round of trap—lose and you don't owe me a thing."

Pete sized up the proposition. "We're all aware that gambling on club grounds is strictly prohibited?" he reminded them. "Your membership privileges could be suspended and I could be discharged."

"The bridge tournament, the golf championship, hell, the beach club regatta—they all gamble. And let's not forget the Calcutta auction I'm hosting next weekend. I don't think there's a member in the whole club who'll give our little wager a second thought," McCashin said, handing the wad of bills to Alex. "Officer of the court: flunked the damned bar exam three times! You're not much, Alex, but I suppose you're honest enough."

Pete held out his hand and all three men sealed the deal with handshakes. "This gun is temporarily off the market, Mr. Vanderstein," Pete said as he picked the SO-4 up off the table. Pete stood on a chair in the corner of the room and with an unsteady hand, reached up to the rafter beam for the closet key. He unlocked the padlock and there, neatly arranged, were the tools of his trade: vests, Hy-Wyd glasses, hats, and four flats of the 24-gram bunker-trap loads that he'd made his name with. Pete shook some talc out of the bottle and rubbed it onto his right cheek.

Word quickly spread throughout the club about the wager. Douglas McCashin was disliked widely enough that people came up from the bowling alley, the paddle tennis and racquet-ball courts—even the barflies from the men's grill stood by, Bloody Mary's in hand, waiting to see Douglas McCashin finally get his comeuppance.

Pete turned to Lou. "Mind if I flambé?"

Lou clearly looked distressed. "Okay if he test-fires, Mr. McCashin?"

"It won't help," McCashin sneered, "but sure."

Pete very deliberately mounted the gun, his cheek coming to rest on the Monte Carlo stock. He'd gained a lot of weight since he had last shot. He couldn't even get his shooting vest zipped around his rotund belly, and his normal comb contact pressure was giving him a high sight picture. He pressed his cheek down deeply, and the front and mid-rib sight beads finally came into alignment. It wasn't a perfect fit anymore, but for one round of sixteen-yard-trap, it would do. He loaded two shells and test fired the gundownrange.

McCashin started from station two, Pete from four. The short squad made difficult work of the round, but as this was by any definition an illegal activity according to the club charter, asking other members to assist had been dismissed as unwise. Pete smoked the first target with the .0025 thin-wall that had been his go-to choke back in his FITASC shooting days. They were both straight for the first station. McCashin was now on station three, and Pete easily ran down a couple of hard-right angles. McCashin was willing to use every tactic at his disposal, and he started wildly varying his timing off Pete's shots. First, he'd be lightning-fast, calling immediately after Pete fired. Next, he'd be standing with a closed action for what seemed an eternity. They were both straight when Pete made the turn back to station one. Again, Pete chased down multiple hard-left angles, but his timing was starting to come back. Instead of working the explosive, reflex-oriented cadence he'd preferred for trench, he resorted to the sixteen-yard timing of his youth. The targets were neither fast nor difficult; an occasional bump here or there from an errant gust of wind, but for not having pulled the trigger in over three years, Pete felt like he was on his game enough not to worry about going straight. *Just make the other guy shoot the targets*, he thought.

Pete moved on to station two. It was now McCashin who was chasing wind-buffeted, hard-right angles, and Pete was holding just above the trap-house roofline, calmly popping clays with perfectly efficient gun movement. They were both straight again and McCashin walked to station one. The wind finally died off entirely, and of McCashin's five birds, only one was a hard-left screamer. By the time Pete fired his last shot on three he knew they'd go another twenty-five targets, if not fifty. McCashin was showing no signs of cracking. Indeed, after his brief attempt at mind games, he'd given up his tricks and was squarely focused on just breaking the targets.

"Dead and out: five and five. Both shooters are straight with twenty-five," Lou announced.

"You're both tied up. I guess we head over to field two for another round," Alex said.

McCashin turned to Pete. "How about we keep things interesting and make this round wobble?"

Pete thought a moment and replied, "It won't help, but sure."

By now the crowd of onlookers had grown larger than sixty, more than half of whom weren't even shooters. Alex and Lou both stood with their backs to the group. Both men knew that creating such a crass spectacle was simply a bad idea. It's one thing to play for a set limit-per-hole at golf, but allowing a grudge-match for that kind of money—and against a club employee at that—Alex couldn't help but allow his imagination to run wild when he considered the potential repercussions.

Out of the crowd stepped Candy McCashin Vanderstein. She was immaculately dressed in a tweed flat-cap, a custom wool whipcord shooting coat trimmed in suede at the shoulder and pockets, and finished with a pair of matching pants that accentuated her length of leg and discretely hinted at feminine angles and shapes. Her maiden name was stitched in cursive crimson above her left breast, and she nonchalantly smoked an unfiltered cigarette in a holder.

"What's Daddy gotten himself into now?" she demanded.

Alex managed a smirk. "A twenty-five-hundred dollar bet at trap if Geiger can beat him: They're straight after the first twenty-five and are beginning a new round at wobble." Candy turned to her father, who was approaching the slate pads on trap field two.

"You can't just go around making these crazy challenges, Daddy! This isn't the army—it makes mother and me feel foolish and it makes you look insane!" McCashin absentmindedly hand-tightened the Extra-Full choke in his autoloader. "Not now, gumdrop. Daddy's about to make short work of this has-been."

Now the order was switched and Pete would start on station two, McCashin on four. Pete called to view targets. They were all over the lot: high, low and extreme hard-angles. This would be a fast round that would favor reflexes and quick timing. "Ready?" Pete asked before calling for the first bird.

Pete smoked his first target and then it was McCashin's turn. He called for the bird, a simple flat-on, straightaway—no wind and nearly no angle. Lost! McCashin stayed in the gun. He couldn't believe it! Pete ink-balled his next target as well, a flat straightaway, so quick he almost seemed to spot shoot it. McCashin called again, and this time it was a high, hard right. Lost! Again, he stayed in the gun, not believing his eyes. Pete called for the next target and broke it, and it was only then the lightbulb in McCashin's brain came on. He had the offset, high-pattern choke in the gun when he'd intended to use a flat-shooting, Extra-Full. He unscrewed the offset tube and dropped it on the pavement at his feet. He then placed the heel of his left foot on the choke and collapsed it.

Out of his choke box he pulled the tube he'd intended all along and installed it in the gun. That did it: Neither shooter missed another target—their timing, for once, working off each other. On the last two targets, McCashin first called over, "Don't tighten up, Geiger!" and then barked, "Don't choke, quitter!" Pete killed the final target with the same obsessive focus he had had in his last, Olympic medal–winning round of bunker. When it was McCashin's turn to shoot, the gun discharged into the ground at his feet when he closed the action bolt. Everyone stopped in their tracks. "There's your misfire, Geiger. Mind if I just kill this last target before I surrender the trigger to you?" Pete nodded. McCashin called for the target, and broke it.

It was over. McCashin let the butt of the autoloader come to rest on his right foot and stared intensely out at where the action had taken place. The crowd broke into wild applause at his humiliation. When the heckling finally quieted down, McCashin instructed Alex to "pay the man." Alex shook Pete's hand and laid the wad of bills in his palm. Douglas McCashin then asked calmly, still without breaking his gaze, "I suppose you think you're one up on me now?"

Pete Geiger cracked a smile. "I'll have that trigger, if you don't mind."

McCashin took the autoloader by the barrel with both hands and flung it down range beyond the trap house, where it cart-wheeled off the fourteenth fairway turf, again and again, disintegrating a bit more each time it made contact with the ground. "Hope you don't mind walking for it!" The crowd let out a long gasp. Guns simply weren't thrown at Little Kill—the offense was automatically punishable by a $2,000 fine to be paid to a police scholarship fund.

It had been a big day for Pete. Not only had he taken the $2,500 from McCashin, but after watching him win so decisively, Alex Vanderstein had been only too willing to pay full price for the SO-4—even though the gun probably wouldn't do his slow, lumbering game much good.

The money made Pete solvent again for at least another couple of months. It was a cause for celebration. Sundays marked the beginning of *his* weekend. He wouldn't be back to work until Wednesday, and such a big Sunday called for a night on the town.

Just over the state line, the bars in Port Easton are open until 4 a.m. every night, and they sell booze on Sundays. You can buy schwag and crack on the street, or good cocaine and black-tar-heroin with a cell phone. The Mexican food is cheap and authentic, and the whorehouses operate discreetly with the grudging acceptance, if not tacit approval, of the community.

Pete had his shrimp taco plate with double guacamole and chips, and washed it down with five Tecates. The cathouse was just two blocks from the restaurant, and as Pete strolled across the intersection, he thought about what sort of girl he'd get.

II

It was Saturday, and Calcutta weekend had finally arrived. The fieldstone fireplace warmed the gun clubhouse while the coffee service and platters piled with donuts and bagels were gingerly trundled over treacherously icy golf cart paths. Alex and Candy Vanderstein arrived in separate cars.

Candy asked to shoot the Midas Grade for the Member-Guest weekend. It was beyond Pete why anyone would pick a competition to try out a new gun, but if he sold it as a result, who cares? Alex was clearly nervous—he'd requested to pay out the SO-4 over three months, but if his wife forced him to buy the Midas too, the household finances would be awfully tight.

"I don't see why it's alright for you to buy yourself a new gun, but when I want one too, suddenly we can't afford it?!" she whined.

"All I said was now isn't a great time. If you'd told me last week, before I bought mine, it wouldn't have been a problem."

"I didn't know I wanted it until . . ."

"Until you saw Ginny Mitchell's new gun," he said, finishing her sentence.

Candy furrowed her brow, deliberately tossed her hair and then finally surrendered, beaming a mischievous smile. "Alright, I guess that's when I wanted it."

At that moment, the door opened and in walked Douglas McCashin. Pete looked at his watch and couldn't believe his eyes: ten o'clock.

Candy threw her arms around her father before he could put his gun case down. "You'll buy me the new gun for Christmas, won't you, Daddy?" she asked playfully.

"That depends, gumdrop, what it is—and why can't your

husband buy it for you?"

"It's a Midas Grade—the best. Alex says we can't afford it—and after he bought a new gun for himself," she pouted.

"That right, Vanderstein: too Jewish to buy my little girl a Christmas gift?"

Alex flushed all at once, and it was all he could do to maintain his composure after such a gratuitous and asinine slur. "Of course not, Mr. McCashin. I just hadn't planned for it. I told Candy if she'd thought of it before I bought the . . ."

"Figures—I've seen your sales numbers, and you can't afford dime-store skivvies!" McCashin said, turning to Candy. "Of course, gumdrop, if it's a Midas Grade you want under your Chanukah bush, then it's a Midas Grade you'll have."

Candy jumped up and down and kissed her father on the cheek, doing her best impersonation of her overindulged, eleven-year-old self. She quickly stepped out to try her newest fashion accessory on the five-stand. Alex, exasperated, grabbed his gun and headed for the trap field.

"Running a little late this morning, Mr. McCashin?" Pete teased.

"Just put the finishing touches on the new trigger," McCashin said as he pulled the rebuilt autoloader out of its slip and held it at present-arms for Pete's inspection. Pete took the gun from him.

"Looks pretty good, considering . . . I've got to hand it to you, I figured it was a complete write-off," Pete said, as he dry-fired the trigger and then nodded.

McCashin placed the gun in the rack, and managed to smile. "So did I, but it's amazing what ten or fifteen hours on the workbench will do."

"I see you're the only member who has yet to announce a partner for the Member-Guest," Pete said, eyeing the sign-up sheet.

"All taken care of. Matter of fact, he'll be here any minute. I understand he's an old friend of yours, and I'm not about to miss the look on your face when he comes through that door."

As if on cue, Bo Harding walked into the room. He was in his mid-forties, stood a shade under six-foot; his wardrobe of matching tweed shooting vest and slacks came direct from the fitting rooms at Savile Row, and his brown cashmere sweater accented his brown eyes. He enjoyed a thick mop of wiry brown hair that didn't have a single strand of gray in it, and only his sterling-tipped ostrich skin cowboy boots betrayed his Tulsa roots. He was the kind of man every woman noticed, and every guy wanted to have a drink with. Pete and Bo locked eyes. Neither smiled, and they didn't shake hands.

"Pete Geiger," Bo said. "This is the last place I ever expected to find you. Back in the day, Peto and I used to shoot FITASC together. Heard you dropped off the planet, but I figured you'd gone into the pigeon ring or back to trench, or maybe even patched things up with what's-her-name . . ."

"That's enough," Pete said, stepping right up. The two men stood close enough to hit each other. "You're on my turf now, Harding—don't forget it."

"Your turf? What are we, back in short pants?"

McCashin relished the chaotic glory of his own creation "You're wrong, Geiger: This is *my* turf, and I won't have you speaking to my guest that way. I'm shotgun chair and I'll have your job any time I want it."

Both men remained eyeball-to-eyeball. "Just stay clear," Pete said through clenched teeth.

Harding turned away to the gun rack. "Glad to, son, but with all that spare tire you're lugging around these days, it won't be easy." McCashin and Harding both laughed. Pete thought it best to leave before he put one of them through the clubhouse bay window.

The format for the Member-Guest event was unchanged from previous years and consisted of a round of sixteen-yard trap, a round of five-stand on each of the two layouts and two rounds of wobble trap, wipe-your-eye. The purpose of Saturday's practice on the day before the competition is not only to permit teams to familiarize themselves with the game formats in which they'll be competing, but also to allow the gun club manager the opportunity to observe each shooter in action and make any adjustments to handicaps. While preliminary handicaps are calculated by the shotgun committee, any final adjustments are at the sole discretion of the gun club manager.

After his first practice round of five-stand, Bo Harding let several club members try out his Westphalia Grade K-32. In between rounds, he opened the trunk of his Bentley convertible and allowed members to inspect demonstrator guns in the parking lot. After lunch, the shooters returned to the practice fields. Half an hour before closing, Bo Harding gave Candy Vanderstein his patented "private lesson," engulfing her in his arms to show her the movement he wanted her to make on the target—artfully hinting at other physical movements in which they might engage together.

Bo Harding was rakish, charming, and his was the name on the tip of everyone's tongue that weekend. Pete knew the routine—Harding hadn't varied it much. In the end, it all came down to a matter of integrity—Pete's. If someone just invited a raccoon into the rabbit hutch, did he have any responsibility to sound a warning?

* * * * *

Even in a town full of beautiful homes, the McCashin residence, Bailiwick, stood out. Its classic stone Frasier Peters design had been commissioned and built by Conrad Winston, the munitions visionary and heir to the Winston Firearms fortune during the Great Depression, when only the most well-off could afford to build. Its architecture, craftsmanship and finish were peerless. At eight acres, the property was twice the size of most other showplaces in town and enjoyed a long uphill meandering driveway covered by towering elms. Mrs. McCashin would never hear it called an estate—she had grown up on an estate, and this home certainly didn't qualify as one in her mind. It had a pool, cabana/guesthouse, tennis court and stables that had been converted into a workshop for Douglas. This compound was ringed by three par-three holes of golf that the Little Kill head greenkeeper had designed and built, and whose teenage son now perfectly maintained three mornings a week in summer. It was Douglas McCashin's dream that his wife, and then his daughter, would win the ladies golf championship. Neither woman ever did, nor had either struck a golf ball on the abbreviated course in years.

Mrs. McCashin answered the front door with a vodka martini in her hand. If the acorn doesn't fall far from the tree, then Vivienne McCashin—"Sugar" to her friends—was where Candy got her looks. Where Candy threw off raw, physical sexuality, Sugar was more statuesque, refined, and carried herself with an air of unattainability. She had a blue-blood's fine features, sable hair, onyx eyes and a demeanor that was simultaneously gracious and made it clear that she was of superior background—and you weren't. It's not your fault, mind you, but don't expect her to pretend she isn't nobility. She wore a burgundy silk kimono, black slacks and needlepoint flats.

"You're looking well, young man."

"I've gone to seed, Mrs. McCashin," Pete said, patting his gut as he stepped through the front door. He was dressed in a threadbare camel hair topcoat, a blue blazer—too tight for him to button—with the U.S. Olympic team patch at the breast pocket and a new pair of gray flannel slacks from Sears.

"Nonsense," she said. "My father had your build, and he was bedding shop girls and cocktail waitresses till the day he died. Besides, any man who can reduce Douglas to a weeklong sulk in the barn has instantly earned my affections." She locked her arm through his and they strolled through the foyer into the living room. "I love the man, but he can be such a horse's ass!"

The furnishings in the room were exactly as Pete remembered them: Louis XIV accents with a large Aubusson rug. Strategically positioned around the room were stakes boards from past Calcuttas dating back a decade. Pete ordered a soda at the bar, reviewed the handicap ratings and waited for the guests to arrive.

Calcutta night was always a catered affair. Platters of cheese puffs, shrimp cocktail, smoked salmon and filet mignon with horseradish sauce circulated endlessly, but the overwhelming emphasis always remained on the bar and, as every auctioneer knows, nothing lubricates free bidding better than flowing spirits.

Candy and Alex arrived. Bo Harding descended from an upstairs guest room, and at seven o'clock sharp Pete opened the bidding. Twenty-two teams were pulled out of a hat, and whoever won the final bid for each team was automatically obliged to offer half back to the actual team members, should they want to buy in. Everything is handicapped—the entire Calcutta was for even-money. Sales started out slow, as they always did, but as the evening progressed, even mediocre teams started to get expensive as bidding was punctuated by frequent trips to the bar. Douglas McCashin and Bo Harding were one of the last teams in the draw.

"You all know how well Mr. McCashin shoots," Pete announced. "He's the reigning club champion in skeet, trap and five-stand, and has successfully defended all three titles for the past four years." Pete looked at McCashin, and smiled. "I have recently witnessed his tenacity up close." This line brought down the house. "So, expect him to finish high-scratch individual. Some of you have expressed reservations about Mr. McCashin's guest, Bo Harding. This event has always been closed to professional shooters, which means a competitor can't have been sponsored by a gun or ammunition company, nor can they have ever worked as a coach. I used to shoot with Bo and, to the best of my memory he never enjoyed any such arrangements." Pete shot a glance at Harding. "I can attest, therefore, that Bo Harding is not now, and has never been a professional shooter in any discipline—and is eligible to compete." The McCashin/Harding team opened at $1,000, then doubled to $2,000, $2,500, $2,750 then $3,000. Up to $3,000, there had been five competing bidders. Now there were just two, and one of them was Douglas McCashin.

"I want to remind you that you're bidding on this year's premier team," Pete announced during a lull. "We've got the best shooter this club has ever seen and his guest, who, if he could have only kept his fly zipped, might have been world class!" McCashin and Bo both shot forced smiles at Pete, as the room burst into uproarious laughter. The bidding started up again at $3,200, and then McCashin stood up.

"They say it's not gambling if you know you're going to win!" McCashin said to his rival bidder. "I'm sorry, but I'm not going to share this with anyone: $5,000!" And with that, Douglas McCashin set a new club Calcutta record price for a team. The last few sales were anticlimactic: Alex Vanderstein and his partner, an ancient State Supreme Court justice who was better known in the box-bird set for his prowess with a deck of cards than with a shotgun, went for a paltry $800. Judge Eastman's skills had atrophied after gradually worsening cataracts prevented him from shooting, but recent surgery convinced him he was fit as a fiddle and he insisted to Alex that, with their whopping 25-target handicap, they had a very real chance at winning.

With the show over, the shooters already felt in themselves the nervous tension of impending competition. The pot totaled $43,000 and most members and guests wished it were already the next morning so they could get on with it. Alex and Mrs. McCashin were in the library hosting their annual Calcutta night bridge game. Music was playing softly, and Bo Harding and Candy were dancing together. Pete sat at the bar and ordered his first Jack Daniel's of the evening. Douglas McCashin bellied up and ordered his wife another vodka martini.

"Record price for a team—that'll be one for the books when we win tomorrow."

"Perhaps," Pete said. "But I wanted to talk to you about something, Mr. McCashin—in private."

"I have a house full of guests—you must be joking."

"It concerns your partner," Pete said, biting the inside of his lip. "Just how much do you know about him?"

"He told me this would happen and, sure enough, here you are," McCashin said with a smirk. "Lost your wife to a better man, and you'll never forgive him for it. I know everything I need to about the situation. He told me something else about you that I happen to agree with: He said you'd be a whole lot better off if you'd learn to leave that glass on the bar a little more often."

"He's a con man, Mr. McCashin. Think whatever you want about me but . . ."

"You're a rummy—a regretful, resentful goddamned rummy. You blew it, and now you're desperate to hang it on someone else."

"He's notorious—a criminal. He'll ruin you."

"He is a winner . . . and you are not." McCashin picked the martini up off the bar and returned to his party.

The music ended, and with the dance over, Bo Harding sat down at the piano and played a soft rendition of "Love Is Here to Stay" while he spoke to Pete.

"Poor, pitiful Cassandra—foretold the future and couldn't get anyone to listen. Why don't you give your conscience a rest, son? This is supposed to be a party." Pete managed to crack a weak smile. "You gotta go a little easier on me," Harding continued. "These nice people don't need to know about some ancient history between the two of us. 'Keep my fly zipped'—not funny!"

"I saw you working them today—taking checks," Pete said. "When was the last time you took a deposit and actually delivered the gun? You roll in here, turn on the charm, fuck their wives and daughters, rip them off and blow town one step ahead of the law. It's amazing you're even still alive—I figured someone's husband would have long since taken the top of your head off."

"Now wait a minute. How long do you think I could operate if all I ever did was steal from people? Let's just say I've had a couple of misunderstandings. Kara and me—that just happened. It wasn't anything against you, and I sure as hell never expected she'd leave you." Pete gave him a mocking look. "I'm serious," Bo said. "You're right—I do this all the time, but she's the only one who ever pulled that on me. And she's the only one I ever tried to go straight for. Longest year of my life!"

"You left her flat broke, with a baby!"

Bo stopped playing the piano. "She threw me out, and it kind of stung!" he said innocently, as he started playing again. "Funny story: brought her cousin, barely north of legal, over to mind the baby. Now, I don't drink and I don't smoke, but damned if I don't got a sweet tooth for them young ones. Caught with my pistol out of its holster, so to speak."

"I hope she was worth it," Pete said.

"I know there's bad blood between us, and I feel for you . . . but what the hell: If you really want her back that bad, why don't you just call her? She learned some hard lessons with me, and you always were the nice guy. Tell you the truth, it was all your damned drinking that turned her—not me." Pete looked into the bottom of his glass and downed the rest. "Now, you see that fine gal over there?" Bo gestured toward Candy Vanderstein, who acknowledged him warmly. "She'll be sharing my bed—and a whole lot sooner than you'd think," he announced, through a neutral, pasted-on smile. "Come next year's Calcutta, I'll be driving one of her old man's Jap cars, to boot."

"You know the difference between right and wrong, and you just ignore it," Pete said incredulously. "The guilt alone would do me in."

"I've been doing bad things to good people my whole life. I was hustling quarters on the trap field when I was in grade school, learned to deal from the bottom of the deck in junior high and screwed my first married woman when I was seventeen. Ripped her off for a blacktop job too! Nothing I love in this life more than doing double dirt!" Pete gave him a look of mildly inquisitive puzzlement. "You know— fucking 'em for sport and then fucking 'em outta their money!

"Getting down to horse trading," Harding continued. "I been talking to McCashin, and he's about ready to cut you loose. You humiliated that old fool one time too many, and don't think he's not gunning for you. I got his ear and can put in a word for you so maybe you can hold onto your two-bits-above-minimum-wage, piece-of-shit life a little bit longer, but you're gonna owe me. Let me get my foot in the door—grease the tracks—and I'll slip you something to make it worth your while." Bo held his hand out to Pete, who continued staring into his empty glass. "I got the power to break you, son, but if you cooperate, this could work out for both of us."

Candy crossed the room to the bar and ordered a Coke. "I gotta hit the hay soon, darling," Bo said to her. "If you want that driving lesson, we better hit it now." He looked at Pete. "Showing the little lady some moves I picked up racing." And with that the two left together.

Pete was in the kitchen putting on his topcoat when he overheard the conversation coming from the pantry.

"What the hell kind of man plays cards with an old woman while his wife runs out on him? You're asleep at the switch, Vanderstein! I swear, sometimes I think it's my wife you want to bag and not my daughter."

"How can she expect the marriage to survive?"

"She doesn't, you simp! She's through with you. You can't cut it, Vanderstein, never could. You were invited to join this family to perform certain, specific duties—and you can't handle any of them. You can't sell cars, you can't run salesmen. You don't know how to make money, and you sure as hell can't hold onto my daughter. You're a flop all around. I figured with time, the natural cunning of you people would emerge and you'd learn the love of the kill, but it's almost like they refined all the backbone right out of you. All you're good for is parlor games and eating finger sandwiches. I never even wanted her to marry you. Sugar was all for that high-society, titled aristocracy. She wanted the name, but I never thought it was a square deal. You're nobility all right, but you're kike nobility—it's got a taint."

"I'm not some wetback you can just fire off your lot."

"That's exactly what you are! You're an employee of this family, and I'm firing you! She needs a real man, someone strong enough to handle her—it's your own damned fault!"

Pete Geiger walked out the front door. Snow was falling through the cold night air.

*   *   *   *   *

*Y*ou're not going to do this to yourself again, Pete thought back in his room later that night. *You don't need another drink, and you sure as hell don't need to read that letter again.* He loosened his necktie and cracked the seal on a fresh bottle of Jack. He poured one—two—three—four, half-a-water-glass full, and downed most of it in one long swallow. The letter was hidden between the pages of a dog-eared copy of Lawrence Smith's *Better Trapshooting.* He removed it from the book and read it.

> *Love,*
> *I'm hoping this letter finds you well and past times*
> *makes your feelings soft for me. I am well and have*
> *taken position of coach for Deutsche Damen equip.*
> *It is nice here in Berlin and there are many chances*
> *for shooting.*
> *I have done many stupid things—I know this and*
> *wish forgiveness from you. The girl is beautiful,*
> *and even though you are not the father, perhaps*
> *you can still like her. I miss you—you are only*
> *one love in my life. Write me please. I want to be*
> *together. You come, I go—I don't care. If you will*
> *drink, I don't care. I miss you.*
> *I always love you.*
> *Kara*

Pete Geiger finished his glass of whiskey, poured and finished another and slept in his clothes.

*　*　*　*　*　*

*P*ete knew the look and saw it in himself: the yellow in the whites of his eyes, the oversized pores on his nose—was that a broken blood vessel? The mirror doesn't lie—all the hard living was catching up to him. His hangover was terrible, though they all felt pretty much the same these days. It was seven-thirty. He was still shaky, but he had time. He showered, drank a pot of coffee and got dressed. On his way out the door, he thought about it and thought better of it, and then changed his mind again. He stuffed the flask of vodka into his back pocket. Pete sang aloud to himself as he walked over fresh snowfall...

"What happened to you?" Lou asked as Pete fumbled with the lock on the gun clubhouse door.

"One drink too many."

"One??? Jeez, you been hitting the bottle awful hard these days. It's not my place to say, but it's starting to get a little obvious."

"Just start the fire and find me some aspirin, Lou."

The pewter coffee service and platter heaped with eggs Benedict breakfast sandwiches came up from the dining room and, for the first time ever, Pete helped himself.

"You sure you wanna be doing that?" Lou asked. "On account of it being special for members . . . and guests?"

"All they can do is fire me, Lou, and somehow I think that's already in the cards," he said, biting into a second sandwich.

"Fire you for pigging out and coming in hung over—they can't. You're famous."

"*Was* famous. You'd better start facing up to reality because the writing's on the wall for me. You're going to be running things next season if you can show them now that you're up to it."

"Me?" Lou asked. "I shot some leagues here and there, but I can't handle the .410 worth a shit, and I'm nowhere in the same . . ."

"You don't have to be. This is country-club shooting. Show them how to be safe and break targets, and the rest of it they can figure out on their own."

"I don't know Pete—I'd kinda feel funny . . ."

"Look—you can step up to the plate now and earn yourself some decent money for a change, or you can hem and haw and wring your hands and lose out to someone who's not as good as you. I'm giving you the heads-up. If you're too stupid to pick up the ball and run with it, well then, I can't help you."

Pete Geiger popped a couple of breath mints. The first teams were arriving, tracking snow onto the clubhouse floor, where it promptly melted into a soup of salt and sand. Pete was mopping the floor when Douglas McCashin and Bo Harding arrived. He didn't have any idea of how the evening had ended for Harding and Candy, but he could tell by the way the two were interacting that something was up.

Alex Vanderstein and Judge Eastman arrived shortly thereafter. They assembled their guns in silence, but the old man had a spring in his step. For a change, he really felt good: He knew he didn't have many days like this left, and was intent on making it count.

The Member-Guest competition is best described as a three-ring circus. All fields run at once, five shooters to a squad and every third team is split, with a team member shooting on a different squad. Douglas McCashin and Bo Harding started on five-stand one with Candy as the extra single team member on their squad. There was a triad of subtle exchanges and body language: the familial way that McCashin regarded Harding, the way Bo doted on Candy, and the way she responded with an intimate touch to his hand or to remove a piece of lint from his vest shoulder. The way McCashin encouraged this and the way it fed Harding's ego and confidence weren't noticed by anyone except Pete and Alex.

The targets on five-stand one were easy; nothing beyond 35 yards, and the only entirely new target was a non-hopping gravity rabbit, lackadaisically dropped by hand down a long ramp onto a rubber mat by a busboy from the main clubhouse dining room. McCashin and Harding both easily exchanged perfectly center-punched pairs, and their only break in concentration came when McCashin warned Harding after it became apparent that Bo was tempting fate by playing with targets, taking them far later—albeit always killing them—than was advisable. McCashin smoked all but two with his flat-shooting I-Mod choke. The lost targets were on the slow rabbit. They seemed so close and easy, McCashin had tried to kill them shooting with both eyes open—and missed both in front. After the two misses, he rifle-shot the rest with one eye, and killed them all. Bo Harding was straight until his last pair, where he nearly missed them both when he took the pair backward and had to race to kill the second target before it hit the ground. "Don't do that again," McCashin admonished.

"The young lady's beauty caused a momentary blindness," Harding retorted, at which Candy Vanderstein flushed visibly.

Next, the squad moved onto their single round of sixteen-yard trap. Candy was always slow to call *Pull!* and late to fire, throwing the squad's timing off, but Harding and McCashin worked around it. When the round was through, McCashin and Harding had a straight and a twenty-three.

Pete enjoyed seeing everything come together for a shooter of Alex's questionable ability. The day was certainly his, and Judge Eastman was breaking his fair share of targets. An eighteen on five-stand two for the Judge was certainly respectable, but Alex had finally found his game and had come off with a twenty-two! Whereas the Judge simply thought it was a fun day of friendly competition, with tens of thousands of dollars in wagers thrown in to keep it interesting, Alex shot like his life depended on killing every target. His life as he knew it was about to end anyway. His wife had spent the night with someone else, and she didn't much care who knew. It was all flowing through his fingers like a handful of water, and the championship was all he had left. If he could beat Douglas McCashin just once and deprive him of his arrogant swagger, he could be the spoiler.

It was plain to Pete what was happening. Alex was spitting mad and shooting far above his abilities. He was really moving the gun aggressively, setting up on tight hold points and killing targets with quick timing. Pete knew that throwing the gun around like this could spell disaster, but for the first time since Alex started shooting, he looked like the real thing. "You keep this up and you could carry the day," Pete said after the first round. Alex looked at him with intense anger in his eyes. "I'm going to burn that bigoted bastard if it's the last thing I do," he said through gritted teeth.

Pete Geiger broke his cardinal rule and took his first drink of the day in the bathroom at one o'clock. He never drank around guns—he rarely drank at all during the day because whenever he had, he was sloppy before nightfall, but today he needed it to steady the shakes and get his blood moving. The quickest way for him to look and feel human rested in the flask. He took two long pulls of vodka off the threaded pewter spout, chased it with a breath mint, and then returned it to his car's glove compartment.

Pete started tabulating team scores and handicaps on the chalk leader-board in the gun clubhouse. Vanderstein and the Judge added a 23 and 20 at 16-yard-trap, bringing their total to 83. McCashin and Harding were on the board with 95, but as they only had a handicap of 10, they couldn't afford to miss much else.

"Looks like the Hebe's got some life in him yet," McCashin said, loud enough for the entire room to hear, after he glanced at the board.

Pete stopped him before he could say another word. "That's totally uncalled for!"

McCashin stepped up to Pete and for a moment; it looked like he might strike him, but he poked a sharp index finger into his sternum instead. "The only question you need to be pondering—Mr. Silver Medalist—is whether you're going to make it to the end of the season or to the end of this weekend." He emphasized his words with a whiff and a raised eyebrow, which made Pete realize that McCashin smelled the alcohol on his breath. Pete turned back to the chalkboard, and McCashin and Harding headed out for their rounds of wipe-your-eye.

Wipe is classic country-club fare. In short, it is a round of wobble trap from the sixteen-yard line shot by two-man teams standing side by side. The lead, or primary, shooter calls for the target and takes a single shot. If he kills it, the secondary shooter doesn't fire. If the primary shooter misses, the secondary attempts to *wipe his eye* with his single shot, hopefully killing the target. If, by chance, the secondary shooter wipes on a dead target, it is counted as lost. Normally, McCashin being the member and primary shooter, would stand on the left and Harding would be the secondary shooter or *wiper* on the right, but as McCashin's custom autoloader would be spitting empty hulls to the right, it was easier on Harding if he stood to the left.

McCashin and Harding played the game the way it's meant to be shot. Bo only ever had to fire twice as secondary, and they were easy kills. McCashin shot quickly enough to leave these targets well within range. When it was Bo's turn to lead, his timing was similar, although his preoccupation with being quick for McCashin's sake meant he missed six times. The only unforced errors were McCashin missing two of these outright and shooting an already dead target, leaving them with wipe scores of 25 and 22.

Alex Vanderstein continued his hot streak into his wipe rounds, having supplemented anger with strategy. Wobble had always been his favorite game at Little Kill and experience had taught him that choke selection, at least for this game, was everything. Whenever he shot wobble he used a Light-Mod for the first shot. He feared this might be too open now, but he also felt his game was shaky enough to merit erring on the side of caution. He expected that with old eyes and slow reflexes, the Judge would be useless when it came to backing him, so Alex took his time and tried to be as precise with his one shot as possible. He couldn't have been more wrong. The old man successfully wiped him eight out of nine times on their first round, popping impossibly long targets with the fixed Full-choke of his antique Ithaca 5-E trap gun. The Judge struggled with his turn as primary shooter, however. He couldn't pick up the targets quickly enough, and by the time he fired (and usually missed), the second shot was fruitless. When they arrived on their fourth station, Alex had wiped the old man twelve times and killed eight.

"What say," Judge Eastman asked, "instead of prolonging this charade, we smarten up. I'll just fire on the call and give you a fair chance at it?" And so for the remainder of the round, the Judge wasted his shot firing downrange on the call of *Pull!*, leaving Alex to chase and kill the target with his wipe. It worked! The pair successfully went straight for the remainder of the round and posted wipe scores of 24 and 21.

Accounting for handicap, the Vanderstein/Eastman and McCashin/Harding teams were tied at 189. The tiebreak would be decided with a winner-take-all shoot-off round of wipe, and would give the Vanderstein team a three-target handicap for the round of 25. It was shooter's choice—either teammate could act as primary: Vanderstein and the Judge decided Alex would shoot lead and Eastman would attempt to back him when necessary.

McCashin would be the lead shooter on their team, with Harding standing to his left to chase down the occasional miss. They needed a straight and for Vanderstein's team to drop at least four to win. All the member/guest teams as well, as a contingent of 25 or 30 Little Kill member onlookers stood by to watch the shoot-off.

"If Misters McCashin and Harding go straight, Misters Vanderstein and Eastman can afford to miss two and still win, three to tie. Four misses and the McCashin/Harding team wins," Pete said addressing the crowd. "There's quite a bit of money on the line here, so please be considerate of the shooters and hold your conversations and applause until the round is complete."

McCashin leaned across the pad to Alex, pointed to Bo Harding and boorishly announced loud enough for the entire gallery to hear, "In case you ever wondered, Vanderstein—that's what a real winner looks like!" The crowd groaned uncomfortably and McCashin momentarily tried to shake it off, but it was too late: His remark had shown him as the mean-spirited bully he was.

Pete showed the teams a couple of targets, and then McCashin started in. For the first three stations it was a fairly even exchange. McCashin and Harding went straight, and Alex and the Judge lost two targets on six wipes. When Alex and the Judge made the turn at station five to head back to one, McCashin whispered "Loser" under his breath to Alex as he passed. By the time they finished four stations, Harding had only wiped McCashin twice, but Vanderstein and the Judge were now only in contention for a tie.

Three targets from the end, McCashin called *Pull!* and tracked the target, a flat, low straightaway, pulled the trigger in his usual timing—and nothing happened. The gun failed to go off. McCashin held the autoloader, barrel pointed skyward, for Pete to inspect.

"Malfunction," McCashin said irritably.

"Hand it here," Pete said, taking the gun as he stepped between the two shooters. He mounted the gun and tried to pull the trigger: nothing. Pete shucked the bolt back, and it ejected the unfired shell. He bent down and picked it up, inspecting the primer. "No indentation," he said. Pete pointed the muzzle at the ground, and closed the empty action. He repeated this, shucking the empty action open and closed, again and again. Finally, he put the shell in the receiver one more time and the muzzle briefly floated over Harding's foot. He closed the action bolt—and the gun discharged.

Harding collapsed like a matchstick man burned to ashes. The toes, the ball of the right foot and what remained of the cowboy boot melded into a bloody mash of shoe leather, pulpy flesh and crimson sterling. Harding fell forward, bouncing the Westphalia Grade off the concrete and badly cutting his cheek and eye socket when he hit the ground. Two doctors raced out of the crowd and applied their belts as tourniquets to the now useless appendage. "It just went off," Pete said, bewildered. "I closed it and it just went off."

"You couldn't leave well enough alone!" Lou badgered. "Pete warned you but you just had to keep monkeying with that trigger—always trying to get the edge on everybody. Look at what your edge got you now!" he said pointing to a now convulsing Harding.

McCashin was flustered. "It didn't . . . I didn't know."

He looked to Candy, who avoided her father's gaze. The doctors were on the phone to the hospital, and Alex Vanderstein called the police.

A life-flight helicopter landed on the fourteenth fairway of the Little Kill Country Club. While Bo Harding's gurney was loaded onto it, Douglas McCashin sat silent and alone in the gun clubhouse with his head in his hands.

TWO MONTHS LATER

On the first day of spring, Pete Geiger stood near the water's edge at the exact spot where the trap house had once been. Twelve combination skeet-trap fields once ringed this peninsula, which jutted out into the waters of the Sound and had comprised the Stratford Gun Club. Civil litigation had forced its closure after an environmental group filed a lead-and-plastic-shot-collar contamination lawsuit against the gun club's corporate parent. It was all gone now: the clubhouse, the pro shop, the fields, trap-houses. Even the people seemed to have all been razed back in 1987.

Pete was one of the last living souls still intimate with this ghostly world, and only the shadowy hint of the concrete pads suggested it had ever been a clay-target shooter's paradise. He stood on field twelve, which had been his favorite. It was closest to the coast guard base and lighthouse and received wild, buffeting winds from every conceivable direction. Trap-shooters hated to be squaded here. In its day it had been regarded as the most difficult field on the coast, followed closely by the waterfront traps at the Field Club at Port Easton—also now defunct. But Pete had marveled at its unpredictability: Twenty-one here was worth a straight anywhere else, and he credited the flexibility that this particular field had instilled in his game with allowing him to excel at bunker.

Today the wind was blowing steady up the Sound. Pete positioned himself on station one at the 27-yard-line. He extended his left arm and index finger to an imaginary hold-point, off the left corner roof of a nonexistent trap house. "*Pull!*" he called. When he closed his eyes he could see the target fly and break, the sights and sounds of a past incarnation. He reached into his pocket and pulled out the Indian-head nickel. He pressed the contours of its center hole into his palm, and then held it up to his eye, allowing the sun to peek through. He walked to the most distant point on the trap field closest to the water.

Pete skipped the coin across the mild, dark waters of the Sound. A green Jaguar sedan pulled up behind him on the handicap trap line, and Alex Vanderstein got out. "Nice toss," he said.

"That'll carry all the way to Europe," Pete replied. The two men shook hands.

"You look good, Pete."

"Two months without a drink will do that," he said, patting his flat stomach through his now-buttoned Olympic team blue blazer. "How are things?"

"Judge Eastman got me the appointment as state's Public Advocate. It's a baby step, but it's politics."

"Things have normalized then?"

"For me? No. But the dust has settled at the club if that's what you mean. Harding is suing: no surprise there, I suppose."

"And McCashin?"

"Wintering in Florida. They rented a house for the season, but she's talking about making it permanent. He went on a two-week bender after it happened. *The great abstainer* drank everything in the house! She finally had to lock him out to get him to sober up! Now he's down there trying to come up with some new sand-wedge design; spends every day on the golf course driving everyone crazy! With all the stories coming out of the woodwork about Harding— did you know he's under indictment for fraud?—it wouldn't surprise me if the McCashins dropped their Little Kill membership entirely."

"And how's Lou making out?"

"You mean Il Duce? Luigi Paisan has become the great dictator. He's outlawed autoloaders entirely: break-open guns only. They call him the safety Nazi—he sent a whole bunch of members home for minor infractions. Lou's got it down, alright!"

Alex opened the trunk of the Jaguar, pulled out a blue plastic hard case and opened it. "I never even got around to changing the pad," he said. Pete put the SO-4 together and mounted it a couple of times. Due to his recent weight loss, the gun fit him again. "With all that commotion, they just split the money. It's funny: I know it's impossible to put a price on a man's foot, but in this case it turned out to be worth a little over $11,000. You're going back to shooting?" Alex asked.

"McCashin was right: I was a quitter. Now I'm going after the World FITASC Championship." Pete took the gun apart and carefully packed it back into its fitted metal airline case. "I know it's the oldest line in the book, but I'll send you the money when I'm back on my feet," Pete said.

"Take your time—it's back where it belongs."

"And Candy?"

"Living at her parents' house. Frankly, I don't think we're going to make it. She wants counseling—I want out." Pete put the case in the back of his car and slammed the hatchback lid shut.

"Because she strayed?"

"She says she's lost without me—concedes we're different and recognizes I'm the stable one in the relationship. She admits she's self-destructive and that the same things that attract her can also hurt her. She says I can keep her grounded and safe. I say marriages either succeed or fail for good reasons. She bailed on me, Pete—I don't think I could ever trust her again."

"I wouldn't be too hard. Bo Harding's had a lot more experience at suckering married women than she's had at fending off sociopath shit-heels. Besides, it's not like the old man wasn't pointing the way."

"She made a fool of me—I won't forgive it."

"That's the ultimate test of character: to forgive someone when you have no reason to."

Alex turned and looked out to sea. "Poignant, isn't it, that when faced with the identical dilemma, *you* walked away?"

"That was the mistake of my life, and I'm about to rectify it," Pete said. "I'm catching a plane to Germany to be with her, to help raise the girl."

Alex was baffled. "Really?!"

"My wife left me because I was—because I am—a drunk. It's *my* fault, and now I just want her back. We're going to take it one day at a time: I'm going to stay the hell out of the bars, and we're going give it another try."

"There's been speculation," Alex said, changing the subject.

"People are insinuating it was intentional—not a misfire: that you actually pulled the trigger."

"Revenge is a dish best served cold? People say a lot of stupid things, Mr. Vanderstein. Besides, it's not like the gun didn't have a history of accidental discharge. Everyone knew it was unsafe—and there were a bunch of witnesses right there. I was cleared by the police." Pete held out his hand, and Alex shook it. "You're the only true gentleman in the whole damned club," Pete said as he got into his car. Alex tapped on the window and Pete cranked it down.

"Say that I'm your lawyer for the next thirty seconds," Alex hypothesized. "Anything you tell me remains privileged permanently. Did you shoot him or was it an accident?"

Pete pointed toward Alex with his index finger extended like a gun barrel and his thumb cocked like a hammer. "Bang!" He said as he winked at him and dropped the hammer.

Alex Vanderstein stood with his mouth open in astonishment as Pete Geiger drove a circuitous loop, taking a final grand detour over all the derelict skeet and trap fields before exiting through the front gate to get on with his life.

THE END

II
THE SHOWMAN

onrad Winston III pulled his rental car into the parking spot of the Salty Sands trailer park designated MANAGER'S OFFICE. The South Florida sun hit his blue blazer and gray flannel slacks and he started overheating the moment he stepped out of the car. He was hot and irritable. After all, it was a totally unnecessary trip. Normal people, even those well into their seventies, used e-mail. His own mother was mindlessly sending him one- and two-sentence e-mails all day long—and she was in her sixties. The fact that Winky and Walter Wagner's last known address in Bridgewater was a pile of charred cinders and that they currently didn't even own a telephone irritated Conrad to the point of exasperation. A little eccentricity in an old couple was one thing, but this was downright reclusive. These two people clearly didn't want to be found, and yet the job had fallen to Conrad to find them. Conrad was an old-line County WASP, thirty-five, divorced with two children. He was beanpole thin which, combined with his stooped posture, gave him the unmistakable slouch of an awkward adolescent. He had a teenager's face, with sad defeated eyes, and hair as black as Texas crude, streaked through with pronounced patches of premature gray at his temples that had earned him the nickname of "Skunk" in prep school.

"She's not exactly all there," said the raven-haired trailer park manager, Ms. Adelman. "*Non compos mentis* in legalese, but *he's* around—out fishing." As to when Mr. Wagner could be expected, she replied, "Every day, he hits the boat ramp at noon and drives to that gas station over there. You can set your watch by it." She pointed with a long slender index finger. "Then he drinks one bottle of beer and I make him his lunch. Come with, if you care to join me."

The Wagner residence was the nearest unit to the beach, sitting on a double lot. It was old, but showed well in battleship gray paint with royal blue shutters. The added-on Florida room made the single-wide trailer feel more like a real house. There was a navy blue Kennedy-era Ford Falcon convertible parked under a carport adjacent to a vegetable garden planted in tomatoes and peppers. A blue tarp covered half the trailer's roof; the ladder ascending to it attested recent work.

The window-unit air conditioner was on when they entered the trailer and, while Conrad was aware that Mitzy Adelman was undoubtedly Jewish, she was also a South Florida siren—a dark beauty with brains to match. As every man over a certain age knows, a beautiful woman is a beautiful woman, whether she's sixteen or sixty.

The tea that had been brewing in the sun on a weathered wooden picnic table near the garden was warm enough to melt most of the ice in Conrad's glass as soon as it was poured.

"He won't be happy to see you," she said, making a sandwich of grouper and tomato. "I assume you're here regarding Winston Firearms?" Conrad confirmed this with a nod. "I'd better stay with you then. He's a hothead anyway, but once he gets started . . . if he tries for you, I'll grab him from behind. You just get out."

Conrad stared at her. "You're joking," he said.

"That man is like a dormant volcano—simmering and seething. Winston Firearms always gets the old lava flowing. If he makes a move for you, I'll get on him and you make a run for it—and don't come back. I don't think he keeps a gun around here anymore, but I wouldn't put it past him."

The front door of the trailer flew open and in stepped Walter Wagner, a deep-sea rig in one hand and a spinning rod in the other. He was wiry, bowlegged and tan. He wore khaki shorts secured by a length of rope tied in a square knot, a white undershirt with a hole the size of your thumb at the shoulder and rank smelling flip-flop sandals. A straw hat, worn through at the peak, with a green vellum visor sat snug on his head and polarized sunglasses were perched on his nose, which was covered in zinc oxide.

Walter removed his hat and glasses, revealing a close-cropped head of white hair bleached to a brackish yellow by the sun. He had fine Nordic features, and his gray eyes sparked. He stopped in his tracks the instant he saw Conrad. Then he continued his stride and proceeded to hang the rods with others in a rack on the wall. "What's for lunch, hon?" he inquired.

"The rest of last night's grouper on toast with tomato. You've got a guest, in case you didn't notice," she said, not looking up from the cutting board.

"Got me a Winston in my house is what I got—you're Double's boy."

"Conrad Winston . . . the Third," he said, holding out his hand, which Walter looked at quizzically for a moment before continuing about his work arranging rods on the wall.

"That kinda makes you a Junior-Junior," Walter half-shouted. "You look just like your grandfather—when he was sick with cancer and realized he was turning the whole concern over to a useless dilettante! I said to myself *that looks just like Senior after he became completely disillusioned with life*, and sure enough you do, Junior-Junior."

"Don't mind the volume," Mitzy cracked. "He's not mad at you—yet—just deaf as a post."

"Too much bang-bang."

Conrad took a moment to screw up his courage to begin his pitch. Daintily, he patted the sweat on his brow with the swatch of paper towel that had accompanied his drink. "You're a hard man to find, Mr. Wagner," he began. "The reason I've come is Winston Firearms would like to cordially invite you and your wife to . . ."

"Let me guess . . . " Walter squinted peevishly as he thought. "Winston Firearms, or what's left of it, has been picked up by one of your Little Kill syndicates, and now they want to make them in

Bangladesh or Mexico or some damned place."

"China," Conrad revealed.

"Yeah? I heard it was Mexico—and they figure it'll sell easier if they got Winky vouching for them that their product won't blow up in your face the first time you pull the trigger. Sound about right?" he asked, raising his eyebrows. "They sent you on a fool's errand, boy."

"There would be money . . . a stipend . . . an honorarium,"

"Stipend! Honorarium! I was a stockholder, goddamn it!" Walter jabbed his index finger into Conrad's sternum, and the veins at his temples started to throb. "No half-assed per diem is ever going to make up for . . ." He trailed off into bitter memory. "Besides, she's the one you really want—and she isn't available."

They both sat down.

"It's not like she would have to shoot or anything. She'd just have to . . ."

"You're about five years too late. She doesn't know who she is, who I am, the day, the year, or the planet she's on. I get up to the home twice a week to visit—to read *Nancy Drew* to her. Might as well be reading to the chair I'm sitting on," he said, bouncing his fist off the arm of his BarcaLounger.

"Empire Capital was really counting on having her attend the big promotional weekend. I guess this really changes things."

"Empire Capital, which one is that?" Walter asked.

"Sid Shapiro—he's invited a group of potential investors down to Onori Plantation for a big catered event—three days of box-bird shooting," Conrad answered. "Empire Capital is Sid Shapiro and Alex Vanderstein."

"Vanderstein? I thought he was some kind of lawyer?"

"Now he's a banker."

"Lawyer, banker: Leave it to the Jews to put the final nail in the coffin of Winston Firearms. No offence, love," Walter said absentmindedly toward Mitzy. She snorted in distaste and handed him the plated sandwich and a glass of tea.

"Well, I'm sure they'll want you to come even if Mrs. Wagner can't."

"Me?! She was the whole friggin' act! What the hell do you want with me? I'm nobody," he said through a bite of his sandwich.

"It was both of you on *Johnny Carson*, and it was both of you on *Wide World of Sports*. Both of you said 'We're the NRA' from the pages of every magazine in America. You were Archie Bunker with a shotgun—you were her punch line. You were both a pretty big deal once, Mr. Wagner, and plenty of people still remember. Besides, it's not like you weren't a champion in your own right."

"Lots of people won at the Grand American, Junior-Junior. Some of them were great, some got lucky, some just hung around long enough for their number to come up. It didn't mean much then, and it doesn't mean anything now. What you want is a famous exhibition shooter who doesn't really exist anymore. I was just the assistant—the comic relief. You wasted your time coming down here," Walter said flatly. "Not interested."

"You're a part of Americana, half of the last great exhibition shooting team . . . ever. The only two trick shooters most people can even name are Annie Oakley and Winky Wagner. If it's the money . . ."

Walter cut him off. "Why do you country-club boys always assume you can solve every problem with money? Think you can buy your way into or out of whatever it is you want . . ."

"Well, I think you should go," Mitzy said to Walter, who shot her an aggravated glance. "You're in a rut, old man. You go out fishing, you drink your beer. I make you lunch, you take a nap. You visit Winky Wednesdays and Saturdays; we go out to dinner and a movie Thursdays and Sundays. You relive the same damned week *every* week. I wouldn't even mind so much if it wasn't such a lackluster week to begin with! When was the last time anything out of the ordinary happened to you?" she asked, adding, "Other than your roof almost blowing off last month and your outboard motor seizing up last week. Take a trip—go on a little adventure."

"Input from the peanut gallery," Walter said, jabbing a thumb toward Mitzy. "What do you expect from a Jersey girl? *We* were Bridgewater people when it was still a place decent people wanted to live. Probably been a rat hole the entire time you've been alive, but there was a time when it was a nice place to call home. I lived my whole working life in Bridgewater. Started with your grandfather when I was discharged out of Korea. *That* Conrad was a great man: a great gunsmith, engineer, designer. Senior made me a machinist and then a tool-and-die man: He taught me a trade. A man can't stand on his own two feet if he hasn't got a living in him, and your grandfather gave that to me, that and the self-respect that comes with it." Walter took the last bite of his sandwich, washed it down with the rest of his tea and placed the glass on top of the plate on the beige shag carpeting. Mitzy picked them up and washed them in the sink.

"Senior gave me the targets to become a shooter," Walter continued. "All I ever paid for at Stratford was ammo. He sold us the guns—factory seconds at cost! And his factory seconds weren't even really seconds. We'd pull them off the line for one little thing or another, but after that: custom-shop wood, engraving, choking all at cost! He wanted his employees to be shooters—"ambassadors to the sport," he called us. He believed that every shooter on the production line was an added level of quality control. Winky cut checkering in the custom shop—fleur-de-lis, 32 lines per inch. Never wore specs a day in her life. Damn, that woman had eyes: shot a twenty-two at skeet the first time she ever picked up a shotgun! Like falling out of bed, I tell you! She thought sixteen-yard was a bore; went right into handicap and doubles. Talk about a natural, she didn't care about gunfit, barrel length, balance, weight. If it had a pad on it, she could shoot it! Genius with a scattergun—one of only two or three I've ever seen in fifty-plus years. As soon as they realized she could shoot, Winston wanted her for all their advertising and public relations. Exhibition shooting? Sleight of hand with a shotgun, I say! She could have been a great competitive shooter instead of a merchandising shill, but she didn't care. She just loved all the attention."

"Why don't I just put in a call to Empire Capital anyway," Conrad said, as he stood up and reached for his cell phone.

"Sit your ass back down, Junior-Junior!" Walter commanded, pointing to the sofa. "I'm a pissed-off old man, and if you want a piece of me, you're damned well going to listen to what I have to say." Conrad sat. "Bridgewater was one of the greatest manufacturing towns this country's ever seen. We produced the arms and munitions that won two world wars—built fighter planes right through to Vietnam. Hell, we invented the damned helicopter! Copper pipes and tubing, steel wire and cable; we made the products that made this country. Bridgewater *was* American industry, number two on the bombing list of industrial sites for the Nazis. And all of that's just as dead as a dodo. Detroit?! I don't need to hear about the heartbreak of Detroit, I lived it in Bridgewater! You know it took them a grand total of five days to burn down my house? Five days for those porch monkeys to torch it! Nothing left. Neighbor said they started stripping the copper out of it on the third day. I never went back, and I'm glad for it.

"I saw the whole thing swirl down the commode myself," he continued. "Political corruption? Sure. Graft? You betcha. Bridgewater civic bankruptcy? Unions shanghaied themselves right out of a job. But that was all fixable. What finished Bridgewater to my mind was Orion splitting the arms division off like a redheaded stepchild and then turning it over to a bunch of stooges. Our guns were made from quality machined forgings, and a pre-1964 manufacture date still means something—because that's when the cheap, so-called *improved* models came out. What killed Winston was turning those employees over to piss-poor management, and then financing it at usury rates! The patient could have been saved: We needed a surgeon who really understood the business to figure out which limbs to amputate—we needed a margin of error, some wiggle room. We needed Senior, but instead we got your father! We lost something of real value, not just to Bridgewater or to me, but to every customer we ever had."

"My father lost too—everything! It was Orion's call—that's what he always said. He made the best deal he could."

"*He* made a bargain with the devil himself," Walter said calmly.

"China?! Who the hell is ever going to buy a Chink Super-X?! Someone who knows bunk about guns, that's who! Those yellow bastards were trying to kill me sixty years ago, and now they're going to produce Winston designs?! It's a goddamned perversion!"

The room went silent for a moment until Conrad finally said, "You must have made a claim on your homeowner's policy."

"Ah . . . but insurance would have defeated the entire purpose, Junior-Junior," Walter said, tapping his index finger to his temple. "All it took was those moving trucks. . . . The natives saw that, and the free-for-all was on. We couldn't sell that house—our home—at any price. With all the plant closings and the taxes through the roof, no one could sell a house in Bridgewater—there were no buyers. We held on, Wink and me—by our bleeding fingernails: iron cages on the windows and doors and a loaded shotgun in every room! We held on till she finally got so sick that the writing was on the wall. Bridgewater was doomed—we were doomed. The only way it worked on paper was to divorce. She bought me out of the house. When it burned, that left her flat broke, which was what we needed to get her into the state home. A hell of a way to run a country: You gotta be out on your ass before you finally get what you need. Bridgewater is a man-made disaster, and your father's one of the men who made it." Conrad looked at his shoes.

Walter finally softened, and added, "Why are you involved with this? I don't think I ever saw you more than twice in the whole twelve years I ran the desk at Little Kill. Why do you pick now to suddenly trade on your name?"

Conrad turned to Walter Wagner directly. "My name is all I have left. I need the money."

II

Raised in a one-bedroom apartment out by the airports, Sid Shapiro had done spectacularly well for himself. Starting in the sixth grade, his mother—a single woman, floating bookkeeper to the garment district—had scrimped to afford his tuition at a Catholic school. There, the scrawny, cerebral son-of-

Abraham was bullied and beaten, taunted and tortured every single day of the academic year by the Mick-Irish children of union heads, precinct bosses and city brass of the fire and police departments. He was pelted with sticks, rocks and curbside trash. He was always being chased—through alleys and backyards, across vacant lots and pedestrian bridges, over brick walls and under train trestles. His mother was fully aware of this relentless hazing, but never spoke of his Sisyphean trials. Her single, silent acknowledgement of his troubles became fundamental to his escape: She made sure he had a decent pair of sneakers to wear to and from school. He was a City College undergrad by sixteen, immediately followed by law school, which seemed like a vacation after this hellish existence, but the scars of these traumas ran deep, and turned him sinister. Sid became the very thing he so despised, and later felt no greater fulfillment than in dominating and controlling everyone and everything.

After his two years of doing mergers-and-acquisition law with a white-shoe Wall Street firm, Sid's mother died, and he was freed of his obligation to her. He quit his law job and started trading coffee futures. He left the law because he'd grown impatient waiting on a partnership track that didn't really pay off even when it paid off. He wanted real wealth—tens of millions, hundreds of millions. He didn't want to linger for twenty years to get it, and he certainly didn't want to be told what to do by people not nearly as sharp as he was.

Sid was tall, with quick black eyes and an aquiline nose which made him look like a hawk. He had a thick mane of silver hair that he wore shaggy and parted down the middle. His fingers regularly found themselves luxuriating in that bountiful mop, slicking the whole thing back over his crown—a tell he unintentionally exhibited when he wanted to emphasize something. Sid became the ambitious, whiz-kid focus of any room he walked into. People wanted to hear what he thought, and the moment he started to make some money in the pits, he began thinking about just what kind of a life he aspired to live.

* * * * *

The man they called "Mr. Market" was a legend. He had risen from humble beginnings—the son of a white sharecropper and fruit picker—and grown up in abject poverty in the deep South. His story of stumbling out of the bitter cold at seventeen from a job tearing up railroad ties into the warmth and bustle of the Chicago Board of Trade, asking for a job and receiving one—writing commodities prices on a blackboard—and his subsequent ascent to Olympian heights of business stature and social prestige had been told and retold, embellished and enhanced, until it read more like something out of a Jack London yarn than anything rooted in reality. He was a fabrication coaxed to life from the wellspring of his own imagination. True, he was a high school dropout, but he was also a voracious reader with an uncanny memory for detail. Like many people with an incomplete education, he overcompensated by trying to be better informed than everyone else, and relished the look on people's faces when he proudly announced he had had only a ninth-grade education.

Mr. Market was small, with short legs, and wore a patchy, white beard to cover acne scars. He had notoriously bad teeth, which were a constant source of pain. The process of acquiring an entire set of dental implants took years, and he was forever recuperating from these ongoing surgeries. In spite of these deficiencies, he was vain about his looks and regularly had haircuts, manicures and facials in his office suite. He was also a clothes horse, preferring silk and cashmere. Everything was custom, right down to his bench-made golf shoes.

He was a quick study, who had taught himself trigonometry and calculus on his way to earning a pilot's license and instrument rating. He had become intrigued with computer technology the moment it became available to the retail consumer. He carried an executive word-processing Commodore-64 nearly everywhere he went before anyone had even heard of a portable computer. It was no surprise then when he took a special interest in the potential of the Internet and what promise it held for the global marketplace He had earned his moniker by creating Stockmarket.com, the original and still largest discount online brokerage firm. This innovation alone made him a legend, but Mr. Market was never satisfied with past achievements—his mind was constantly percolating *big ideas*. Stockmarket.com offered a wide range of à la carte online services from banking to insurance to brokering mortgages, but Mr. Market eventually felt the irrepressible compulsion to "play the game"—to manage money for global clients and compete against the best and brightest.

He asserted that his Infinity Fund used stock options to hedge equity positions that were decreed by his proprietary black box trading system—a massive mainframe computer called FELIX, which he'd co-created with a Nobel laureate. All the market data from the online brokerage was fed through this mainframe, and when it was distilled, the condensed information gave him a *market intelligence*, an edge that allowed Infinity to consistently outperform. When he first opened the fund, annual returns as high as 25 percent weren't unheard of, but now, twenty years on, he confessed that he'd grown conservative in his temperament. He simply wasn't willing to take those kinds of risks with client nest eggs anymore.

Mr. Market insisted on vertical integration throughout his operation. The online brokerage, acted as custodian for all securities held in Infinity customer accounts, and no one was permitted access to the black box. He was adamant that signature tails had been built into the trading software, like the contrails left by jet aircraft at altitude. Mr. Market said that anyone duplicating his trading platform would leave these *signature tails*, and every time he used an outside custodian or allowed an auditor access, he saw his platform signatures creeping across the tape for months afterword. For this reason, he used an obscure accounting firm in Port Easton. Their entire business was dedicated solely to Stockmarket.com and the Infinity Fund.

When Sid Shapiro had his initial meeting, Mr. Market was already rich from taking the online brokerage public, and was the current president of the National Chamber of Commerce. Sid had $250,000 to invest, and he wanted the best manager in the world to run it. A well-connected friend on the coffee exchange arranged for a golf outing—a foursome. Sid rented a car, drove out from the airports and got off on the north side of town. Then he backtracked toward the Sound, which took him through one of the choicest neighborhoods of homes in the entire country. The big houses were all set back from the road, with manicured lawns and multiple outbuildings. They had architectural style—that one looked like a French chateau and this one looked like a Jeffersonian Federal. Every home was a reflection of its owner, and every owner was obviously rich and had taste. By the time he turned onto the Post Road and headed back over the state line, he'd driven through a wonderland of world-class affluence and was star struck.

Sid Shapiro was woefully under-informed for his round of golf with Mr. Market. Sid thought he was meeting just another money manager—albeit a famous one—in hopes that Mr. Market might run his quarter million for him. Not being a golfer, Sid envisioned the Links at Port Easton as just another highbrow country club. He couldn't have been more wrong.

Recognizing as a young man that the way to get ahead quickly was to socialize with financial movers-and-shakers, Mr. Market had caddied weekends at a suburban Chicago country club. He learned the game there, and now played to a five handicap. Mr. Market had played Little Kill exactly once when he first came to the County and had made such a devastating social faux pas that he forever poisoned his chances of becoming a member. He was unaware of, and very well tripped over, the arcane process of being invited to join. He'd simply blurted it out in a drunken, humorless remark, belligerently asking the club president *whose dick he had to suck to get an application for membership*. He was never invited back, and the member he'd been playing golf with was officially reprimanded.

Utterly humiliated, Mr. Market swore that if he couldn't go to the mountain, he'd make the mountain come to him. The Links at Port Easton was Mr. Market's private nine-hole golf course. The idea struck him when he spotted the fifty-acre island with a causeway, a dilapidated Mediterranean-style estate, from the pitching deck of his motor yacht. It jutted out into the Sound, and was unlike anything else on the coastline. It would provide him with his palette—an opportunity to create something so exclusive and rarified he would become a social sphere with a gravitational pull entirely unto himself. It was a country club dedicated to one man. It had tennis courts, a swimming pool with snack bar, a men's grill, as well as a formal dining room, not to mention an oak-paneled locker room with Turkish baths and tanks of water for hot and cold dunking, tended by a full-time masseuse to serve guests.

And there were the links, designed in the oldest Scottish golfing tradition of a course built into the craggy, undulating shoreline with dune bunkers and firm, sea-grass rough. It was the real thing, imported directly across the Pond and plunked down less than 30 miles from the city. Some of the first high-profile guests to begin an audience with Mr. Market in hopes of playing the course were PGA superstars warming up for links matches in the British Isles.

When Sid Shapiro arrived ten minutes late for the golf date, he found his coffee-pit buddy nervously waiting alongside Mr. Market and a former British Open Champion from a dozen or so years back. Sid got out of his rental car, looked over the rest of the foursome and asked, "I don't want any trouble with the valet—where do I park?"

Mr. Market replied without so much as the blink of an eye, "This is my course, this is my house. We don't use valets here. Park anywhere you like." A Scottish caddy popped the trunk of Sid's rental and immediately noticed there weren't any golf clubs inside. "I'm happy to loan you a set," Mr. Market invited. "There are several to choose from."

Sid finally came clean. "I don't play—not at all. The only golf club I ever held in my hands was at one of those miniature putt-putt deals. But I'm not about to let that stop me from spending a couple of hours picking your brain."

"I admire your candor," Mr. Market said. "But when I play golf, I talk politics. Like to argue ideology, Mr. Shapiro?"

"I'm a businessman—I have no ideology."

"Clever," was Mr. Market's only comment.

After nine holes and an hour-and-a-half of discussing the role of the black male in the African-American matriarchy, the suspension of due-process for terrorist suspects, when the first female president of the United States would materialize and who she might be, an examination of the fine line between enhanced interrogation and torture, and just what Thomas Jefferson, Abraham Lincoln, Charles Lindbergh and Martin Luther King would say about the current state of the American experiment if they played a round of golf together—players always walked the Links at Port Easton—Sid Shapiro was wrung out physically, conversationally and intellectually. Mr. Market seemed to know everything, and demanded informed opinions able to withstand a rigorous cross-examination. The PGA pro mostly cracked wise with the caddies and occasionally held up the British end with a few select witticisms. Sid felt transported back to law school, arguing the fine points of the law before a skeptical professor. Sid would not be staying for lunch, as Mr. Market had booked the meal and the afternoon round with the secretary-general of the United Nations and the former exchequer of the Bank of England. The golf pro would remain in residence for the entire week.

As Sid and his coffee-pit compatriot drank tall glasses of sweet iced tea and snacked on a fruit-and-cheese plate awkwardly held aloft by two dining room waitresses, Mr. Market delivered his verdict. "I always advise my clients to only invest what they can afford to lose. You're precocious, Sidney. You've got guile and intelligence, but I can tell just by looking at you that you couldn't possibly absorb any quarter-rack bust. My advice to you is to live a little more and learn: Add experience and money to your bag of tricks and come back to me when you can better afford my services." He held out his hand for Sid to shake. "I refuse accounts all the time. This isn't a fuck-off," Mr. Market said warmly. "I's a comeback now, y'all."

* * * * *

fter discovering paradise, Sid Shapiro spent the next several years with his nose pressed up against the glass looking in. He was like a rat in an affluence maze. Wrong turns and dead ends abounded, and this started with marrying the wrong woman. What Sid aspired to was an upgrade. He had found one professionally after the open-call coffee exchange closed and he landed on his feet, securing a position in the County, trading precious metals for one of the Swiss banks. *But why stop there?*, he thought. Why not an upgraded home to go with that new job? He finally immigrated into town and bought the right house, albeit on the wrong side of the tracks: an undersized mansion with six bedrooms, guest house, greenhouse, gardener's apartment, swimming pool and cabana. To him, it all seemed perfect— but it was in the wrong neighborhood and less than a half mile from the Post Road and the town's dealers' row of car lots. Snickers abounded over the silly Jew from the airports who overpaid for a white elephant.

Salvation came in the form of Victoria Vanderstein. The moment that Shapiro's yenta wife saw him talking to Victoria at a party, she knew right then her marriage was probably over. Victoria was like the immigrant descendant two generations removed: She was a Jewess, but she looked more inclined toward *Howard's End* than Howard Beach.

Victoria had been raised in the County and had gone to private school there. When she met Sid, she was fundraising for the 92nd Street Y and lived in the city during the week. She seemed to know everyone and fit in everywhere. She was statuesque, with red hair, freckles, green eyes and an athletic purity—she'd been on the diving team at Pepperdine. Placing toned, healthful wholesomeness on a pedestal in such a rarified air, she seemed erotically virginal. Married men looked at a point in the distance when talking to her for fear of losing themselves in her ethereal presence and risk having to hear about it from their wives for the next six months. To Sid, it couldn't be more clear: Victoria was a woman to navigate through society and life with, a woman whose company would make him incalculably more attractive and bankable.

Sid's wife took the humiliation in stride—for a while. She hoped the phase would pass, and suffered as a second-class citizen in her own home while Sid waged his campaign. Finally, she sought refuge in a visit to her parents. It was a one-way trip out of the County and back to the neighborhood where she grew up. Sid offered no excuses: It had all been a terrible mistake with her. He gave her the entire proceeds of the sale of the house and half of his trading portfolio. He wanted her happy in her settlement—and gone from his life for good. Sid Shapiro started over from nearly nothing with only a vague notion that he might land Victoria Vanderstein. Sid's ex-wife married a rabbi, and they bought a house out near the airports.

It was a relationship founded on real estate: Sid asked for Victoria's help viewing homes, pleading a truthful ignorance in understanding the subtle cultural qualities that distinguished one property from another in a county that placed an unappraisable value on setting and address. Victoria had other men in her life and made no pretense to deny it. Sid was just one of many in a grand horse race. She was helping him partly out of curiosity—to simply let the game play out and see if he could in fact land her— but also because she enjoyed spending money, even if it was only other people's. For a good while, they were like two prizefighters circling each other in the ring in anticipation of who would land the first blow. The exchange was finally consummated in the master bedroom of a five-bedroom Georgian estate on seven acres. Sid and Victoria stood facing each other like two teenagers at a high school dance and asked the broker for a "minute" to get a feel for the room. While the broker made calls from the front foyer, Sid Shapiro finally took it all—everything he wanted or ever would want—inside *the* girl, inside *the* house, inside *the* County, and started on the new life he now chose for himself. "I think you should make them an offer," Victoria quipped as she pulled her panties back on under her summer dress, leaving Sid Shapiro, sexually spent, to contemplate a number.

Sid Shapiro bought the property and was engaged to marry Victoria within a year. His prospective brother-in-law, Alex Vanderstein, had also become similarly disillusioned with a law career, abandoning it for professional freedom—and financial limbo. The more Alex got to know Sid, the more intrigued he became with the entire field of financial services—an industry he'd largely ignored up until this point. He pestered Sid about investing and hedge funds—shorting this company's stock, buying that country's currency. Sid humored him, for a while. One night at a luau dinner at the Little Kill beach club with Victoria, Sid finally leveled with Alex.

"You're a gentleman, Alex—to the manor born, but you don't know shit about business! You know rich people—lots of them. You probably know two-thirds of the membership of this club by their first name. Deliver me access to that caliber of client—twenty-four carat leads—and then we'll have something to talk about." The die was cast. Sid had the hands-on, Alex had the connections. With all the free money floating around the County, the two ex-lawyers put their heads together and came up with *the* idea: a hedge fund-of-funds. Empire Capital hung out a shingle at the top of the Avenue and started taking deposits.

* * * * *

id had been bitten by the shooting bug, first participating in intra-club events at Little Kill, but quickly progressing to the sporting clays circuit. He shot a matched pair of Perazzi

MX-8s with deep relief engraving in a Celtic theme, and owned a dozen or so London Best guns—he wasn't really sure anymore. He also bought several of the Winston Firearms custom shop's finest pieces, the jewel in the crown being a Grand American Model-21 originally built for Herbert Hoover. Shapiro hired the best coaches, and used company block-time in a corporate jet lease to fly around the country for clinics. Box-bird shooting was his newest passion, and he'd already shot both the Pennsylvania circuit and the World Championship in Spain.

Sid's rationale for the Winston Firearms acquisition was multifaceted. First off, he legitimately saw a potential for profitability by resurrecting a legendary name that had gone to seed. Secondly, as an officer of the New Winston Firearms, all of his costs related to shooting would become a write-off—a legitimate business expense. Why didn't he simply finance the deal himself? Why bother to chase private equity investors for such a relatively paltry sum? Because that's not the way the game is played. The first rule is you put the deal together and raise the money, and *then* you cut yourself in for free. You never put your own money at risk, and recognize that the true measure of a deal-maker is how long the line of investors stretches to throw in with him. Sid's ego simply wouldn't allow him to pay for the brand himself. First, he had to sell the dream to someone else.

Shapiro's interest in Winky and Walter Wagner was simple. He was hosting an invitational box-bird event at his private quail plantation in the Red Hills north of Tallahassee. The prospective board of directors for the newly re-formed Winston Firearms would attend, as would a slew of high-net-worth individuals who might enjoy meeting a legendary exhibition shooting team. Invited to enjoy a weekend of box-birds, gratis, these wealthy benefactors would also be solicited to join Empire Capital as clients.

III

Conrad Winston III had gone to school with Alex Vanderstein, and they also knew each other from Little Kill. Conrad had started his career in the nonprofit world at the National Kennel Society. Then he moved into trust management, insurance and, most recently, yacht brokerage. He was meek and affable—a natural for the soft sell, but he never earned the big money he expected. He also wasn't bold enough to learn these businesses from the ground up and strike out on his own. He was, as such, chronically dissatisfied with his underemployment. His connections were just as promising as Alex's, but they were also largely the same connections. Conrad wanted in on Empire Capital, but he had nothing to bring to the party—no money and no expertise. The only thing Conrad Winston III had to offer was his last name.

All that remained of the formerly august Winston Firearms was the brand, which until recently had been pasted on everything from clothing, to beer can cozies, to thermos bottles and sunglasses, and even a power boat. While the design patents for the most recent generation of guns were still active, the real value of Winston was not in the current patents but in the original, pre-1964 designs themselves. Sid Shapiro reasoned that by blending the contemporary design with the best of the original, augmented with cheap Chinese handwork, the Winston line could be reintroduced profitably as a quality firearm built to a price. As to Conrad he would be if not the front man, then at least the public face of the deal. He would be a figurehead chief executive, with a cushy position overseeing an informal dealer network. Conrad hoped to parlay this role into a permanent position in the hedge-fund business.

Conrad assumed that Sid Shapiro wanted Walter Wagner. In addition to winning the Grand American in trap-doubles, Walter had also been a formidable competitor in the pigeon ring. It was Walter who acted as assistant in all those old color films of Winky's exhibition shooting act. She shot empty 12-gauge paper cartridges off his fingertips, and it was also Walter who clenched the cigarette in his teeth when Winky extinguished it with a .22-short from twenty feet. It was Walter who engineered and built the contraption that allowed Winky—standing on the roof of a trap house—to launch a dozen clays into the air at once and break them all with a Model-12 pump. Walter had been the creator and choreographer of the act, and had taught Winky how to make every shot. He was her assistant, then her straight man, and finally the male-chauvinist buffoon to her liberated Annie Oakley.

Sid Shapiro offered Walter an honorarium of $300 per day plus hotel expenses. Walter countered, demanding a flat fee of $500 for total expenses as well as a daily rate of $500 to be paid—cash-in-hand—each morning. Walter wasn't enthusiastic about the trip: It meant missing one visit to Winky and three days away from his fishing. Sid Shapiro let out a chuckle over the phone when he heard the demand. Sid admired audacity in all its forms, particularly in a cantankerous old man. The New Winston Firearms Corporation could afford Walter Wagner. He was part of American lore—one of the few quasi-celebrities Winston could still claim as its own.

IV

Conrad Winston arrived at the prescribed date and time with an engraved invitation to the event and $1,000 in his pocket. Out in front of Walter Wagner's single-wide sat a sixteen-foot long, tear-drop-shaped tow-behind camper made of varnished plywood hitched to a stylish white 1959 Chevrolet El Camino with tail fins. A Boston Whaler, with the helm console and cockpit stripped out for fishing, rested on a trailer in the yard. Walter was filling the camper's water tank with a hose.

"I don't think I've ever seen a wooden camper," Conrad said in salutation.

"Bought it second-hand right after we were married. Used it for all our shows—drove it all over the country."

"It looks brand new," Conrad said, noting his reflection in the varnished bright-work.

"Never spent a night outside she didn't need to. A fishing buddy of mine lets me use his warehouse down here."

"I just can't believe anything this old . . ."

"Take care of your equipment, Junior-Junior, and you'll be surprised how long it'll last," Walter said interrupting him. "You see that frame and axle? It's the gun carriage off a Howitzer. When the original apparatus let go, I replaced it with that. Bought 'em as scrap from Winston Firearms. That's number two—don't suppose I'll ever get to number three."

Conrad poked his head inside the trailer's open door. It was a marvel of compact hominess. The upholstery, curtains, bedspread and tablecloth were in a matching royal-blue-and-white nautical theme. "Winky made all that. That woman was a whiz with a needle and thread. She made all her own shooting clothes—mine too. At one point, Winston even thought about having her do a clothing line for lady shooters."

Conrad would accompany Walter up to the event. He worried about the old man driving at all, but particularly at night. Shapiro wanted to make sure Walter showed up. On Saturday, Sid would show his guests four half-hour films of Winky Wagner in her prime, and Shapiro wanted to have at least half the act on hand.

When they finally pulled onto the highway, Conrad explained that Walter's duties would be to press the flesh with the crowd, wear his Winston Firearms regalia and be generally agreeable. Both windows were down in the un-air-conditioned truck, so the men had to shout to be heard. "You don't mind if we make a quick stop?" Walter asked.

As the caravan pulled into Palmetto Glades Trap and Skeet, Conrad's interest was piqued. "This'll only take a minute." Walter said, as he double parked the El Camino over two handicapped spots, leaving the flashers on. Conrad followed the old man inside to the front desk.

"You got a couple of guns here on loan from me," Walter said, pointing over his shoulder to a glass case containing a shrine to Winky Wagner. The woman behind the desk looked confused.

Walter turned around and pointed to the case. "Those guns in there—they belong to me. There's a note inside the barrel of each of them to that effect. I want to borrow them back for the weekend." The woman was flustered. Walter surmised he was dealing with a mental defective.

When the gun club manager finally appeared, he shook Walter's hand politely and told him he knew nothing of the agreement. As far as he was concerned, the case and its contents were club property, but he would call the previous manager to enquire as to the specifics. When the manager retired to his office to place the call and the desk clerk left her post for the bathroom, Walter Wagner produced a key from his pocket with which he opened the glass shrine. He motioned to Conrad and handed him a Super-X trap gun and a 22-pump gallery gun, and draped an open over-under, 101 live-bird-combo over his right forearm. He then placed a nickel-plated Model-12 pump with a custom, extended, riveted alloy magazine tube and a military surplus canvas web sling over his shoulder and took with his left hand a Model-37 single-barrel hammer gun with an aftermarket rib and a highly accurate Model-52 target rifle with his right hand. All five guns were adorned with custom shop, feather-crotch walnut and pink, yellow and white gold inlays of songbirds. An 1873 lever-action .30-.30, a Peacemaker revolver and a 1911 Automatic pistol were the only things that remained inside the case. Conrad walked gingerly to the car with a gun in each hand as Walter locked the glass case and slipped out.

"Isn't this illegal?" Conrad asked as they laid the guns onto the bedspread covering the floor of the trailer.

"That's my handwriting, ain't it?" Walter proclaimed, removing a rolled-up, yellowed index card from the muzzle of the Super-X and showing it to him. "That's my signature. If they want to prosecute an old man for borrowing back his own guns, good luck." Conrad got in the El Camino, and Walter started the engine.

"I thought those were Winky's guns?" Conrad asked.

"They are, but they were mine first. She always used my guns from when she started shooting: always my dimensions. She never changed, so I just set up all her guns to shoot for me." Conrad looked over his shoulder, expecting to see someone come rushing out of the club house door. "Don't worry Junior-Junior. They'll get 'em all back after the weekend."

Conrad was puzzled. No one expected Walter to shoot. Why did he feel the need to bring his own guns? "It never fails," Walter enlightened him. "Anytime I don't bring a gun, I always wind up wishing I had. If I'm going to pull a trigger, it's damn well going to be with a gun I can hit something with."

The El Camino rolled north over the Florida peninsula at a steady 70 miles per hour. The vehicle was white, with patches of royal blue coming through what looked like house paint. It was musty and unkempt. The driver's-side seat cushion had collapsed through the wire framing, and there was a small decorative chintz throw pillow from Sea World that covered the hole. When they stopped to refuel at a particularly inexpensive truck stop, Walter filled four additional jerry jugs: enough gas to run his portable generator for the weekend.

"You take over, Junior-Junior," Walter said, opening the passenger's side door. "This old fart needs to close his eyes for a bit."

* * * * *

Babysitting was just one more in a long line of humiliating, peon assignments that had comprised Conrad's professional career. He'd lost enough pride and social standing in his adult life, so at this point there wasn't much that was beneath him. But this, he felt, was. He'd been born during the final crescendo of the Winston family's powers. His great-grandfather had founded the company, and his grandfather made it a household name. His father sold a controlling interest to the Orion Corporation, and they eventually took the remainder from the family as collateral on a bad loan.

Conrad ("Double") Winston II had never quite accepted that

once he conceded even partial ownership, Winston Firearms was no longer really his. As chairman, he was regularly confronted by internal auditors who questioned his repeated use of company accounts for blatantly personal expenses, and he was incensed that they expected reimbursement. Even though his name was on the building, Double couldn't stand that he had a board of directors to answer to.

The board expected Winston Firearms to be profitably run by career professionals. Double thought otherwise. Things finally came to a head when an oilman-cum-corporate-raider took a fourteen-percent stake in Orion and demanded a seat on the Winston board of directors. Double denied the request out of hand via a press release, but the raider filed a class-action lawsuit on behalf of all Orion shareholders, charging embezzlement.

At the time, Continental Distillers day-to-day operations were headed by Double's business school roommate, and he saw a surefire way to diffuse the entire situation and keep his position as chairman. If Double could convince Distillers to purchase the controlling interest in Winston Firearms from Orion, the sale might quash any legal proceedings while allowing him to remain in place as CEO. The plan was foolproof; that is, until Continental Distiller's chief operating officer—his former roommate—died of a heart attack on the ski slopes before the deal could close.

In the process of preparing Winston Firearms for a possible sale, the Orion bean-counters determined that it was in fact the ammunition side of the business that was the most profitable, the most highly automated and therefore the most promising in the long term. The arms business was limping along, barely surviving off its past glories and making due with old designs and very expensive union labor. The solution was obvious: figure out a way to spin off the gun business. The Japanese firm that produced the 101over-under expressed immediate interest in an acquisition, but it was only the brand name and the designs they were interested in. The real estate, tooling and most of all, the union employees with their eye-watering legacy costs—these the Japanese weren't interested in retaining.

Double Winston was faced with a crisis of conscience when the board of directors threatened that the way forward lay in completely shuttering the arms division in one fell swoop and pink-slipping its entire workforce. A shrewd businessman would have forsaken sentiment, set his jaw and expediently done the dirty deed. In the end, Double Winston was neither shrewd nor a real businessman and did what he thought his own father, the great company patriarch, would have done in the same circumstance: Against his better judgment, he acted as guarantor for the refinancing of an employee buyout of the arms division of Winston Firearms.

Double Winston served as chief executive officer and chairman of the board to the newly recapitalized entity, and when the city of Bridgewater was forced into civic bankruptcy, valuable incentives and tax subsidies that the company relied on for its very profitability, were nullified by a federal bankruptcy manager. When the leveraged company inevitably missed a debt-service payment to Orion, it was Double who suffered catastrophic personal ruin. With the company in receivership, he became just another ruined executive with a drinking problem. Due to further disastrous financial calamity and the divorce from Conrad III's mother, Double Winston died alone and relatively young, of a heart attack in a hotel suite in the city. All this had played out when Conrad was in prep school. When he started at boarding school, he was the heir apparent to a firearms dynasty that was a household name. By the time he left for college he knew his degree would be preparing him for life as just another working stiff.

Conrad III's mother was still very much alive, remarried, with a daughter from the second marriage and unwavering in her assertion that her substantial wealth, including a valuable stock portfolio she took in the divorce, was hers to spend. The remaining fortune, upon her death, would be split between Conrad and his half-sister.

Downward mobility had been gradual at first, but had gained in momentum. Conrad recently took a leave of absence from the club. It killed him to do so, but his modest trust fund had always subsidized Little Kill. With his own divorce, subsequent alimony and child support, the numbers had become quite impossible. A leave of absence stemmed the hemorrhage of club dues and minimums, but it was only a temporary salve—he had two years to either get his finances in order or resign from the club altogether.

He went from buying new cars, to buying demonstrators from McCashin Motors, to finally purchasing used cars off a lot over the state line in Port Easton. He too had moved to Port Easton, into a cramped studio apartment. He retained his old in-County cell-phone prefix as well as a post office box, hoping to perpetuate the illusion that he was still living in town. His clothes mostly came from eBay or the thrift shops in Palm Beach or Nantucket. It was a stark change from a lifestyle he had lived even a few years ago, but the labels still had the right names on them. He liked to imagine that he remained essentially the same person and continued to make the same outward impression on the rest of the world. To the keen observer, however, he had an impoverished sheen about him, like the worn elbows of his blue blazer.

*　*　*　*　*

P ull over here," Walter said, suddenly wide awake, pointing to a roadside orange and grapefruit juice stand. "This was Winky's favorite. Best juice in the Sunshine State. We always hit it coming and going."

The juice lived up to its billing. It was freshly squeezed from Florida's finest before your very eyes. No ice, no straw: simple service in a white paper cup. Walter ordered two cups and a quart jug to go. He drained the first cup before Conrad's had even been squeezed.

"Ms. Adelman seems nice," Conrad suggested.

"Mitzy's okay," Walter replied, starting on his second cup.

"Manages the whole place, does she?"

Walter very deliberately put his drink down on the countertop, showing his growing irritation. "Yes, she manages the whole place—owns nearly half of it in fact: the community center, post office, pharmacy, shuffleboard, docks and the office." He eyeballed Conrad and asked, "Is there something in particular you're trying to get at here, or is this just a feeble attempt at small talk?"

"Just small talk, I guess," Conrad said as his juice finally arrived. Walter looked away and then finally turned back.

"You were prying—at least admit it," Walter said. "We can talk about lots of things. We can talk about my special friendship with Mitzy while my wife is vegetating away upstate. Winky liked Mitzy. She wanted it this way, and told me as much. How about we talk about your old man, Junior-Junior, and how he ended up drinking himself to death? I see you wearing a wedding ring, but I'd bet cash money she divorced you—how would you like to talk about that?!" Walter stared into the bottom of his empty paper cup. "We all got scabs, boy—you don't pick at mine, and I'll do likewise." Conrad paid the tab. Walter picked up his quart jug off the countertop, and they both headed for the car.

V

The Onori Plantation was renowned, and Walter knew it well. Onori was an anagram of Orion, as in the Orion Corporation, which had bought a majority stake in Winston Firearms directly from Double Winston. Orion repurchased the old place to use for corporate entertaining when it acquired Winston Firearms. In its heyday under the ownership of Conrad Senior, the plantation had hosted the Duke of Windsor and Herbert Hoover. Gary Cooper, Ted Williams and Robert Ruark were repeat guests.

Dogham plantation, as it was known then, was a simple, spartan facility for outdoorsmen. Guests were well entertained, but the shooting always came first, and the creature comforts second. For more than a decade after its repurchase, the Orion Corporation attempted, albeit unsuccessfully, to use it for business entertaining, but it was always an awkward fit. Executives from unrelated industries within the Orion conglomerate didn't naturally gravitate toward blood sport.

Onori was a place Double could treat as his very own, a place where a man could ride Tennessee Walking Horses or shoot quail, and entertain business associates or even the occasional extracurricular lady friend in complete privacy. Most importantly, Double Winston would finally be able to drink as much as he wanted at any hour of the day or night, far from prying eyes— particularly those of his wife.

Eventually, Orion couldn't justify the eye-popping expense of its own private quail plantation any longer, and sold it. Situated near the state border between Tallahassee, Florida, and Thomasville, Georgia, Onori was a bona fide biscuits-and-gravy Old Southern plantation. Conrad Senior had cobbled it together by purchasing an antebellum mansion and its outlying 500 acres, and then securing the lease of 10,000 additional acres of surrounding farmland.

In the years since Onori's final sale, the mansion and its surrounds went through varying incarnations, finally ending up as a bit of Southern pomp and circumstance for the wedding industry.

Sid Shapiro had stumbled across the history of Onori in his research for the Winston Firearms acquisition, and vowed to not only put the plantation back together but to make it better than ever.

Onori's present size was down to just over 2,000 acres—not nearly big enough to sustain wild quail, which made necessary regular weekly releases of pen-raised birds in order to let them learn to fly *wild*. The amenities at Onori were the best they'd ever been. The main house was surrounded by 25 acres, a swimming pool, tennis court, stables for eight horses and/or mules and kennels for two dozen hunting dogs. And there was "The Branch" flowing through the property, for bass fishing and swimming.

When Sid bought it, the mansion was a patchwork of additions and utilitarian elements grafted haphazardly onto classical Greek-revival architecture. Victoria Vanderstein Shapiro made the restoration of the estate her project. For the better part of two years she shuttled back and forth to Onori using up valuable time on Sid's private jet account and oversaw much of the work herself.

While she didn't pretend to be an expert on architecture, she did know what the fancy Northeast set—what a Little Kill member—would expect from such a place. She had taste and style, and she intuitively knew the checklist Onori needed to qualify as a Southern clubhouse for the *big swinging dicks* of the Northern business world.

The main house had six bedrooms, each with a full bath and Jacuzzi tub, central air conditioning with independent climate zones and antique beds with Swedish mattresses. Each room also had its own Acoustic Wave music system—Sid had flatly refused televisions in the guest rooms. The library held every book the Winston Firearms publishing division had ever printed, as well as a full complement of first editions of every other obvious outdoor literary work. The dining room could seat two dozen. The game room had regulation pool and billiard tables, and the bar was an alcoholic's wet dream. The grounds were maintained like Little Kill's. Two full-time and countless part-time staff dedicated themselves to this immaculate presentation of corporate staging designed to intimidate a peer—practically whispering in his ear, *this is what real money looks like, hayseed; these people are out of your league.*

Sid and Victoria eventually felt the innkeeper's lament when in residence at the plantation. They entertained in the mansion beautifully, but the nights often ran too late, to the point where Sid established a rule—last call at the bar was midnight, no exceptions. They also determined that while over-the-top Southern white-glove entertaining was fun, they liked their privacy and found a practical simplicity in doing the smallest things for themselves. They converted a suite of rooms in the south wing into a supremely comfortable, self-contained private apartment. Never much of a drinker, Sid simply concluded an evening at the stroke of midnight by dead-bolting a lock on the bar and soberly retiring to the warm bosom of his intimate quarters within his grand home and into arms of his waiting wife.

Sid lived a larger-than-life existence among his impressive

possessions, but he surprised even himself in that after he'd *arrived*, none of it really turned his head. *This* Onori had never really existed until Sid dreamed it up, and the modern Onori was far better appointed than had ever been the original. This new incarnation was the businessman's equivalent of a bachelor's closing restaurant: the last establishment a would-be suitor would wine and dine his young lady at before he closed the deal in the bedroom.

VI

t noon, Walter awoke with a loud snort and started searching on the car's AM radio. He fine-tuned the dial until the vocal ranting boomed over variable static.

"I should have known," Conrad said, half-condescendingly.

Walter shot him an irritated glance, confirming this was in fact one of his guilty pleasures. "Politics, religion and anything else that's even mildly interesting to talk about, Wink was always steering me away from. I'll tell you one thing, Junior-Junior, if you voted for that commie piss-ant, you deserve to be just as flat broke as the rest of us."

"I'm a moderate," Conrad said.

"No such thing." Walter paused a moment and recomposed himself. "I'm not gonna harangue you, boy. Wasn't that long ago I voted the union ticket right on down, but when people say it doesn't matter who's in charge, I know right down to the marrow they couldn't be more wrong. When Ike said *go to Korea*, I went. I sure as hell didn't want to, and there's times even now I wish I hadn't. But he was my commander, and I was just a snot-nosed kid. The best military mind of the twentieth century says go—you go. It was the right thing to do even if I didn't understand it then. We forged a half-assed peace that by some miracle has lasted."

"I think we're best off when we try to see things from all the points of view," Conrad replied. "Be realistic and not condemn compromise."

"Commendable sentiment, son, but Wink and me barely survived the seventies, and *this* time reminds me of that. I'm already hard up against it: I'm making it on fish sandwiches and tap water. I suppose it doesn't really matter whether it turns around or not—I won't be a part of it anyway. I'm doing this thing for the same reason you are, Junior-Junior. I need the money—for a new roof, a new outboard motor, and I need to get that bench seat you're sitting on re-covered."

Walter stuck his arm out the open window and marveled as his hand undulated, porpoise-like, in the slipstream. "I'd probably be better off junking this old girl and buying something newer, but I'd miss the familiarity of it," Walter said, as he pulled his hand back inside the cab and looked over at Conrad. "I'm a twentieth-century man, Junior-Junior, a mid-twentieth-century man really, and I'd just as soon go out that way—keeping up the illusion. If I squint a little bit, it all goes just fuzzy enough so I can almost pretend things aren't really so different. Hey, there's a Wal-Mart," Walter said, pointing out the window. "Get off. I need a few things for the weekend."

He bought some generic motor oil and windshield washer fluid, as well as a twelve-gauge Beretta 391 autoloader from the hunting and fishing department. "How can you possibly need another gun?" Conrad asked. "You just hijacked an entire museum exhibit of firearms!"

Walter was hunched over the counter filling out the paper work. "Maybe I want to get back into trapshooting—or try out that sporting clays I've heard so much about. Or maybe I just want it for protection. What the hell difference does it make to you?"

"It makes no difference to me," Conrad replied. "But Sid Shapiro is going to go ape if he sees that—totally mental. He asked you along because he feels you were a big part of the Winston Firearms family, but he also views it like he's doing you a big favor and he expects some consideration for that. He's going to treat you like an employee—he pretty much treats everyone like an employee. Listen to me, Walter—*let him*. You said you need the money from this. Don't start off on the wrong foot by showing that gun to anyone."

"We'll just see about all that, Junior-Junior. It's still a free country—for the time being at least," he said as he shook the sales clerk's hand.

VII

Sid Shapiro spent the morning in Thomasville picking up an over-under—a pigeon gun by Ivo Fabbri. It was the Majestic Model, a single-trigger, seven-pin side-lock with 29-inch Phoenix steel barrels and bouquet engraving over a coin finish. He knew he'd overpaid for it at auction. It wasn't anything he particularly lusted after or even wanted to shoot, especially for the event this weekend, where he wanted to shoot well. It was a strategic piece, and was to play a specific role in his gun collection: He would shoot it a bit simply to be seen with it.

A Fabbri pigeon gun speaks wordlessly to just the right people. To the untrained eye, it looks no better or worse than any other upscale shotgun. But Fabbri, even more than Purdey, Boss, or Holland & Holland, conveys a powerful message to firearms cognoscenti. It's simply the best handmade—best designed, highest quality, most reliable—and therefore most desirable competition gun ever made. A Fabbri is rare—virtually unheard of in the clay-target disciplines. This gun was purpose-built for the big-money game of killing live pigeons on the wing. The Fabbri is unrivalled in balance and handling and for a man who lives for box-bird shooting, it's the only gun he'll ever need to own, provided he can afford one. For most, the thrill of owning a Fabbri is as much about the cachet as it is about shooting it. Some people are so intimidated by the mere sight of one that they refuse to handle it. If anything happened—they dropped it, scratched it or damaged it in some way—the repair bill could run into tens of thousands of dollars. For that kind of money, it really is just as nice to look at.

For someone who predominantly played clay-target games, however, it usually made more sense to shoot the gun they're intimately familiar with for fliers or perhaps just switch to a lighter set of barrels. The optimal solution for the occasional box-bird shooter is to procure a proper set of pigeon barrels. By design, these throw the bottom, first barrel, high and the top, second barrel, spot-on. A live pigeon unfolding its wings and rising into flight would, therefore, have some built-in vertical allowance on the first shot, and the second would be a dead-flat rifle shot.

Sid had been around shooting circles long enough to have divined all this for himself. He was first and foremost a shooter, not a collector. His newest acquisition, priced at a shade under six figures, would add to his image. A man who owned a Fabbri was a particular type of man—even if Sid hadn't quite figured out what type that was. He knew that this gun, at least for the weekend, would send the right message to the right people. It really was just another part of his business calculus. If he decided later, as he suspected he eventually would, that being the kind of man who owned a Fabbri wasn't all that it was cracked up to be, he could always flog it at auction to another unsuspecting image-conscious buyer, at a hair under what he paid, less commission.

* * * * *

Sid was a statistician in business, preferring small, steady margins and equally manageable risks. In baseball terms, he considered himself a good hitter of doubles. *Keep getting on base*, he reasoned, *and the runs will take care of themselves.* Sid's weakness—the glaring white light that blinded him to rational thought and fed an insatiable financial blood lust—was for the deal that ensured the ruination of the counterparty. To gut a man at the poker table, in the coffee pits or in the fine print of a contract, and watch him absorb the monumental impact of total annihilation, that he'd been utterly taken: That feeling of complete domination was what Sid Shapiro lived for. It made even the smallest deal priceless, and without it, even the biggest transaction seemed unsatisfying— like a paid sexual encounter: better than nothing, but lacking the savor of a true conquest. Sid knew nothing more gratifying in life than counting the other guy's money while he's on his knees, begging for mercy.

Sid was a deal junkie. He still prided himself on his personal trades and continued to look for private equity deals for himself and a few select clients, but most of his *sheep*—unless he was bringing them into the inner sanctum—were fed directly into the funds. He had long since concluded that the best way to make money was to skim management commissions off investment portfolios. By managing a growing pool of assets and charging not only a management fee, but also a percentage of the profits, Sid had built a better financial mousetrap. It's what attracted him to hedge funds in the first place. There was also the nagging problem of actually managing a fund. Sid was patient for quick-turnaround deals, but the long-term buy/sell discipline wasn't his strong suit. Besides, why expend all that energy when it was just as easy to feed clients into multiple other funds who would do all that heavy lifting for you?

His fund-of-funds model was a great success. Everyone made money. The clients, the funds themselves, all the way up to Sid Shapiro and Alex Vanderstein, each of whom skimmed a layer of rich cream off the top of everything. The only thing that ever kept Sid awake at night was that Mr. Market's Infinity Fund was secretive about its trading practices to a point that seemed paranoid. Because Sid had a background in mergers and acquisitions and Alex had been a prosecutor, Empire Capital emphasized—even heralded—their due diligence capabilities. Empire went far deeper into a balance sheet—they claimed—than was typical. When they vetted a manager, it was the kind of colonoscopy usually reserved for a takeover bid, as opposed to a trading partner. And the due diligence was comprehensive for every single manager—except Mr. Market. Unbeknownst to anyone, Sid eventually panicked: One day out of the blue, he insisted on a face-to-face meeting, where he literally begged to see documentation on Empire Capital's holdings in the Infinity Fund. Mr. Market smiled his Cheshire Cat smile, stood up from his desk and gave Sid Shapiro a bear hug.

"Of course, of course," he whispered in Sid's ear as they embraced. "You're upset and I'm to blame. It's this bugaboo of mine about control—if you want to keep something a secret, don't tell anyone. My shop is a closed-circuit without a single person knowing more than the absolute minimum of what is required to keep this thing up in the air and flying. Unfortunately, this also means my counterparts sometimes feel vulnerable; their imaginations run wild. My suspicions feed their suspicions. I deeply regret that I've made you uncomfortable, Sidney. My business associates are like family to me—it's as if I've upset one of my own daughters."

Just then the cherubically youthful head of IT for Infinity appeared and stationed himself at Mr. Market's computer terminal. "Simon's about to put your mind at rest," Mr. Market said reassuringly. A cacophony of keystrokes later, they arrived at the National Depository Trust Co. website. "Our custodial holdings are all registered. Now I'm only going to do this for you once. . . . Give me two positions in your account, and I'll show you the holdings," and he did. Sid knew the approximate size of two growth-stocks in Empire Capital's fund-of-funds that were exclusive to Infinity, and there they were, just as big as life. It wasn't exactly proper due diligence, but it allayed Sid's fears and put his mind at rest—at least for a time.

Attempting to probe any further would have been futile. Sid certainly couldn't audit Infinity: Mr. Market would never allow that, and he set the ground rules. If you wanted in on Infinity, you didn't ask too many questions. Take the leap of faith, keep your cool and Mr. Market will make you rich. The double-digit returns continued to roll in, just as they had for decades. Everyone got fat. What worried Sid was that as overall economic conditions gradually shifted, he abandoned his balanced approach to the funds. He let this single winner take over a larger and larger portion of the investment. So far, his plan had worked and his clients didn't seem to mind that his formerly conservative model had morphed into a concentrated, aggressive strategy in a brief three years.

* * * * *

id signed for the Fabbri, put it in the trunk of his vintage Mercedes-Benz Silver Arrow convertible and locked it. He pumped the accelerator three times and turned the key. The straight-six fired briefly and sputtered. He turned it over again, and the engine started to idle roughly. Sid coaxed the car to life like a father coaxes a baby to eat strained peas. *This car was always a pain in the ass to start,* he thought. Finally, the engine seemed to clear its throat and began to hum sweetly. This image-enhancing toy, this unforgivably finicky and breathtakingly beautiful automobile, drove worse than a new Toyota sedan, and got just under 13 mpg on premium.

Sid would be the first to admit that he was a bad driver. Growing up near the airports, he'd never even owned a car until he moved to the County. He lacked reflexes and situational awareness. He found the coordination of multitasking while simultaneously maintaining his concentration difficult, and he had the nerve-racking habit of turning his entire head away from the road to talk to a passenger. He'd long since curb-rashed all four rims on his Lexus, the only car he drove regularly. He clipped protrusions with the tires and regularly gave love taps to other cars' bodywork when backing up. He constantly found himself in the wrong gear when driving the Mercedes, with its tricky stick shift, and often stalled it when starting out in first. As he worked his way through the gearbox, he invariably found himself either over-revving the engine in third or lugging the motor at low speed in fourth. When he came to a stop, he would forget to downshift. He would often arrive at a stoplight still in fourth gear standing hard on the brake pedal, trying to prevent the car from creeping forward, and would ultimately stall the vehicle. He'd already replaced the clutch in this car once, and it had cost him a king's ransom.

Though his name was on the title, it was Victoria who'd really wanted the Mercedes. It was ostensibly a bribe, as Victoria didn't care for plantation life. She found some small satisfaction in the rehabilitation of Onori, but Sid knew she always found a quiet gratification in spending large sums of money. She considered

Southern living, with its slower pace, slower way of talking, heavy food, soft and not-so-soft bigotry and graduated degrees of cultural literacy, stultifying and cringe-worthy. Victoria was interested in *ideas*. At home, an evening's entertainment might be a dinner party with a billionaire banker, an avant-garde multimedia artist and a political activist. Her dinner guests might argue acrimoniously, but all would have something interesting to contribute, and the opinions would at least be informed. Southern charm was lost on her.

Victoria's single foray into plantation society had been the Christmas party at another plantation. The women's conversation ran to hairstyles (the bigger, the better), nail polish and its relationship to eye shadow and, of course, to church life. Though none of them worked, each woman had an "idiot" black maid whom they kept on out of a sense of duty. *Her* family had once been owned by *their* family five or so generations back, and the bonds of responsibility from overseer to chattel, slaveholder to slave, far outlived the Confederacy or any law of man. The males drank beer and Maker's Mark Old-Fashions, spoke of hunting—everything from the bobwhite quail to the snapping turtle—college football, the prices of soybeans and peanuts, and conservative Southern politics.

At nine o'clock, the local church choir arrived on the front lawn to sing Christmas carols in minstrel chorus. After the recital, the master of the house discreetly passed the deacon a check, and the choir was treated to refreshments at the back door. It was all very down-home and picturesque—something so saccharine it could only be staged. It was rare that Victoria ever felt out of place, but plantation society was beyond her adaptable range. She would never fit in, and vowed that evening to stop trying.

This Mercedes was a quid pro quo to Victoria for accompanying Sid to Onori. While she was still lukewarm on Southern living, she did like to brag about her prowess behind the wheel. Although the convertible was just another bit of image-enhancing corporate stagecraft to Sid, it was a never-ending source of exhilaration to

Victoria. To slip behind the wood-rimmed steering wheel and into distressed leather seats older than she was, to heel-toe down into third gear through a long, fast bend, all the while keeping the rear end on the verge of sliding, this was a thrill that only came from doing something inherently dangerous. *Anyone can drive a safe modern car well*, Victoria thought. *It took nerve and a light touch to get the best out of that Mercedes.* Though children with Sid were already penciled in on the calendar, until her official title became Mommy, flirting with the ragged edge behind the wheel of that gunmetal Silver Arrow was one of the only motivations for Victoria to take the jet down to Onori.

VIII

Alex Vanderstein looked tanned and fit, fresh off the courts and still dressed in his tennis whites. He tipped the valet two dollars and got into his rented Volvo sedan. A junior suite at the Ritz-Carlton was his home away from home whenever he was in south Florida, and it suited him. He liked the fact that, while the hotel was easily accessible to Palm Beach, it was situated in Manalapan, the better part of five miles south of the cashmere district. The Ritz-Carlton was convenient, opened out onto the beach and was slightly under the radar: perfect for someone who was pretty well known in financial circles but generally preferred to remain as anonymous as possible. Many of his associates stayed at the Breakers resort when they were in town. Quite a few had even bought beachfront homes. Alex had briefly considered it, and taken a pass. His mantra was simple and timeless: Unto thine own self be true. The self-aggrandizement—the trappings of wealth—were prisons in themselves. He knew who he was and left the window-dressing to others.

Alex crossed the bridge leading from A1A into West Palm Beach. It's barely a stone's throw from the barrier island of Palm Beach, where a wealthy Jew in tennis whites and a rented Volvo might feel a fundamental part of the social fabric, to the marginal, mostly black neighborhoods of West Palm Beach, where that same person might feel like a target. Alex self-consciously locked his car door at the first stoplight on the mainland and followed the GPS directions. St. Gilbert's Christian Academy was in one of the worst neighborhoods in the city. Alex parked his car in the visitor's spot of the school parking lot.

A black eighth-grade boy in the academy uniform of a crisp white short-sleeved shirt, black necktie and black pants led Alex through a maze of corridors and stairwells into the basement of the complex, past the massive climate-control air handlers and finally into a large, darkened storage room. The farthest wall was spot-lit with floodlights trained on five regulation bull's-eyes. Of the five students, there were three black boys and a Hispanic boy and girl. They all wore padded, multicolored riflery coats and were shooting air rifles from the offhand position. A timer counted down from fifteen minutes.

"Breathe in, breathe out," Douglas McCashin said, just above a whisper. "In—let it halfway out and hold it. Calm the mind—calm the heart. Let the pendulum of your pulse guide you, and squeeeezzzeee." The air rifles fired in near unison onto the bullet traps. The students stayed in position, continuing the subtle pendulum motion based on their individual cardiac rhythms. Douglas McCashin, bald as an autumn gourd, wore wire-rimmed, vermillion-tint, aviator-style prescription shooting glasses, and was dressed in khakis, court sneakers and a short-sleeved cleric's gray frock and white collar. He turned and acknowledged Alex with a cheerful wave. The students finally lowered their firearms and broke open their barrels, recharging the pneumatic systems.

"Time," McCashin called, and each student paused their timers. He turned to warmly shake Alex's hand with both of his. "How are you, son? You look well." Douglas turned back to his charges. "What I want you all to sense is not that you must shoot a perfect score under a hard time limit, but that you may shoot a good score within that limit, provided you take each shot individually. Every score is built: It has a beginning, a middle and an end. A rough start often means nothing, and a score isn't complete until you finish."

He strolled down the line of shooters.

"That jerky trigger work makes me think you wish you were in a hip-hop video, Markus. Rita, you need to keep up with your upper body work—an elbow on your hip is useless if you can't control your fore-end. Allen, I know that knee is bugging you, but kneeling is one of the three positions, and you're going to need it."

Douglas stopped walking, and addressed the students. "The point I hope to make is that perfection is something to strive for. It's certainly not an all-or-nothing proposition. Before any of us will ever know perfection in life, we'll know mediocrity, then competence, then perhaps excellence and then—and only then—might we ever taste perfection. It's that journey that makes us who we are. How often do we hear that only the Lord can know true perfection? Yet we hear of pitchers and bowlers throwing perfect games—a mathematical measure of perfection, yet they are mortals. I don't exactly know how God feels about human beings achieving perfection, but I do know with every fiber of my being that he wants us to try." Douglas turned and walked behind the firing line. "Hail Mary time," he called out, and the students loaded their air rifles and went back into their trancelike offhand stance. In less than ten seconds, each student had fired their shot. "Time," Douglas called. "Class dismissed. You all stay safe this weekend!"

"Thank you, Reverend," the class sang in unison.

"Impressive," Alex commented.

"I do believe you're right," Douglas proudly proclaimed as he killed the floodlights.

"When I heard you were doing this, I honestly didn't think you could pull it off."

"This happened because I paid for it, Alex. I don't have much to offer these kids except for the mystery of my history and maybe this," he said, gesturing to the range. "I always believed that many of life's best lessons are tied up in shooting. Young people need to know early on that not everyone can be a pro basketball player or an R&B artist. They need to see that there is a lock in this life that their individual key fits. If I show them that they can be disciplined—maybe even be good at something that's a little bit different—perhaps they can apply that lesson elsewhere."

IX

C onrad and Walter pulled through the red brick pillars and a hand-painted, filigreed cast-iron archway that spelled out ONORI PLANTATION in a brilliant flourish of Technicolor. The long, white pea-pebble drive was lined with magnolias and Southern live oaks draped in Spanish moss. Their canopies formed an archway to the historic red brick antebellum mansion at the end of the shaded lane, which sat amidst a grove of Flowering Dogwood and Sweet Bay Magnolia.

"Brings back memories," Walter grunted from behind the wheel.

"I wouldn't know," Conrad countered resentfully. "This is my first time here. He never invited me, not once."

Walter turned to face the younger man. "Really? That's pretty raw, but I think I understand, and can't say as I blame him. I ran into him a couple of times down here and it was when he was already on his way out of the company. They say he never drew a sober breath down here. Staff used to call him "Make-it-a-double-and-leave-the-bottle Winston." Probably couldn't bear to have you see him like that."

"It's not like he was exactly holding it down to two drinks with dinner at home."

"These were major-league benders—not much fun to be around."

"I know," Conrad added regretfully. "But it would have been nice to be asked."

✳   ✳   ✳   ✳   ✳

A n attendant directed Walter and Conrad to the gun club area, with its three pigeon rings. They were told they could set up camp anywhere, but if they wanted power and water, they'd need to park by the kennel office. Walter navigated his rig next to a stand of turpentine pines, and unhitched the trailer.

Walter went right to work. Everything had its place, and every task was executed in its particular order. A military surplus tent with screened side-flaps retrieved from under the bed served as a de-facto outdoor living room replete with folding canvas campaign chairs, ice chest, a card table and several Coleman propane lanterns. An Astroturf rug underfoot completed the décor. Walter then retrieved his guns and started cleaning them. He smothered the 391 with lubricant and laid it out in the sun to dry.

"I usually do that in the oven," Walter said. "Best thing for an autoloader is to really hose it down once when it's new and completely clean, then let it all bake right in." Conrad was glowing in the afternoon heat, and streaks of sweat bled through his navy blue polo shirt. Walter sat cleaning his guns in his boxer shorts, and when Conrad noticed several distended, bulged vertebrae running through the center of his shoulder blades, the old man shrugged and quipped, "Occupational hazard."

Conrad picked up the Model-37 and broke it open. "That's really heavy," he noted.

"Nearly twelve pounds," Walter said. "It's the tube insert that does it. Pull it out and it's lighter than most trap guns, but tubed down to a .22, it adds a lot of weight."

"It must be hard to swing," Conrad stated.

"That's not what it's set up for, though I did once put a round through the tear duct of a red-tailed hawk with it."

Walter reached into the ice chest, pulled out two sweating bottles of Miller Lite, opened them with a church key that was tied to the cooler with bailing twine and set one on the table next to Conrad. "It's a little later than usual, but my gut says it's Miller time. You get into the habit—even if it is just one a day." He drank the long first swallow and went back to cleaning his guns. "This is my first time out in this rig without her."

"Without Winky?" Conrad asked.

"Carrying on without someone, be they completely gone or

just lost to you, you kind of keep on in the same routine, only without them. Setting up—we were a well-oiled machine. She had her jobs, I had mine. We could strike camp in twenty minutes. Getting it done this time was difficult, though. It's tough going it alone—doing both jobs."

"I feel the same way since my divorce. I still live in the same town—well, almost the same town. I still go the same places, only she's not with me and neither are my girls."

"Breaks your heart—one way or the other," Walter said, slamming the bolt closed on the Super-X and dry-firing it at the tent flap. "And it's a shock to the system to be on your own again."

"She said we had a deal and I didn't hold up my end," Conrad continued. "She was a spoiled daddy's girl—a princess—from the Caribbean. The house, private schools, Little Kill. She said we had an *implied agreement*, and never understood that all that costs real money and you don't just snap your fingers," he said, snapping his fingers.

"She thought being a Winston meant you'd always be rich."

"I married a girl from old San Juan," Conrad snorted. "A pretty brown girl from Puerto Rico: I should have known better, and Mom said as much. 'You're an attractive boy with a good name and a proper upbringing,' she said. 'But you really should marry someone from your own background. Money and status are the lingua franca of the world, and you don't want to wind up married to a girl who only speaks Portuguese.'"

"She was probably right. I've never seen one of you country-club boys make it with someone from outside of the County. You got this whole hidden thing going on that's like one of those silent dog whistles, only you're the only ones that can hear it. I never could make heads or tails out of that Morse code. Just as well, I suppose: Wink and me never wanted that kind of life anyway," Walter said, taking another pull from the bottle.

"Well, I did want that kind of life—expected to have that kind of life. And I'll get back to it, I hope."

"Riding Shapiro's coattails?" Walter asked.

"It's as good a way as any."

Walter drained the last of his beer, put it on the card table and let out a belch from the deepest regions of his constitution.

"Let me tell you something, Junior-Junior, and I'm not trying to castigate you. One thing I know is that fighting to get something back that you've already lost is like trying to retake high ground: very difficult if it can be done at all. When you've hit the skids, you can't go backward to put it right. All you can do is move ahead and try not to make the same mistake again. You're a bright boy and decent to the core. You're a gentleman, and in a world full of shit-heels that's got value. You play it straight—right down the line— and something good'll come of it. You get into bed with gangsters for money and that makes you a whore. Plenty of people in the County won't do business with a whore. You think about that."

Conrad's beer remained untouched on the table.

X

Alex and Douglas ate dinner at what had been in the past McCashin's favorite steakhouse, an old-school establishment unlikely situated in West Palm Beach's dealers row of auto sales lots. It was a red-leatherette, shrimp cocktail and aged-prime-rib-as-thick-as-your-forearm kind of bar and grill, out of place and time, and probably only continued to thrive in this neighborhood because it provided free valet parking in a secured lot. Douglas McCashin finished off his meal with exactly one single-malt Scotch.

"You're tempting me, Alex," Douglas said, "trying to lead me astray."

"I promise you, a good meal and one after-dinner drink won't lead to eternal damnation."

"You know I never drank—ever. All through the army, and with my business. I never touched it until . . ."

"You still think about it?" Alex asked quietly.

"Every day—all the time. I imagine I will for the rest of my life."

"I don't suppose you ever really get over it," Alex agreed. "That's what they say, anyway."

"I hope," Douglas said, clearing his throat, "that in time you'll move beyond it—find yourself someone else. You're a good man, Alex. A great reservoir of love resides within you. You're still young enough to have it all, or nearly so. I just hope you won't let it become the defining moment of your life. It really wasn't your fault."

"How do *you* live with it?" Alex asked.

"By serving God and man . . . and by becoming a new man. Atonement and repentance. I was wicked, full of avarice and conceit. I sneered at God's gifts and abused everyone around me. I rejoiced in the misery of others—in your misery, Alex. Ego was the essence of my being; I had to be the best at everything and everyone had to know it. I was a miserable wretch living in a prison of my own creation." Douglas sighed as he gently chimed the side of his highball with his wedding ring.

"All this blood is really on my hands," he continued, "not yours. My daughter—your wife—learned all her bad behavior from me. The arrogance, the willingness to take it all for granted. It's no wonder she could finally only find contentment in a heroin fix. She was raised in an illusion—a snow-globe paradise so grand not even the best possible version of reality could measure up. And I was cheap, criminally cheap, with my wife. Not with money but with myself—my attentions. She was so good to me, and I was such a snotty bastard to her all those years. You know what she wanted from me most of all, and she must have asked for it a dozen times? She wanted to go on an ocean liner; she wanted to take a ship across the Atlantic. But the thought of being trapped with her and all those jerk-off passengers for a week—that, *the great Douglas McCashin* couldn't tolerate! I was such an idiot!" he said, dabbing his eyes with his dinner napkin. "The idea of making her happy, of doing that one simple thing entirely for her, meant being away from my business. I thought the sun couldn't rise on those dealerships without me telling it to. An eighth-grader can run those lots, that much is proven to me every quarter. No, Alex, when I am finally called home, I'll confess that it was entirely my fault. Sugar's stroke was my fault too. Between being run out of the County like that and the overdose, it was all just too much. She didn't deserve any of it, and I'm just glad it all ended quickly."

"There's plenty of blame to go around," Alex said.

"And I think that's how *you* should cope with it. I just know that in my gut, it was mostly me. The only two people in God's creation who could stand to love me, and I made life impossible for both of them. West Point made me hard and the *hard sell* made me cruel," Douglas said wistfully, as he drained the last of the Scotch from his glass. "Anyway—that life is over." He blew his nose into a red bandana long since laundered pink. "And a new one has sprung from the ashes. I don't have much time left, but I hope to make something of myself yet."

XI

Walter set up the portable gas grill, sliced ripe tomatoes he brought from his garden, dressed them in vinaigrette and herbs, seasoned two grouper fillets and let them marinate in white wine and lime juice. From the camper he withdrew two push brooms, a customized clay-target thrower, a duffle bag, three guns in soft cases and a five-gallon plastic bucket.

"I will require your assistance for the next hour," Walter announced to Conrad. Both men carried the equipment out to the combination skeet-trap field adjacent to the three pigeon rings. Walter then closely inspected the conjoined skeet and trap pads. They were connected by concrete, billiard-table flat and in immaculate condition.

"Cracks are what get you: cracks and pebbles," Walter said as he handed a push broom to Conrad. "You go first, starting with the trap stations. I'll follow right behind you. Don't push the pile, sweep from side to side. Every square inch of this area needs to be swept twice." In half an hour, their work was done and the superbly constructed pads were immaculate. The attendant opened the houses. Everything was already loaded, but after Walter pulled targets from all the traps, he took the hoop from in front of the cinder-block trap house and held it upright at the stake. "Hold that, boy," he said, handing it to Conrad.

"Why are we even doing this?" Conrad reiterated. "They don't expect you to shoot."

"I told you I'll be damned if I'm going to make a fool of myself because I couldn't take the trouble to have the right gun or to prep the grounds. They're going to ask me to shoot. In fact they're going to pay me to perform the old act—and you're going to help me, Junior-Junior." Conrad looked positively bewildered.

"The moves for something like this—you don't just pull 'em out of your ass," Walter said, more congenially. "I haven't so much as picked up a scattergun in nine years. I wanna know if I can still make the shots." Walter stood back at skeet station four and pulled both the high-house and low-house. The high was low and the low was three feet outside the center stake. "Bunch of country-club yahoos," Walter said under his breath. He adjusted both traps until the targets flew through the top third of the hoop. Then he adjusted the 16-yard trap for height and to reduce the hard right and left angles. "Now they're set to regulation," he said.

"How could you tell?" Conrad asked.

Walter looked down his nose condescendingly at the younger man. "How can you tell it's your wife's cooter in the dark? It just feels right, that's how!" Walter pulled a couple more trap targets and put on his shooting glasses and vest. He produced three boxes of 12-gauge papers in shot size number eight and a box of .22 short rifle cartridges from his duffle bag. "Just pull me a couple of trap targets so I can get my bearings."

Walter picked up the 101 live-bird-combo and walked to the center station of the trap field. He dry-fired the gun, reacquainting himself with the trigger pull, checked that the bottom choke was screwed tight and loaded a shell. He took a hold-point a foot over the center of the back roof of the trap house and called *Pull!*. The muzzle rose slightly and to the right to intersect the flight path of the clay; Walter made an involuntary lurch with his forehand, and fired the full payload into the back of the trap house. "Jesus H. Christ!" he said as he broke open the gun. Conrad stood with his mouth agape. "You okay, boy? Didn't hit you, did I?"

"I'm fine," Conrad reassured him. "What the hell was that?"

"That," Walter said, "was a flinch for the ages—old shooter's curse. After pounding myself all those years with 12-gauge loads, sometimes my brain says *oh no you don't*, and won't let me pull the trigger. Usually it's not so pronounced, but that was one for the history books." Walter started dry-firing the gun again, pointing it over the trap house. Finally he said, "Okay, let's try that again." He loaded, called *Pull!* and fired. This time the target broke into several pieces. He pulverized the next nine into dull metallic smoke. Walter shot ten targets from trap station one, then ten from station five, throwing his empty hulls into the bucket. "That's enough of that," he said. He laid the over-under on its slip on the turf and reached for another gun case. "This'll be a little more challenging," he said, removing the 30-inch, tubed Model-37. He consolidated his twelve-gauge shells into one pocket and reached for the small box of .22 shorts. "You can't do this just anywhere, but with a safe background it's pretty impressive." The planted field in front of them was empty as far as they eye could see. "Look safe to you?" he asked.

"Safe enough for what?"

"Safe enough to shoot trap with a rifle."

"You're kidding."

"Just watch me," Walter said, as he closed the gun and cocked the hammer. He took a hold-point on the trap house and dry-fired. He continued to dry fire while moving the gun, mimicking the trap shots he just made.

"Isn't this really dangerous? I mean, don't bullets fly really far?"

"By modern standards, it's pretty dangerous. But considering that me and Wink barnstormed this stunt at every two-bit gun club and county fair that would pay the freight with nary an accident excepting the errant woodchuck, I'd say it's safe enough. Your grandfather is spinning in his grave that a Winston would even have to ask a question like that. You got a lot to learn, Junior-Junior, if you can't even figure how far a .22 will carry." Walter broke open the gun and turned to Conrad, looking him straight in the eye.

"Let me ask one more time. Do you see a house, car, person, dog, mule—we did pepper that mule one time—or anything else that I could otherwise kill or harm by unleashing this peashooter on it? Really look hard, boy," Walter said.

Conrad scanned the background and saw nothing but the sorrel brown of a soybean crop. "I don't see anything," Conrad confirmed. "I guess it's okay."

"Alright," Walter said, as he placed a live round in the chamber and closed the gun. "Let's see if I can still do this." He cocked the hammer, shouldered the gun, took his hold-point and called *Pull!*.

XII

It was just warm enough for the morning sun to begin burning the dew off the grass that was now seeping into Sid Shapiro's leather boating moccasins as he walked across the lawn to the kennel. The black kennel boy who walked with him was middle aged and light-skinned, with a pencil-thin moustache and straightened hair. He wore canvas-faced brush pants, a white undershirt and a broad straw planter's hat with a dark sweat stain around the band. He held an unlit Tiparillo between his teeth.

"I'm not sure I'll be able help you with this, Mr. Sid."

"I have every confidence in you, Jazzmo," Shapiro replied.

"Only ever did it the one time—couldn't really live with myself afterward. Pastor says it's the same to sin against an animal as a person. I ain't no sinner. No sir. They my friends."

Sid stopped him at the kennel door. "Don't snow me, boy—I've heard the stories. Don't say this isn't done around here anymore, because I know better. Every plantation does it every season."

Jazzmo collected himself and spoke slowly. "No sir. I don't believe I'll be able to . . ."

Sid cut him off, "Listen, this is a dirty job—I realize that much. But it's *your* dirty job. If you want to keep it and the fine salary I pay you, I suggest you protest a little less and get on with it."

Jazzmo seemed resigned to his fate, and held the door open for Sid. The two men started walking down the kennel runs, inspecting the dogs. They walked to the end and stopped.

"Five," Sid said, gesturing to the kennel runs. "Which ones are they?"

"Four," Jazzmo replied. "Four. Old Duke, he'll make another year."

"Duke'll make another year . . ." Sid said, looking through the chain-link fence at the English Pointer. "How old is this dog—and don't lie; I've got his papers in the house."

"Be twelve this winter, but I tell you, sir, he'll make it another season."

"Hunting every other day, maybe. Duke makes five," Sid said. "What about the others?"

"You got Lila and Daisy," Jazzmo replied, gesturing to liver-and-white and orange-and-white Brittanies. "They old brood bitches, seven and nine. Lila ain't taken seed for two years, and Daisy . . . Daisy's just old."

"The others?" Sid demanded.

"Slick," he said, sticking his hand through the fencing to let the Vizsla lick his hand. "Got the jones for running rabbits, but he's only four. Maybe he'll grow out of it. Jake," he said, referencing a liver-and-white Shorthair. "He's seven. He's good enough, but he won't go in a brace—fights with the other dog. Don't like people much neither, except for me," he said in a retreating tone that petered out into silence.

"That's it then, Monday morning. Dig the hole," Sid ordered as he headed for the door.

Jazzmo followed him and screwed up his courage again. "I just don't know, sir . . ."

"Well, I do," Sid said, not breaking his stride.

"Duke—I done whelped him myself, raised him up. I'll take him off you, Mr. Sid, if I just can get me a cup of dry here and there."

Sid stopped and turned on his heels to face the black man, eyeball-to-eyeball. Jazzmo raised his hand and then slowly removed his unlit cigar. "Let me tell you something about the way I work," Shapiro said. "Every relationship in my life, and I mean every single one—whether it's business or personal—is conditional. You give me something and I give you something back. That goes for my employees, these dogs and even my wife. I like you just fine, Jazzmo. You're conscientious, and you obviously take a lot of pride in your work. The dogs look well, seem to like you and show a lot of style in the field. But the minute you stop doing your job, I can't use you anymore. A bird dog that can't hunt to my standard isn't fulfilling its function. A manager who isn't willing to run this kennel to my standard isn't fulfilling *his* function. Those are the conditions of *our* working relationship. If these dogs can't cut it— they're gone, period. You want one? You want them all? Take them. They don't work for me anymore. Everyone and everything around here is going to earn its keep."

Sid put his hand on the black man's shoulder, gentle at first, and then it gradually tightened into a claw grip. "I'm sure you locals see me coming a mile off: Rich Yankee with the jet and the car and the wife, and maybe you think money doesn't matter to me anymore. Well, think again. Money means as much to me now as it ever did. I'll leave you dead in a ditch before I'll let you cut my pockets."

"I understand, Mr. Sid. But Duke, he's like family to me."

"Take him," Sid said waving his hand dismissively. "But if I ever hear of you bringing my food out for him, you're fired." Sid turned and started walking again. Jazzmo followed.

"I don't know," Jazzmo repeated. "I just don't know if I can do it."

"Your backbone *will* materialize when the time comes," Sid said, walking through the door.

XIII

This is something I really could have helped you with," Douglas McCashin said through the voice-activated microphone in his headset, over the drone of the aircraft's single engine

Alex Vanderstein let the thought sink in before he replied. "I wasn't interested in flying back then anyway. The important thing is you're helping me now."

Douglas had sold his twin years before and hadn't been in

the cockpit since, but as soon as Alex initiated the preflight-check McCashin began sharing his wealth of knowledge, teaching what he knew to the younger pilot. Douglas protested a bit when Alex gestured for him to take the left seat, but his opposition was brief: Douglas missed flying, as he missed many of the familiars of his former life, and the opportunity to take the yoke and revisit this part of who he'd been proved irresistible. "They're like boats," he said. "You think bigger is better, but it's really not true. Fixed gear, VFR—if you know when to stay on the ground, this is all the aircraft you'll ever need."

"I want an instrument rating and a twin," Alex proclaimed.

"And I'm sure you'll get them," Douglas agreed. "But you really have something right here. Rugged airframe, good glide characteristics. You could set it down anywhere in a fix and, most importantly, your approach speeds are low. Fast is fun but unforgiving."

"Says the man who had a turbo-prop."

"I did indeed." Douglas was cheerful as he scanned the horizon. "And now I'm flying your 30-year-old Cherokee and realizing I really didn't need any of it."

"Religion has warped you, old man," Alex said. "It's bad enough that I have to be nice to you at all, but to hear you wax on about the simple life—from a man who owned a King Air and a Fabbri. You look back now and say you didn't need any of it. Well, now it's my turn and I want some of those things, so go easy with the vow-of-poverty spiel. I made some money and now I'd like to spend some of it, thank you very much."

"Quite right: I just hope that you'll discover long before I ever did how little any of it means." Douglas changed the radio frequency as they entered new airspace. "I need to make a minor confession to you, Alex," he said with a puckish smile. "I know you thought that by kidnapping me for the weekend, you'd get me around shooting and I'd miss it—maybe enough to start up again." He looked across the cockpit and Alex nodded in silent affirmation. "Well, the real reason I'm doing this is because I need you to take over the dealerships, and I wanted the weekend to talk you into it."

Alex grimaced. He turned away from Douglas and looked toward the ground below. "We already played that game once, remember?"

"That was then. We're both different people now."

"I can't work for you, Douglas. I never really learned the business when I was in it and, frankly, I don't need the money or the aggravation. If you want out, why don't you just sell them?"

"That's exactly what I intend to do: I want you to buy them." Alex didn't know whether to laugh or turn away; he finally went back to window-watching. "Be a sport, Alex—you already bought my house. Purchase the dealerships and complete the set."

"Bailiwick was a once in a lifetime opportunity."

"And so is this. I know what you're thinking," Douglas continued. "But I just want you to hear me out. First of all, it's a wonderful business—a business I spent a lifetime creating. Now, I can sell it all in one shot for a lot of money, or I can keep letting those monkeys run it into the ground—neither prospect is very satisfactory to me. What I propose is . . . strike that. What I require is a million dollars a year." Alex turned in disbelief toward Douglas, who then added, "in perpetuity."

Alex snapped back, "You can't do it—not in this economy anyway. If you try to cash-flow that much out of those dealerships, you'll bankrupt them."

"It would be a staggered payout. I only need $250,000 for the first year, then a half-million and so on. I want to create a foundation—the Lollipop Fund—named for the girls."

"What you need is a money manager, Douglas. You need someone with the expertise and time to build you a balanced portfolio with enough fixed income to spit out that much annually. It's really not my thing; I couldn't help you even if I wanted to," Alex confessed.

"I'm not sure you'll understand any of this, but I'll try to make sense of it for you: God spoke to me—in a dream, just as you're speaking to me now. *Educate them and I'll do the rest,* he said. Now that's my mission. The smartest way to do it is to have the kids themselves pay for as much of their schooling as possible by serving a hitch in the armed forces. Our foundation will give grants to St. Gilbert's alumni taking a college education through the GI Bill. I want each of them to leave for college with a grant for $10,000 a year toward living expenses, to be spent as they see fit. Ten thousand a year for as long as they remain on schedule for an undergraduate or graduate degree."

"God said this . . . to you?! Have you lost your mind, Douglas?!"

"That's a trick question, Alex," McCashin continued. "It depends entirely on the yardstick you use to measure a man's life. I will leave behind many assets, things: nothing else. You will remember me for a while. Others will too, I imagine, but mostly for all the wrong reasons. An annuity that pays out indefinitely for the good of mankind is the only meaningful legacy I can possibly leave. What I'm proposing is you take over the dealerships, set up the foundation and pay yourself whatever you think is appropriate. I'll buy a big-ticket life insurance policy and name you as sole beneficiary. When I die and the insurance pays out tax-free, you purchase the dealerships from the estate, and the proceeds then go directly into the foundation coffers and on to the money managers you mentioned. You'll wind up owning a tremendously profitable business, virtually for free." Alex was unconvinced. "This is the gift horse of a lifetime, son: the ultimate part-time job. You could find yourself someone, raise a family and do this—all with your eyes closed. It's fate, Alex—mine and yours. It's God's will and your future all rolled into one. I'm certain of it."

XIV

P igeon shooters are generally also compulsive gamblers. Wherever there is a tournament throwing fliers, there is a high stakes poker game somewhere in the vicinity. The game at Onori was held in the storage pantry of the gun club snack bar among the floor-to-ceiling shelves holding gallon cans of sweet corn, baked beans and cooking oil. A green plastic picnic table sat in the center of the narrow room, surrounded by metal folding chairs. The room had a small window to provide ventilation, which was wide open due to the cigar and cigarette smoke. The overhead ceiling fan—set on low—seemed only to push the smoke around the airless space in opaque waves. A solitary overhead bulb provided the only light for the game, and Walter resorted to putting on his reading glasses to make out the cards he held in his hand. It was 10:20 in the morning. Walter held an unlit crook in his free hand, occasionally chewing on the uncut tip as the game of seven card stud unfolded. He had a tin cup of black coffee with a pint bottle of bourbon sitting next to it, $600 on the table and another $1000 in his wallet. It was a $50 ante, and the biggest pot he'd seen was just shy of $900. It was early yet, but he was already up, having won two pots right out of the gate, the first with a straight—Jack high—the next bluffing with a pair of sevens showing. Walter knew he was playing with fire, but he also remembered what he'd heard: Sid Shapiro sat in on this game for an hour every morning like clockwork. He usually arrived at ten, but today he was obviously running late. Finally, the door opened and Sid poked his head in.

"Got room for one more?" he asked.

"You're the house, Mr. Shapiro. The house is always welcome," said "Tom Thumb" Stratton, the morbidly obese pigeon ring manager. In addition to providing Onori with all of the fliers, Tom Thumb ran and maintained all the rings, interpreted the myriad arcane rules of box-bird shooting and was the regular puller on ring one. Stratton was also a compulsive gambler, as insatiable in his appetite for box-bird Calcuttas and stud poker as he was for toasted Po-Boy sandwiches. He had a full head of gray hair cut in a flattop, and he wore his shirt wide open, revealing a gold medallion that danced in the hairless valley between two copious man-breasts. Shapiro erected a chair at the far end of the table directly next to Walter, removed the rubber band from his cabbage roll of money and peeled off $1,000.

"Can't stay long," Sid said. "I break out in hives if there's a game around and I'm not part of it." Shapiro dropped his ante in the middle of the table. Tom Thumb expertly tossed the cards around the horn with dexterous yet sausage-like fingers, covered as they were in egg yolk and bacon grease left over from breakfast.

Sid perused the room, making mental notes of the players, all of whom he knew and had taken money off, with one notable exception. "Who's the youngblood?" he asked Tom Thumb, as he pointed in the general direction of Walter.

The fat man took multiple puffs on his Churchill, blew a few precise smoke rings toward the ceiling fan and addressed Walter quizzically.

"You been shining me on? Cause that's the boss man, and if he don't recognize you, you ain't welcome."

Without saying a word, Walter laid the unlit crook on the edge of the table and threw another fifty into the pot.

"Walter Wagner," he said holding out his hand for Sid Shapiro. "You sent young Winston down to dig me up." Sid shook his hand unenthusiastically.

"Winston," Sid repeated in a disinterested monotone. "You're . . . the exhibition shooter?" Walter nodded his head silently as Sid dropped a hundred in the pot, raising the stakes.

"Sort of: my wife, really—but yes, I'm an exhibition shooter."

The fat man dealt another round of cards, face up. Shapiro sized up his cards—and Walter Wagner. "Funny thing, running into you at the pantry game like this," Sid said.

Walter put the crook back into his mouth and grunted, "I suppose."

"What I mean is I thought I hired you to come out and socialize around the gun club. Talk with the guests and represent Winston Firearms."

Walter laid his cards face down in a neat stack on the table in front of him, and looked at Sid. "I *am* socializing. I'm in here playing cards. I'm talking and representing . . . and I'll be damned if I'm not ahead!" he chuckled.

"Hey, gottrocks!? Who the hell said playing cards and drinking bourbon at ten in the morning was any part of the deal?"

"Who said it wasn't?" Walter protested. "The boy said come

up and enjoy the hospitality, so here I am—per his request. I just saw an opportunity to supplant my stipend. I've been shooting live birds for near on sixty years, and I sure as hell made a sight more money playing cards than I ever did in the ring."

"Fancy yourself a poker player then, do you?" Sid inquired.

"I do," Walter said as he dropped another fifty in the pot. "A regular artiste."

"This is your last hand, old man. I'm not paying you to hide from my guests. You want to get along—you're going to do what you're told. Call," Shapiro announced, simultaneously dropping another fifty in the pot, meeting the bet.

The cards were laid on the table. When Shapiro saw Walter's spade flush, he swore sharply with a "Fuck!" and threw his three tens—face up—onto the pile of cash.

Walter collected his winnings like he was scooping up a windblown pile of autumn leaves, then stood up.

"Where are you going?" Tom Thumb demanded.

"You heard him—I've been banished. Gonna take the money and run."

The fat man took enough draws from his cigar so that the smoke, ever so briefly, appeared to be rising from the flat top of his closely shorn skull.

"All due respect, Mr. Shapiro, but Father Time over here's into us for nearly a grand. You run him off—we got no chance of getting even."

"All due respect, Mr. Shapiro," Walter added mischievously. "You're not really paying me all that well in the first place, and I was counting on this game as a way to make my end work out. Got a room here flush with stud poker players—that's gotta be worth something."

Sid flashed a smirk, like the fox being cornered by the raccoon, and announced to the rest of the game, "Back in the neighborhood, this is what we call a shakedown. You can't seriously be suggesting what I think you are?"

"I'd have walked out of here Sunday with a couple grand, easy.

Hell, I've only been here forty-five minutes and I'm already up $900! Granted it was a couple of lucky hands, but Porky Pig over here's got more dollars than sense when it comes to figuring probabilities," Walter said, gesturing to Tom Thumb. "You want me to cut out—you want me to refrain from playing cards and drinking liquor? For $500, I'll put a cork in the bottle and walk away from the card table. Otherwise, don't blame me for not getting specific enough with young Winston. You want a Boy Scout for the weekend—pay for one!"

Sid Shapiro was pissed off. The very idea that his hired help would even try to play in the hush-hush pantry game was bad enough, but this was ridiculous. "This is extortion!" Sid shouted, pulling the cabbage roll out of his pocket and peeling off $500. "If you think you'd have walked out of here with one red cent to your name, you're fucking delusional! I'm saving you from yourself. *You* were the mark, and the $900 was part of the setup. The fat fuck dealing the cards would have gutted you like a mackerel!"

"Guess we'll never find out," Walter responded, folding the bills daintily in half and placing them in his shirt pocket.

"I ought to let them have a go—just to burn you," Sid said, standing up. "But I got a conscience, and Winston says you're already flat broke as it is." Sid put the bankroll back in his pocket. "Got a regular set of millstones on you, old man. Paying you not to get fleeced by this rogues gallery is charity of the highest order. Frankly, I'm not sure that being able to sleep at night is worth it," he added as he headed for the door.

"Thanks just the same," Walter called after him, as he stuffed his winnings into his pocket and began to shake hands with the rest of the players. He swiped the unopened pint of bourbon off the table and tossed it to the fat man. "A little John Barleycorn for General Tom Thumb Stratton," he said.

"Kiss that little gal for me when you see her," Tom Thumb said somberly, as he fished the pint bottle out of his cleavage.

onrad was quartered in a bedroom of one of the outbuildings, an actual former slave cabin that was reserved for plantation employees. It had a single bed, bureau, chair, lamp and a clock radio. There was a common bathroom down the hall. Conrad showered, dressed and headed across the dew-soaked lawn toward the gun club and the catered breakfast that waited.

He surveyed the room after he entered. Standing at the sign-in desk with a fistful of hundreds was Walter Wagner, counting money off to the cashier. A busty redhead took the bills and read back his à la carte bets.

"That's the fives, tens, fifteens, long-run front and back, thirty-straight jackpot and the Great Eastern purse. Sure you don't want to round it out with the overall race too while you're at it?" she asked.

Walter's ears pricked up. "What makes you think an old fart like me could get anywhere near the race purse?"

"I was a trapshooter once. I know who you are, Mr. Wagner. I saw you shoot in Vandalia, and I'm sure you'll skin your share of youngsters this weekend."

Walter beamed. "That may be, but I've already seen some of these sharpies shoot practice birds, and I know I'll have my hands full. No, ma'am: Youth counts for an awful lot, and these old bones say wager on fourth or fifth—that's where I'll stick."

"What the hell do you think you're doing?" Conrad demanded as Walter completed his transaction.

"Just laying in stakes before I shoot practice."

Conrad hadn't had his morning coffee yet and he snapped temperamentally. "You're here to meet and greet, Walter. Play nice with the rich people and nothing more! You're the minor—*very minor*—attraction. I'm willing to play babysitter, but I'm not about to have you screw things up for me by letting you shoot."

"Funny thing," Walter replied, pulling the engraved invitation out of his shirt pocket like he was drawing a weapon. "But this fancy greeting card entitles me to shoot the event as a guest. All I'm doing is exercising that entitlement, and laying on a little green in the hopes that fate smiles on me."

Conrad recomposed himself, put his hand on Walter's shoulder and desperately tried to pull rank. "We've been pretty generous with you, Walter. Show a little appreciation. You could have a future with Winston Firearms. Who knows? There may be more events like this and you could be a part of them. I'll put in a good word for you."

"If I *behave*?" Walter added sarcastically. "Yeah, the hell with that and the hell with you while we're at it! You pull me away from my home, my fishing and my wife to go on some half-assed panhandle hayride, and now you want me to be seen and not heard? You're going to harangue me for jeopardizing your meal ticket, screwing with your future? I got no future, Conrad: I'm all used up. You drag me way the hell up here, the least I'm going to do is have some fun and see if I can't take a little money off these country-club fops while I'm at it. Per diem? Hah! I'll make enough in these rings to see me all the way through, die on my feet with some dignity. It's all right here this weekend, and I sure as hell intend to take some of it home with me!"

*　*　*　*　*

The standard pigeon ring takes the rough shape of a baseball stadium. Its dimensions are based on the numbers nine, two, seventeen and thirty-two. There are nine electronically controlled boxes or traps with electrified spring floors. The floor of each box is charged, and when a bird is released on the call of the shooter, a spring under the floor throws it four feet into the air before it takes to flight. A theoretical plumb line, anchored dead center to the station on the concrete shooter's pad, stretches to the center of the designated shooting area and measures off thirty-two yards. That's where the center number five-box is positioned. Box numbers four and six are five yards to the left and right of box five—still thirty-two yards from the shooter's pad. Boxes three and seven sit outside of boxes four and six, and so on. The row of boxes fans out like an eyebrow, around the killing range of the shooter's gun. The whole area is ringed by a fence that runs another seventeen yards behind the boxes. The fences stand two feet high and are usually a permanent structure of chain-link mounted to galvanized steel bracing poles. A shooter feels like he's standing at home plate because he's looking down what appear to be foul lines, which then converge into an outfield fence.

Fifteen feet or so behind the shooter's pad is the puller, who sits in a booth with windows on the front and side. The "race" scorecard is a long, narrow strip of paper with score boxes, and while dead birds are tallied in pencil, lost birds are more permanently marked by a hole punched through the paper. Shooters begin from 32 yards. If they kill five birds in a row, they slide back to 33 yards, and so on after every five birds killed, until they reach a maximum of 36 yards.

Pigeon rings are also similar to ballparks in that each has its own unique personality. They can be built anywhere, down in a hollow or on top of a rise, in a wooded clearing or in an open field, or even on the side of a hill where one side of the ring is slightly higher than the other. A competitor steps out onto the pad, starting 32 yards back from the center trap. The shooter loads two shells, calls *Trapper ready!* and then *Pull!* and uses both shots on the bird. If he misses, and the pigeon flies beyond the confines of the fenced ring, the bird is lost. If the shooter kills it and the flier hits the ground stone dead within the confines of the ring, the bird is scored dead. If however, the shooter kills a pigeon on the wing that, albeit dead, lands outside of the ring, the bird is scored as lost. Any bird that crosses the fence-line in flight but returns to the confines of the ring to die is counted as lost.

Pigeons also regularly drop within the ring, appearing lifeless, only to then miraculously revive, walk themselves to the border, and hop the fence. That bird is scored lost. If a competitor kills a flier stone dead with the first shot, might they use their second round to dispatch one of these walking wounded? No. Each brace of loads is destined for one flier only, and may not be used on another. Dead birds are gathered by "bird boys," who retrieve fliers that have actually died and capture those with still enough life in them to pose a threat of hopping the fence. Often a shooter who's working on a straight of five or ten will tip a bird boy for hustling to run down a "zombie bird."

Bird boys capture "runners" with a large hoop net affixed to the end of a pole. The metal box traps are refilled from what looks like a six-pack for long-necked bottled beer fashioned from sawed off PVC tubes glued together with a carrying handle. Live birds are stuffed snugly into the tubes for safekeeping until they are needed, whereupon a hand shoved through the pipe unloads them into the trap.

Feral pigeons come in all colors: gray, black, brown, white and infinite combinations thereof. An entirely black bird against a dark background like a shaded tree line will be a much more difficult target than an ivory-white flier against the same, and such is the gambler's luck of the draw. The puller holds actual playing cards—ace through nine. He shuffles them thoroughly then selects five. Those five cards correspond to the box traps he'll pull for that ring.

To the shooter it's a mystery, and the line of traps seems impossibly wide. A hold-point at or just above the center five-box seems an awfully long way from the one or the nine-box, particularly if the bird flushes directly away from the shooter. A flier coming toward a shooter is completely exposed, and a kill is simply a matter of executing a reasonable shot reasonably well. The explosive flush directly away from the shooter is the most difficult of all shots. It requires a split-second reaction, precision and nerve, in equal measure.

* * * * *

id Shapiro walked past the practice ring and saw Walter kill three straightaway birds in a row. The last one, dark as a crow, beat a direct course for the tree line. It exploded like a handful of black confetti on the report of Walter's second barrel.

"Jesus!" Sid said, loud enough for the showman to hear.

As Walter turned around, Conrad was already making the introductions. "This is Walter Wagner, the famous trick and fanciful shooter."

"That's trick and fancy shooter, you nimrod," Walter grumbled, as he extended his hand self-consciously. Sid regarded it like it was some kind of vestigial extra appendage. "We've already met," Walter added uncomfortably.

"Jesus!" Sid repeated. "You're shooting?"

Walter held up the 391 for Sid's inspection. "Can you believe anything so cheap can thump fliers like that? This Wal-Mart special is the Grim Reaper's own scythe. Anything that lethal oughta be outlawed!"

Sid turned to Conrad. "He's shooting a 391—who said he could shoot a 391?! Who the hell even said he could shoot?! What do you think you're doing, Wagner?! This is by invitation only, and unless I'm losing my fucking mind, you're the hired help!"

Conrad cut in. "We sent him an invitation, Mr. Shapiro. He insisted. Technically, he *is* your guest."

"Talk about building loopholes into a contract," Sid said to Conrad, who confirmed it with a nod. "Alright, grandpa," Sid stated. "You want to take your best shot against the post–WWII generation, fine, *be* my guest. But don't come crying to me when you lose everything I'm paying you, plus your social security. Just one other thing: I'll be damned if anyone working for me is going to shoot a 391 at Onori—Winston products only. Old goat like you should know that."

"It's news to me." Walter feigned ignorance.

"It's been the unspoken rule here since Conrad's grandfather's day."

"That would explain it," Walter qualified. "Winston Firearms was compensating Wink and me handsomely to shoot their products. For obvious reasons, we were very agreeable back then. You just saw me drop how many birds with this dime-store popgun?

And now you want me to throw her over as some sort of *favor* to you? Come now—a man's got to have confidence in his equipment."

"We picked a plum, Winston!" Sid brayed to Conrad. "It's like 'The Ransom of Red Chief,' for Christ's sake! Alright, old man—what do you want? How much to ditch the *wop* auto?"

Walter, now fully in control of the negotiation, regained his plucky disposition. "My price for not shooting the stovepipe that I just cancelled the air-freight on three outgoers in a row with is $500."

Sid reached into the pocket of his khakis and removed his cabbage roll of hundreds. He wetted his thumb. "Another fin?" he asked.

Walter nodded and added "That's five hundred for the whole weekend, mind you. A one-time-payment kind of deal." Sid peeled off the bills and laid them into the old man's hand. "Good to be back on the old home-team again," Walter said, sealing the deal with a smirk and a handshake. "Yes, indeedy," he reiterated, pumping the rich man's arm like it was attached to a spigot.

Walter returned to the trailer. He meticulously cleaned the 391 and placed it back in its blue hard-plastic case. Then he reached for the soft case containing the 101 live-bird-combo. He grabbed the slip by the barrel, letting the worn canvas slide through his fingers until the receiver came to rest securely in his grip and jumped from the camper floor to the Astroturf-covered ground. The old man had a spring in his step as he loaded some items into the El Camino and drove it across the grounds to the gun club. As Walter stepped onto field one for the first crank of fliers that morning, he left a looped DVD playing on the banquet table in the clubhouse which, for six hours, showed Winky's four half-hour trick-shooting films. An old laminated sign in front of the screen read WINKY WAGNER TRICK SHOOTING DVD, $20. With a grease pencil, the $20 had been crossed out and $25 handwritten in.

XVI

cross the room from Walter, Alex Vanderstein and Douglas McCashin stood together, looking at the gun lying on top of the soft case on the table. It was a highly modified 391 autoloader that had a synthetic thumbhole stock with an adjustable carbon-fiber cheek piece and an extra-high custom rib.

"I brought your gun. I figured once you got here your resolve would weaken and you'd want to shoot it."

"Hell's bells, Alex!" McCashin said at the sight of it. "I figured the police had long since taken it."

"I had it. They called after the season ended. It was still sitting in the rack of the clubhouse where you left it."

"I'm not sure I'd even want to shoot it now, Alex. I don't know if I'm comfortable shooting live birds at all."

"I had the trigger changed, if that makes any difference."

"It's still the same gun."

"Yes," Alex confirmed. "And superstitious beliefs are completely irrational; it's also the same gun you won all those other championships with. It worked for you then, just as it'll work for you now."

"I suppose. I just feel a little like I did the other night at the steak house: This was a big part of my life for a long time—a part of my life that has rightly ended. I don't know how healthy it is for me to revisit that side of myself. Say I did shoot and started to feel the old competitive juices flow again—suppose I liked it? Do you really want that Douglas McCashin back in your life?" Alex gazed at the cursed shotgun.

"The Lord guides us in many ways," McCashin continued. "Mostly he lays the choices out in front of us like a trail of breadcrumbs, so there can be little doubt when we are doing His will. But this is just such decadence: catered meals and cocktails, blood sport for high stakes. None of this has changed a whit, but I sure have.

"Lord," Douglas McCashin said, looking toward the heavens and then closing his eyes, "if you could just give a sign." When he reopened his eyes, they came to rest upon the seven-pin side-lock sitting in the gun rack. "Is that my Fabbri?" he asked Alex.

XVII

Walter Wagner chose to shoot last in the rotation for the entire event, partly to gauge who had shot what score, but more importantly, because he wanted to see birds fly over and over in the three rings. He wanted to map out in his head how he would approach each flier, spot-shooting that one with a first barrel, then taking time to finish it off as a crosser. Killing the screaming white one with the first shot and revoking its walking papers with a second on the ground. Finally, fanning the trigger reflexively, putting both barrels into the fast inky outgoer before it beats for a hole in the tree line. He could not escape the fact that no matter how fast and aggressive he was, luck would do as much to determine his success as any preparation. The best box-bird shooters may win more often than anyone else, but they can still only work with what they're given.

The easiest money in the pigeon ring is on the fives, tens and fifteens—killing five, ten or fifteen fliers in a row. If you can string together three rings, you won't likely have more than one or two other competitors who also tied. A $100 option played by most of the contestants creates a $4- or $5,000 betting pool. If two or three hit on perfect fifteens, that's still at least a $1,000 payout. Given that a perfect fifteen already counts as a perfect ten and three perfect fives, you've already hit on three purses. If the 30-bird race is the mountain, the tens and the fives are the individual steps ascending to the summit.

Fate smiled on Walter, and he was playing the box draw well. He had a sixth sense for the probabilities of which side of the field would most likely present the next bird. More than once, Walter wasn't just in the right area, he was on the exact trap, and dispatched the pigeon before it could even unfold its wings. Light and color worked to his advantage as well. The overcast sky burned off into a hazy sunshine, which allowed Walter to see even the darkest birds reasonably well. Only once, in the very first ring, was he given an outgoer which he moved on so aggressively that he clipped it in the head and sent it spinning, as his second shot unloaded into the cartwheeling carcass. If anything, the whiter birds in the open rings flared his eye with their brilliance. Walter tucked a darker set of Hy-Wyds into his breast pocket and switched to them for the brighter rings. His first miss was on the twelfth bird of the Friday morning crank. His second miss was the first bird of the afternoon crank. He claimed two shares in the ten-in-a-row purse—a little over $1,000.

All it took for Alex to borrow the Fabbri for Douglas was to ask: Sid didn't point the gun particularly well and it was putting a damper on his enjoyment of the event. Shapiro was the kind of man to shower his affections on any and all when things were going his way; he was also perfectly willing to rain down misery when they weren't. Walter had officially gotten under his skin. Sid had seen the morning scores, and it didn't take a mathematician to recognize that the old coot not only had a knack for box-birds, but that Wagner hadn't lost a blink of reflex time in retirement. Walter wasn't just good for a seventy-something-year-old shooter, he was good for a shooter of any age. The old codger could really point a shotgun—and Sid hated him for it.

Douglas McCashin was also shooting well. He considered being presented with his old Fabbri as divine providence. The Lord, Jesus Christ, did in fact want him to reenter the ring to slay pigeons, and he did so with ruthless dispatch. The rose-colored glasses with blinders at the temples, the faded-clays vest with USMA, WEST POINT NY embroidered on the back, the gun, the shooter: The man—or at least the remaining benevolent parts of him—was back. Douglas enjoyed what he was doing—the challenge excited him. After not handling a shotgun for nearly five years, he didn't think he could win any of the purses, and didn't concern himself with score. His timing was off a bit, but he made up for it by missing only two birds on the morning crank and another two in the afternoon. His day's total was 26. There were two 30-straights on the board, so McCashin's 26 tied him for fifth along with Walter, who was shooting in the final slot directly behind him.

When Sid Shapiro entered the clubhouse, a group of a dozen or so was gathered around the banquet table watching Winky Wagner's trick-shooting video. Walter was making change for forty dollars when Sid approached him.

"What the hell is this, Wagner?" he demanded.

"Entrepreneurship at work: I found a niche in the market, and I'm filling it," Walter said, tucking the money into his shirt pocket. Sid put his fist to his forehead as though he was forestalling a migraine.

"The plan was to show those movies at the big house tonight," he said with quiet sincerity. "It was gonna be the prelude to a big sales talk. If all the people I wanted to join me tonight have already seen the films, why would they bother to come?"

"I see what you mean, Mr. Shapiro, but that's the first I've heard of it. I got a garage full of these films, and I just thought I'd take advantage of the captive audience."

"If Winston didn't tell you about tonight, he's about to be out of a job."

Walter backpedaled. "I honestly don't remember what he told me. He may well have laid the whole thing out for me, and I just forgot. There's a lot of *in-one-ear, out-the-other* at my age. Don't take it out on the boy—I'm sure he's done everything you've asked of him. In regards to tonight, I can't make these people un-watch what they've already seen, but I can put it right. I'll get them to the clubhouse by performing the act live and in person."

"Why do I have the overwhelming suspicion that it's going to cost me at least another five bills to rectify a situation you single-handedly screwed up? Can you even make those shots anymore?"

"Seven-hundred-fifty—props included. It was my act before it was hers, and yes, I can certainly still perform it. I'm even willing to bet on it."

"Bet on it?" Sid asked.

"It only seems right. I need to get paid, but I did pretty well jam things up for you. In my mind, a wager is the only way. If it was a bet, I'd have no qualms in collecting, but I'd kinda feel funny charging you up front for it."

"You're worse than the damned unions," Sid grumbled, shaking his head. "Large attachments, old man—a regular set of brass clappers. The only question is whether you're going to run through all my pocket money before I throw you and that shit-box gypsy caravan the hell out of here." Shapiro counted out $750 and slapped it flat onto the table top loud enough to silence the room. "When?" he demanded.

"Four-thirty—before the light goes. I'll be there with bells on." And with that, Walter Wagner scheduled his very last exhibition of trick and fancy shooting—the last-ever performance of the original act.

XVIII

Walter turned off the gas cook-stove and removed the boiling kettle, into which he ladled two heaping spoonfuls of coarse black tea. He laid a camp plate full of cookies on a pressed-metal tray, along with three mugs, a metal creamer of milk, a mason jar of sugar and a fine mesh strainer. Alex Vanderstein and Douglas McCashin sat in the canvas campaign chairs enjoying the comforts of outdoor living when Walter exited the trailer, expertly balancing afternoon tea and cookies in his hands.

"Nice to have company over," Walter said, as he laid out the spread on the card table inside the screened tent. "Wink used to have her lady friends over for afternoon tea. Usually the gun club manager's wife. She always served these butter cookies," he added as he picked one up off the plate and bit into it.

Douglas poured milk and sugar into his mug while the tea steeped, and said, "Sorry about Winky, Walt. She's a fine woman—certainly the best shot I ever saw."

"And I'm sorry for your loss," Walter reciprocated. "I always joked she was too good for you anyway."

Douglas managed a smirk. "And I resented the hell out of you for it, but Lord knows you were right."

Walter poured the tea, first for McCashin and then for Alex.

"Happiness is fleeting," Alex added morosely. "Savor the good moments, because they're sure not to last."

"Amen," said Walter.

"I'm just glad you're still around to apologize to," McCashin said, placing his hand on Walter's knee. "I'm sorry for the lousy way I treated you, Walt."

Walter clapped his other thigh in slapstick poignancy. "Live long enough and you'll see it all, no matter how unlikely. The great Douglas McCashin, apologizing to me after all these years—and as a man of God at that! The very thought would have kept Wink in stitches for months," Walter cackled. "Truth is, you were the pain in the ass of a lifetime, but I'll be damned if you weren't entertaining. Always reaching for the moon—clawing for something better. Sure, you were a disagreeable son of a bitch most of the time, but I'd be lying if I said I didn't admire you for all the success you wrought. You were a man in full, just as big as you could be. So maybe you had to crow to everyone that you were the cock of the walk. I don't blame you for it."

"It's no way to live," McCashin replied, topping off Alex's mug for him. "Having to hate in order to call upon the best that's in you is juvenile. I try to steer my students well clear of it even though I lived my entire adult life that way. I can succeed *and* still respect my adversary. Unfortunately, I've learned this all too late.

"Alex is the only family I have left," he continued, "and I hated him with every fiber of my being. I would have destroyed him in time had fate not intervened." Alex, unperturbed, drank his tea. "I would have ruined him because he wasn't good enough to marry my daughter. I would have heralded his downfall because he's a Jew, and because doing so would have fulfilled me. Candy would have left him eventually. I would have felt she was choosing me over him, and that would have made me feel like a winner. That's pretty sick thinking, Walt."

"We all got weak rivets."

"I was a pretty terrible human being. I'm not going to run from it or try to fool myself about it now. Talking to you makes me realize . . ." McCashin said, turning to Alex. "Let's find Pete Geiger. I need to apologize to him as well."

"That little bastard broke my heart," Walter said bitterly.

"He quit drinking—finally," Alex said as he reached for another cookie. "Anyway, it's easy enough to track him down," he added through a mouth full of crumbs.

"The amends become a regular job in themselves," Douglas said to no one in particular.

Jazzmo appeared from the kennel leading Lila, the liver-and-white Brittany brood bitch, on a leather leash. As they approached the camp, the dog wagged her tail so thoroughly that her entire hind-end swung to-and-fro like a pendulum. The dog nuzzled each man affectionately in greeting. "This here's Lila," Jazzmo said. "She's a finished gundog—done trained her myself. Natural retriever right to hand. We making some room in the kennel, so if any of you gentlemen would like a fine shooting dog to take home, I got Lila and some others I can give to you."

The men looked at each other inquisitively.

"Making room?" Walter asked.

"Yes sir," Jazzmo replied flatly.

"They're going to kill them," Walter said. Jazzmo looked at the ground. "When?" Walter asked.

"Monday."

"How old is this dog?" Walter gave the animal the once-over.

"Seven. Started as a plantation dog—done trained her myself."

"I don't want to get home and find out this bitch won't hunt," Walter said. "Shoot her myself if that happens."

"No sir," Jazzmo assured him. "Got a kennel chock full of broke gundogs. Got me a Shorthair dog, a Vizsla dog and another Brittany bitch. I swear by 'em all—go in the field just as pretty as you please. Need to place 'em pronto, and was hoping one of you gents might take one."

"I might be interested," Alex said, as Douglas prepared to

protest. "What?" Alex asked defensively. "I might like a hunting dog. We could hunt it together. Why not, if it's a good dog?"

"Because nobody ever gave a nice dog away for free, but hell's bells—alright, we're interested," McCashin, said addressing Jazzmo. "But only if we can see them work. We won't even consider taking one unless we can shoot over them all."

"I'll put you on some coveys in the morning," Jazzmo said.

"Two," Walter said, holding two fingers up. "We're interested in two dogs."

XIX

At 4:30 that afternoon, Walter appeared, freshly scrubbed and immaculate in his showman's uniform of white flannel slacks, royal blue boating moccasins, a white short-sleeved shirt, and a braided horsehair bolo tie with the brass end of a Winston 12-gauge shotgun shell fashioned into a keeper, topped off with a cream-colored linen shooting vest trimmed in blue suede at the pockets and shoulder patch. The iconic royal blue W was hand-stitched like a high school letterman's patch on the vest back, and Walter's name was embossed in cursive over his left breast pocket. He wore a cream linen flat-cap with another, smaller royal blue W at the peak. A card table was covered with a Winston Firearms promotional oilcloth displaying the royal blue W. Laid on top of it were all the tools of Walter's trade: the nickel-plated Model-12 with extended magazine tube, the Super-X autoloader, the tubed-down Model-37, the 101 live-bird-combo, the .22 pump gallery gun and the Model-52.

Walter and Conrad took one last sweep of the skeet and trap stations with the push brooms. They looked as perfect as the day they were poured, and Walter retired behind the skeet high-house. Sid Shapiro, dressed in a white shirt with pink bowtie, pink Bermuda shorts, horse-bit loafers without socks and a navy blue blazer with the Little Kill club crest at the breast pocket, began moving toward the infield, where his wife was already waiting.

Victoria Vanderstein Shapiro stood confidently. Her wholesome freckled visage was in striking contrast to her brilliant eyes, sparkling as deep green as emeralds. Her shoulder-length auburn, rose-gold hair was pulled back in a ponytail and held with a black velvet bow. She wore a Chanel dress in a brilliant yellow that had a modest slit up the side and showed just enough thigh to keep things interesting. Her choice of white flats for walking the infield turf was sensible. She was there in a supporting role as a kind of prop, to charm prospective investors into believing that even though the Shapiros were in a social league unto themselves, the happy couple did seem just like regular people.

An amphitheater of folding chairs was set up behind the sixteen-yard trap stations for the fifty or so event competitors, as well as for many of their wives who were in attendance. There was an open bar and a table dedicated to bottle after bottle of ice-cold champagne in crystal flutes. Male guests were dressed in church-social casual—khaki pants, penny loafers and short-sleeved dress shirts open a button at the collar. White-gloved, liveried waiters circled the guests with sterling platters arrayed with hors d'oeuvres and finger foods. Some of the more rotund guests trailed after these platters like parasitic fish following a predator host, grabbing more than their fair share whenever the opportunity presented itself. Other men sat off to the side with their stogies, cigarettes and bourbon, and talked politics and the markets. The ladies privileged enough to draw an invite were a bit more self-conscious and formal, yet all could point a shotgun convincingly, even if they weren't necessarily partaking of fliers this weekend.

Finally, when the moment seemed right, Sid Shapiro gave his prepared speech from the infield.

"Ladies and gentlemen, treasured friends and guests," he began. "I can't begin to tell you how gratified I am that you've honored me with your company this weekend. Life is short, and loving friendships, both old and new, are the only things that make it worthwhile. Family traditions spanning generations: father-to-son, grandfather-to-grandson. Hunting and target shooting in our nation's great open spaces, a manufacturing industry that makes a product you can be proud of. That's what made this country the economic powerhouse of the world. It's all that Winston Firearms once stood for." The audience began to applaud steadily in agreement, and Sid punctuated his sentiment. "And that's exactly what she'll stand for again! The New Winston Firearms will be alive with innovation. Its products will be at the vanguard of the sporting firearms market. The China initiative forges synergies between the old West and the emerging East; between a lethargic, marginalized capitalism and an unbridled, vibrant entrepreneurialism; between the demands of just-in-time manufacturing and the compliant work force required to gear up a major production run, and then gear it right back down again once it's completed.

"Everything in entrepreneurship is relative. The man who created the Swatch sold hundreds of millions of them." Sid held up his left arm and peeled back the cuff of his shirt sleeve to reveal his platinum moon-phase, repeating chronometer. "The man who created this watch built 24 of them over his entire lifetime. The Swatch created multigenerational wealth. The creator of this bit of celestial perfection died a solid member of the middle class. The son makes a career repairing and servicing the timepieces the father created for me and 23 others just like me. Not much of a legacy.

"The China initiative will give us the best of both worlds," he said, rebuttoning his shirtsleeve cuff. "The design and engineering aspects are clearly the realm of the West, and we intend to poach the very best the industry has to offer. Industry knows about the New Winston Firearms and is excited about it. There are countless talented young risk-takers eager to create a new dynastic tradition with Winston. Our Eastern counterparts are every bit as enthusiastic. While arms manufacturing is relatively new to China, metallurgy and precision machining are old hat to Guangzhou City. Our Eastern partners are hardworking and entrepreneurial. They want to join us because they admire and respect American ideals, and want the same for themselves. The Germans taught them how to make cars to a global standard. Now the Americans will teach them how to make guns. We will give them the best-engineered designs, and they will manufacture them faster and more cost-effectively than we ever could. In short, our partners in Guangzhou will give us a less expensive, better quality Winston firearm. I hope that you will all join me in the entrepreneurial adventure of a lifetime, and perhaps your grandchildren's lifetime. Thank you for your kind attention, and without further ado, I give you the husband of the great exhibition shooter Winky Wagner, as well as the 1962 Grand American trap-doubles champion in his own right. Here he is, folks: trick and fancy shooter extraordinaire, Walter Wagner!" Walter appeared from behind the high-house with the Super-X in hand, stepped gingerly onto the concrete skeet pad and turned a kind of pirouette. He was on a pair of roller skates! He stopped mid-turn and addressed the audience.

"Conrad Winston III has been kind enough to join us. His great-granddaddy started the company and he will be acting as my assistant."

Conrad, dressed in his threadbare blue blazer and gray flannels, emerged from the crowd dragging the skeet and trap field controllers, hardwired on long cords. Walter loaded two shells into the auto and said to Conrad, "If you please—*Pull!*" Conrad hit the PAIR button and the two skeet house targets took to flight. Walter tracked the high-house dropper from his low gun, READY position, killed it without ever mounting the gun to his shoulder, then swung from the hip and killed the low-house crosser in perfect timing and position, as if he had been shooting a proper round from the shoulder for score. Before the second empty hull had even hit the concrete, Walter skated onward, and reloaded the gun. On station two he repeated the drill, killing a pair from the hip and skating on. At station four he killed pairs both ways, breaking the easier high-house-target-first pair and then the more difficult diving low-house-target-first pair. Walter skated with a jaunty slight-crossover step around the half-moon of concrete, always arresting himself on the rubber stops at the tips of the skates.

Finally he arrived at station seven and announced to the crowd, "Let's shake things up." He conspicuously reoriented the gun in his hands and shot the pair left-handed from his shoulder. Then he commenced to skate backward just as expertly as he had been doing forward. When he arrived at station four again, he shot the pair off his left shoulder both ways and announced, "This is getting boring." Conrad dropped a pillow in the grass behind Walter just beyond skeet pad number four. Conrad leaned the barrel of the auto against his crotch and braced himself. Walter suddenly somersaulted onto the pillow and, with Conrad's help, stood on his head. Conrad awkwardly worked the Super-X into Walter's hands and held his legs so that the old man could support his entire weight without the use of his arms. Walter loaded two shells into the chamber and called *Pull!*. Conrad hit the trap singles button and Walter dispatched one trap target, then another, shooting them on the rise before they ever had a chance to drop—or from Walter's perspective, rise. Conrad then removed the old man's skates by unzipping the heavy brass hardware, custom sewn into the leather. Walter leaned the autoloader against Conrad and did a reverse somersault back to a standing position. He took the gun, walked to the Winston Firearms promotional table behind skeet station four, wiggled into his waiting pair of blue suede boat shoes and reached for the gallery gun. He inserted a preloaded tube of .22 shorts into the barrel-tube magazine of the pump and unloaded a shot-bag full of props into his pocket. He walked onto the infield grass of the skeet field, and addressed the crowd.

"Everyone wants to know, are in fact demanding to know: Who shot the president?" Walter shucked the pump action of the gallery gun, and boldly announced, "I did." He turned and threw a vintage silver dollar up into the air, mounted the gun to his shoulder, tracked the coin over the top and plugged it dead center. The vibrating timbre coming from the plugged coin sounded like the beating wings of a large bee.

"James A. Garfield," Walter continued. "A leading proponent of the bi-metal monetary system—read 'money based on silver and gold,' kids. Yup—I shot him," Walter said as he tossed another coin into the air and plugged it too. Walter ejected the spent shell casing, and again addressed the audience.

"William McKinley," Walter announced to the crowd. "Died of gangrene from a gunshot wound sustained in Buffalo, New York. I shot him," Walter said as he shot another two coins on the drop.

"What about Jack Kennedy? I hear you ask. You can't be claiming him as well?" Walter barked, as he produced a smaller Kennedy half-dollar coin from his pocket and held it up for the crowd to see. "I'm not saying it was easy, but I got him too." With that Walter shucked a fresh cartridge into the rifle, launched the half-dollar into the air and made contact, the impact of bullet against coin sounding halfway to a ricochet. Walter produced another fifty-cent coin from his pocket for the crowd to see. "Told the Secret Service boys I'd shoot him again if I ever got the chance." Walter threw the coin up in the air, tracked it till it just came over the apex and rang it with the short projectile. "You're a violent man, Wagner," he said. "Liberals like to harp on how we exterminated the Indian—intentionally annihilated the red man, giving him blankets crawling with smallpox and killing him indiscriminately. They're wrong." Walter produced an Indian-head nickel from his trouser pocket. "I shot Geronimo," he said holding the thumbnail-sized coin up for inspection. "Dropped the buffalo he was chasing with the very same shot," he added, reversing the coin face in his hand. Walter tossed the coin aloft, slightly misjudging the throw, and shot it just before it nearly came down upon him. It flew upwards and disappeared into the settling dusk.

"Honest Abe," he proclaimed. "Freed the slaves. Killed off King Cotton and bankrupted the South. Contrary to popular belief, old Abe was diminutive in stature: a little bitty guy—so small you could barely see him," he said, holding up a highly polished copper wheat-penny. "Wasn't no actor that did him in, of that I'm sure," Walter said, sliding the action closed on the gallery gun and feigning intense concentration.

"I shot Lincoln," he said, as he threw the penny into the air, lower than he had with the others but still high enough so that at the peak of its flight no one, not even Walter, could see the coin.

He tracked what was invisible to the eye but what he was certain was still there. He envisioned its arc through the thickening dusk, followed his sixth sense to where he knew it would reappear, and used an intuition, honed razor-sharp through a half-century of putting cheek to comb, finger to trigger, master-eye to sighting plane. The plugged coin flew erratically out onto the infield, audible at a higher pitch and more distinct vibration from the others.

Walter held up the gallery gun for consideration and addressed the audience. "Ladies and gentlemen, I give you the Winston Model-61: the finest .22 pump rifle of its kind. Guaranteed to make a man out of even the most effeminate boy, equally adept at killing a coon or a commie—a lethal threat to both the red menace and the yellow horde. A young person can plink out a bedroom window with one of these fine rifles, hunting songbirds, chipmunks and even the wayward feral cat. Why, it's so quiet . . . " Conrad stepped forward from the audience—a mere twenty feet away—and silenced the old man with a stern hand clenched into the soft flesh of his shoulder, turning him on his heels and walking him away from the snickering crowd.

"You're ranting like a fascist, Walter," Conrad whispered. "What do you think you're doing?!" The old man was taken aback, oblivious to the outrageously off-color nature of his outdated remarks.

"I'm doing my original solo act, boy. What the hell does it look like I'm doing?"

"You can't talk like that, not in front of this crowd. Not in front of anyone! Effeminate boys and assassinating presidents? Are you insane?!"

"I spoke those lines for years, and they always brought a laugh."

"A lot has changed since then, Walter. This is an audience of wealthy people that Mr. Shapiro wants to attract to Winston Firearms—not as potential customers, but as equity investors. These people now think you're a bigot and a racist."

"Just 'cause I call Chinamen 'chinks'? That doesn't mean anything."

"It means everything if you're Asian! No one in this century is willing to tolerate that kind of thinking. Apologize—grovel even, and no more running commentary."

Walter recomposed himself and looked shamefully at Conrad. "Really?"

"I'm sure: no more jokes."

Walter turned back to the crowd. "My young associate informs me," he said, reticently, "that I pulled a massive boner with my remarks."

"Walter!" Conrad called in a stage whisper. "Boner?! That's the best you can come up with?"

By now the audience was openly heckling the buffoonery of the old man, who suddenly realized he was being laughed *at* and not *with*.

"He says my jokes are going over like flatulence in the vestry. Thing is folks, you go right along and the whole world just kinda changes around you—only you don't. You just keep on the way you always have, or as near as possible. Then someday, someone tells you you're all wrong. Your attitudes and sentiments are no longer acceptable—are actually injurious in the way that you're telling em. Well, I'm sorry. I'm a little out of my depth here. I apologize for my insulting remarks." Walter turned dejectedly and headed for the table of guns.

"Finish the act!" Sid Shapiro demanded from the audience ranks. "For Christ's sake, do the finale."

Conrad made eye contact with Walter. "Let's go," the younger man encouraged.

Walter turned to the audience. "Let's try this again. The wife and I used to do this bit where she'd shoot things out of my hands. Seeing as how I'm the one doing the shooting"—Walter squinted for comic effect and put his arm awkwardly around Conrad's neck—"Conrad's been kind enough to volunteer his services, and perhaps his fingertips, to the cause."

The younger man writhed with apprehension as he tried to worm out of Walter's embrace. "Hold on there, Junior-Junior," Walter mugged to the audience before speaking to Conrad in hushed tones. "This act requires an assistant, and without one, we got another half-hour of chirping crickets! You're the only person I can ask. You want to ingratiate yourself with Shapiro? Here's your chance. I did this with Wink for nearly thirty years without so much as a scratch. I've done these tricks a thousand times. You got nothing to worry about; I'm not going to hurt you, boy. Have a little faith in me and stand perfectly still. Close your eyes when I tell you to and it'll all be over in a minute." Walter was finally able to corral Conrad to the infield, where he handed him three graduated lollipops. "Start with the big one and work your way down. Stand perfectly still."

Walter picked up the .22, shucked a fresh shell into the chamber and nodded to Conrad, who stood in profile thirty feet away holding the first red lollipop in his right hand. The younger man closed his eyes on cue, and a quiet came over the crowd. When Walter took a bead on the candy, he noticed Conrad's hand shaking visibly. Walter took a breath, let it halfway out, and squeezed. At the sound of the rifle, Conrad opened his eyes and was left holding only the cardboard stick. The crowd erupted in applause, and Walter flashed an approving grin. Conrad calmly went to a smaller lollipop. When each of the three candies was reduced to bits of white pressed paper, Walter approached Conrad and hung a harness around his neck. The strip of bridle leather ran down his front like a necktie and was studded with six brass sockets, into each of which was fitted a piece of blackboard chalk.

Walter chambered a bullet in the .22 and gestured for Conrad to stand in profile and close his eyes. Conrad stood ramrod straight and tried not to breathe. Walter held his half-breath and waited for Conrad to exhale. The chalk exploded in clouds of white dust. When Conrad opened his eyes, Walter was approaching him. He removed the harness from around Conrad's neck and, with a theatrical flourish, produced a cigarette from the breast pocket of his shooting vest. Conrad looked at the undersized object in front of him and blanched. He took a step back and felt his knees weaken. "No! This is bullshit—I won't, and you can't make me!" Conrad walked back to the concrete pad where Sid Shapiro was standing.

"I can!" Sid Shapiro insisted, loud enough for everyone to hear. "If you want to play cowboys and Indians, prove to me you got the stones, preppy," Sid said, gesturing toward the infield. "Get out there and let's see how well you play for high stakes."

The old man spoke privately to Conrad. "I've got you, son. Trust me once more and you're in. You made it—he's saying as much." Conrad allowed the old man to guide him over to the cinder-block wall of the skeet high-house. Walter placed the cigarette in his trembling lips and commanded him to bite. Walter manipulated Conrad so that his legs were splayed and he was leaning against the wall with his full weight with the back of his head firmly in contact with the painted concrete blocks. "Don't move a fucking muscle! Do this and we're finished," he whispered tersely. Walter picked up the heavy, highly accurate Model-52 bolt-action rifle, paced off twenty feet and turned to regard his target.

Conrad closed his eyes and felt the damp cool of the blockhouse against his skull. In his mind, he counted off the mile markers to a distant past: being tossed about like a ragdoll inside the cockpit of his car as it descended the embankment—the warm, slick wetness running down his thigh, soaking into his pant leg from the hole where the door handle ran through it. The rapture he felt at twenty-two, looking down upon the seventeen-year-old virgin as he pushed himself deep into her, sweat dripping off his nose onto her girlish chest and dark ringlets—he eventually married the girl. He loved her deeply, but she divorced him anyway. There was the prep school trip to the city when by chance he saw his mother coming out of a theater on the arm of *the other man*. She turned away from him in embarrassment, and they never spoke of it afterword. There were his two daughters frolicking in the South Florida surf, being chased by the froth of an incoming wave and squealing with delight. The cancelling of the contract for the seven-figure Hatteras, and going through his father's wardrobe after his death. Then he was back in time, all the way back to a sinister green sky violently pelting the surface of the lake with rain. Conrad was diving deep under churning waters, fruitlessly searching in the cold darkness, straining blindly to see something. He dove deeper and deeper without ever touching bottom and finally looked back upward to the surface and to the light.

His jaw clenched. His life played out all at once in a condensed sensory overload. All he could hear was the sound of his own heartbeat from the blood rushing in his ears. A tear worked its way down his cheek, and he felt the irresistible compulsion to lift his head off the concrete block wall into the bullet's path. Then he suddenly heard the crack of the rifle, and a burst of applause from the audience. Conrad opened his eyes. The cigarette in his mouth was now just a paper tube, perfectly shredded at the tip. He removed it from his teeth to regard Walter, who flashed him a satisfied grin and gave the okay sign.

XX

Conrad resumed his duties as puller at the controls, and Walter picked the tubed-down Model-37 shotgun off the sponsor table. "People often ask me how I keep trapshooting interesting after winning at the Grand. I just take out my old Winston hammer gun and shoot a round with a .22." Walter walked out to the center pad at the sixteen-yard line and proceeded to weakly break five trap targets in a row. As he walked back to the table he deadpanned, "Half of the secret to getting old is knowing when to quit." The crowd erupted in applause as Walter reached for the Super-X, positioned himself on skeet station four and loaded three shells. "The other thing people often ask is which game do I prefer, trap or skeet? My answer to them is I prefer both—in the air and at the same time." Walter punctuated the words by calling *Pull!* and Conrad launched the trap target, followed a nanosecond later with the launch of a pair of skeet targets. Walter spot-shot the trap bird on the rise and moved right onto where the high-house bird would appear, acquiring the target, tracking it briefly and killing it just past the edge of the trap house. He then made the big turn toward the other end of the skeet field and took the low-house bird, as it was beginning to stall and descend.

Walter then reloaded three cartridges into the auto and called again, vaporizing the trap bird practically before it even showed itself above the roofline of the house, and then turning onto the low-house crosser, as it was rising on a mild gust of wind and then aggressively going directly to the far right side of the skeet field and, holding very low, as the high-house bird dove into his line of fire he chipped the very back edge off it.

Walter returned to the Winston promotional table of guns to a sea of applause. *The old fool might be intolerant, temperamental and thoroughly disagreeable*, the crowd seemed to surmise, *but he sure as hell was one trick-shooting SOB*. Walter reached for the nickel-plated Model-12 pump with extended magazine tube and canvas web sling, and addressed the crowd.

"Time was when the final extravaganza for most showmen was seven clay targets in the air at once. 'They'd show you three and four, and then some more. I'll show you seven, then eleven and then something even nearer heaven,'" Walter sang like a nursery rhyme, as he loaded a box of shells into each pocket of his vest and proceeded to the back of the trap house. Spires of clay targets stood neatly stacked in graduated increments. He loaded two shells into the pump and reached for the first stack of two with his left hand. He threw the clays aloft; the brace crested over the trap house and he broke them near the top. He then loaded three shells and did it again. Each series of shots required that he throw a larger stack of clays that much higher into the air to make sure he could get to the last target before it hit the ground. Not only that, but with every extra cartridge placed in the long magazine tube the gun got heavier and more ungainly.

Walter loaded seven cartridges and reached for the last stack of clays. He rolled the smooth, round edges of the targets back and forth on the pads of his fingers. Seven clays is all about the throw: It has to be precise, and the full force of the toss has to be directed skyward. Like a baseball pitcher throwing a slider, the motion very much depends on muscle memory and feel. Walter well recalled the feel of a good throw, and replayed it in his mind. He wound up, took two compressed steps and launched the stack high up into the air. The Model-12 was firmly seated into his shoulder when the flock of clays fanned out. He shot them one by one while they were still on the rise. He killed three by the time the clays reached their apex. Walter rapidly shucked the trombone slide of the fine-tuned action in a staccato rhythm and followed the targets downward as they disappeared into puffs of granulated pitch. Just as the crowd counted off the sixth ink-ball, Walter killed the final target less than a foot off the grass. The old man playfully shucked the empty hull from the chamber into the air and turned to address the crowd.

"*That*, ladies and gentlemen, illustrates the problem with this trick. You run out of throwing arm and blue sky before you run out of shells or clay targets. If we could only get that whole mess a little higher over the horizon, we might maybe even be able to tack a few more on." Walter gently laid the Model-12 on the trap house roof and then jumped onto it with remarkable dexterity. "That's why Winky and I came up with the idea for this contraption. If you please, Junior-Junior." Conrad appeared from behind the skeet high-house with a remarkable device in his hands. It was screwed together with a sleeved joint and was made from an antique set of ski poles. At one end, an ancient spiral-wrapped leather grip constituted a kind of a handle. At the opposite end—eight feet away—was an ingeniously fabricated aluminum alloy throwing platform that looked a lot like a sink-side drying rack for dinner plates. The rounded edge of each individual clay target was held precisely in place by a dished recess, its fragile dome loosely held down by a flap of automobile tire. Conrad carried the cumbersome device to the edge of the trap house and held it up, handle first, to Walter.

The old man spoke to the crowd. "There were always some that felt we were cheating with this—that the trick only counted if you were throwing 'em by hand. Bear in mind it was my wife that was doing all the shooting back then. She worked out with a medicine ball regularly, and we still couldn't reliably get her beyond six. I don't believe you can cheat at exhibition shooting, anyway. For those of you wondering why the devil I have a sling on this gun, like I'm gonna sneak off rabbit hunting, you're about to find out."

Walter leaned the handle of the bull rake against his thigh, loaded eight cartridges into the pump and looped the canvas sling over his right shoulder. Then he took the handle of the thrower in both hands with the head of the dishrack resting on the grass, shooter's left. He turned ever so slightly to the audience and quipped, "Here goes nothing," then gave a lazy heave to the contraption. The steel pole created a whiplike action that increased the force of his exertion exponentially. The clays fanned out into a well-spaced flock. They reached a nearly uniform height at roughly the same time. With the added leverage of this unique device, eight clays was easy work. In fact, he had so much time in the air that eight didn't really seem like much of a trick.

Walter then loaded nine and broke them—and then ten, and finally eleven. With every additional clay the dish rack got that much heavier, and with each extra cartridge in the extended magazine tube, the gun became that much more ungainly and awkward. By eleven Walter faced a timing-physics problem. "Forgive me if I need an extra step for this," he said, as he took the thrower in his hands. He initiated a kind of two-step running start, and heaved the dishrack skyward. He gently dropped the head of the device onto the grass, while reaching under his right armpit for the slinged pump. Grasping it by its pistol grip, in one fluid motion he inverted the firearm right side up as he brought the stock of the mercilessly barrel-heavy shotgun into his face and started blasting at the soon-to-be falling targets. Even though it was a good clean throw, it was all Walter could do to kill the last target mere inches off the turf before the clay hit the ground. His wiry frame struggled epically, his ropey arms straining against the unwieldy pole. His biceps were spent, and his trick back was beginning to flair.

"There's twelve inches in a foot, and twelve lunar cycles in a year," he began. "Twelve astronauts walked on the moon. The condemned man swings at midnight, failing an eleventh-hour reprieve, having been convicted by a jury of twelve. There's twelve days of Christmas and red grouse season opens on August twelfth. Twelve clays in the air at once was the best Wink could ever manage, and I suspect it's the best any human being can handle. Besides, twelve shells are all this gun'll take!"

Conrad loaded a dozen clays into the dishrack. Walter loaded the pump and counted off the shells as he wedged the cartridges into the spring-loaded alloy tube. "That's twelve," he pronounced. "One more time on a flock of a dozen—for the last time!" Walter took two full steps and heaved the machine, his sinewy muscles fraying a bit under the strain. The clays rose and fanned out of the rack. Walter let the bull rake come to rest softly on the turf as he fished the unwieldy pump out from under his right armpit in an automatic motion. He reoriented the gun vertically, comb coming to cheek, master-eye looking straight down the rib. All that front-heavy mass resting in his left hand. One, two, three, four on the way up; five, six, seven at or just over the apex; eight, nine, ten, eleven on the way down. Twelve hit the manicured grass and bounced back up in the air an inch or two by the time Walter fired and broke it.

"Fuck all!" the old man croaked. He shucked the last empty hull from the chamber and turned to the crowd. "I'll confess I'm a bit out of practice. Gotta put a special kind of English on this thing to make it all come together—kind of like cracking a buggy whip. Let's give her another throw and see if we can't do better."

Conrad reloaded the dish rack, and Walter counted off the cartridges as he reloaded. He very deliberately placed the canvas sling over his shoulder and let the pump shotgun come to rest on the right side of his torso. He took the handle of the big contraption in both hands. Walter swung the thrower to-and-fro—pendulum-like—trying to cheat gravity by building in some momentum. He shifted the weight off his back foot, took two steps on the trap house roof and let loose. The bull rake flexed like a pole-vaulter's punt. The *ping* of metal shearing under enormous pressure sounded like a stressed steel cable snapping. Walter was already in the middle of the throw when the both ends of the conjoined metal tubes collapsed in on themselves. The drastic change in weight put the old man catastrophically off balance. He was going down—falling. It was just a question of whether he would come to rest on the trap house roof or take the long header onto the turf of the infield. He twisted up like a pretzel and fell onto his left shoulder. The Model-12 bounced off the roof, barrel first. The fragile, fully-loaded custom alloy magazine tube tore free of its mounting hardware, popped most of its rivets, and disgorged its ordinance all over the concrete.

The crowd gasped in sympathy. The moment he saw Walter go down, Conrad leaped onto the trap house roof to attend to him. Douglas McCashin also rushed to Walter, and applied a red bandana to Walter's bleeding forehead.

"Let's see what you got here; hold still, Walt," McCashin said, calming the old man. McCashin removed the compress, and the blood started flowing down over Walter's temple and into his eye socket. McCashin put the compress back on the wound to stem the bleeding. "What you've got there is a world-class raspberry. Clean it up, get some styptic powder into it and you'll be all right." Conrad and Douglas got Walter disentangled from the smashed firearm and onto his feet.

"Ambulance is on the way," Sid Shapiro informed them as the two men helped a disoriented Walter to sit on the edge of the trap house. The front of his white linen shooting vest was covered in blood. He'd torn his pants at the knee and was missing his flat-cap with the royal blue W, as well as one of his shoes. "You're going to get checked out," Sid Shapiro announced.

"The hell I am," Walter blustered feebly. "I haven't been on a hospital litter since Korea!"

"You're not going to die on me, old man—not tonight and not on my property," Sid persisted. "You're going to be examined by a real physician at a hospital, and then you're free to go—or to stay— or do whatever the hell you like."

"I'm not gonna die on you," Walter initiated through the bit of froth in the corner of his mouth, as he returned to his feet. "I won't give you the satisfaction."

"You're easily as big a horse's ass as I *ever* was, Walt," McCashin snapped. "And that's nothing to be proud of!"

Walter reinitiated his enfeebled retreat, with McCashin at his elbow. Sid watched the old man limp toward the direction of his trailer. Walter mumbled under his breath something that sounded vaguely like "Carry on, beaten faggot."

"What did you call me?!" Sid demanded.

Walter turned around to address Sid face to face, awkwardly dabbing the clotting wound on his forehead with the bloodied bandana. For a moment it seemed the old man was going to take a swing at him.

"I called you a carrion-eating maggot, Shapiro. You've fattened yourself on the corpse of American industry—and now you're picking over the dried carcass of Winston Firearms, sucking the last marrow out of the bleached bones of Bridgewater. A Winston shotgun manufactured in Red China—it's a perversion!"

The crowd grew uncomfortable at the abrasive exchange. One by one, spectators slowly wandered off and started to clear out. Sid reached under a tablecloth and withdrew a soft gun case from which he produced a Model-12 pump shotgun—a preproduction prototype manufactured in Guangzhou, China. It was the only one in existence, and had only arrived Federal Express that morning. Sid climbed onto the trap-house roof and held it aloft for the crowd to see.

"Behold: I give you the New Winston Firearms Model-12!" The crowd stepped in for a closer look, and Sid climbed down from the trap house and passed the shotgun around for inspection. Then he calmly spoke. "Call me a vulture capitalist, Walter—call me anything you like. The important thing is I always make money for my investors—*always*. You want to talk brass tacks about Winston Firearms in front of these nice people, fine. Let's talk about *your* Winston Firearms. It might as well be dead. Only the name survives—and just barely. People often say to me, 'Sid, wouldn't it be great to revive the old trademark and build it here in America again? Maybe even go back into Bridgewater, reactivate one of the old plants and have a little presence there, for old time's sake?' The ledger of any successful business doesn't have a column entitled 'For Old Time's Sake.' The reason Winston Firearms became the gold standard of the industry was because it over-delivered. It had better designs, was manufactured to a higher standard and was fairly priced relative to the rest of the market.

"Sure, we could build it here in America. Reopen the same plant you used to work in," he said, gesturing to Walter. "Build a quality product just like before '64—and we'd have to charge $5,000 for a Model-12! How many guns do you think we could sell at that price? Zero. We face a choice, plain and simple: manufacture an overpriced product with union labor in Bridgewater that no one will ever buy, or manufacture the exact same product in Guangzhou at a competitive price. The Chinese gun *creates* wealth for the investor, and jobs for the importer and distributors. It revives a mythical name and breathes new life into an American legend. Is it the same as a pre-'64 Model-12? Of course not. That shotgun wasn't particularly profitable even in its own time, and the first job of any business is to make money. If you aren't profitable, you don't have a pulse. You can't build a better mousetrap, cure cancer or even sustain yourself. Winston Firearms went the way of the dinosaur because it couldn't adapt to a changing environment," Sid said, regarding a now seething Walter. "I know it's not the world you wish we lived in, but people expect a modern pump shotgun to be both good quality *and* affordable. The only question you need to answer is, do you want a live upstart or a dead legend? Because Winston Firearms can't be both."

The crowd applauded—Sid's enthusiasm was infectious. Walter stood bitter, beaten and drunk with rage. "Screw you, bub!" was all he could muster. Sid Shapiro had liberated himself from the very snapping jaws of a devastating public relations disaster, and he had also succinctly crystallized the plight of contemporary American capitalism. In short, he had won both the admiration *and* the venture capital of his guests. Sid had closed the deal—there would be a New Winston Firearms. Walter bypassed the waiting ambulance and, with the aid of Conrad and Douglas, managed to navigate over dew-soaked lawns into the enveloping twilight.

XXI

Sunrise created the stark, uniquely Southern contrast of shade to light. The warming sun raised steam off the surrounding terrain that nurtured life for all sorts of fauna—the bobwhite quail in particular. In the shade, frost crystals reminded guests that the Georgia border was a world away from the Palm Beaches.

Jazzmo pulled into Walter's campsite with the four dogs in crates on the back of his most unusual vehicle. It was a retired funeral car, actually a flower car that had been used in cemetery processions. It was a half-car, half-pickup-truck arrangement just like Walter's El Camino, only decked out with black paint and chrome.

Douglas and Alex were warming themselves over the camp stove, drinking coffee in the screened-in tent. Walter emerged from the trailer with a bandage over the wound on his forehead and the beginnings of a black eye. Like a remorseful drunk after a particularly unforgivable bender, Walter was all but mute. He was as cowered as the dog that messed the rug, as Walter, in his fit of rage, had nearly sabotaged the New Winston Firearms deal, and it was only the improvisations of a nimble mind that salvaged the evening.

Jazzmo was dressed in a thin, quilted thermal jacket to ward off the morning chill, and joined them long enough to fill his battered stainless-steel travel mug with coffee. When it came time to load up for the drive out to the bird cover, Walter slid behind the wheel of his vehicle and Alex looked at his feet awkwardly. Someone would have to ride with Jazzmo, as both Walter's El Camino and Jazzmo's flower car could only accommodate two. Without even considering the racial overtones, Douglas slid into the passenger's seat of Jazzmo's truck. This man of God—a bigot of the worst sort in a former life—was now color-blind. Walter and Alex followed.

Douglas rolled down the window a crack and took in the sights and smells of plantation country.

"Taking you onto my own place," Jazzmo announced, gesturing beyond the next rise. "Don't want no trouble shooting into Mr. Sid's birds."

McCashin nodded. The two trucks pulled onto the farm, past Jazzmo's neatly kept single-wide trailer and tobacco barn. They followed the dirt road through a field of planted soybeans and then into the uplands, past stands of turpentine pines and native wiregrass that had never felt the bite of a plow. Jazzmo burned this cover seasonally with a controlled fire in an effort to create a habitat suitable for sustaining bobwhite quail in high style. The trees and downed deadwood were charred from where the flames had licked at them.

Douglas stretched and yawned as he stood taking in the vistas from the high ground. "Nice spot you've got here," he said.

"Ain't much," Jazzmo gushed. "Just shy o' fifty acres, but the soil's black as peat and mostly dry. You can grow anything in or on it—vegetable or animal. That's Onori," Jazzmo said, pointing out to the east. "Over yonder's Sweetbay Plantation," he said, gesturing south. "Covey don't know property lines or who owns 'em. Only knows the hawk, the fox, the snake and the gun. Likes to settle in here on account of I keep it so nice and I only shoot into my own coveys once a month. My birds fly wild 'cause I leave 'em be."

"Sanctuary," McCashin said to no one in particular.

"Hell of a trick," Walter noted snidely. "Having your rich neighbors go to all the trouble of releasing all those expensive birds only to have them come to roost on your land."

"Sure is!" Jazzmo sang out as he unlatched the dog crate and pulled down the liver bitch, Lila. "Farm done come down through Ruby—my wife's side. Both plantations been after it for near on thirty years now, but we ain't selling. Finished enough gundogs in these uplands to last two lifetimes. Money in the hand—year in year out—steady like." Jazzmo secured a small brass bell to the orange collar around the neck of the liver-and-white Brittany. The dog was fussing and yelping and starting to tremble in anticipation of being set loose. "Got me a 28-gauge if one of you gents prefers to shoot a little less gun?"

"I'll take you up on that," Douglas McCashin volunteered, and the black man produced a 28-inch Francotte boxlock, side by side with double triggers and scroll engraving. It had a worn patina that wasn't just well used, but distressed. The bluing was worn through at the breech and muzzle, the case-hardening was completely worn off the receiver-action, and only the slightest hint of checkering remained on the straight-grip stock and splinter fore-end. The red Old English pad looked like a chewed pencil eraser, and what traces remained of the original oil finish had mellowed to a deep muted tone, like the color of a well-seasoned, burled tobacco pipe.

"That's seen better days," Walter said.

"Give her a tickle and she's as good as new," Douglas countered. "Not many wing shooters appreciate a classic game gun anymore."

By now the bitch was ready to jump out of her skin, she was so excited. Jazzmo handed Douglas half a box of shells and added, "Continental gun wasn't worth a lick back in the day. Took it as down payment on a made dog. Ruby's daddy thought I got rolled when he done seen it. Well, who's laughing now, fool?!" Jazzmo gesticulated comically toward the heavens, as he released the Brittany.

The dog took off like a shot down the dirt road, yelping and yipping all the way. She couldn't contain the unbridled joy and excitement in her newly gained freedom. Just as she was getting out of eyesight, she stopped and defecated. Then she worked her way back, crisscrossing the road back and forth, urinating in carefully spaced intervals all along the way and came to heel at Jazzmo's feet, anxiously awaiting her marching orders. "Gonna run Lila alone first, then put down Daisy so's you can see 'em go in a brace. Load up, gentlemen," Jazzmo ordered.

Alex put a shell into the chamber of Walter's Super-X, closed the bolt and put another shell in the magazine. Douglas closed the empty 28-gauge and mounted it to get a sense of the fit and how much comb-pressure would be required to get a correct rib alignment. He reopened the gun, slipped two slender cartridges into the breach and closed it. Walter, injured as he was, demurred. He would walk and watch, and try to rekindle his love of upland bird dogs.

Jazzmo produced a staghorn trainer's whistle on a braided leather lanyard from around his neck. He placed it between his teeth and held his right hand aloft to gain the dog's attention. He took a moment to highlight the bitch's discipline, sitting at heel despite her nervous anticipation of what was about to happen. After Jazzmo was satisfied that each man had duly noted the dog's steadfast patience, he blew the whistle, dropped his arm like a flag and released the animal, sending her out on a wide cast into the cover.

The bitch ran fast and hard, conscious of the light cross-breeze and its ability to carry scent. She ran a bit manically, addressing likely hunting objectives in no particular order. She was elated and athletic, demonstrating an innate intelligence that was impressive to witness. In less than four minutes Lila was locked up tight—motionless and intense—with her stub of tail standing erect and her left front leg instinctively giving direction. Her cheeks were billowing, wafting in volumes of air to concentrate the scent. The Brittany was pointing a covey of quail, doing what it was bred to do, rejoicing in a kind of genetic nirvana—the total fulfillment of instinct and function.

Jazzmo approached the pointing bitch, stroked her affectionately and addressed the men. "That's a $3,000 bird dog any other day. A dog that won't hunt—that's one thing, but these are high-class, finished gundogs. Nothing will break that point— not till you release her. Now come on with me and let's put the other dog down," Jazzmo said, gesturing for the men to return with him to the truck.

"I'll own up to showing off," Jazzmo boasted as he pulled the orange-and-white Brittany through the tight metal gate of the dog box. "A little bit of yourself rubs off on every animal you finish. Lila's a stone-cold pro—makes me proud to see her go. Even after all that time in the kennel, she hasn't lost a step. This 'un too," Jazzmo said stroking the orange-and-white vigorously. The bitch responded by panting enthusiastically.

Jazzmo sent Daisy into the cover. She started off in a plotting, pacing trot—her left set of legs working in unison, but separate and independent from her right. "This dog moves a little funny— quail don't seem to mind." The bitch began quartering back and forth, working a methodical, deliberate pattern. It wasn't as sexy to watch as the first dog, but in very short order, Daisy had found her way over to Lila and was holding at a sensible distance, honoring the point of the still-frozen liver dog. "They go together—they go apart. Daisy's just as staunch: Stay on point till the sun comes up again lest you release her." Jazzmo unfastened the flushing whip from the brass D-ring on his bull-hide belt. He gestured for the men to get ready while he beat the grass cover softly, sending the covey of birds exploding into the crisp morning air—frantic wings drumming a majestic vibrato upward into an impossibly blue sky.

Douglas picked out a bird from the rest and, in one fluid motion, tracked it, flicked off the safety with his thumb and mounted. By the time the stock came to rest in his shoulder, his cheek was already oriented on the comb and his head was erect. He had mounted onto the beak of the quartering bobwhite hen, and increased the lead slightly before he fired on it. In the same quadrant of his hard focus, he acquired a second objective and killed it too: a double in the time it takes to snap your fingers twice. "Preacher's quick on the triggers!" Jazzmo declared.

Alex had tracked a bird and gone to fire, only to discover that he'd forgotten to disengage the safety. He hung on the trigger a moment, leaned into the shot and then nearly fell over when the gun didn't discharge. "I think quail heaven just got two more customers," Jazzmo regaled cheerfully to McCashin, as Lila retrieved one bird to Jazzmo and Daisy gently delivered its package neatly into McCashin's outstretched hand. "All they want to do is please," Jazzmo pleaded, "and maybe keep you company."

Alex flicked the safety on and off several times in practice for the next covey. "Hell's bells, Alex! Be sure that safety's back on before we move off," McCashin sternly warned.

After another twenty minutes, Jazzmo picked up the liver dog and put down the Vizsla to run him with the orange-and-white Brittany. The moment Jazzmo released the young ginger dog he was off at a breakneck pace, wearing a loopy expression, running a cottontail down the dirt road and into the tree line. "And there he goes, shit-for-brains!" Jazzmo lamented. "He picks *today* to run rabbits! Maybe that animal is too stupid to live! I'll get him tonight if I don't luck out and some hapless brother finds him and tries to run him for the season." Jazzmo was clearly disgusted. "I guess it don't matter none. Anything's better for him than . . ." He trailed off.

As he reached into the last remaining dog box to bring out the liver-and-white German Shorthair, Jake, the dog leaped out of Jazzmo's arms and landed in the soft soil. After inspecting the men briefly, he proceeded without fanfare to lift his leg on an unsuspecting Alex Vanderstein. It was only after the warm liquid soaked though the back of his pant leg and onto his calf that Alex realized what was happening. He sprang forward awkwardly, into the arms of the black trainer. "Easy there, young squire," Jazzmo said to Alex, allowing him to recompose himself. "Shoulda told you: Jake'll piss on you, piss on me, piss on the other dogs— got no respect for anyone or anything. Downright antisocial if you ask me, but I'll be damned if he ain't the bird-findingest fool you ever did see. Won't run with another dog—tears 'em up. And he don't retrieve much neither—just kind of mouths 'em. But if there's anything in a section, he'll find it."

The Shorthair was down, and this male ran the biggest of the group. Walter's first thought when he saw the mostly white dog range out so distantly was that this animal had all the hallmarks of a *drop*—a cross-breeding of a German Shorthair back to an English Pointer. The objective in such breedings is to produce an animal with a better nose and more *go*. The natural retrieving instinct sometimes suffers in such pairings, and the resulting offspring often has so much range it's easier handled off horseback.

"That dog's into the next county," McCashin commented.

"Busting birds all the way," Walter added.

"Serves me right: aiming to show you gents how sweet they goes without even a shock collar and two of 'em running wild. Hand it here," Jazzmo ordered, taking the opened side by side from Douglas. The black man confirmed that it was loaded, closed the gun and flicked off the safety as he shouldered it and fired two shots up in the air to gain the dog's attention. "Run his damned fool head off, lest you remind him he's got a job to do!" The Shorthair returned to the hunting party moments later, frantically trying to sniff out dead birds on the ground he was certain must be at their feet. Jazzmo took the flushing whip from his belt, folded it in half, and grabbed the dog by the collar. Jazzmo hit him hard once on the rump with the blunt object, and the dog yelped sharply. "You hunt close!!!" he commanded, just inches from the animal's snout. "With the hardheaded ones, it's all they understand. He's a good dog; just doesn't see enough work, so he forgets himself."

"Picked the wrong day to hunt for himself, I'm afraid," McCashin lamented.

"I reckon so," Jazzmo remarked.

XXII

Walter Wagner pulled his caravan—the trailer was now fully packed and rigged, and he was ready to leave—onto the sandy shoulder and engaged the warning flashers. The orange-and-white Brittany was restless and cramped inside a makeshift wooden crate anchored to the bed of the El Camino. Walter looked as if he'd been in a brawl: His left eye was the color of freezer-burned calves' liver, and the circular bandage covering the raspberry on his forehead had soaked through. His shoulder was bruised, and he was sore all over. He hobbled around the front of the vehicle on his game knee and made a beeline for Sid Shapiro, who sat on the edge of a one-piece wooden picnic table. Sid rested his feet on the bench seat, smoking a cigar and reading the *Journal*. His vantage point allowed him to casually observe the steady stream of shooters circulating through ring one.

"I pulled up stakes," Walter announced, slightly out of breath. "I'm leaving, but not till I put things right. My father always said *it's not the things you do—but what you do about the things you do.* I'm obliged to apologize, Mr. Shapiro. I got angry and tried to wreck your event. I'm sorry—I got no defense for it." Walter reached into his shirt pocket and withdrew $750. "I bet I could make all those shots, and I failed. Here's your money back."

Sid sat looking at the wad of folded notes in Walter's hand. "I don't want your money," he said.

"You gotta take it—I can't live with it if you don't. Square us up, and I'm out of your hair for good," Walter pleaded.

"Do you have any idea of how much I'm worth? What the hell difference do you think chump change makes to me?" Sid said, looking at the money with distaste. "Take it. It's my retirement gift to you. Spend it on Geritol—or penis pills. *Mazel tov!*"

"No," Walter replied flatly as he stuffed the folded bills into a crack between two boards in the top of the picnic table.

Shapiro slapped his newspaper down on the table. "Walter, it pains me to admit this, but your act was terrific—just gangbusters. I could have done without the Aryan Nation diatribe, but what the hell—it was all pretty entertaining to watch. So what if at the end you couldn't make twelve and almost killed yourself trying? You exited with plenty of drama, and your temper tantrum actually created an opportunity: I said everything I needed to about the New Winston Firearms in under a minute, and reinforced all the reasons why we're doing things my way. It turned out fine, really. I *got* what I wanted. As far as I'm concerned, you earned the money—keep it."

"It's the principle of the thing," Walter said, plucking the wad of cash out from its nook between the boards and unfolding it lengthwise. He pinched the bills between his thumb and fingers and fanned them out. Then he reached for Sid's lighter. "Seems we're deadlocked," Walter said as he sparked the flint. "Guess the only way to settle this is for neither of us to have it." He held the bills to the flame and they ignited.

Sid was dumbstruck as the money burned. "If you think you're going to get a rise out of me, you're in for . . . Oh shit!" he shouted, as he sprang off the picnic table, knocked the blazing currency out of Walter's hand, and stomped out the flames. "Are you really that stubborn, old man?! Flat broke and you're burning money—you're an idiot!"

"Self-made bootstrapper," Walter noted. "I knew you wouldn't sit still for it."

"This fucking guy!" Sid announced to no one, as he picked up the charred remains of the currency. There was a little more than half left of each bill. "*My Ma* always said that people who don't respect money don't deserve to have any. Seven-hundred fifty dollars was the world to me at one time. Yeah, I grew up poor and to see you do that . . . it just hurts too much," he said. "The good reverend has been trying to put the touch on me all weekend for his ghetto school; let's give it to him."

"He started in on me at the crack of dawn, sermonizing about righting a wrong, individual integrity and being in the good graces of God," Walter said, as he fished out of his pocket one of the warped silver dollars he'd plugged in the act the night before. He held it out for Shapiro. "Used to hand out Indian-head nickels to the all kids after the show. Thought you might like one of these. Won't be making any more of them—what with the price of silver, I don't suppose anyone will."

Shapiro unclenched his fist, and Walter dropped the coin into his palm. Sid contemplated the silver dollar briefly and then said to Walter, "You paid good money for all those options and you're still in the hunt. Shoot if you want—I won't say you can't."

Walter pondered Sid's words for a moment, then muttered "I'll be damned" under his breath, as he walked back to his trailer to get his gun.

XXIII

W alter moved his caravan over to some level turf within visual range of all three rings. He pulled out the plastic camp table and set it up. He let the orange-and-white Brittany out of the crate, but kept her leashed to the bumper as he put his gun together. The animal was tentative and skittish toward the strange old man. Walter did his best to reassure her, showing her a soothing, firm affection, giving her a pat here and there, and talking to her in a calming tone as he went about his business. When he was finally ready, he took the bitch for one last walk around the vicinity, put a fresh bowl of water in the box and kenneled her back into the makeshift wooden crate.

Tom Thumb Stratton held the scorecard for Walter's thirty-bird race between his sticky fingers and called, "Douglas McCashin shooting—Walter Wagner on deck."

McCashin stepped up to the 32-yard line and rolled his head a couple of times in a circular motion to get his neck vertebrae and muscles loose and working. He closed the empty Fabbri and mounted it to his shoulder to get some perspective on hold-point, and to reconfirm the comb height. As he might expect of a firearm that had been tailor-made to him personally, everything was perfect. McCashin loaded two shells into the chambers of the over-under and called "Trapper ready?"

"Ready," Tom Thumb called back from the puller's house.

Douglas closed the Fabbri and mounted it. He took a bead just to the right of the center box, and screwed down all of his powers of concentration at once. *Pull!* he called, and a gray bird with green accents went airborne, beating its wings frantically, climbing skyward toward the high mid-morning sun. McCashin drilled it with the first barrel, killing it stone dead. The bird sank like a foundered vessel headed straight for the bottom. The pigeon landed behind the center box. McCashin waited a moment for it to move. When it didn't, he expertly took two steps off the left side of the pad, gaining a direct line of fire around the metal box trap, and unloaded the second round into the lifeless fowl as insurance.

McCashin was focused, he was *on* and at times it seemed as

if he was *willing* the fliers out of the sky with sheer tenacity and competitive desire. His timing was quick, but not frivolous or uncontrolled. He wasn't wasting any of his second shots—if a bird didn't drop with the first barrel, he waited a *Mississippi* or two and got a line on it in a measured way. The quick-first-shot-slower-second method paid dividends: Tom Thumb called "Pick up five!" McCashin had cleared the first ring.

"You're living right, Padre!" Walter shouted, pointing to a bird caught by the chain-link fence just inches from going over the rail. "Somebody up there likes you."

"I'm a shooter, Walt," McCashin said through a beaming grin. "From the heels forward. It feels fine to have a shotgun back in my hands."

"Even the pope's gotta have a hobby."

"You'd think."

"Walter Wagner!" Tom Thumb called through the open window of the puller's house.

"I'm gonna burn two and then we'll start," Walter said as he loaded two shells and fired both down range in the blink of an eye, to mimic his rapid trigger-timing for box-birds. He reloaded and held at the *low gun* position. "Trapper ready?!" he called.

"Ready!"

Walter mounted the gun, took a hold-point halfway between box five and six, and called *Pull!*. In the time it takes to knock twice on someone's door, he dropped a pigeon with the ruby hue of a Rhode Island Red. Walter worked his way through ring one and for anyone who knew both men, the contrast in their life histories was stark. Both had been military men in the infantry. Walter had been a noncom draftee, Douglas a West Point cadet.

Walter detested combat and felt deeply ashamed of the intense fear he felt under fire. He'd led soldiers reluctantly and only out of a heavy sense of obligation. It tore him up to see his men become casualties, and he took their individual fates personally. When a transfer came from on high reassigning him to the divisional rifle team in a rear area, he took it—and was haunted by regret for having abandoned his men. When his hitch was up, he vowed to put the entire unpleasant experience behind him, but like many veterans, he never could.

McCashin had been an exemplary cadet and officer. He was a natural leader of men who understood and fit well into military life. Douglas regarded warfare as sort of oversized game of chess—the ultimate intellectual challenge. He personified the ideal blend of tactical theory and practical application, was unflinching in the execution of his missions and recognized that armies purchase objectives with casualties. *That* is the currency of warfare and a commander's job is to see the funds are well spent. Like Wagner, McCashin had also known fear, which he rationalized as simply a leader's healthy concern.

Major McCashin gave every man in his command an added edge of professionalism and training. He lived the military creed that the more you sweat in training the less you bleed in combat. Every one of his frontline soldiers knew how to swim, climb a tree, navigate using a topography map and could shoot offhand into a six-inch group at a hundred yards with battle sights. Rudimentary survival and medical training were also compulsory. He taught his men battle-craft, from how to move through cover without leaving signs they'd been there, to something as simple as tying a tight square knot in a bootlace, cutting off the excess and then taping it over—one less thing to loosen up, snag or trip over at the wrong time. McCashin rarely put a foot wrong or made a miscalculation. His no-nonsense management style was straightforward and easy to follow. His men trusted his judgment, knew he wouldn't ask of them what he hadn't already asked of himself, and they gratefully noted that he didn't disappear once the shooting started. Douglas McCashin bled olive drab and would have happily made his career in the army had the war not petered out.

Douglas was a widower, having lost his wife, Sugar, to a stroke. Walter might as well have been a widower, with Winky having lost all sense of self-awareness. Douglas had outlived his daughter, Candy, who died of a drug overdose. Walter's infant son had suffered a crib death. Both men had spent their entire professional careers in the County. Both had decamped to South Florida, and now lived less than a half-hour's drive from each other. Both were intimately associated with the Little Kill Country Club: Douglas as a member, occasional shotgun chair and perennial intra-club champion. Walter had been the seasonal gun club manager at Little Kill each winter for more than a decade. McCashin had lived his life by his wits, first as a warrior, then as a salesman, finally as an entrepreneur. He prospered most of his adult life and was now richer than Croesus, but had since renounced the trappings of wealth. He now lived as an ascetic and taught physics and geometry to mostly inner-city children.

Walter had lived a quintessentially working-class life, first in manufacturing and then as a performer. Now he was retired and trying to stretch his meager savings into a modest life of leisure. Most importantly, Walter knew the love and companionship of Mitzy Adelman; he had someone to share his life with. Although Douglas hadn't taken a vow of celibacy, he'd nonetheless resolved that living out his life alone was God's plan for him. He determined his purpose was educating poor children and the times of living for himself were entirely in the past.

The two men circulated through all three pigeon rings together, collegially encouraging each other and sharing their fondest memories of how it used to be back in the good old days. By the time they arrived back at ring one, Walter had managed to clear the first two rings, and had missed only one bird on ring three. Douglas had run one ring and shot fours on the other two. It was a thirty-bird race and scores of 14 and 13 at the halfway mark were impressive.

Then the sky suddenly closed up and clouded over. It didn't feel like rain, but a dark bird was certainly not the forgone conclusion it had been at high noon. Douglas was shooting from 33 yards, and in the overcast light he was slow in his reflexes and off his timing. He wasn't seeing the birds—he was seeing silhouettes of birds, and his quick-first-shot-deliberate-second timing had degenerated into two fairly late, poorly placed attempts. He shot a three on ring one before it was Walter's turn.

"I'm gonna burn two and then we'll start," he said to Tom Thumb through the open window of the puller's house.

The fat man laid the five freshly shuffled cards on the console in front of him and said, "I know your routine, Walter. You don't always have to announce you're going to flambé."

"Safety needs to be automatic. Just like *you* double-check every sandwich to see that it's swimming in butter and mayonnaise, *I* say my spiel every time I step into the ring. You might not need to hear it, but I do—just to confirm my intent."

"Your intent is clear, for Christ' sake. Test-fire and let's get on with it!"

Walter fired two shots down range and then reloaded. The light was even worse now than it had been for Douglas. Walter held generally over the left-side third of boxes, as that was where the ring was darkest and where he'd have the hardest time seeing a bird get up. He estimated his chances correctly. Two out of the first three fliers came from that side. The fourth bird came from the hard right-end, and he swung over to it in his usual timing and made a weak hit on the brown bird with his first barrel. Then he went to track it for a second attempt, but as he went to shoot he flinched—hanging on the trigger before he was finally able to fire. The bird fluttered on, landing on a tree branch just outside the ring, where it lasted less than sixty seconds before keeling off its perch, dead.

"Someone's ready for a release trigger," Tom Thumb remarked cynically from the puller's house.

"Goddamn it!" Walter cursed. "Sorry, Douglas—please excuse me," he said, turning to direct his flustered apology toward the pastor. Before Walter could reload for the next bird, a crack in the sky opened up and a ray of sunshine shot through to the pigeon ring.

"How's that for a little divine intervention?" Douglas joked, looking toward the heavens.

Walter reluctantly loaded the live-bird combo, held it at the *low gun* position and called "Trapper ready?!"

"Ready!"

Walter sighed reservedly, mounted the gun, and took a hold-point between box five and six. *Pull!* he called, and when the ivory-white bird was released from box six, he was nearly already on it. He tracked the climbing target, but lurched uncontrollably when it was time to shoot. He hit one of the metal traps, causing the shot pellets to ricochet. Walter took a moment to gather himself and tried to track the alabaster bird, but when it came time to fire the second barrel, he blew a hole in the ground not six feet in front of him. Walter stood on the pad at 34 yards and watched the pigeon, as pale as powdered sugar, fly over the trees and onward toward the next rise. He broke the gun open, and the spent hulls flew over his right shoulder.

"I think I'm done for," Walter said, turning and walking back toward Douglas. "My pigeon shooting days are over."

"No argument here," McCashin agreed. "Quit before you hurt someone."

XXIV

Walter hastily stowed his equipment in the trailer. He put the 101 live-bird combo back in its soft case and carefully hung up his shooting vest, a duplicate of his showman's garb. He gently folded the matching flat-cap inside itself and put it in one of the vest pockets and then covered the whole thing with clear plastic from the dry cleaners. The El Camino was already running. He was ready to leave when he heard a knock on the trailer's plywood wall. Sid Shapiro poked his head through the open door.

"You've tired of our hospitality?" Sid asked.

Walter looked up and smiled weakly. "Not exactly," he said as he tried to exit the camper. Sid had to take hold of the old man's arm as he feebly stepped to the ground. "Thanks," Walter said as he started toward the cab of the truck.

"Why are you running off then?"

Walter stopped and grasped the gunwale of the truck bed to steady himself. "I'm not running off. I'm just going home."

"You've only got two rings left on the thirty-bird race. Don't you want to finish?"

"No . . . thank you," Walter replied as he tried to go about his business.

"I heard about your flinch—tough break. I know what that's like. All I'm asking is that you finish with a Winston firearm— any Winston firearm. If you're shot out, try the Super-X, why don't you?" Walter looked at his feet. "Look, you're only down three birds—you could win the Great Eastern purse."

"The only purse I needed to win was the sow's ear, and I already collected on it," Walter said as he turned and started for the cab.

Shapiro stopped him. "First you elbow your way in here when nobody wants you and now, when you're actually about to make good with my product, you want to go home?!" Sid reached into his pants pocket and pulled out his cabbage roll of money. "I need you in ring two shooting a Winston shotgun now, goddamn it!" He peeled off five hundred dollars and tried to forcefully insert the money into Walter's shirt pocket. The old man was all arms-and-elbows, as if he were fighting off a knife-wielding assailant. When they were finished, the cash was strewn about on the ground and Walter was out of breath. Sid wet his thumb and relentlessly peeled off another five hundred. "A thousand—that's a hundred a bird. All I'm asking is that you to try."

Walter was exasperated. "I know you can buy and sell just about anyone or anything you want, but I'm gonna leave you with this rag to chew on: I'm not for sale—not anymore. I used you just like Winston Firearms used me—screwed me outta my pension. I got what I wanted from you, and now I'm leaving." Walter turned his back on Shapiro and started to get into his truck.

Sid's demeanor visibly shifted. All the charm in him evaporated and he went snake-eyed. "That looks like one of my brood bitches you've got strapped to the back of your shit-box. Funny thing—I don't remember giving away any dogs recently. Don't remember selling any either. Could it be that you're trying to sneak it out of here—like stealing?"

Walter now leaned heavily against the vehicle to stabilize himself. "That Negro gave her to me, but if you want her back, take her. You're not gonna blackmail me, though. Just tell me what kind of a shit-heel would rather kill an animal than give it away?" Walter started to reach for the rope that anchored the dog crate to the truck bed.

"Don't make me be a son of a bitch, Wagner! Shoot the fucking gun and let's be done with this!" Sid commanded. Walter continued to untie the crate. "Stop with the dog for a minute, will you?" Sid said collecting himself. "I asked you here to promote this product and here you are, about to do something remarkable—and you're just quitting. I don't get it?"

Walter looked Sid in the eye. "You may find this hard to believe, but I made a promise. I sat on the edge of that good woman's bed and promised that if I could just have it back for the weekend, my abilities, my skills—if I could just have it back the way it was when I could really shoot, I'd quit when I hit my number: I'd cut out when I had $12,000. Well, I was less than five-hundred short when I counted it last night and that's close enough. I held her hand and swore on it. Fate's paid out, and now I'm gonna hold up my end."

Walter pulled out his wallet. "I'll pay you $500 for the dog," he said counting out the bills.

"For a finished gundog?"

"Don't go getting any Hebrew notions that I'm some kinda money tree you can start shaking. Five hundred is my one-and-only offer."

Walter held the money out to Shapiro, who finally accepted it. With infuriated eyes, Sid managed to snarl, "Get the fuck out of here!"

<h1 style="text-align:center">XXV</h1>

alter crawled toward the front gate at a snail's pace. There were lots of intricate turns and kinks to negotiate. Seeing as this was probably his last-ever road trip in the rig, he'd be damned if he was going to bang up his pristine trailer by rubbing it against a tree because he cut a corner too sharply. The road came to a fork in front of the slave cabins. The old man was making an awkward three-point-turn, and it was lucky that Conrad stepped out the front door. Just as Walter was getting flustered, looking first in his mirrors then over his shoulder, Conrad suddenly appeared. He banged the side of the El Camino with his hand to get the old man's attention.

"Shit!" a startled Walter barked. "You scared me, Junior-Junior. I thought I ran into something."

"Put it in reverse," Conrad said confidently. The young man directed the old one and got the caravan onto the main drive, pointed toward the front gate.

"Everyone's been talking about how great you're shooting—why are you leaving?"

"Because I know when to quit—that's why," Walter snapped back before he caught himself. "Actually, I started flinching. I'm now officially a danger to myself and to others; I stopped before someone got hurt."

"I'm sorry to hear that."

"Don't be. I had my moments, both alone and with Wink—enough to last a lifetime. I got what I came here for, and I'm grateful to you, son—for helping me, for trying to look after me."

"Don't thank me, Walter, it was my job."

"*It was your friggin' job*—I'm thanking you for trying to protect me . . . from myself, a task at which you didn't exactly succeed, I might add! What I'm trying to say Junior-Junior . . ." Walter collected himself and then finally gave the younger man the respect he was due. "What I'm trying to say, Conrad Winston III, is that you're a good boy—I mean a good man, a patient, virtuous man. You showed me a kindness, and I'm beholden'.

"You're welcome—I guess." Conrad said contemplatively. "I

don't suppose we'll be seeing much more of each other."

"Guess not."

"I'm surprised he's letting you leave without a bigger fuss."

"I think it finally dawned on him that I'm probably a bigger pain in the ass than I'm worth. Besides, I think our parting words have pretty well burned that bridge for all time," Walter said.

Conrad placed his hand on the old man's shoulder. "Take care of yourself, Walter."

The old man pondered the goodbye and words left unsaid on his tongue. Then the courage of his convictions sounded sharp within him like the crack of a rifle. He put the car in neutral, engaged the parking brake and placed his hand over Conrad's. "I wanna tell you something, son, and I'm dead serious: This Shapiro strikes me as the sort that's got flunkies doing his bidding, his skullduggery, for him. Mind you don't sell him your soul for the price of wages. And don't ever go doing things in *his* name that you can't live with. I got blood on my hands in the name of God and country, but that doesn't make it any easier to live with."

"I'll try to remember that."

"I don't want to seem ungrateful, seeing as I'm leaving with so much of the man's scratch in my pocket, but one of the great curses of growing old is you can see—sometimes how a situation will play out, and sometimes you can see right into a person. You watch yourself: He's got your number—knows it by heart. He's gonna try to play you like a broken banjo. Don't let him. He's got a mean streak, and it's sure to end badly with him." Walter shook Conrad's hand awkwardly in farewell. "If you ever make it down my way again, look me up and I'll take you out fishing," the showman called to Conrad, as he rolled off toward the front gate.

XXVI

Sid Shapiro was elated and exuberant—the weekend was finally over. It was a crisp, sunny Monday morning and all his guests had finally gone. He crossed the manicured lawns between the main house and the kennel, carrying a soft case that contained the Guangzhou prototype. In his other hand, Sid carried a twitch he'd taken from the stables. A twitch is a heavy pole about four feet long, with a loop of rope attached to one end, used to distract a horse when it's being groomed with clippers or being given a shot. The upper lip of the animal is pulled through the loop of rope, and the pole is turned several times to isolate and put pressure on the lip. The idea is that the animal is preoccupied by this mild distraction, so that a groom or vet can work close on a skittish animal. Figure-eighted into the short loop of rope on this twitch was a larger loop, which acted as an oversized extension of the first.

The objects in Sid's hands counterbalanced each other, and the noose at the end of the twitch flopped back and forth with each step he took. Sid made his way to the kennel's back door. Smoke rose from the chimney, indicating the morning feeding was underway. When he entered the building, the entire kennel erupted thunderously in loud barking. A small, light-skinned mulatto woman with Caucasian facial features tended a cooking pot on the wood-burning stove, and Jazzmo made his way to the door with the old pointer, Duke, on a leash.

"Jazzmo," Sid greeted.

"I'd like to speak to you outside, sir," Jazzmo replied.

Sid laid the pump in the gun rack and the twitch next to it, and followed out the front door to where the black man's funeral car sat. Jazzmo loaded the dog into one of the metal dog boxes mounted to the truck bed. The liver-and-white Brittany was already in another box.

"I'll be leaving you today, Mr. Sid," Jazzmo said delicately. "Done drove some stakeout chains on either side of the kennel so's they can't see each other, but that's it for me. My wife Ruby's given 'em something special, seeing as it's their last . . ." He trailed off. "I appreciate all you done for me, but I just . . . can't."

Sid took a moment to absorb what Jazzmo was saying to him and puzzled over it like he'd been asked to square a circle. "You're quitting—over a couple of broken down, useless dogs?"

"Ain't neither of 'em useless," Jazzmo said. "Find homes for both if I had the time, but somehow I get the feeling you ain't very particular about doing the Christian thing. I think you gonna smite these animals—just 'cause you can."

"Stupid shine," Sid taunted. "You're walking away from the best part of six-figures because you don't have the stones to pop a couple of worthless gundogs. Good riddance—trainers are a dime a dozen down here; I'll have the position filled by lunch."

Jazzmo's eyes went wide at the slur. He grabbed Shapiro by the lapels of his field coat and lifted him a couple of inches off the ground. "You want to see those dogs slaughtered for your entertainment," he said through clenched teeth. "You want me to do it for you so you can go to sleep at night with your pretty wife, makin' like the blood ain't on your hands." Catching himself, he lowered Sid back down gently, seating him on the tailgate of the truck. He patted the white man's lapels flat and took a step back. "And I'll be back, hired onto another plantation before the season's half gone. Maybe not for the same money—but there's some things you can't rightly put a price on."

"No one will hire you. Not after they hear what I have to say."

"That I wouldn't do your dog-killing for you? That'll be a selling point. Most people in these parts find that way kind of primitive."

"Primitive?" Sid asked.

"Barbaric," Jazzmo clarified.

"Big words," Sid noted, "for a dog trainer."

"I limit the one-syllables to the Stepin Fetchit routine. I just quit your employ, *Masta Sheeny—Ahhh dons't gotta fake it no mo!*" Jazzmo said in his best chitlins-and-watermelon accent.

"Ever hear how I got my name?" Jazzmo asked. Sid shook his head. "I play some pretty fair jazz piano—studied formally. My daddy was kennel boy over at Magnolia. Taught me all about running bird dogs. Had me a job at a hotel bar up in Manhattan playing in a quartet. It weren't no Café Carlisle, but it was all right. I was eating, and I sure loved that town. Then one night Daddy lost his damned mind and got good and drunk—put out his own eye.

Then he says he's been struck with visions and can see the future out of it. Magnolia called to see if I'd take over the position.

"My given name is Pendegast—Benjamin Harrison Pendegast: a white man's name. No kennel boy's ever been named Benjamin Harrison. So on the first day, this ignorant nigger overseer says, 'Piano player—your new name's Jazzmo,' like he's naming a slave. That's thirty years ago: I still play some down in Tallahassee, but bird dogs and quail shooting have been my living ever since. And I still go by the name Jazzmo—it's what *Rich Whitey* expects. *Ya'll done made it too damned easy for us coloreds!*" he continued, briefly relapsing into his minstrel sing-song. "Just gotta play your part— stay on script. Well, Mr. Sid, Jazzmo may be my slave name, but I'm nobody's slave. You shoot your own dogs."

The mulatto woman came out the front door with her cook pot and spoon. She walked around the back of the truck and snarled "You go to hell!" at Sid as she passed and got into the passenger's seat. Shapiro stood up from the tailgate, as Jazzmo conscientiously put an empty soda bottle into the trash can, turned off the outdoor light and closed the front door of the kennel. He waved a vague farewell, slid behind the wheel of the funeral car, and rolled down the window to speak. Sid cautiously approached, and Jazzmo added, "Comes a time in life when none of us can fulfill our functions anymore. Gonna keep the bar just as high as you're holding it now for these dogs when *your* time comes?" Jazzmo unwrapped a fresh Tiparillo and placed it between his teeth at an optimistic angle. Pea-pebble gravel crackled under his tires as he rolled off onto the tree-lined drive toward the front gate.

XXVII

Conrad sat eating his bacon, egg and cheese breakfast sandwich off a paper plate, and tried to get a good look at the woman in the navy blue alligator shirt and mid-thigh-length shorts. She wore ancient, old-school canvas tennis sneakers, and her hair was covered by a blue bandana. Amy Winehouse was blaring from a boom box in the gun club snack bar kitchen, and the woman kept time, swaying her hips to the beat, as she mopped the tile floor. The clubhouse was otherwise empty, and Conrad found himself bewitched, transfixed by the raw sexual pull in which this woman held him. She was what they used to call in the Jim Crow South "high-yellow." Her apricot complexion could have made her anything—Italian, Greek, Hispanic, Lebanese or even Polynesian. Only the telltale kink in the dark wave of hair that lay beneath her scarf hinted that she was of African descent. She was lanky but small, and also unnaturally top-heavy. Her buxomness, while pleasing to the eye, was slightly out of proportion to her square hips and spindly legs. The size of her breasts and their pronounced shape highlighted a symmetry that could only be conjured into existence by a surgeon's scalpel. With unwelcoming eyes as black as olives, Caucasian facial features and a cruel, radiant smile, she was a strikingly beautiful woman.

Climbing out from inside the low white tennis sock of her sneaker, somewhat faded but still unmistakable, was an ornate, tattooed vine of roses ascending her right leg. It started simply as a thin green thorny vine above her ankle and blossomed and bloomed as it worked its way over her shin and knee into a full-flowered shrub that enveloped her thigh. The climbing trellis eventually disappeared into the pant leg of her shorts. The embellishment's crispness, as well as its vibrancy of color, had faded like a photograph forgotten on a window sill. The tattoo was being removed, and she was only partly through the treatments. Any man, regardless of race or age, seemed to feel a deep instinctual desire for her—a primordial yearning. No man, however, would mistake her for a white girl.

As the music blared, the yolk of Conrad's sandwich ran down his forearm as he ate. The young woman noticed his predicament and provided him with a stack of cocktail napkins.

"It's all that's left!" she shouted apologetically above the music.

"Thanks," Conrad replied softly.

"What?!" The young woman asked.

"What's your name?" Conrad inquired.

"I can't hear you!" She shouted pointing to her ears in frustration. "Let me turn it down," which she did.

"What's your name? Conrad reiterated.

"Rosalie," she replied. "I'm Rosalie."

"I'm Conrad," he said inspecting his hand to make sure that it was clean enough to offer in greeting. She took it softly in hers and he noted the pearlescent sheen of perspiration on her upper lip. She was beautiful in an ageless, exotic sort of way. She could have been nineteen or thirty-three—it was anybody's guess. "What do you do, Rosalie," he asked, "when you're not making egg sandwiches?"

"Nursing school—up north," she snapped curtly, as she wheeled to turn the music back up, but Conrad interrupted her.

"Can't we just enjoy the quiet? I'd like to talk to you," he confessed.

"You want to talk?" Rosalie asked with a clipped, terse diction that made clear that her patience was waning. "To me?" she added, perching her hands defiantly on her hips, causing her cleavage to jiggle ever so slightly. "I got a plane to catch—and you want to talk."

"I'd just like to get to know you," he replied.

"Why?" she demanded. "Because you've got ideas—that's why," she said, satisfying her own query. "If I got turned around every time some dirty white boy got the jungle fever, I'd still be living here in a rented trailer with two redneck curs on each nipple. I've got news for you Mr. Conrad, this isn't a Spike Lee movie, and I'm not Halle Berry. You want some colored tail? I suggest you rent it."

With that definitive social disengagement, Rosalie turned the volume back up on the boom box and returned to her job of mopping the floor. Conrad was unfazed by the decisive rebuff. He finished his sandwich, slurped the remains of his coffee, balled up the cup into the paper plate and sank a hook-shot into the corrugated metal garbage can from halfway across the room. Rosalie didn't notice.

XXVIII

T he cell phone call to Conrad was short and to the point: Sid required his presence at the kennel. He was waiting when Conrad came through the kennel door and shook his hand warmly in silent salutation.

"You've been steady at the helm throughout this whole weekend, Winston. Don't think I didn't notice a job well done."

"Thank you," Conrad replied. He was uneasy, suspecting there was another reason he was being summoned.

"Now, I need to ask you a favor, and it's a real heartbreaker."

"I'll help if I can, Mr. Shapiro," Conrad said in earnest.

"Well it's like this. I got two dogs outside and both of them are riddled with heartworms."

"God, Mr. Shapiro," Conrad said weakly. "That's really a shame."

"I gotta destroy them both. This is the true burden of leadership, Winston—of being an owner. They're my animals, and their welfare is my responsibility. As much as it hurts, I've got to do the right thing—by them. You gotta help me, Conrad—be a mensch."

"I don't think I can."

"Neither do I, but it's still got to be done. It's a wonder the entire kennel isn't lousy with it. One pill a month—how useless do you have to be to fail in that simple task? I fired that shiftless darkie for incompetence this morning."

"Nothing can done for them—not a vaccination or anything?"

"A vaccine after the fact would kill them instantly. The worms have bored into the heart and now control the blood flow. Kill the parasites and the animal dies immediately. I'm sorry, but they're doomed—they'll both be dead in a week or so anyway. It really tears you up, though, don't it? I shot a ton of birds over those dogs. I just wish I'd been around to have the vet do it humanely when he was here, but *Little Black Sambo* didn't have the chutzpah to call that shot when the time was ripe."

"Mr. Shapiro . . ." Conrad started to say.

"This is the first really difficult thing we're doing together,"

Shapiro said, melodramatically putting his hand on the Conrad's shoulder. "But somehow I don't think it'll be the last. Help me, Conrad—please."

Sid walked to the gun rack, picked up the pump shotgun and the twitch, and headed for the door. Conrad followed a few steps behind.

They exited the kennel, stepped out into the crisp morning air and onto the manicured turf. The contrast of the Vizsla dog, the color of a ginger snap, against the lush green of the lawn reminded Conrad of Christmas. The dog was attached to a chain anchored to the ground and turned its head toward the two men as they approached. Sid handed the twitch to Conrad and dry-fired the pump shotgun several times to make sure it was working properly. Then he reached into the pocket of his field coat and withdrew three solid rifled 12-gauge slugs. He put one in the chamber and closed the action. He inserted the other two into the magazine tube. He flicked on the safety and handed the gun to Conrad.

"I need to handle the dog," Sid said as he took the modified twitch from Conrad and slipped the loop over the dog's head. The Vizsla was preoccupied by a rabbit that was feeding across the lawn at the tree line.

"All right, Winston," Sid said as he put a turn on the twitch to tighten it up enough to control the dog if it tried to bolt. The animal was intent on the cottontail. "Put the safety off. Do it now."

Conrad awkwardly clicked off the safety on the trigger guard of the Model-12 and brought the gun to his shoulder. "Do I shoot him in the head or what?" Conrad pleaded.

"In the lungs—shoot him through the side."

Conrad put a bead on the animal's ribcage at a distance of about ten feet. He put his cheek to the comb of the shotgun and his finger on the trigger. He began to shake uncontrollably and his hand became unsteady, but he managed to screw up his determination, steady himself and pull the trigger.

When Conrad opened his eyes, the animal lay on its side, a red mist emanating from the gaping wound. The dog was motionless and calm, even dignified, as it lay dying. It blinked several times and then strained in increasingly labored breathing. Blood began to run from its nose, pink foam bubbled from its mouth and a brilliant scarlet froth seeped forth from the wound. It was all over in a moment, and Sid Shapiro—as big as life—stood over the dog watching intently as the pitiful animal died.

"Gimme that," Sid commanded as he took the gun and unloaded it. "That's one down," he stated with a grim efficiency. As Sid turned for the other side of the building and the other dog that waited, Conrad stood over the lifeless carcass. A fly landed on the dead dog's nose and it seemed odd that there was no animated reaction: no reflexive twitch, no motion. "Come on," Shapiro called.

"Are we just going to leave him? Don't we need to cover him or something?"

Sid returned to Conrad's side to view the dead animal. "It's a dead dog, Conrad. It'll be in the ground soon enough." Sid nudged the carcass and the toe of his boat shoe came away covered in blood. "Fuck!" he muttered as he awkwardly tried to scrape the blood on his shoe onto the grass, as if he'd stepped in shit.

Jake, the liver-and-white Shorthair, was panting and pacing in circles around the circumference of his chain. The men approached and the dog started to strain against his collar.

"Smells the death on us," Sid said coldly through a smirk. He reloaded the pump shotgun, put the safety on and handed it to Conrad. "Do it again. Right in the bread basket," he said with a sickening, upbeat lilt. Conrad and Sid exchanged the gun and the twitch. Sid walked in on the dog and tried to put the loop over its head, but the Shorthair was frantic and ran spastically within the chain's tight confines. After several failed attempts, Sid lost patience with the terrified animal and kicked it violently in the ribs. As the dog briefly paused to catch its wind, Sid slipped the noose over its head and put a few turns on the pole to secure the animal. "Alright—do it!" he demanded. The dog had recovered enough to start struggling again and Sid was getting jerked around by the seventy-pound animal. Conrad flicked off the safety and raised the gun to his shoulder. The dog saw this. His eyes went wide with fear and he fought off the pole even harder. "Shoot him!" Shapiro demanded, but Conrad could not.

Conrad reengaged the safety and lowered the shotgun. Sid lost all control. "You finishing-school faggot!" he said as he started turning the pole, tightening the noose. "I need men who can kill!" he added as he continued to put turns on the twitch. The dog could no longer draw breath and its eyes were bulging out of their sockets. The animal was clawing at the rope with its front legs and its jaws were snapping manically for air.

"You're broke because you're soft. People like me took it all away from you!"

The folds of skin at the dog's neck were abraded and bleeding from the noose. Finally, the animal stopped struggling. Second by agonizing second the life bled out until all the vitality was drained from him. Sid gave one last vindictive jerk to the pole for good measure and flashed a smile through gritted teeth.

Conrad was stunned by the brutality he'd witnessed. He laid the loaded shotgun at his feet next to the animal's lifeless body and began wandering toward the kennel door, which suddenly opened. Alex Vanderstein poked his head out and surveyed the gruesome scene.

"Don't look," Alex said regretfully to someone just inside the building. "He already did it. Go back to the house."

Victoria Vanderstein Shapiro barged out the kennel door, dressed in her nightgown, bathrobe and slippers. "What have you done?!" she demanded indignantly as she looked at the asphyxiated dog. "What have you done, Sidney?!—Damn you!" she cried as she slapped her husband across the face. "Goddamn you, bastard!" she shouted as she tried to hit him again, but he ducked the blow.

Conrad was shaken out of his stupor and spoke. "Worms, Mrs. Shapiro. The dogs have heartworms. We had to do it—to put them out of their misery."

"Is that what you told him?" Alex inquired incredulously. "I shot over these dogs yesterday. Jazzmo was desperate to give them away because he knew you were hell-bent on killing them. There was absolutely nothing wrong with them."

"Is that true?" Victoria asked her husband. "Is any part of what he is saying true?"

Sid Shapiro was flustered. He pointed a finger toward Conrad. "It's what he said."

"You're a liar," Alex accused. "I always knew you had a screw lose—the way that you had to humiliate people and make them grovel after you fucked them over. I've known some eccentrics, but you're a downright savage."

"Is he right?" Victoria pleaded. "Tell me he's completely wrong—that it's all just a terrible mistake," she said through flowing tears.

"It *is* a mistake," Sid began feebly. "It's worms. We had to."

"Monster!" Victoria screamed hysterically. "Blood sport: quails, pigeons! Where's the sport in this? This isn't blood sport—it's bloodlust! What kind of sadistic man kills a domestic pet?! What kind of monster tortures a dog to death?!" she said, as she beat on Sid's chest with her fists. "The human world isn't enough for you—you've got to take their world too!" Victoria spat on him contemptuously. "You possess everything: everything except mercy. You're unworthy . . . of them," she said, gesturing to the dead dog and then broadly to the surroundings. "Of all this . . . of me." She turned on her heels and walked away. Her rose-gold hair covered eyes full of tears.

"You lied to me!" Conrad accused.

Sid lunged for him "I oughta fuck you in the ass, white-bread!" he snarled as he violently pulled Conrad to the ground. Alex turned from Victoria and jumped on the two men, separating them.

"Get out of here!" Alex ordered, and Conrad ran off.

"You're fired!" Sid commanded Alex. "You're out of Empire Capital—through in the business."

"The hell I am!" Alex shot back. "I'm an equity partner, not your damned employee! You want me out—buy me out."

Alex Vanderstein left Sid Shapiro standing next to the lifeless body of the big-going German Shorthair Pointer, Jake, who had a superb nose but didn't retrieve much. He wouldn't go with another dog, and liked to lift his leg on any unsuspecting human that happened to be around. His dead eyes were wide open and glazed over, milky blue. His motionless tongue unfurled from his gaping mouth onto the perfectly manicured turf.

XXIX

The Bridgewater landscape looked like the scorched earth of a battlefield. Derelict foundations and chimneys rose from the savaged terrain. Concrete staircases led nowhere. Here and there, bits of brick and rebar, pipe and insulated wire poked through gravel, rock and pulverized concrete. The land—the very earth itself—seemed infertile, even toxic, incapable of providing sustenance to any living thing. Block after block of this desolate moonscape of vacant lots was interrupted only by the occasional dilapidated industrial building or abandoned apartment house. A human being in such an environment seemed a rare and exotic creature—one of the last of its kind and sure to become extinct if it didn't migrate to less threatening territory.

Conrad regarded every stoplight as a potential ambush, every pedestrian as a would-be carjacker. The doors of his rattletrap BMW were locked, and he ran every red light at Walter's insistence. It didn't matter anyway. No police officer spent a minute more in this purgatory than was necessary, and receiving a moving violation while running this gauntlet was as likely as receiving a sermon on virtue from a streetwalker. Into this lawless ghetto Conrad drove, a silent, thoughtful Walter Wagner his passenger.

The old man brushed aside some of the cobwebs in his mind and the View-Master slideshow of his twentieth-century life came into focus. *On this block, the five-and-dime used to be there, and Wink just loved the chop suey house on the next avenue over.* Walter directed two or three turns in quick succession, which brought them to a half-acre lot that was just like every other in size and configuration. A chain-link fence ringed the property and the burned-out hulk of a raised-ranch house. A charred brick chimney and hearth that looked as pristine as the day the mason's trowel last caressed them rose from the blackened foundation. There was a lawn and a dormant vegetable garden. Backing up to one corner of the lot was a small battleship-gray outbuilding that was still intact, the former kennel to generations of gundogs: Springer Spaniels for the uplands and Chesapeake Bay Retrievers for waterfowl. A thin ribbon of gray smoke spilled out of a stovepipe fitted through a section of plywood inserted into the quarter-pane of the kennel window. Walter got out of the car and regarded it all from the sidewalk.

"Jesus!" he said, bewildered. "Look what they did to it." Walter was dressed in his best navy blue worsted wool suit—the one he had gotten with Winky at Marshal Field's in Chicago. It came with two pairs of pants, and the alterations were free. He wore an old-fashioned gray topcoat that went clear down to his calves—just like Bogart wore in all the gangster pictures. He also sported a gray fedora with the brim-front cheerfully turned up. His weddings and funerals suit—the only suit he owned—was a garment far too heavy for the tropical climes of South Florida. Conrad was dressed in his thrift-shop best and prep school tie—the same outfit he wore the first time he ever met Walter Wagner. The old man turned and reached for the rear-door handle of the sedan, but it was locked. "Open up," he said to Conrad, who remained nervously behind the wheel.

"I don't know, Walter. This is a really rough neighborhood—what if something happens?"

The old man reached into his coat pocket, produced a nickel-plated .38 revolver and tapped its snub-nosed barrel on the passenger-side window. "Nothing is going to happen," he said confidently, as he replaced the pistol in his overcoat. "The faster you get out of the car, the faster we can get the hell out of here."

Conrad unlocked the doors. Walter reached onto the floor of the backseat and removed the twin-handled sterling silver trophy cup, its lid firmly secured with duct tape. The two men squeezed through a hole in the chain-link fence and found their way across the earthen bank and onto the concrete staircase that delivered them to what had been the front door of the house. On the left side of the front stoop stood a heavy cast-iron birdbath with an inch or two of melting early spring ice in it. On the right side of the stoop was a charred metal flag pole; a weather-beaten Stars and Stripes flew on a light breeze.

"I think somebody is over there," Conrad whispered, gesturing toward the kennel.

"You may be right," Walter agreed. "Don't want any trouble with the natives. Supposing we just sneak around back."

The two men did their best to slink across the lawn unnoticed, but just as they were passing between the garden and the front of the kennel, the door opened and a pit bull bitch the color of a Brown Swiss cow lunged at them, barking ferociously in a pathetic, muted pantomime. The dog had been debarked—had its voice-box crudely altered—and although the terrifying visual remained, the blood-curling audio did not. While Walter and Conrad were held at bay, hard against the garden fence, a bearded young man in a camouflage fatigue jacket stepped outside the shack. He struck the concrete stoop, metallic and hollow—again and again—with an aluminum baseball bat. He swung his club with only one arm.

Walter had a bead on the animal with his .38. "Don't make me shoot your dog!" he said nervously.

"I'm not leaving!" the bearded man shouted. "I'm not going back to the VA hospital—squatters have rights. You can't put me off without an order signed by a judge!"

"Nobody's putting you off, son," Walter said, calmly pocketing the pistol. "We're not here for that."

"Two white men poking around this shithole can only mean police or lawyers, and you're too old to be the fuzz," he said, waving the bat toward Walter and then bringing it back to rest on his own shoulder.

"This was my home," Walter said quietly. "For nearly fifty years my wife, Winky, and I lived here. We built all this," he said, gesturing to the kennel with a wave of his hand. The bearded man finally called off his dog, which came to heel at his side in the doorway. "We poured the kennel runs and threaded that sideways-chimney through the window frame together," Walter said as he stepped closer. "That's what's left of her," he said holding out the sterling trophy. "I've come home to spread my wife's ashes. I'm Walter Wagner," he said, as he hugged the trophy to his chest and held out his left hand for the left-handed, one-armed man to shake.

The name on the bearded man's fatigue jacket read BAKER. An improvised explosive device embedded in the path of his Humvee had taken his right arm. A bluish-green tattoo of a cougar showed beneath his collar, and needle marks perforated this crude animation, betraying Corporal Baker's drug addiction. He pulled out a soft pack of generic cigarettes and offered one to each man. Then he planted one between his lips and lit it. There was a wide, dark gap in his lower bite.

Baker laid the bat in the corner of the doorframe and retreated inside the shack with his dog. Walter and Conrad looked at each other. Baker returned with an ancient metal pitcher in his hand, red rust marks bleeding through the cracks in its blue enamel. "I'm making tea. Want some?" he asked. Baker walked to the corner of the building, placed the pitcher on the concrete slab and worked the well pump handle so water flowed generally into and around the vessel. "One of the best things about this place," he said picking up the pitcher. "Got my own running water."

"City water never tasted right," Walter agreed. "Wink and I made the coffee with that. It's the only water we ever drank."

Baker filled a dodgy looking kettle and put it on the potbellied stove to boil. He pulled a colorful tin of drugstore cookies down from the shelf, inspected the sell by-date, shrugged and unsealed the cellophane wrapping. "Sorry about the state of things—housekeeper's day off," he cracked. He emptied the overflowing ashtray onto the hot embers of combusted wood pallets and produce crates. "You're the only visitors I've had—ever," he confessed.

The wood building wasn't much bigger than a garden shed, but it managed nicely for Corporal Baker. He had a metal cot with a soft mattress, a couple of lumpy pillows with actual cases over them and several warm wool army-surplus blankets. There was a beanbag chair zipped into a child's sleeping bag in the corner for the dog, and a sheet of plywood set upon two sawhorses served as a table. A low-backed upholstered armchair was missing one of its hind legs. Baker adjusted the block of wood that served to support his throne and invited Walter to sit on it. Then he pulled a solitary kitchen chair down from a hook on the wall for Conrad. The men drank tea with condensed milk. Their host spiked his with rotgut vodka, and they all ate stale butter cookies. The dog, J-Lo, warmed up to the guests enough to mooch from them. As Walter's eyes flitted about the room, they came to rest on ordinary articles that had once been his personal property—artifacts of his daily life in Bridgewater. He lovingly picked up some of these pieces—a mug with the handle broken off it, a coffee tin of mixed nuts and bolts, and felt them radiate their warmth of familiarity.

Baker said, "I don't pretend to have a rightful hold on this. If you're wanting any of it back—if you want me off your place, just say so. I thought it was abandoned or I never would have . . ."

"It *is* abandoned," Walter stated. "Seized by the city of Bridgewater for unpaid taxes. As far as I'm concerned, you *are* the rightful owner of any of the remaining contents you care to have. I'll attest to that in writing, if you like." Conrad produced a pen and Baker handed over a brown paper bag. Walter pulled the kitchen chair up close to the makeshift table, tore a section off the bag and began scribbling. When it came time to sign his name he added, "You gave me the best gift I coulda hoped for. You let me stick my big toe back into familiar waters. Let me live a little bit of the old place one more time. Just being here reminds me of how much of life is in the *here and now*. I had this old property fixed just about the way I wanted. Everything had its place and purpose, and it all worked just the way it ought to. Then fate dropped a Chiclet in the works: Stratford gun club closed, Wink's mental fog thickened into navy bean soup and this town abandoned every value it ever held dear. This was my home for most of my life, but I don't belong here anymore. I'm just glad a part of it still exists, and I'm grateful that you're looking after it, son."

Conrad drank about half his cup of tea and then poured the rest out onto the lawn. It tasted funny and he didn't trust the aquifer under his feet. He stood outside the open doorway, keeping an eye on the car and enjoying the sun's warmth. The dog stretched out in the long beam of sunshine at Baker's feet and fell asleep. Her legs pulsed rhythmically; her eyes were wide open and darting about, and her breathing became dramatic between silent intermittent barks as she luxuriated in animated slumber.

The men spoke for at least an hour. They discussed Bridgewater and baseball, growing tomatoes and peppers, and Walter betrayed some of Winky's best-kept secrets for jarring her September spaghetti sauce. They talked about fishing and the army, and different sorts of addictions and their various treatments. They spoke of battlefield injuries—the kind that kill and the kind that just maim—and they talked about how a dog wasn't afraid to snuggle right up to a stump, when a woman was utterly repelled by it. They talked about having friends and living alone, and of what kind of a shit-heel would silence an animal only to abandon it to the pound. They laughed and then got quiet. They cried out in desperation, and then silently said everything they needed to with a look. They drank cup after cup of the strange-tasting tea and finished the colorful tin of cookies.

Finally the afternoon sun gave way to impending dusk. Conrad continued his surveillance over the background noise of conversation until a black boy wearing an oversized satin Chicago Bulls jacket with matching wool cap pedaled slowly past the car on an absurdly undersized BMX bike that was missing its saddle and seat-post.

"Someone's checking out the car," Conrad nervously observed.

The dog awoke. Baker rose and went to the door. "I know that punk. Scared shitless of the dog—freaks him right the fuck out. You lock J-Lo in your car and I guarantee he won't fool with it."

Baker led the pit bull down to the car on the street and withdrew a sturdy rope chew-toy from the pocket of his field jacket. He threw it onto the passenger's seat and the dog jumped in after it and curled up serenely. "The only car alarm that works in this neighborhood," he deadpanned.

The men climbed back up the concrete staircase and past the stoop into Corporal Baker's home, and retrieved the sterling silver urn. Walter led the procession. He cradled his wife's remains in his arms, carrying them over their brief, final journey to a corner of the lot that had some landscaped shrubs and perennials to help mask the rigidness of the chain-link fence. Small slates set into the earth were crudely inscribed with JENNY, KELLY, KATIE, SUSIE, SKIPPER, SANDY, PIPER, SALLY, CINDY and GYPSY. A larger, professionally cut granite monument was already in place and inscribed BABY WALTER WAGNER, JR. Underneath was written MARGARET"WINKY" WAGNER—GONE TO THE DOGS. There were no dates or any mention of Walter. Her only other sentiment was a simple rendering of a flock of geese on the wing, in a V-formation— the kind you see so often near the Sound, rhythmically beating through gray skies during the migration.

The men stood in solemn silence before the headstone. Walter noticed a flowering purple crocus, the earliest of the spring bloomers, coming through the softening soil. He carefully broke off the stem at its lowest point, near where it anchored itself to the ground, and ran the stem of the tiny flower through the buttonhole of his lapel. Then he sat the trophy in front of the marker, delicately peeled back the duct tape that secured its lid, and began having a conversation.

"Here we are, old girl—my love. I brought you back just like we always said. Conrad drove me. You never met him, but he's my good friend. He keeps an eye on me . . . for you." Tears started flowing—just a single drop at first, then more. "Got another friend here—a young man by the name of Baker who says he'll be looking in on you till I come around again. You'd like him. He's got a green thumb, been cultivating the hell out of your raised beds. Told him about your September sauce. I know you don't want your secrets getting around, but I figured, seeing as how he's a good egg and you're both sorta connected now . . ." Walter dug his hand into the urn and took out a fistful of ashes. As the silt began to sift through his fingers, he added, "God, I'm gonna miss you, woman. Seems like only yesterday, we were pondering over the plans for this old place—figuring how to swing it. Well, we sure swung it! And it'll be home to all of us again before too long," Walter said as he picked up the trophy and finally began to liberally spread the remaining dregs directly from its wide, gilded mouth. "All our wonderful dogs," he said with a shake, "And you, and me—and baby makes three," and with that, he upended the chalice. The last mortal remains of Winky Wagner were now one with her baby boy, her beloved dogs and the wasted earth of Bridgewater.

* * * * *

The musk of the pit bull clung to the upholstery of Conrad's BMW and he drove with his window open a crack, albeit with the doors still locked. Walter was silent as Conrad backtracked his route to the turnpike, running all the same red lights in reverse order without any urging from Walter.

"Think you can find your way back here?" Walter asked solemnly, as he turned to Conrad. "I hate to ask, only I got no one for when it's my time."

"Consider it done," his young counterpart said definitively. The two men entered the turnpike driving south, back into the heart of the County and into the enshrouding darkness.

XXX

Whenever the authorities reconstruct one of these things, the mystery is always how, in retrospect, ordinary details take on extraordinary prescience. That Sid Shapiro was flying alone wasn't unusual. His wife had abandoned him suddenly, before the Christmas holidays, and a petition for divorce was imminent. That he took a corporate jet down to Onori after the close of business Friday also wasn't unusual. That it was May, and so far removed from the quail-shooting season, was highly unusual. That he brought a fast-food hot roast beef sandwich from the airport terminal for his supper wasn't unusual—he liked them growing up. That he didn't bring any luggage, not even a briefcase— that was a first. That he channel-surfed the business news stations for the entire flight wasn't unusual. That the coverage was entirely dedicated to a bombshell of a story rocking the world of high finance was irregular, indeed.

At the center of the story was a visionary—the architect and inventor of all online financial services, preeminent hedge-fund manager, friend to foreign heads of state, occasional golfing partner to the president of the United States and financial advisor to the surviving members of the Beatles, the Who and Led Zeppelin. Mr. Market's Infinity Fund had been exposed as a fraud, a global Ponzi scheme. A minor cyclical correction in the equities market had overwhelmed the fund with sudden redemptions, and Mr. Market had come clean. He was cooperating with the authorities in the hopes of receiving leniency.

FELIX, the black box trading system he'd co-created, never worked. What limited *market intelligence* it did produce was a poor substitute for common sense. The Nobel laureate co-creator explained at the time, in his computer-nerd best defense, that the initial massive financial loss was nothing more than a statistical anomaly. As the dataset fed into FELIX expanded over time, the system would become more predictive and accurate. With that first round of bad bets, the hole was already dug. The wicked plot was hatched shortly thereafter.

This worldwide spider's web of financial entanglement, from the individual investor to the feeder funds, to the fund-of-funds, to the institutional clients, to the sovereign banks—waves of financial ruin spread outward in rings like wavelets racing toward the shore. Mr. Market's tentacles seemed to be everywhere and on everyone. Some would suffer professional humiliation and breathtaking financial loss—but miraculously manage to survive in the business. And some would be utterly savaged. The devastation would be total and irreversible.

Sid half-thought, at some point, he'd redirect the jet to Miami and its international hub. He had his passport in his pocket, a money belt around his waist and several numbered offshore accounts. Of course, you could always spend the rest of your life in exile in one of those banana republics with a dodgy extradition treaty, but what the hell kind of an existence would that be? You'd be the biggest swinging dick in Haiti or Zimbabwe, but who cares? He knew deep down he'd take his just lumps, but he'd do it on his own schedule and in private. He had a little time—half the weekend. He could take that time to enjoy some simple pleasures. He'd also use the time to get the letter just right; Victoria deserved that much. He missed her—actually yearned for her. He had the name of a leading midtown psychotherapist in his wallet and had intended to call—just to see if a meaningful personal change was even possible. He'd planned to put things right with himself and then win her back, but he ran out of time.

Sid knew Alex was looking for him—his voicemail messages were stacked up on the cell phone he left sitting on the back seat of the limo. Sid also knew that Alex would make an announcement to the media and turn himself in to the authorities on Monday morning, regardless of the fact that he was technically no longer even a partner in Empire Capital. The buyout had been executed, and Alex had just received his first of many payment installments. *That was the way country-club boys behaved in these situations,* Sid thought. They admitted their culpability. Sid had shown willful negligence in his due diligence and vetting of Mr. Market's Infinity Fund. His visit to Infinity was the first time he'd ever even been on the National Depository Trust Co. website, and the positions he saw were—in hindsight—obviously illegitimate. Sid had indisputably failed to fulfill his function in a professional capacity.

It wasn't that Sid lacked character, or even that he was particularly afraid of prison. The "Club Feds" weren't really so bad, at least that's what he'd heard. It was the public admission of failure—the groveling and the contrition—that Sid rejected out of hand. He refused to face the media gauntlet, rife with embarrassing questions, that he'd seen Mr. Market have to physically fight his way through that morning in front of his townhouse. He wouldn't have his picture plastered all over the tabloids, and he couldn't face the humiliation of a criminal trial. Sid Shapiro had enjoyed a meteoric run, but he'd played to an inside straight and not drawn the card. He was gutted, and now it was time to leave the table.

Sid spent the night in the apartment suite that had been his and Victoria's home when in residence at Onori. Some of her clothes still hung in the closet. He pulled out one of her Hermès scarves, green with a foxhunting motif. He removed it from its place in the top drawer of her wardrobe and took in its smell. The scent of her hair, her perfume, of her—as if she'd just stepped out of the room. He breathed her in deeply again and then reminded himself of his task.

The house was closed up properly, with bedsheets covering the furniture and the Persian rugs in cold storage. The housekeeper had opened the apartment for him, and all he wanted was his privacy. He sent her home and spent the remainder of the evening listening to music. Just before he turned off the lights, he turned on the television and perused the business channels. Mr. Market was still front-and-center and additional details were trickling in. He looked at the Tiffany silver-framed black-and-white photo of him and Victoria on the Pont Neuf on a trip to Paris when they were both gorging themselves on new love. The frame was inscribed To My Uptown Girl, With Love, Sidney. He turned off the bedside lamp and thought of his numbered accounts, passport and money belt. He *could* leave—he *had* resources. He'd protected himself even if he'd failed to protect his clients. He had the street smarts never to trust anyone enough to commit entirely to them. He still had time to leave the country. It was simply a matter of having the will.

The next morning, Sid Shapiro sat at his antique tiger-maple desk and committed his mortal sins to paper. He documented his professional failings and confessed to his personal ones. He tried his best to explain why he was the man that he'd become. He recounted the early forces and traumas that had formed his personality and how he'd become a prisoner to them in adulthood. Finally, he told his wife in no uncertain terms that he loved her. That winning her affection had been his greatest achievement, and losing it was his most bitter failure. Life without her had barely been worth living, and she would remain on his mind, first, last and always.

He took the Mercedes Silver Arrow for a spin through the lush spring countryside, green and fertile in anticipation of coming summer. For the first time, he drove the car enthusiastically and well. He worked his way up and down the gear box, double-clutching into the corners and matching the engine's torque to whatever undulation of road he was negotiating, spiritedly riding the long sweepers on a knife's edge. For a brief moment, he was one with the automobile—confident and its master. The wind rushed through his luxurious mop of silver hair, and dappled sunshine radiated through the canopy of budding trees and into the lenses of his sunglasses. He finally understood why Victoria loved driving this car so much. For a fleeting moment, he was happy.

Sid ate a dinner of cold fried chicken, lukewarm collard greens, baked beans and corn bread with butter and honey. He listened to some more music. After dinner, he brushed his suit, the one he'd worn on the plane. It was a blue chalk-stripe from Alfred Dunhill in London, and was one of his favorites. He hung his white shirt on the hanger covering the suit pants, and then hung the suit jacket over it. He folded his crimson necktie and placed it in the jacket breast pocket, then carefully zipped the entire thing into a garment bag. He draped it on the bed and laid his black Bally loafers at the foot of the suit bag on top of the note. The envelope was addressed with the rounded flourish of a fountain pen and read simply, "Vic."

Sid Shapiro was alone in the setting sun as he carried a folding metal chair out to the kennel. The stakeout chains were still in place where Jazzmo had driven them all those months before. He erected the chair, set the photo of Victoria and him at his feet and poured a glass of wine. It was a special vintage he often used for entertaining. Then he sat and read selections aloud to himself from *A Tree Grows in Brooklyn*, a book about an early twentieth-century Irish girl fighting her way out of the slums, which he heavily identified with as a child.

In the dusk, it became too dark to continue reading, and he knew it was time. He closed the book and held it briefly to his chest in a gesture of endearment. He placed the picture frame and book inside a plastic bag. He drank the last of the wine and laid the crystal goblet beside it. He stood up and took off his platinum moon-phase repeating chronometer, one of only two dozen in the world. He removed his wedding ring and kissed it. Then Sid took Victoria's green Hermès scarf and breathed her in one last time. He threaded the scarf through the watchstrap and the gold band and tied a knot in it. He carefully placed the jewelry and the scarf inside the plastic bag with the other items and sealed it. He removed his burgundy silk dressing gown—Victoria had given it to him. He folded it neatly and laid it on the ground next to the bag. He stepped out of his leather bedroom slippers and reached for the gun case, unzipped it and fished out the two loose shells. *Why did he bother to bring two?* he thought. "Better safe than sorry," he said aloud to himself. He removed the Model-12 pump— the Guangzhou prototype, the only one in existence. Production would never begin on any New Winston Firearms design. Sid Shapiro held out the gun and admired its fit and finish. He shucked the pump action closed, mounted the gun on an invisible target and dry-fired.

The gun was a wonderful product—period. It was well-made and finished to a high standard: a shotgun anyone, including a one-time paper billionaire, would be proud to own. He dry-fired it one more time. *Oh well*, he thought, *that's one that should have been.* He picked up one of the two shells, loaded it into the chamber, slid the action closed, and put the safety on: He damned well wanted to be in position before he put it off. Sid braced the rubber butt pad of the gun against the ground and began to hyper-ventilate a little, as the thought of what he was about to do started to sink in. *It was his only way out.*

In time, Victoria would come through. She had some family

money, and there were always the numbered accounts. The instructions were there in black and white, secure in a safety deposit box in Nassau. Victoria didn't know exactly what that box contained, but she was a signatory and had a key. It would be a terrible shock to her, of course, but she was young enough to find someone else. She could remarry and maybe even start a family. Sid's eyes welled up, and the tears began to flow. His nose stuffed up and, briefly, he laid the loaded shotgun on the turf and turned away to crudely blow the nasal congestion, first out of one nostril and then out of the other.

"Come on, Jew-boy!" he bawled, trying to pull himself together. "Grow a set!" Sid picked up the shotgun again, flicked off the safety and carefully wedged the rubber recoil pad against the turf. He stood over the barrel and slowly lowered himself onto the muzzle until it was firm up against the area directly over his heart. Sid sat down slowly on the metal chair and took a deep breath. He lifted his right foot, held it briefly suspended in midair, and brought his big toe down on the trigger blade. The gun discharged, blowing an ounce-and-a-quarter of 7.5-sized copper-plate birdshot into his chest—a hole the County Coroner would later fit four fingers into. His heart was crushed to pulp instantly. His last thoughts as he fell off the chair and came to rest on the ground were of her.

XXXI

Alex Vanderstein reported to his lawyer's midtown office and surrendered himself to the authorities at 10:30 on Monday morning. In a statement given to the press, he pledged to cooperate fully with the investigation. He also vowed to return the management fees he collected over the years from clients of Empire Capital's fund-of-funds. Alex had made some money investing these fees outside of Empire, but he refused to surrender that profit. While this relinquishment made him immeasurably poorer, it did leave him with a proverbial pot to piss in. He had his house, Bailiwick, with a mortgage that he'd bought from Douglas McCashin, and he had an offer on the table to purchase the auto dealerships. He didn't know what his future held, but he was certain that it wouldn't be in finance or law. The last call he made before he was taken into custody was to his former father-in-law.

XXXII

Alex Vanderstein led his mother up the stairs of his home to the door of the master bedroom suite. Mother was a pixyish woman with flushed cheeks, a ski-jump nose and blond de-gray hair with a naturally curly wave. His father sat in a chair in the hallway, distraught. His freckled face was in his hands. Mother carried a breakfast tray with eggs, coffee and toast. There was a single pink rose in a long-necked vase. Alex's hand came to rest on his father's shoulder, which pulled the old man out of his stupor.

"We're going in, Pop. Are you coming?" Alex asked. His father—gaunt and hollow-eyed—looked into his son's face. Tears were still wet upon his cheeks. He sat exhausted, devastated in heartbreak, and mouthed, "I can't."

Alex, with a dishtowel draped over his shoulder, led his mother through the door and into the darkened bedroom. He pulled back heavy curtains drawn over the windows to welcome the gray autumn day and to spread the morning light around the room. His mother sat the tray on the cedar blanket box at the foot of the bed.

Victoria lay in repose, under the covers with her eyes wide open. "I have a town car taking me to the airport," she said.

"You picked a good day for it," Alex noted as he went about his chores. "It's supposed to snow later."

"That's exactly what *I* thought. Onori's always so beautiful this time of year. It's as if they're a full season behind us. We're entering winter up here, and it's still Indian summer down there. A hardy soul might even brave a swim in The Branch."

"Might be awfully cold—with the flowing waters."

"I didn't say it wouldn't take determination. Just have to go right in. Like diving off the platform, just jump right in," she said, with a childlike lilt.

Alex reached for the breakfast tray and moved it to the bed

next to Victoria. He unfolded a white linen napkin and tucked it under her chin. Her mother inserted a straw into the coffee, which Alex awkwardly directed toward his sister's mouth.

"No sugar!" she protested.

"No sugar," Alex said, quieting her. "Milk only." She drank a swallow or two and Alex seemed pleased. He used the edge of the fork to cut the eggs into bite-sized pieces.

"I don't suppose the Flowering Dogwood or Sweet Bay Magnolia will be in bloom."

Alex brought a forkful of eggs to his sister's mouth and replied softly, "It'll be too late in the year for that."

Victoria set her jaw. "No!" she insisted through clenched teeth. "I won't eat! You can't make me!"

"We're not going to start with that again?" Alex asked patiently. "These are cooked just the way you like, and if you'll just try a bit . . ."

Victoria kicked violently, and the entire bed bucked. She peddled her legs and feet, and drove the feather duvet from her chin and shoulders, exposing the restraints that anchored her to the bed frame. The headboard and four posts were padded, and her wrists were held in place by leather bracelets lined with soft shearling, stained with dried blood. She had recently slit her wrists, and the healing wounds were still weeping. Alex took the dish towel from his shoulder and mopped up spilled coffee from the tray.

"You need to eat, Vicky. You don't want to waste away."

"Lord, we know what we are, but know not what we may be."

"You don't want to go hungry on the plane, dear," Mother said. "Eat your breakfast."

"They have food on the plane—better than this!" Victoria snapped.

"The driver won't take you until you eat," Alex said tersely. "He's downstairs waiting, and that's what he said." Alex tried to finesse the fork to his sister's mouth. "They won't drive willful girls who haven't eaten their breakfast—period. It's company policy. You don't want to get the man in trouble, now do you?" Victoria opened her mouth grudgingly. Mother smeared butter and strawberry jam onto the toast, cut it into bite-sized pieces and handed the plate to Alex. Victoria chewed her food well and swallowed, washing it down with coffee through a straw. As he fed her breakfast, Alex's mind proceeded to the next pending tasks, which would be the bedpan followed by a sponge-bath.

XXXIII

The governor of Florida was also formerly the state's attorney general. He has in his possession a most remarkable shotgun with a highly dubious provenance, a 29-inch, seven-pin, side-lock over-under built by Ivo Fabbri. It's a Majestic Model live pigeon gun with Phoenix steel barrels. The gun was ordered destroyed—reportedly melted down by the state police and the serial numbers have been expertly removed. This firearm was found at a unique crime scene.

Early one morning, a policewoman stumbled upon a convenience-store holdup in progress. A standoff ensued, during which a bald pastor, dressed in a cleric's gray frock and white collar, emerged from the back storage room wielding this twelve-gauge shotgun. He snuck in, treading quietly on court sneakers. When he had a clear line of fire and took a bead on the assailant, he whistled loudly. The criminal turned and fired his nine-millimeter pistol, hitting Douglas McCashin squarely in the chest, but not before the reverend let off one round, clipping the entire right side of the holdup man's skull. Brain matter splattered all over the wall, and the stickup man slumped to the floor, stone dead.

Douglas McCashin departed this earthly realm nearly instantaneously. Crime scene investigators couldn't imagine an explanation for the expansive, peaceful smile on the reverend's lifeless face. They also couldn't fathom any reason for a man of God to possess such an ornately engraved handmade shotgun. And why he did he have it with him at the crack of dawn at a gas station in a seedy part of West Palm Beach? The fact was, Douglas McCashin had planned to leave for a box-bird shoot right after school let out, and he was gassing up for the trip in a modest Japanese car recently off lease from his own dealership.

The governor, who never knew Douglas McCashin in life, now slays pigeons with ruthless dispatch using the dead reverend's shotgun. It's all under the radar of course—very hush-hush. And he never recounts the story of how he got this firearm. According to the authorities, this particular Fabbri doesn't even exist. Douglas McCashin would be gratified to know that his pigeon gun lives on under such rarified stewardship—especially after the violent circumstances of his own spectacular demise.

* * * * *

Three days out of Portsmouth, the North Atlantic seas picked up and the ocean liner cut her speed in an attempt to make the passage smoother. The ship pitched and rolled and the passengers and crew—at least those not seasick below in their cabins—developed a sixth sense for the rising-and-falling decks and companionways. It became standard for every pedestrian to walk in serpentine to compensate for these high seas.

A light-skinned black man with a pencil-thin moustache and straightened hair, nattily dressed in a tuxedo, removed the heavy brown duck canvas cover from the baby grand piano. He checked that the musical instrument was well anchored, its brakes firmly locked to prevent it from sliding, before he sat down and opened his book of musical arrangements. Without being asked, a cocktail waitress brought half a cup of black coffee and half a glass of club soda, and placed them in cupped coasters anchored to the piano. The bass player, the drummer and the trumpet player literally staggered into the nearly empty lounge. There were a handful of drinkers on one side of the piano and a handful of smokers on the other. It would be a quiet night in the Britannia Lounge, but as long as even one passenger wanted to hear live jazz, the quartet would play their regular set.

Jazzmo pulled a fresh Tiparillo out of its cellophane wrapper and set it in the ashtray. He took a sip from his coffee and replaced it on the coaster. He did a cursory check of his fingernails and smartly adjusted his bowtie. Finally, he opened the keyboard and hit a middle-C, once, and then twice. The quartet confirmed the pitch with their instruments, followed by a casual nod, and then they all came out together—on key—for "Love Is Here to Stay."

* * * * *

The worst part about working for McCashin Motors is that no matter how many cars you sell or how hard you try to ingratiate yourself with the boss, Conrad Winston III is the only salesman Alex Vanderstein will even speak to. Everyone else on the showroom floor is livestock. Hit your numbers, show up sober and on time or Conrad will see to it that you're gone. Granted, he'll do it in his awkward, adolescent way that will make you feel guilty for having made him fire you in the first place—but he *will* fire you.

Conrad is a floating salesman at the dealerships and keeps a kind of a cubbyhole desk in each showroom. When an old classmate or a Little Kill member wants to take a test drive, Conrad pops over and cheerfully obliges. The best thing about dealing with Conrad is that he's low-pressure, a master of the soft sell. He remembers your name without really having to think about it. He can also remember your spouse's or ex-spouse's name—and divine whether it's appropriate to ask after them.

Conrad does a hell of a lot of business out of Little Kill, which is ironic. Just as Alex Vanderstein tendered his resignation without having to be asked by the membership committee, he suddenly realized that if he was going to have Conrad act as his proxy at the dealerships, the Little Kill connection would be vital. Conrad now floats through his old haunt like he never suffered a leave of absence. He is toying with moving back into town, but as it turns out, his one-bedroom in Port Easton is very convenient to the dealerships. Besides, when he finally saves up enough money for a down payment on something back over the state line, he wants it to be just the right thing.

Alex doesn't show himself much around the showrooms. Mostly, he comes in afternoons. He brings that liver-and-white Brittany bitch, Lila, with him, and he looks over the sales reports. Then he attends to foundation business. The Lollipop Fund awards grants of $10,000 to one hundred—give-or-take—St. Gilbert's alumni who are also former servicemen and -women pursuing undergraduate and graduate degrees.

Alex is a social outcast, a notorious pariah in the County. He cooperated fully on the Infinity fraud case, but it remains to be seen whether he'll make it through without serving at least some token jail time. He lives his life in a vacuum, surrounded by immediate family and a handful of old friends. These people know the particulars of his circumstance and don't judge him a criminal, but rather recognize him for the financial dupe he in fact was. Conrad is the only person, other than the dealership's secretary, whom Alex deals with.

Alex daydreams a lot. He's got a vague notion that, perhaps, when his legal troubles are behind him, he'll take a trip to New Zealand to see if it's a place where he might reinvent himself. He could sell the dealerships and become anonymous—just another Yank expat. Who knows? Maybe there's already a Kiwi girl down there waiting for him. Perhaps they could even start a family together. He goes onto the greater-Auckland-area real estate websites and looks at pictures of houses. And then he daydreams some more.

* * * * *

The first thing Walter Wagner did with all the money he took away from Onori was to buy himself a secondhand 25-hp Evinrude outboard motor, along with an extra power head. He still had the lower shaft-unit to mate it to from the motor he previously seized. His second expenditure was to get the bench seat of the El Camino reupholstered in a sturdy burgundy vinyl. Then he sprang for the $299 to have Earl What's-his-name properly repaint the old girl in ivory white—a lot more dignified than leftover house paint.

The day after Winky died, Walter bought Mitzy Adelman a wedding ring. He used his own gold band as a down payment. He had never worn a wedding ring to begin with. He knew too many physical types who lost that finger catching the band on something, and he knew that once remarried, he wouldn't wear that ring either. Winky's wedding band would forever sit in her jewelry box among a modest selection of other keepsakes.

Walter took a run up to Palm Beach to the fancy Catholic charity second-hand store and bought himself a wedding suit more appropriate to Southern Florida, a beige wool-and-polyester number in a very fine weave—something that really breathes. He bought a deep blue, short-sleeve shirt and a yellow tie to go with it.

He also put a new roof on his single-wide—much needed deferred maintenance. Since his remarriage, the trailer is now a rental property and provides just enough additional income so that, in combination with his social-security remittance and meager pension, Walter and Mitzy can spend the rest of their lives together going Dutch.

After Walter's big adventure up to the panhandle, the Brittany bitch Daisy immediately bonded with Mitzy. The two are now inseparable, which irks Walter to no end. He had it in his mind that the dog would be at the boat ramp every day, loyally awaiting his return from fishing. Right now, Daisy is asleep under Mitzy's feet as she sits at her desk, cutting the monthly batch of checks for the Salty Sands trailer park. Never mind; Walter is fond enough of the dog, and he's planning on taking her back up to quail country this coming hunting season.

It took a while for Walter to get used to sharing a bed with someone again. It's an odd feeling at first. Kind of like being unfaithful, but also exhilarating in that this dark beauty consented to be his mate. He misses Winky and always will, but he's in love with Mitzy and takes every opportunity to show it. They take tango lessons on Friday nights at the old Colony Hotel ballroom and most weekends they catch a concert at the Delray band shell or drive up to the dinner theater in Lake Worth.

Walter's just cut the engine on the Boston Whaler and he's gliding in, onto a piece of floating wooden crate. He's lathered up in sunscreen and zinc oxide, wearing his rope-belt tied in a square knot around khaki shorts that are decidedly a cut above what he ever wore as a quasi-bachelor. His white undershirt is clean and free of holes, and his sandals no longer smell like anchovies. He looks out from under the green velum visor of his straw hat that's worn through at the peak, focusing hard from behind dark polarized sunglasses. Walter's got a hunch there's dolphin congregating underneath that floating box. He wants to make a few more casts before he hits the boat ramp for his daily Miller Lite at the gas station, followed by lunch and a nap at the apartment he shares with Mitzy. It's the owner's place—she used to live there with her husband.

Life is for the living, yet another place awaits Walter where he'll be reunited with his first love, an American cultural icon and the finest woman exhibition shooter of the second half of the twentieth century. It's a place where a ferocious canine growls silently at things that go bump in the night, and a one-armed man reaches for a metallic club—just in case. The seasons come and go and always the purple crocus returns with the spring thaw.

THE END

III
THE RICOCHET

onrad "Double" Winston, Jr., heard the traffic blaring on Seventh Avenue far below his suite at the Hotel Pennsylvania, and snapped out of his daydream. He glanced out the window at a minor fender-bender between two taxicabs. He would turn forty next spring: not terribly old for a show jumper, but not young anymore either. In a meaningless political gesture, the United States had recently boycotted the 1980 Moscow Olympics. The Western powers had staged an alternate event at Rotterdam, The Netherlands. Though he certainly had another Olympic cycle in him, Westley Richards, his thirteen-year-old thoroughbred Nation's Cup team event horse, did not. Westley wasn't the same animal he'd been before the injury that sidelined them at Rotterdam. The trauma had visibly aged him, and he was starting to gray around the white blaze running down his nose. While the spirit in him was still willing, the swaybacked old bay was at the beginning of the end; it was time to retire him.

Westley was the best horse Double had ever sat on. He was intelligent and conscientious, stylish and versatile. He intuitively knew what was required, and strived to deliver. Above all, Westley was honest and brave. Jumping six feet was beyond his limit now— but whatever was asked of him, he committed to unconditionally. It was a relationship of mutual trust, and while the fences didn't always stay up anymore, that horse had never once stopped or run out at a fence with Double in the saddle. The old gelding was now only marginally sound and needed to be handled with kid gloves. Tonight would be his farewell performance. Westley would live out his remaining days at the Little Kill Country Club stables as a pleasure horse: a trail-riding nag extraordinaire, an equine pensioner that had been the toast of virtually every major horse show in Europe.

Double's wife, Francesca, was asleep on her side, and their seven-year-old son, Connie, was napping on a cot in the living room. Double tiptoed to the bedroom door and turned the knob, which made a sound, waking his wife.

"Look for us," she whispered without looking at him.

"I love you . . . both of you."

"I know," she replied.

* * * * *

In less than two days' time Double would assume the role of chairman of the board of Winston Firearms. Double's father, Conrad Senior—the company's patriarchal leader—had died at the family's ancestral lakefront house, Sun-Up, at the Big Pine Club two weeks before the horse show started.

Big Pine is a 5,000-acre lake community just a 75-minute drive west of the County and over the state line. Overlooking Big Pine Lake, the club is an Adirondack-style private enclave of weekend homes, with a main clubhouse hosting bedrooms and dining facilities. There's a sandy beach, tennis courts, a gun club with skeet and trap fields, as well as a 100-yard rifle range that can be reconfigured to shoot out to 1,000 yards. Roughly one-quarter of the Big Pine Club members also belong to the Little Kill Country Club, and legacy memberships often date back generations.

Ravaged by cancer, Senior wanted to expire in the full flush of autumn color, so he moved into Sun-Up. There, he lived out of a hospital bed in the great room where he could spend his days regarding a panorama of fall colors so vibrant it was hard to believe he'd ever wished for any relaxation other than to sit on that porch and take in the sights and sounds and smells of the lake. On the days when he was unable to leave his bed, nurses positioned him near the big bay window so he could still see nature's fireworks from indoors.

Senior was gaunt, his visage skull-like. His scalp was an intermittent patchwork of hair and bare skin. His eye sockets were hollow and his temples concave. His jaw seemed to have narrowed, and the loss of muscle mass and baby fat now conspicuously pronounced his teeth and gums. These long teeth seemed to protrude outward beaklike, which, along with his balding head, gave the lasting impression of a helpless baby bird. His nose seemed big and bulbous, and his ears looked comically oversized, their superfluous lobes likely to flap on the breeze. This legendary industrialist, a designer of firearms and ammunition—a man on whom presidents and secretaries of defense once called upon hat in hand—had transformed into a reasonable facsimile of Jimmy Durante.

Conrad Winston, Sr., was at peace with his imminent death because he was at peace with his life. He'd left his indelible mark on the world, and had personally influenced global outcomes. He showed foresight in the late 1930s by going to Washington D.C. to personally lobby the War Department for a loan on favorable terms in order to construct one entirely new plant building and to generally improve and expand ammunition production. His initiative was nothing short of prescient. This meant that at the dawn of America's involvement in World War II, from the .45 cal., to the .30-06, right up to the 155mm Howitzer, the United States armed forces had adequate ammunition production capacity, thanks to Winston Firearms. That small head start gave America an ever increasing and decisive advantage in war production, and the Allies out-produced the Axis powers every bit as much as defeated them militarily. In addition to being an innovative arms and ammunition designer, Senior was also a visionary—a transcendent figure; in later years he befriended General Douglas MacArthur, who told him this personally.

* * * * *

s the rest of the city seemed like it was either coming home from work, starting the night shift or ducking into a corner bar for a drink to start the evening, Double emerged from the lobby doors of the Hotel Pennsylvania. He stepped out into midtown's glaring florescent light show that is nightfall on the West Side, dressed in his show-jumping outfit—the equestrian's traditional riding habit of polished high black boots, white britches, scarlet Melton wool hunt coat and a white shirt and tie. His black velvet–covered helmet—his hunt cap—along with his spurs and crop (whip) were at the temporary stabling directly across Seventh Avenue in the Garden.

Conrad Double (as in Double Gun) Winston II had a dark crown of hair, blue eyes, a chiseled jaw and a scar in the shape of a pony's hoof on his cheek. He stood five-foot-ten-inches with a 30-inch inseam—perfect proportions for a show jumper.

The opulent gilded silk sash pinned across his shoulder, signifying his status as the leading jumper rider of the entire International Horse Show, made him look like the winner of some sort of Odd Fellow's pageant. People stared, and some even snickered. At the crosswalk waiting for the light to change, Double felt a towering presence behind him like one is prone to sense in any big city. His personal space was being invaded, and just as he was about to turn to confront the threat, he heard the voice whisper in his ear, "Giddyup," in a particularly deep but effeminate drawl.

He smelled her well before he saw her as he turned toward the voice, which was attached to a large transvestite. She had a platinum bouffant, frosted lips and eyelashes and stood about six-foot-three. All the makeup, hairspray and eau de cologne in the world couldn't cover up an Adam's apple the size of a tangerine and hands large enough to palm a basketball.

"We're busting broncos over at my place tonight," she hissed.

The light changed, and Double started across to the Garden.

"What's the ribbon for?" she now catcalled brazenly, making a spectacle of herself worthy of the crudest construction worker,

"The last virgin on the West Side?!"

She turned on her high heels and strutted uptown in an exaggerated gait. Double finally cracked a smile at the bizarre scene. *Only at the International Horse Show*, he thought to himself.

Double entered the arena through the side entrance, showing his exhibitor's credentials to the uniformed cop guarding the door. He ascended up through the basement of the arena, climbing a spiral-shaped, winding concrete ramp from street level, finally emerging into the schooling area adjacent the temporary stabling. There Westley—his only remaining horse at the show—awaited him. Their last moment together in the spotlight was just a few hours away.

* * * * *

In staging a horse show in a major city there are disparate and opposing smells. Immediately outside the building is the asphalt jungle, an artificial environment devoid of any smells that reference the cycle of life—hot pavement, auto exhaust, roasting chestnuts, rotting garbage and tobacco smoke. Follow that with the temporary stabling area at the Garden and the smells of a horse's life at its basic level: alfalfa and timothy, oats, corn, bran, sweet-feed and lots of fresh water go in; manure, urine and soiled bedding (wood shavings and wheat straw) come out. Manure smells particular, but no horseman would ever suggest it was vile. The same goes for equine dander: An absent-minded hand across their flanks comes away perfumed with memories.

Double sat on his tack trunk, a kind of supersized steamer trunk that acts as a horse's suitcase when it travels. Other riders, men and women he'd competed against for decades, streamed through like the bereaved at a wake. They all knew he was retiring tonight and would be embarking on a business career. The horse world is a place where that kind of departure, a definitive break—a veritable divorce from the entire lifestyle—virtually never happens. Even when riders get too old to continue in the saddle they usually fall back on instructing or become show judges or ground stewards. Virtually no one who'd committed the best years of their life to this pursuit ever simply up and quit the scene entirely.

He'd be around, Double assured them: He'd pop in from time to time to check up on them. But somehow, both Double and his friends recognized that this was wishful thinking. Assuming the mantle of executive leadership for a global brand like Winston Firearms meant that he wouldn't be informally popping in anywhere anymore. He was crossing a kind of Rubicon tonight, and once he was out, he would no longer be a part of the culture. He would become a stranger to them—an outsider.

They would continue their traveling road show but he was stepping off onto terra firma—permanently. They might see him again in the city or perhaps down at the polo club in Palm Beach, but when they did, he might be unrecognizable. Would he suddenly become gray and aged? Would he be unfit to even sit on a horse, perhaps even become obese? Would they shake their heads in disapproval at his appearance, and scold him for becoming middle aged? They would most certainly all walk away from him with the same unspoken sentiment lingering on their tongues: *He was once one of the best, but look at him now—just another bloated, pasty-faced businessman.*

* * * * *

What was unique about the course of fences for the International Team Jumping Speed Stake at the Garden was that it only contained two straight lines, where one obstacle lead directly on to another. Indoor arenas are always tight and the Garden was especially narrow, so a course designer was always limited in options. This course was a switchback kind of layout: a straight line of two fences along one wall, followed by three individual fences each turned 180 degrees from each other, followed by another straight line of two fences, finished off with two more individual obstacles turned 180 degrees from each other.

Double walked this course of fences with the other riders competing in the class, pacing off the strides—four human steps to one horse's stride. He walked this measured march from one fence to the next, whenever they were in a direct line, but then he took extra pains to count the potential strides in the sharp turns. He tried to calculate the shortest possible distance and therefore the fastest line through the course. Double also examined individual rails and, in particular, the concave steel cups in which they rested. Some cups were very shallow, to the point where he could roll a rail off an upright standard and onto the ground with the tip of a finger. If a horse made any contact whatsoever with these rails, they would come down and cost the rider four scored faults.

Seeing the distance to takeoff for a fence, accurately divining the exact number of strides it will take to deliver a horse to the base of the obstacle at its sweet spot and at the correct speed so as to have the optimal chance to clear it, is the trick to the entire thing. Get it right and the near impossible looks easy. Get it wrong and it comes off looking like an act worthy of the Roman Coliseum. A rider can regulate the striding going into a fence by reining in the horse or increasing speed with leg pressure. Less often, a rider may intentionally open or close the angle of approach to a fence, coming in at a bias, thus deliberately manipulating and fine-tuning the arrival distance into the fence. Finally, the horse has a mind of its own: Most want to go well in the ring and avoid hurting themselves or injuring the rider. The horse may simply use its own judgment and leave out the last stride, leaping farther out from the base of a fence than optimal, or they may add a stride where the animal takes an emergency half-step to set up for the fence. Neither are very satisfactory alternatives to an accurate eye, and every show jumper regards judging stride and seeing distances precisely as their single most valuable asset.

When he had examined each fence and counted off the strides in between them, Double tried to grasp a strategic overview of the entire course and decide where to take his one calculated risk. *Which corner would he cut sharper than any other? Which line would he try to gallop through so aggressively so as to leave out a stride altogether? Which fences would he approach at an extreme angle so as to set himself up for the next element?* Riders not only memorize a course, they visualize and mentally choreograph the ride in their mind. The horse has never seen this exact arrangement of fences, and part of the course designer's art is to showcase individual elements of oddly themed or spooky looking jumps often based on obstacles encountered in the fox hunting field. The idea is that a horse cantering headlong toward a flashy, colorful presentation may take a second look and try to avoid jumping it.

There are procedures to the way that an over-fences class plays out, and all it begins with the order in which the horses will go, which is posted at the in-gate where they enter the ring. Double always liked to go as close to last as possible: He was a seasoned competitor and preferred to know exactly what was required to win. The jumping order was supposed to be randomly selected, but perhaps on this his final night, the fix was in: He would go dead last.

Senior's only demand in exchange for providing Double's show jumpers had been that the horses be named for famous gun makers, and Westley Richards was named for the venerable English Best maker. Double's horse stood calmly on cross ties in the temporary stabling area as Double teetered on a stool and quickly rebraided the two lowest and smallest knots on the horse's mane. Braiding is a traditional embellishment on a show horse, which dates back to fox hunting. The idea is that when a horse goes in the field, a braided mane and tail are less likely to come away covered in briars, brambles and thorns.

By the early 1980s, braiding show jumpers had fallen out of fashion, as they aren't in any way judged: They win or lose entirely on how high and how fast they can jump. Their appearance never enters the equation, therefore most grand prix riders had quietly let the arcane tradition slip away, preferring instead to show the horse au naturel. Besides, it takes at least half an hour to braid a sixteen-hand horse, and most opt to pay a specialist to perform the meticulous chore. For a show like this, once the braids are in a horse's mane, they stay in the entire week, which can irritate the animal. Many horses take to rubbing up against the stall walls to scratch an itch; the knots come undone. That's exactly what happened to Westley as Double, dressed in his horse show habit, stood on a stool with precut strands of blue wool yarn dangling from his teeth. He untangled the knotted hair, removed the old yarn from the mane and with expert and nimble fingers, rebraided the short stretch of neck nearest the horse's withers.

His last moment in the saddle would have to last a lifetime, and Double wanted to make it as perfect as possible. The braids probably wouldn't have even been noticeable to anyone else, but *he* would have known, and it would have become a distraction. He was as compulsive in his sport as his own father had been in business, and he rebraided his horse simply to silence the critical internal monologue constantly streaming through his head. His two Argentine grooms looked on nervously. They knew there really wasn't time to be fooling around with this, but Double was a perfectionist: It would be done right—period. He would damned well make his final exit on a perfectly turned-out horse!

Double scrupulously snipped off the excess yarn, stepped down from the stool and headed for the in-gate to watch the first couple of horses go from ringside. As this was a speed class, it would only be one round as fast as you can go. While the fences weren't overwhelming in size or spread, the tightness of the course and all those sharp S-turns were clearly catching out the majority. The trick was to have the horse in hand but also be responsive enough to increase and decrease speed as the course unfolded. Just as humans can jog quickly in place, a horse can show a lot of action without necessarily covering much ground—*impulsion* is the technical term for where the horse is literally raring to go, but also highly maneuverable.

As he approached Westley to begin their warmup, one of the Argentines held out Double's spurs. Double made a point of never wearing spurs when he was walking around. He'd known a bunch of cases where people hooked the neck of one spur inside the fork of the other and fallen catastrophically. These spurs—the same spurs he had loaned to Lady Metcalf, the show-jumping team alternate, at Rotterdam—were special to him, and quite specific to his horse.

He had picked them up when he was fourteen, at the Pony Club swap meet held each year at Little Kill. They were the first pair of adult spurs he ever bought, and they were roweled. The small pie-cutter wheels had frozen solid with rust, and while they weren't anything fancy, they were English and he had paid fifty cents in quarters for them. He had Senior cut off the rowels and grind down and polish the remaining stub of neck to create a very mild short spur, no longer than a pencil eraser. The finishing touch was when Senior had the Winston Firearms custom shop's chief engraver cut a curlicue flourish of scroll inside of each spur. Now they were truly one of a kind.

Double wore these spurs occasionally as a teenager, but they were too mild for most horses so he put them away. When he bought Westley, they came back out. This horse was so honest and true, he didn't need to be spurred into anything. He just needed to be signaled, and Double's adolescent spurs did the trick perfectly.

One Argentine brother now held Westley as the other gave Double a leg up onto the horse. Then the men vigorously ran a rub rag over Double's black dress boots, polishing them one last time. Now he too was immaculate.

One of the peculiarities of riding jumpers at the Garden was that the warmup area was so small and cramped, it was only feasible to set two practice fences—a simple vertical and an oxer spread-fence on either side of a large concrete structural pillar. The other distinguishing feature was the low ceiling, which was very intimidating because riders went so high in the air over a fence, one marveled at how they weren't scraped off the horse and onto the ceiling. It was really only safe to have two or three horses going in the schooling area at a given time. The mayhem of half-dozen horses warming up at once in that postage-stamp-sized area was chaotic to the point of being dangerous.

Double started out riding a simple posting trot where the rider rises and falls in the saddle, keeping synchronized time with each of the horse's steps, making an easy loop in one direction and then repeating the process in the other. He did the same thing with an energetic, collected canter though Westley grew antsy, as the horse well knew from both sight and sound what was coming, and grew excited with anticipation.

Just as with humans, a really good jumper can become overconfident in its abilities. The best cure for this is, right before they enter the ring, for them to knock a fence down or hit a rail hard enough to get their attention. It was with this intention that Double turned his horse and took two impossibly short strides into the vertical jump, intentionally putting Westley in too deep to its base so that he took down the top rail. As expected, they finished the rest of the warmup without ever even grazing a rail.

Finally, when it was two horses from his turn, Double jumped the vertical once, then quickly turned his horse nearly in place and jumped the oxer. Then he jumped both fences going around the pillars in the opposite direction, intentionally employing the kinds of quick turns he'd make in the ring.

The feeling of jumping is the feeling of harnessing brute force and transforming it into graceful motion. A rider steers his mount into a fence, guiding him with the reins but also with the steady alternating pressure of both legs through the calf muscles applied to the horse's barrel. As the rider arrives at the last two or three strides before a jump, he will sit deep in the saddle to better feel the distance to the fence and encourage the horse onward, but also to assume a sort of safety-seat to protect against the outside chance of the horse refusing the fence at the last second and pitching the rider off. While it doesn't happen very often, every jumper rider is conscious of this possibility, and always builds in a margin of error with this defensive seat.

As the horse arrives at the base of the fence and his front legs leave the ground, the rider stands slightly in the stirrup irons, rising out of the saddle, his upper torso meeting the horse's forward motion, folding the upper body and leaning into the crest of the horse's neck. In the air, the rider's upper body should be somewhat parallel to the horse's neck, with his heels down, his legs with a break at the knee and his hands releasing the horse's mouth via the reins. As the horse clears the obstacle and the arc flattens and the descent begins, the rider comes back in the saddle with his torso unfolding in anticipation of the landing, at which point he absorbs most of the shock through his heels and knees, softly regaining his deep seat and cantering onward.

Victor Kralik, the Olympic show-jumping team coach, stood alongside the Argentines, turning in place as he watched Double prepare. Victor was a former Hungarian nobleman and cavalry major who'd graduated from the leading Prussian cavalry school in Germany before WWII. He had also been a junior member of the middling Hungarian show-jumping squad for the 1936 Berlin Olympics. His old-fashioned elephant-ear wool breeches and high-top Reitstiefel cavalry boots had the traditional cut, and he exhibited all the spit-and-polish of a former military man. He wore his graying hair short and slicked back, with a blue silk cravat under the collar of his long-sleeved white dress shirt, and a dueling scar was on prominent display along his right jawline. Victor remained entirely silent, as he had long since grudgingly conceded that Double knew nearly as much about show jumping as he did.

Finally, Double stopped the horse and backed him up three steps to recompose him. Then he eased the skittish horse over to the in-gate. Double was on deck and could see the horse and rider in front of them riding hell-bent for leather, going fast but taking the turns wide. Victor quietly stood next to his horse and rider. He put his hand on Double's thigh in a final silent farewell gesture of respect. The in-gate door opened and a flushed, ginger-haired man on an animated dark horse tipped his hat to Double as they came dancing through.

"Goodbye," Double said through a taciturn smile as he rode off. Victor's hand gently fell away, and Double headed out into the ring through the in-gate door, riding Winston Firearms' Westley Richards at a near gallop.

It's quite disorienting to both horse and rider to leave the quiet dark confines of the grotto-like warmup area for the blinding lights of the Coliseum. Passing through the in-gate is almost like being pushed out the birth canal and into the bright light of day. The orchestra box, which was festooned with the orange-and-black bunting of the International Horse Show colors, struck up a jaunty instrumental of the first few bars of Cole Porter's "You're the Top." It's a song which, if the silly lyrics were sung, would have heaped praise on Double, comparing him to the smile of the Mona Lisa, Napoleon brandy, Cellophane and a turkey dinner, to name just a few items on the bizarre laundry list.

As Double and Westley streaked across the ring, the announcer said glibly of the previous round, which was both fast and clear, that he didn't expect anyone could beat that performance. Hearing such a challenge set the bit in Double's teeth: He was going take a big chance well beyond his usual solitary calculated risk and try to run the table like ball of fire.

The first real coach who taught Double to ride jumpers gave him a handful of golden rules to live by, the first was to always gallop into the ring: It guaranteed both horse and rider were wide awake and ready for action. The other happy by-product was that it took you from one end of the ring to the other and back again. The result was the horse had a good look at every fence it was going to jump. It wasn't always practical to try to pull off this grand tour, but tonight's event was an international team speed class in a small ring. Double was well within the rules as he trotted back to the middle of the ring, stopped his horse and heard the horn blast signifying the timers were set. His round could begin, and he set off.

There were just eight fences to the entire course, ranging in height from four-foot-ten inches to five-foot-three—not terribly big, but only four of them were in a straight line. Everything else was placed somewhere along this serpentine switchback. Double and Westley picked up a canter on the right lead as they rounded the far side of the ring. They hugged the wall and came out of the long sweeping curve onto the straightaway and through the timers. Double saw the distance to the first fence and cantered on without checking his speed. He cleared the first low vertical, a single rail over a brush box followed five strides later by a double-railed cylindrical hay-bale oxer with the back rail set at five-foot, four inches with a five-foot spread, front-to-back.

Upon landing, Double reined in Westley, collected him and then turned the horse hard right 180 degrees and, in three short strides from a near standstill, met the four-rail vertical at an acute angle. Double then checked his stride again and quickly spun the gelding, this time to the left, and galloped onward five strides to jump another hay-bale oxer, this one being lower front-to-back and with a narrower spread.

Double quickly checked his speed, and two short strides after hitting the ground was again wielding Westley, turning him toward the next fence, a vertical of three brightly painted flat planks over a wooden flower box. He cleared it three strides from a near standstill. Then he galloped down only the second line of fences on the course for five long strides, where he cleared the single rail over a green roll-top, a fence which acts like a right-angle triangle, forcing the horse to jump high and long to clear it. Double took this fence at a slight angle as he was now at the very bottom of what would be the S curves for the next two fences.

He pulled Westley up sharp upon landing, and the horse briefly tossed his head and stumbled at feeling put upon. The horse swung to the left and galloped headlong for three strides at the wooden box wall painted to look like stone—a square vertical fence that stood five-foot-two.

The next obstacle was a triple-bar oxer of painted rails. The high back rail stood only five-feet-tall, but the spread was nearly square. To compound the challenge, this triple bar was right next to the horse and rider when they hit the ground after clearing the stone wall. The rider now had to canter on in the opposite direction from the fence he was about to jump, judge the critical distance to close and then pick the right moment to turn and gallop into this big triple bar with the gaping spread. If the horse came out of the last turn in the wrong striding or more likely, without enough room to take a real run at it, the monster width would end all chances of going clear.

Double hit the ground and cantered on for three full strides, pulled up short and wheeled Westley into the top of the S-curve. When they came out square onto the fence, they had only two short strides to accelerate from a dead stop to a near gallop to gain enough speed to clear it, which they did in the fastest time of the class.

When a round is going exceptionally well, it begins in a hushed silence from the audience, which is haunting in such a large interior space. With ongoing incremental success, chatter steadily builds and gets louder and louder until the last fence, at which point, if the obstacle remains standing, the applause erupts like a thunderclap in the ears of both horse and rider. A really thrilling class-winning performance like Double's can sound like an artillery barrage. The spectators in the supplementary bleachers stomped their feet on the metal alloy floors like it was the biggest kettledrum in the world. Flashbulbs popped like twilight fireworks on the Fourth of July, and the frantic clapping lapped over him like waves breaking on a beach.

It's rarified air, a moment thrilling enough to bring a crowd of seven or eight thousand people to their feet in rapturous applause, but it doesn't so much make a man feel he's touched greatness as humble him. It's a privilege to live one's dreams in a way that most people living a workaday existence never can, an exclusive club for those who have known the feeling of that bright spotlight tracking them as they ride a victory lap to the soundtrack of a standing ovation. It is simultaneously both an extroverted and extremely private moment—a sea of adulation experienced in a darkened arena. All Double could really see was the blinding white oval of spotlight, the outline of the various fences in the ring and his horse. If his life ever meant anything at all, that brief victorious moment in the dark was the best evidence for it.

Thoroughbreds are a high-strung breed anyway, but all that commotion—a standing ovation for nearly a minute in a darkened Colosseum—had Westley ready to jump the rail and into the box seats.

"Greased lightning, ladies and gentleman!" the announcer cried. "Double Winston riding Winston Firearms' Westley Richards are your stake winners and overall International Jumper Champions for the show." The applause continued unabated. "Take a good look, folks, because you won't see their likes again: Horse and rider are retiring tonight. Is that true, Double? You still want to turn him out after a ride like that?"

Double smiled broadly and nodded his confirmation in pantomime.

"That's it, then. Our champions and the end of a great pairing: a once in a lifetime combination." Double rode back out through the in-gate where Victor waited to shake his hand. Horse and rider turned around and waited patiently as the formal presentation red carpet was rolled out and the trophy stand was set up.

A crowd of riders stood silently behind Double and Westley. He glanced over his shoulder and saw out of the corner of his eye wall-to-wall white shirts and dress breeches. He briefly flushed: He was a quiet, cerebral competitor who wasn't always that well liked in the riding community. Now the entire field of horsemen began to applaud in his honor as the first six winning horses entered the ring, with Double leading this victory procession.

The class was pinned in reverse order, starting with the sixth-place horse followed close on by the international team results. When it came time for Double to accept the trophy, he rode up on Westley and accepted the large silver platter, blue ribbon and overall International Jumper Championship trophy and rosette—the American show jumping squad finished second. Then he handed the sterling and silk off to Victor, who was waiting with a navy blue woolen cooler blanket. Double slipped out of the saddle and onto the ground. He rolled up the stirrup on his near side as Victor did the far side, unbuckled the girth, removed the saddle and handed it off to Victor.

A smattering of applause responded to the symbolism of this mundane task—the ceremonial retirement. Double took the blue cooler, embossed with the equestrian team logo, from Victor and spread it over the horse, looping it over his ears and threading his tail through the loop in the back. He took the reins from over the horse's head, laid a collar of roses across the horse's withers and proceeded to hand-lead Westley out of the ring on foot. Both horse and rider were simultaneously victorious and vanquished as they walked out to a muted and respectful standing ovation, after which the international teams took a turn around the ring. As Double came through the in-gate, the Argentines took the saddle from Victor and the horse from Double.

* * * * *

F rancesca met her husband at the in-gate dressed in a black gaucho-look outfit with a vest and a low-cut white silk shirt. It was a bizarre but popular period fashion that was equal parts matador and pirate, but she looked terrific in it. She embraced her husband with a long kiss to commemorate this triumphant moment. A kiss of victory: No one at the Garden that night doubted Double Winston was the best show jumper in the country. Also a kiss of relief: It was all finally over, and he wasn't leaving the ring in a wheelchair.

"Lobster Newburg," she whispered invitingly in his ear. "Connie's back at the room with the housekeeper. They're holding a table for us at the Astor House, but we have to hurry."

Double and Francesca strolled down the spiral concrete ramp to street level and hailed a cab. Except for his velvet helmet and crop, Double was still dressed exactly as when he'd hopped down from Westley, right down to the silk leading rider's sash and spurs.

Double had always stayed at the Astor House with his parents before the Garden moved downtown. This masterpiece of art deco architecture had been just a few blocks from the old arena, and all the horseshow balls and after-parties were held there, so it made sense for most of the riders to stay there. In those years, Senior had grown especially fond of the hotel's Lobster Newburg, a dish the Astor House kitchen had created.

*　*　*　*　*

Francesca was Swiss, and had grown up in the Italian-speaking lakefront city of Lugano in the region of Ticino. Charming and coquettish with dark sable hair and olive complexion, she was the daughter of a notorious Nazi neuropsychologist on one side of the family and a wealthy industrial war profiteer on the other. Her German parents had quietly slipped over the border into Switzerland, one with much of her fortune still intact before the war even ended, and the other fleeing one step ahead of the Allied war crimes tribunals.

Francesca's childhood home was a private psychiatric clinic, a small twelve-bed sanitarium with sweeping views of the lake, in a picturesque terra-cotta-roofed Mediterranean villa cut into the hillside. The sanitarium specialized in electroconvulsive therapy (ECT) and offered deluxe accommodations in a private setting. Many of the affluent patients were also public figures, and for this reason, registered under assumed names and identities. The clinic staff was discreet and confidential: They'd all refused countless bribes to confirm that one celebrity or other was in residence. For this reason the Berger Clinic was revered, and enjoyed a long list of prominent patients rotating in and out for periodic treatments. Those without issues of confidentiality were often treated on an outpatient basis and stayed at area highbrow resort hotels.

The scientific community was vaguely aware of Dr. Heinrich Berger's wartime activities, and it was widely presumed that his later-published neurological papers were derived from research and data gleaned from that period. His recall was uncanny, and many of Berger's peers questioned just how such statistical analysis, now some forty-odd-years-old, could not only be revisited so comprehensively but also how he could seemingly rearrange and cross-reference his vast catalogue of empirical findings seemingly at will. In the era before personal computers, information came on written pages inside manila file folders. This kind of statistical dexterity was all but unheard of at the time. "During the war I was quite aware that such unique scientific conditions couldn't last," was Berger's standard response. "Therefore I developed into a very thorough clinician."

* * * * *

Perhaps it was too much cognac, or the late hour, or maybe it was simply that he wouldn't be riding the next day or any day after that, but after dinner Double's cheery disposition suddenly shifted. He stood curbside at the main entrance of the Astor House, and Francesca, who held an empty Perrier-Jouët bottle adorned with hand-painted flowers as a keepsake from their victory dinner, slipped two quarters into her husband's palm. The hotel doorman, uniformed in a forest-green peaked cap and brass-buttoned dress tunic worthy of a Prussian field marshal, flagged down a yellow cab, a Checker Marathon. The fleet of once predominant, oversized hacks was in the process of being phased out of service, but many city dwellers still preferred them for their spacious interiors and auxiliary jump seats, which swung up from the floor on a hinge and could easily accommodate two extra passengers. Double pressed the coins into the doorman's white-gloved hand and followed Francesca into the backseat.

Before he could get himself situated, the overeager doorman slammed the cab door right onto the outside fork of Double's right spur. It snapped halfway down its scroll engraving like a capon's dried wishbone as the cab drove off.

"Damn it!" Double reacted, reaching down and unbuckling the two fractured pieces from his instep by their leather strap. "I should know better after all these years than to tie one on without taking off my spurs." He held the shattered steel pieces up for Francesca to examine.

"I'm sorry," she said. "Perhaps it can be mended."

"Mended?! It's shit!" Double snapped bitterly. "They were always junk—a cheap pair I paid two bits for. It's not like I'm ever going need them again anyway." He started to hand-crank open the window to toss them out into the street when Francesca stopped him.

"Don't you dare!" she said, snatching the shards away. "You've been carrying on like an old woman all the night, and now you throw a tantrum and want to . . . You are such an ass! Someone else may appreciate them someday." She stuffed the broken pieces into her clutch.

Double brooded, aware that he was becoming surly, but he just couldn't help himself and added, "What the hell difference does it make now?"

His sudden dark mood was typical of the prickly pear he became whenever he drank too much. He was a serious man of ambition and accomplishment; presently, he was neither. He would no longer be the well-known show jumper—the successful athlete with an ongoing future in the sport. He'd spent his whole life looking forward to the next season, the next horse, the next opportunity. That was all over now. Currently, he was nothing more than an unproven executive behind in both age and grade with no real-world business experience. This disoriented feeling of being a nowhere man made him loathsome and resentful.

Yet on this particular night he was the toast of the town, closing out an accomplished show-jumping career by decisively dominating an international field of the best. He was a sore winner who had nothing to be bitter about: In the horseshow world he was a great success. He'd lived a charmed life from his first breath until that very moment.

"No one is making you stop," Francesca pleaded, as she withdrew a handkerchief from her purse and put it to her nose and eyes. "Your father always said it was your choice and that you didn't need to . . . Why not just sell the damned company and continue riding?"

"Shut up about my father!" Double fumed under his breath, as cold-blooded as a cobra.

They finished the journey in crestfallen silence, and when the cab arrived curbside at the Hotel Pennsylvania, Francesca sprang forth in tears, showering the sidewalk with a flurry of money as she dashed inside the hotel. She left the empty hand-painted champagne bottle on the backseat of the cab, and Double scurried around on the filthy pavement in his britches, boots and scarlet hunt coat with the silk leading rider's sash, fighting off stooping pedestrians to gather up enough money to pay the fare. When he finally had enough, he handed the bills through the open passenger's side front window and the hack handed him back the empty bottle. As the cab sped off into the night, Double stood on the street corner pondering his options.

If he left her alone, Francesca would stew for a while and probably cry herself to sleep. If he returned to her now, the argument would only escalate with a higher force of magnitude. He didn't want to risk waking his son, and he certainly didn't want to say anything more tonight that he'd later regret. He felt like a heel, but calculated that if he just left his wife alone, the situation would improve by morning, when combustible tempers would have long since burned themselves out.

A convoy of horse vans came through the Seventh Ave. intersection and made the wide right-hand turn into the loading area at the base of the spiral concrete ramp leading up into the stabling area. These horses were being brought in for Sunday's equitation classes, a division where junior competitors under the age of eighteen are judged on their riding ability and style, both on the flat and over fences. Many of the show horses that had already finished the week were heading home in those same outgoing horse vans, and Westley Richards was among them.

At the street corner, Double stuffed the hand-painted champagne bottle into a wire garbage basket seeped through and overflowing with the weekend's refuse. As he waited for the crosswalk light to change, an old black vagrant with white hair scurried over and removed the painted bottle from the basket. The homeless derelict was oddly dressed in a fool's motley, clothes still pungent with the odor of mothballs. He wore a black derby, string-backed riding gloves and full-length woolen elephant-ear jodhpurs with the conventional leather straps at the knees. He also sported a houndstooth tweed hacking jacket and ankle-high riding boots. He had a round cardboard rider's number clipped in back of his black turtleneck collar, and the stub of an unlit cigar was wedged into the corner of his mouth. A pint bottle of rotgut bourbon bulged from his coat pocket. He fished out of his handkerchief pocket a monocle tethered to his lapel buttonhole and daintily placed the looking glass into his eye socket to better inspect the painted bottle.

"Don't come down off your high horse," he muttered.

"What?!"

The vagrant turned to him and removed his cigar. Double could see that behind the monocle, the man was missing his eye. His right socket was just a gaping hole with a flapping eyelid.

"Don't get off your horse, and don't give the long gun back to the boy. Y'all seen what he done with it out yonder —ought to know better." Obviously, the man was spouting gibberish, but Double found it unsettling just the same.

"Young boy ain't got no sense," the man insisted, growing more animated in his gesticulations. "Can't figure for when wind blows and the trees get to swayin'. Don't give him back the long gun, no sir. Let 'im leave that girl alone: Take Fran and the boy down the seashore instead."

Double grabbed the man violently by the arm and spun him. The champagne bottle fell out of the vagrant's hands and shattered on the sidewalk.

"What the hell do you know about me?"

"Pickwick? Bailistock?" The prophet directed his attention to the glass shards on the sidewalk in front of him. With slender fingers he stroked his chin and told the future like he was divining chicken entrails.

"Greedy man gonna live in your house—angry white man with the money right in his name—a man of God? No, that can't be right. You gonna lay with another woman—a beautiful giant she is." He removed the pint bottle from his coat pocket, took a long pull and then boldly turned to Double and predicted, "But she don't stay: Ya' drinks too much."

"Who the hell are you?"

"It's a ricochet!" The seer foretold the vision as clear as day. "A goddamned ricochet like a flat stone skimming 'cross de branch. She's down there—oh, she's down there alright, and she be found too. You take him away, but he don't come back the same—no sir." Double now shook the man by the shoulders and the prophet finally seemed to snap out of his trance.

"Be forewarned!" the black man thundered as the monocle fell away from his vacant eye socket. "I seen it all." Then he gave Double a broad, toothless grin and a diabolical belly laugh that revealed naked gums as vibrantly scarlet as the flesh of a ripe watermelon.

"There's a riverboat down in the subway—comes drifting past at midnight all lit up. I lost my money at the tables last night, boss. Stake me so's I kin' get it back." The old man held out his palm and Double laid the only money he had left in it—a ten dollar bill. His fingertips brushed the black man's gnarled calluses, and it reminded Double of the sensation he once felt as a child when a cow licked him.

"Sawbuck," the vagrant marveled, holding the bill up to his remaining eye. He replaced the cigar stub back in the corner of his mouth with a flourish "Looks like Old Man River's got me playin' in the first-class salon tonight," he sang as he shuffled back down the block toward the next cross-street.

Double was haunted by the tramp's dire revelations and uneasy with his prophetic gibberish. The whole thing had a nightmarish quality to it. *Just another crazy panhandler,* Double concluded, trying to shake off the encounter, as he quickly crossed the intersection to the Garden. When he reached the opposing sidewalk, he glanced back over his shoulder toward the opposite block—it was completely empty.

* * * * *

D ouble followed a single-file of horses up the spiral concrete ramp from street level like he was bringing up the rear of a train of pack mules. When he reached the top, the two Argentine brothers were slowly walking Westley around the schooling area. The horse was prepared for shipping, his legs wrapped in cotton bandages for support and wearing a thin wool blanket underneath a heavier canvas turnout sheet. On his head was a leather halter covered in shearling for added protection against chafing.

Double approached the brothers, silently took the leather lead-line and fished around in his coat pockets for the sugar cubes he'd purloined from the coffee service at the Astor Hotel. The bay thoroughbred with black points gingerly plucked the cubes from Double's palm with miraculously dexterous lips that seemed to have a life of their own. Double stroked the horse's jaw and led him on a lazy loop through the warmup area.

Double was calm and nearly sober again, feeling remorse for the sharp words spoken to his wife earlier, but also content in performing this menial task. It had always been that way with him: Working around horses soothed his temper and quieted his burning brain, and this moment was no exception. The show horses began funneling down the spiral ramp as the PA system called out the names being shipped. When Westley Richards was finally called, it drew a short burst of applause from the warmup area as Double personally walked his horse down to street level and loaded him onto the van headed to his new home at the Little Kill Country Club.

* * * * *

D ouble sent the Argentines back to the hotel to sleep. Now that he had retired, their business relationship was officially over. The brothers would begin work again in just a few hours in the employ of Lady Metcalf, the team alternate, who had already parlayed an expectation-busting sixth-place finish in the individual standings at Rotterdam into a burgeoning teaching career. She had three junior riders competing in Sunday's big equitation class.

Similar to racing stables, it is common practice for show barns to be represented by a distinctive set of colors. It is also common practice that each show stable has a set of ornately embroidered, heavy duck canvas drapes custom-made in these colors, which will fit any standard box stall.

Double's colors were Kelly green with yellow, and his tack room had two color-coordinated canvas director's chairs and a cot made up with a woolen championship cooler from the Hickstead Derby. His soiled scarlet hunt coat and leading rider's sash now hung on the back of one of these canvas chairs, and Double was prostrate on the cot. He was feeling grimy after his long raucous night, trying to nod off with his eyes closed. He was doing his best to ignore the coliseum sound system informing the junior riders about their four a.m. warmup, which was the only time when they could familiarize their horses with the sights and sounds of this chaotic arena venue. This was interrupted every three minutes by the stabling area speakers nagging him that he was now in a no-smoking zone and should wait to exit the building before lighting up.

Double finally managed to relax. He always took comfort in this special environment, but he also felt like a heel for snapping so viciously at Francesca. He could be such a prick whenever he drank, and it was always over the smallest things. He had a brief, fleeting flash of clarity—an epiphany of resolve: The only real long-term solution to his problem was to stop drinking entirely.

Suddenly the great snort of a snore, the kind we all make when we've had too much, violently roused him back to consciousness.

"My, my . . ." Lady Metcalf said as she stood over him. "Look what the cat dragged in."

Double opened his eyes, fog-headed and disoriented, and peered up at Lady, who was draped in an emerald velvet evening gown. Her swanlike neck was adorned in the shimmering sparkle of a diamond necklace choker, her honey-blonde hair illuminated by the glow of overhead fluorescent lights. The former centerfold and Bond girl was leaning against an invalid's wooden cane, her entire right leg encased in a plaster cast that ran from her ankle to the top of her thigh. She was tall, standing six-foot-one in stocking feet, and was naturally busty, with the rest of her being lissome and willowy. She was long of leg and naturally lithe, but also wiry. She had cobalt-blue eyes and chiseled features with a light Nordic complexion, a bewitching, slightly gap-toothed bite and natural butterscotch hair that edged toward pale highland Scotch whiskey whenever she was in the sun.

"Lady," Double sputtered, eyes blinking feebly against the light. "I dozed off—what time is it?" He began to swing his legs off the cot, but then found he couldn't when the spur on his left heel caught the bedding and prevented him.

"Easy there, cowboy. It's 3:30," Lady said, trying to help guide his feet to the floor. "Passed out is more like it. . . . I'm the one in the cast, but you're the one who can't stand up. Jesus, you're a mess. Those stains'll never come out," she said, pointing to the soiled knees of his britches. "You been worshipping at every brass rail in town?"

"I fell getting out of the cab," he said. With Lady's help he was finally able to stand. They were now face to face—she towered a good three inches over him—and were well inside each other's space. Intimately close, his line of vision came to her nose. He could have kissed her by just leaning in and up. "I see you're still dressed from the night before. Where'd you slink off to?" he asked.

"Dinner party—big client. Fell asleep in the soup. You're missing a spur, Double. How'd you manage that?" she asked, taunting at their awkward, overly familiar juxtaposition by breathing the words directly into his face.

He finally side-stepped out from her immediate presence and sought refuge behind one of the canvas director's chairs. "Cab door snapped it off; Franny's got the pieces."

Lady hobbled over to the chair, set her evening bag on it and began to dig through its contents. "Got a bank check for your farm in here somewhere, but I'm starting to think I should hold out for more," she said, withdrawing a plain white envelope.

"I hate to sell it, but I won't need the King Street farm anymore, what with the big house on the hill and the company."

"Are those the spurs I used on Sequoia at Rotterdam? 'Cause I'd sure like to have one."

Double came around the front of the chair and put his boot up on the footrest. As he unstrapped the spur, he began to get testy. "You want this spur that I've had since I was fourteen years old, the one my father cut down and had engraved—the one I rode Westley in all those years, just because I let you borrow it once?!" he said, as he presented it to her.

"Yup," she chirped, taking it from him. "Help me take a load off." She hooked her cane onto the armrest of the director's chair, and Double lifted her up by her hips and awkwardly helped her into the seat.

"How long till that thing comes off, anyway?" Double asked indifferently.

"February."

"Who's riding Sequoia in Palm Beach this winter?"

"No one. I'll probably just turn him out. Lunge him every couple of days—let him rest a while. I'd let you show him if you wanted . . . but only you." Her words were at once both painfully pragmatic and telling. They honored his prowess, but the underlying affection was also undeniable.

"Consider yourself lucky," he said, glancing at her cast. "I saw someone swim through an oxer like that once. After the horse got off him I don't think he took another breath. I ran into the ring and stayed with him—talked about his life and his family to him. I don't know if he heard any of it, but I wanted his last thoughts to at least be something pleasant."

"I can walk, and I'll ride again, but right now my students need babysitting." She stood up and reached for the cane hanging on the armrest, and once again she and Double were standing too close for comfort. He held out his hand for the envelope, but she withdrew it and held it to her breast.

"What else could you possibly require, Lady?!" he demanded.

Suddenly, she broke into an impish grin and pulled him directly into her. Her arms rested on his shoulders as awkwardly as if they were two mismatched children in a dancing class. He was in her embrace, his head cocked upward ever so slightly now to account for their differences in height. "You're leaving us. I want a goodbye kiss," she announced.

Their lips met apprehensively at first, and then suddenly his hands went exploring as they clenched together in a kind of intense, slow-motion, writhing grind.

It was a revelation. Mismatch aside, they had real sexual chemistry. It was the sort of moment that could easily go off the rails. She looked great and felt even better to him, and that cot would more than suffice. Double started to back up toward the bed, pulling her along into him, but she broke free of the clinch. She looked at him, her fingers going directly to the scar of the pony's hoofprint on his cheek as she traced its outline.

"Ain't that a kick in the head?" she said. "With this leg, I don't think I could ball you even if I wanted to, and this girl's got a long day ahead of her. I'm not about to have you dripping back out of me for the next fourteen hours." She handed him the cashier's check. "Three-hundred-eighty thousand—even," she announced as she reordered her dress and peered in the mirror to check her makeup.

Double held the envelope up before him as if trying to divine its contents. "Most people close a deal with a simple handshake."

"That was to see if there's any juice flowing through that live wire of yours—there is," she said, meticulously reapplying her lipstick and pursing her lips. "You're a married man—for the time being. That may not always be the case." She turned toward him and leaned heavily on her cane. "I don't need a husband. I can afford to go it alone now, and I'll never let anyone have it over me like that again. I got a handful of rich students and more coming all the time. I figure you go where the dough is, and Port Easton is about as close to the County as I can stand: close enough, but far enough. But if I ever was to hang my hat on a man's bedpost again," she caught herself and then chose her words carefully. "I'd shack up with you." She teetered unstably over the cedar chips out to the entrance of the ceremonial tack room, turned to him as her hair fell, covering over one eye in a come-hither look. She flipped it away and said, "Ever find yourself feelin' lonesome for company, look me up."

II

On Conrad's ("Connie") Winston III's eleventh birthday, Double presented him with a first-generation Winston Model-52—a .22 caliber, bolt-action target rifle. More than once Double second-guessed himself and questioned whether his son was mature enough to handle the responsibility of owning a deadly firearm. *Might it not be prudent to wait another year?* Senior had famously pronounced that a boy was ready for his first .22 when you could send him to the market with a grocery list and cash money and he would return having perfectly filled the order with the correct change. Double speculated that if his son were put to that test now he would fail in spectacular fashion. The boy was regularly rifling through his father's pockets for loose change, pen knives, nail clippers and a favorite pen—a fourteen-carat stub that was just long enough to write with and neatly fit into the fold of Double's wallet. The housekeeper regularly fished these items out of the boy's bedding when she made his bed. Apparently Connie would inventory the day's haul each night before he fell asleep.

This same rifle had originally been a gift from Senior to Double on his fourteenth birthday, when it was presented by the famous female Winston Firearms exhibition shooter, Winky Wagner. It was the same model she used in her act for one and only one shot—to shoot the cigarette out of her husband's mouth. Hers was restocked in fancy walnut and decorated with ornate inlays of songbirds in pink, yellow and white gold. The gift rifle was unadorned, but otherwise identical.

Senior had colluded with the legendary trick shooter in a final attempt to pull the boy away from horses and gently nudge him toward guns and the firearms business. So much did Senior care about the big birthday surprise that he sent the company's lone DC-3 corporate aircraft to shuttle the sharpshooter from a weeklong engagement at the Ohio State Fair back home to Bridgewater and then back again in a single-day round trip.

Winky arrived in her showman's outfit, just a snip of a woman in her cream-colored skirt embroidered with a royal blue W, matching cream shooting vest with the W on back as well as on the upright brim of her white cavalry trooper hat. Winky spent the afternoon at the plant firing range plinking away with the boy, trying her best to establish a rapport and fan the flames of enthusiasm. And Double did enjoy himself—to a point. He enjoyed shooting when it was the only activity in the offing, and Winky Wagner was clearly someone special. She showed him all sorts of tricks, and she'd spent so much time around children of every sort that she could charm even the most withdrawn, shy youngster among them. She wore celebrity like a loose-fitting garment, comfortable in her own skin to the point where she could play away a day with a shy adolescent—a boy perhaps not so very unlike the infant son she inexplicably lost during a mid-morning nap only a few years earlier.

Double had enough insight to realize what was going on, and dutifully humored both Winky and his father by feigning enjoyment. When it came time to say goodbye to her, Senior told him to give her a kiss. Unsure of himself, Double awkwardly held out his hand to shake. Winky gathered up the boy in her arms and held him tight her to her bosom. "You don't get off that easy, buster," she said, kissing his cheek.

After that day, Double rarely ever shot the rifle and remained indifferent to the gun culture generally. Double gave the Model-52 back to his father for safekeeping and largely forgot about it. Only after Senior died did Double rediscover the gift gun in his father's walk-in cedar closet, as oiled and immaculate as the day it left the custom shop. Senior never neglected a firearm or any mechanical device, and couldn't bear to see others do so.

It was with apprehension then, that Double and Francesca made the rifle a birthday gift to their own son, their only child. Double was reassured however that the boy had proven himself a good shot with an air-rifle: Double always stressed safety whenever they plinked with pellet guns in the basement range at home. Occasionally, Connie would visit his father at the Winston Firearms manufacturing plant and the two of them would shoot .22s at the company firing range.

*   *   *   *   *

Double's private office was a deeply burnished wood-paneled room with vibrant Persian carpets, Frederick Remington bronzes, Charles Russell cowboy oil paintings and full-size taxidermy mounts of an African lion and a Bengal tiger. The room was framed by a brace of 100-pound elephant-ivory tusks as tall as a man. The main offices were on the Winston Firearms campus, a 40-acre harbor-front complex of industrial buildings totaling some 1,500,000 square feet of factory space.

The centerpiece of the campus and long a focal point for the city of Bridgewater was the great shot tower, a ten-story red brick structure with vast banks of frosted windows that filled an entire city block and was capped by a flagpole flying an oversized Stars and Stripes. Molten lead was poured through copper sieves at the very top of the building, which was then dropped into cooling vats of water at the bottom. The act of liquid metal freefalling 250 feet chilled it, forming solid spherical balls which could be varied in size depending on the graduated sieves used. The building was an orienting landmark for the citizens of Bridgewater, who often established their bearings relative to the Winston shot tower.

Double's workplace was in the executive office building, a light-filled beaux-arts-style structure designed by the architectural firm of Warren and Wetmore, one of the two parties that built New York's Grand Central Terminal. Winston Firearms' founder, Marion Davis Winston, designed the private office himself, with a working fireplace and a private bathroom with shower, as well as a pocket bedchamber built right into the side of the building as an oriel window overlooking the factory complex. Heavy burgundy velvet curtains could be drawn to cover over the stained-glass window, as well as to close off the bed from the rest of the office. Senior regularly took his after-lunch nap there to stay fit for the afternoon, and during the war he often stayed in it overnight.

The five-story limestone building had an immense glass atrium covering the center stairwell that was trimmed in brilliantly colored stained glass by Louis Comfort Tiffany. These executive offices were located directly across the street from the newest of the Winston Firearms plant buildings. Senior fitted a pedestrian footbridge, an enclosed suspended catwalk of steel grating that led from his office over the street and directly into the plant building. With this modification, Senior could literally pop his head into his largest and most modern plant in less than two minutes.

It was from the landing of this catwalk at noon on August 15, 1945, that Senior addressed the entire workforce of Winston Firearms over the company public address system regarding the unconditional surrender of the Japanese and the end of WWII, which had been announced the prior evening. Double, who was only five at the time, was present: It was a historic occasion and his mother wanted him to hear the speech.

What Double remembered most about the day was the stifling heat and that his father wore a sky-blue-striped seersucker suit with a straw boater. The sudden silence which overwhelmed the enormous plant was haunting. Every machine was turned off, some for the first time in years, and Double remembered how the slight audio delay over the primitive speakers seemed to project his father's words, echolike, as if he were speaking in some great cathedral.

It was a strange feeling to have so many people hanging on his father's every word, and it left a big impression on Double. There were more than 5,000 employees working that factory shift alone. They stood scattered among the great machines that pinged and popped as they cooled after their prolonged service—industrial presses and routers, milling machines and duplicators, long slack canvas belts attached to cast-iron wheels driven by steam that powered the entire plant: a big, complicated production line of armaments—the very arsenal of democracy of which our leaders often spoke.

Senior talked briefly, but his words were poignant. He spoke of the future, not just of the world and the United States of America, but of his company, his employees—the city of Bridgewater and all its citizens. He conceded that many war workers would choose not to continue their employment or would be outright pink-slipped now that the critical need for defense work was over. He asked them to stop and take stock of themselves: to look each other in the eye and shake hands in victory, but much more importantly, in peace—just as they would in church.

Winston had turned out millions of small arms ranging from their own Model-12 trench shotgun to the (built under license) British .303 Lee-Enfield rifle and Vickers water-cooled machine gun, the Russian Mosin-Nagant M91/30, the Colt .45 1911 and the BAR Browning automatic rifle. In addition, there were two extra production lines, one dedicated to building a special Browning .50 caliber machine gun used exclusively in fighter aircraft and the other for manufacturing the 105-mm Howitzer mobile artillery cannon. The custom shop dedicated its entire production to turning out highly accurate Springfield 1903 sniper rifles on old reclaimed tooling left over from WWI. They also re-barreled and refurbished large numbers of pre-existing surplus Springfield rifles.

The company and the entire country had risen to meet a daunting existential challenge: a war of outright survival—win or perish. They had toiled and persevered through hard times and bleak moments, working round-the-clock shifts, living with the daily nuisance of endless rationing of seemingly every consumer staple from sugar and coffee to meat and butter, from rubber tires and gasoline to nylon stockings and even shoes. They had grown the victory gardens, raised the chickens and rabbits, fished and hunted the wild game to round out the larder and always they conserved and reused things, repaired them or set them aside for spare parts.

All throughout the great undertaking was the omnipresent suggestion box hanging on the factory wall, into which any war worker could unleash his or her creative initiative and brainpower. Anything and everything was open for consideration, from an improvement for carpooling to production shortcuts that could be widely disseminated throughout the rest of war production. Winston employees substantially improved both the production quality and reduced the manufacturing time on everything they made. Winston's war workers not only worked harder, they worked smarter.

They had overcome adversity by creatively adapting. The values learned in the Depression and reinforced by war were Christian-American values. A person was never really poor if he had skill in his hands, thrift in his conscience and the love for his fellow man in his heart. Each Winston employee standing on the plant floor at that moment possessed those virtues and would carry them to the grave.

They embodied all that was great and virtuous about a free society, Senior said, and they, right along with the soldier in the field, represented the very best America had to offer.

"Look each other in the eye, and shake hands as friends and neighbors," he implored. "As you are the finest people I ever expect to know: The most resourceful, the most conscientious, the most industrious."

Many of his workers had been separated from family members throughout the war years and some had lost loved ones—offspring, siblings, spouses. The war was over, and now that the Allies had fought and bled and died to ensure the peace, it was the job of every American to build a society worthy of that peace.

Although production would continue unabated for the

short term, this was a moment to celebrate and give thanks for deliverance. To facilitate this, cash money would be handed out by supervisors at the close of each shift on Friday: $5 for every worker, an additional $2 for every child dependent, and $3.50 for every adult dependent. Everyone got the same, executive and line-worker alike.

Senior closed by saying that no matter where life took them, each employee should always remember that they were once a part of a great enterprise that saved the world from itself—that toppled the despotic, freed the downtrodden and allowed the natural law of man to once again flourish. They needn't ever again question their own motives, integrity or moral certitude. The balance of accounts was correct—their freedom had been paid for in full. "Go home. Kiss the children, cook a chicken and hoist a beer on Winston Firearms. You earned it," he told them.

With that, Senior turned from the crowd and took the handkerchief he'd been using to mop the sweat from his brow to dab his eyes. As he did so, one of the shop stewards cried out, "Three cheers for Mr. Winston!" And 5,000 or so employees, fully half of them women, sang out "Hip-hip-hurray!" three times in masculine/feminine harmony.

In time, elderly strangers, former Winston Firearms employees, once they realized he was Senior's son, would often recount the story of that speech to Double. To a person, nearly all of them said it was an unforgettable moment in their lives—like the birth of a child or death of a parent. Most of them got choked up just recounting it.

* * * * *

Now Senior's office had become Double's and, with the exception of trading up to a new desk chair and modern lamp, the décor of the room remained unchanged from his father's tenure. Double also inherited his secretary, Mrs. Beeberstein, a thirty-year employee and former schoolmarm who knew the entire history of the company. She was a war widow and frustrated thespian who lived for the theater, taking roles in two or three different amateur productions a year. When she wasn't spending her weekends on stage as an actress, she would take the train down to the city and catch a theatrical matinee, very often a show containing a particular role that she had her eye on. Mrs. Beeberstein was a shameless mimic—if she saw a performance she could crib, an audience was likely to see a striking facsimile of the original reappear at an amateur county playhouse within a year. She would scribble detailed shorthand notes in the darkened halls, and she had boldly stolen from the best—some said her Jessica Tandy as Blanche Dubois in *Streetcar* was as good as the original, and at a fraction of the price.

She co-owned, along with her sister, a mint-green aluminum-sided two-family home in Blackstone, a suburb bordering Bridgewater. In the war, her husband had been in a construction battalion in the South Pacific building aircraft runways. There were still ongoing skirmishes taking place with the Japanese, and he was felled with a head-shot as he rode on his bulldozer—death was immediate. She used her husband's life insurance benefit as a down payment on the house and never remarried.

Mrs. Beeberstein—it was always Mrs. Beeberstein and never Gilda—was a literate, educated woman who spoke in a clipped, professional tone but also with efficient economical diction. She used four words where others might use ten, but they were always precisely the right four words. Her secretarial skills were beyond reproach—she could take shorthand faster than you could think and she had a phone presence that was simultaneously authoritative and welcoming—no one ever dreamed of phoning up Senior's office with gum in their mouth. Her penmanship was so ornate and appealing that employees often showed off a quick note she'd jotted as if it were some sort of art form to be admired. Had she been born fifty years later, Mrs. Beeberstein might easily have become a top executive in her own right, but as a prisoner of her era, she had to settle on being Senior's right-hand and confidante, the person who best knew his personal agenda and business priorities. She was also the only woman whom Senior ever deferred to on occasion in business.

Mrs. Beeberstein acted as a kind of surrogate parent and corporate wet nurse to Double, patiently explaining the blatantly obvious to him in the way that a nanny might try to instruct a child. She was tasked with breaking him in, fulfilling a promise she made to Senior. She had a couple of years left to go before retirement, and now regarded as her first duty preventing Double Winston from self-destructing long enough to actually learn the business—a fifty-fifty proposition at best, she posited.

III

Another holdover from Senior's era was Winston Firearms' general counsel, Nathan Clarke. In addition to generally overseeing the legal department and providing an overarching set of broad principles and parameters for the company to operate within, Nathan also managed all the product liability litigation, hired the outside trial lawyers and directly intervened in all settlement negotiations. He was born a Boston Brahmin—a Harvard-educated lawyer whose second love was the sea in general and the *Halcyon*, his 39-foot Concordia Yawl, in particular.

Halcyon was a two-masted wooden sailboat with classic, elegant lines. Every man knows that beauty, whether applied to a woman or a sailboat, is all about proportionality: What is relevant is neither the errant exquisite mark nor the flaw of imperfection, but rather the way the entire package of qualities comes together. If a marine architect has ability and aesthetic taste along with a sense of balance and proportion, the result can be as viscerally impactful as a quick look at a woman on the platform through the windows of a moving subway car. In that fleeting glance you can tell that she's beautiful without ever really seeing what she looks like.

The Concordia's lines are heralded as one of the single most graceful designs ever created, and Nathan Clarke plied the waters of the Sound and the Cape in his white-hulled *Halcyon*, more often alone than not. Nathan was an old bachelor. His one-and-only marriage at the age of fifty had ended in a humiliating divorce in less than a year.

He was tall and thin, and wore his hair slicked back with a close-trimmed brush of a moustache. He wore owl-eyed glasses with tortoise-shell frames, and was partial to his father's gold pocket watch, an antique, 21-jewel, 14-carat Elgin with a clamshell double-hunter case decorated in heavy engine turnings with a matching gold chain. Whenever he faced a particularly vexing problem, Nathan made elaborate ceremony of removing this gilded instrument, opening its face to check its accuracy against another clock in the room and then winding its watch stem. Most often when he snapped closed the watchcase he had the makings of a solution ready on his tongue. A Phi Beta Kappa key adorned the watch chain, but he rarely wore vests, preferring instead the boxier cut of a double-breasted suit. Most often, the watch resided in his jacket handkerchief pocket tethered by its chain to his lapel buttonhole.

He wore bow ties exclusively and the same brown crushed fedora, regardless of the color of the suit or overcoat. In summer he switched to a straw Panama hat which he'd picked up in Cuba. He smoked a black walnut pipe, its partially burned loose flakes of unflavored Virginia Burley tobacco mingling nicely with his Bay Rum aftershave lotion, provided him with a distinctively pleasant aromatic signature whenever he walked past.

* * * * *

ℕathan's father had suddenly died of a coronary in the midst of the stock market crash of 1929 when Nathan was in the sixth grade. His father had been a compulsive Wall Street speculator and perennial bear. So sure was he of impending economic doom, he frittered away most of his fortune by sitting out the Roaring Twenties—obstinately fighting the tape of a raging bull market in short positions and treasury bills. He fully expected to be momentarily forced to confess to his wife the secret of their dire financial predicament.

He had spun a spider's web of explanations to his wife regarding the sale of his own father's inherited stock exchange seat as simply taking a profit on an already overripe investment. Besides, an office with a ticker-tape machine was less expensive and imminently more practical, more easily allowing him to expertly track any number of financial issues. Then he justified closing his business office as yet another cost-saving measure: He could just as easily follow the markets in the clubby environs of his broker's office anteroom or in the gallery of the stock exchange itself for free.

It was a godsend—manna from heaven—when the markets initiated their relentless selloff on Black Monday, October 28, 1929. Nathan's father had bet big against the market and sold short U.S. Steel, General Electric, RCA, Atlantic Telephone & Telegraph, Ford Motor, and Goodyear Tire and Rubber. The precipitous decline in the Dow Jones Industrial Average meant that not only was Nathan's father back in the chips, he was once again legitimately wealthy. The staged false-façade of effortless success and luxury was instantly real again to the touch.

With the markets in total free fall, the loans taken long ago were now about to magically evaporate back into the ether. Pawn shop tickets would be redeemed in full. The back rent on the Park Avenue apartment would be made current—the lone remaining servant, his gentlemen's club and Nathan's private school would all continue. As other investors panicked because the sky was falling, Nathan's father joined the phalanx of panicked shareholders thronging Wall Street, blocking traffic and assembling at the front steps of the New York Stock Exchange.

While this sea of the financially distraught gasped in their tortured ruination as snippets of the devastation trickled forth by word of mouth, Nathan's father became so elated in his sudden relief that, overwhelmed with emotion, he finally took to his knees in the slick pungent mire of the filthy sidewalk, strewn with scrap paper, cigar butts, discarded plugs of tobacco and even vomit, to thank

God Almighty for his mortal deliverance. His pipe stem shattered when he hit the pavement, face first, after his heart stopped cold.

After his father died, Nathan became the central focus of his mother's life, and they became inseparable. She grew intense and moody, overdramatic and melancholy—even hysterical at times. Nathan grew up in a hurry. There were prolonged periods when his mother was an inpatient at a series of sanitariums. Crude, first-generation antidepressants, along with Freudian analysis, provided only temporary relief, but the bipolar whipsaw always resumed. It was only after he returned from the war that advances in electroshock therapy began to widely disseminate out of Europe and long-term relief was finally procured for his mother.

IV

Electroshock therapy was propelled into the public conscience by the release of the bestseller *On the Children's Ward*, the memoirs of an anonymous Nazi neuropsychologist writing under the pen name of Hippocrates Misanthrope. A protégé of German electroshock pioneer Dr. Friedrich Meggendorfer, the author had followed his esteemed mentor from a prewar position in Hamburg to his wartime post in the Psychiatric Department at Erlangen-Nuremberg in Bavaria. There, under the direct authority of Doctors Karl Brandt and Viktor Brack—top leaders of the medical command of the entire Third Reich as well as the architects of the Action T4 euthanasia program—the pediatric electroshock trials commenced. With an initial pool of sixteen sets of triplet and identical twin children, many of the medical subjects had no history of mental health disorders.

Extensive clinical trials were conducted on the effects of electroshock therapy on these triplets—abnormal German children slated for euthanasia, as well as Jewish, Gypsy, Polish and other so-called social undesirables. A premium was placed on the value of triplets, as they provided a unique opportunity to compare electroshock therapy against drug therapy against a nearly identical untreated control subject. When the study was complete, the children were summarily euthanized, usually with injections of phenol or chloroform directly into the heart. Their brain tissues were then studied in postmortem comparisons.

Hippocrates Misanthrope canvassed the administrations of the largest Nazi extermination camps with form letters giving a layman's explanation of the study's objectives and a formal request for subjects. He received efficient, timely responses from all, including one from the Auschwitz death camp in Poland signed by the Angel of Death himself, the notorious eugenist Dr. Joseph Mengele. Mengele, chief medical officer of Auschwitz, expressed his enthusiasm and encouragement for the clinical trials which so closely mirrored his own medical trials on identical twins.

Mengele selectively culled the prisoners personally upon their initial arrival at the camp, deciding who would die immediately as opposed to who would be put to work as slave labor for another three or four months before being executed. Mengele made use of twins and triplets in his own trials, but promised he would henceforth interview prospective subjects to determine if they might be more suitable for the electroshock trials. Mengele was making large-scale scientific studies of *heterochromia iridum*— cases of subjects who had eyes of different colors, dwarfism and a range of other hereditary deformities. Psychological disorders, however, were not in his purview.

The Third Reich, under their sinister T4 Action euthanasia program, sought to entirely eradicate the psychologically infirm in an attempt to prevent them from consuming valuable state resources and reproducing impaired offspring. The chronic and incurable, the spastic and mentally retarded, the senile and epileptics were all sanctioned by the state for elimination. Many of these unfortunate souls were non-Jewish German citizens who were indiscriminately euthanized, their death certificates falsified to reflect a myriad of plausible natural causes of death.

The request for twins and triplets was easy to fill. The extermination camps were killing thousands of people each day, and it was simply a matter of spreading the word. Twins and triplets invariably remained inseparable right up to the end of life, so SS underlings were put on the lookout as the mortally condemned filed past. The Jewish internal camp *kapos* were happy to comply, in the hopes that producing suitable subjects might result in a reward—cigarettes or perhaps some of the brandy and food these unfortunates so often brought into the camps with them inside their luggage. Mengele took a genuine interest, as one scientific colleague to another, in any promising new research project, and hoped to continue to receive regular updates on the progress of the electroshock study.

On the Children's Ward was equal parts layman's scientific text and moral confession, and it kicked off one of the great cocktail party ethics debates of the 1950s. The pertinent questions discussed were: Are the murders of some 1,500,000 innocent children in any way morally offset by the positive advances derived from medical research related to those deaths? Was the science gained worth the sacrifice?

If the evil act was certain to be committed anyway and the only question was by whom, wasn't it the duty of all eminent scientists to avail themselves as willing participants on the grounds that if they didn't volunteer, some less capable clinician who couldn't make nearly as much of the unique opportunity would be assigned the task? Does science at the expense of one man justify science that benefits all mankind?

If the world was taking leave of its senses, albeit temporarily, and the rules of civilized society were momentarily suspended, then mustn't the enlightened scientist conclude that it was best to make hay while the sun shines and resolve to do it better than anyone else? Can peacetime ethics be applied to the irrational environment of war?

The book and its ethical quandaries made their way into the popular zeitgeist, and for decades represented the single best explanation for how a sophisticated society at the very pinnacle of high culture could degenerate to such a point where the murder of innocent children was justified under the guise of scientific research.

For the first time in the short history of electroshock therapy, its outer limits were fully explored. Before the war, psychologists had worked entirely at the low end of the therapeutic scale, discovering how little voltage over a short duration was required to produce a convulsion. No one had ever probed the upper limits of what the human brain could tolerate before the subject died or became permanently impaired. And no one had ever explored the effect these treatments had on recall and their potential to generate retrograde amnesia, to wipe clean entire swaths of memory. These trials nearly perfected the process for erasing short-term memory—events taking place in the 48-hour window prior to treatment could reliably be voided from a subject's recall.

This was only one of the areas examined in the triplets study.

What was intellectually inconsistent about the study in general, but the epileptic trials in particular, was that one of the core objectives of the T4 Action euthanasia program was to exterminate all of the mentally impaired in order to eliminate their drain on government resources. The attempt to gain a better understanding of these medical conditions and to engage in experiments with potential cures was a contradiction in terms. Many have since suggested that this approach was germinated by the mental health care industry itself in order to justify its own existence: If T4 Action euthanized every psychologically infirm person, there would no longer be any call for psychological therapies.

The outcome of this research provided some promising leads. Electroshock proved immediately effective on a wide variety of psychoses, and the remissions generally lasted six months. The positive findings were tainted, however: The stigmatized results chronicled in the book were based on a flawed scientific method that was applied sporadically and in a needlessly sadistic manner.

V

nathan Clarke lived with his mother throughout college and law school. It was only his service in the navy during the war that finally interrupted this oedipal nightmare, but his mother even tried to derail that. A woman of significant social standing and influence, she pulled strings and managed to gain him a complete deferment on the grounds that he had a dependent—namely her. Then, when he volunteered for duty, she saw to it that he was posted to the Governor's Island Naval Base in New York Harbor as a lawyer to the Judge Advocate General—one of the plummest assignments in the entire fleet. Shore duty at Governor's Island meant a man didn't have to feel awkward about being out of uniform. He could feel gratified that he was doing his part for the war effort without actually risking life or limb, all the while enjoying the Big Apple in his off-duty hours. It was a posting millionaires would have given their fortunes for, so it was an added humiliation to his mother when, after less than a year of desk duty, Nathan threw it all away by applying for sea duty and a transfer directly into the shooting war.

He spent the remainder of the conflict as executive officer on board a destroyer escort and saw duty in the North Atlantic shepherding Liberty ship convoys and their cargos of war materiel to the European theater. Eventually his ship became part of the D-day Normandy invasion armada. After this Nathan was redeployed to the Philippines, and was awaiting his first command in anticipation of the invasion of Japan when the war finally ended.

With V-J Day, Nathan, along with every other citizen soldier, expected to return stateside and be discharged back into civilian life. He was somewhat less than enthusiastic at the prospect of returning to his mother, however, and found himself intentionally lingering overseas, first in the Philippines and then later in England, looking at the various options for remaining in the service abroad. His timing was fortuitous.

Nathan recognized his legal education was incomplete. He had been awarded his Juris Doctor degree in the spring of 1942, just as the war was getting started. More importantly, many elite Ivy League law graduates clerk for a Federal judge or, if they're really exceptional, for a Supreme Court justice as a professional rite of passage. Because of the war, Nathan had done neither.

The liberation of the concentration camps was well documented on film, and the entire world was witness to the vicious brutality of the Holocaust. The outcry for justice was universal, and it soon became clear that the Allied powers would conduct war crimes tribunals prosecuting the Axis leadership for depraved criminal acts committed on an industrial scale far beyond the demands of orthodox warfare. This would be a first in the history of civilization: The Leipzig War Crimes Trials after the First World War were limited in scope and quickly forgotten.

The initial Nuremberg Trial of top Nazi leadership would come to be known as "the greatest trial in history." No one had ever proposed that all humanity held a moral authority over the leaders of an individual nation-state and that this authority could actually be exercised in a court of law. As an attorney, Nathan imagined it to be the chance of a lifetime, not only making up for his lack of a clerkship but permanently cementing his criminal-law credentials. He felt compelled to pursue this unique opportunity and sacrifice that little bit more of his civilian life in hopes of playing a part in finding justice for some six million lost souls, the only evidence of their ever having existed being a thin layer of ash covering the topsoil in select parts of Western Europe.

* * * * *

Nathan arrived in Nuremberg at the end of March, 1946, holding the rank and drawing the pay of a lieutenant commander. In immediate postwar Germany, this amounted to a king's ransom. His security clearance was reinstated, and he was ordered to attend the initial trial of Nazi leadership conducted by the four Allied powers: America, Britain, France and Russia.

Some two dozen defendants—military officers, politicians, a publisher, an economist, a journalist and a banker—were put on trial for their personal involvement in the war. The sole industrialist, Alfried Krupp von Bohlen, was charged but later released on a technicality. (Krupp eventually became uncle to

Francesca Berger—Double Winston's wife and Connie's mother.) Legal precedent was being set every day of this initial trial, and it was obvious that more trials were in the offing. Nathan Clarke would play as a minor figure in one of them.

Nuremberg was a bombed-out shell, and Nathan was billeted at the only hotel left standing in the city center. The Grand Hotel was formerly one of the great hotels of Europe and had only recently played host to Adolf Hitler and his top lieutenants during the Nuremberg rallies. Air raid bombs had cut the hotel in half, but the U.S. army spent a million dollars to repair the damage and make it habitable for U.S. personnel. The Grand Hotel was the center of American life during the trials: It had the only properly stocked restaurant in the entire city, the only full-service bar and the best band, with ballroom dancing every night. Nathan lived in a small suite of rooms with its own bath. Tap water was unsafe to drink, and chlorine tablets accompanied every meal. Electricity was intermittent, and there was no central heat. Overcoats were worn both in and out of doors, eight months out of the year. Nathan slept on a featherbed with down duvets in wintertime and took a cold shower twice a week.

The German people lived amongst the rubble, most often in the basement foundations of their former homes. The smell of rotting human flesh emanated from that same rubble. Crews would begin work on a new pile that used to be a building and would invariably unearth entombed remains or otherwise expose corpses to the air, which would then create a new stench of rot. This was prevalent all over the city, and everyone learned to live with it. Water came to the Germans in a bucket when it came at all and the concept of bathing the entire human body all at once was but a distant memory.

Nathan had access to food, coffee, sugar and cigarettes, and could buy hard liquor at the Post Exchange. These staples were unavailable to German citizens, and American personnel were forbidden from eating in local restaurants. The Germans couldn't feed themselves, let alone an occupying force and besides, the established agricultural practice of the time was to fertilize produce with human feces, which promoted parasites and amebic dysentery.

So desperate were the German locals that a job at the Grand Hotel became a prized post. It was worthy of a generous bribe in order to secure a position, for it meant access to waste—table scraps of meat and fat, bruised fruit and vegetables, potato peels, stale bread and half-eaten sweets. Curdled milk and cream could be made into a mild farmhouse cheese. Tea and coffee could be reused, their grinds re-steeped. Old newsprint could be used for just about anything—especially toilet paper. Nothing went to waste, and with a little ingenuity, a hotel job could sustain an entire family. Such scavenging in modern peacetime is unthinkable, but in Nuremberg in 1946 it meant all the difference. Unfiltered cigarette butts so nonchalantly left smoldering in hotel ashtrays had great value— unburned tobacco from two or three of these could be rolled into a thin pin of a new cigarette that could then either be smoked or sold. Americans also occasionally threw away alcohol—sometimes as much as a half-bottle of wine.

The occupiers traded on the black market for antiques and curios—fine art and jewelry. Things which held great value in America and had also once been cherished in Europe before the war were now commodities the Germans no longer valued: You can't eat a diamond broach or drink a painting. You can, however, convert them on the black market into life-sustaining nourishment and a bit of warmth and comfort for your family. Food and coffee, sugar and cigarettes and any form alcoholic spirits are the things that have real value to the vanquished. The previously haughty war profiteer will sell his soul for a little warmth and comfort. The pretty girl who wouldn't even speak to you before the hostilities will let you have your way with her all night for a few basic necessities from the PX.

United States Supreme Court Justice and former U.S. Attorney General Robert Jackson was the lead prosecutor for the initial Nuremberg Trial of top Nazi leadership. He had a master list of armed services members with law degrees and was extending the enlistments of a select few deemed worthy of such an awesome legal undertaking. When Nathan, with his Harvard-law pedigree, volunteered his name to the pool of applicants, the Division of Judge Advocate General cut orders attaching him as aide to Florida State Supreme Court Associate Justice Harold "Tom" Sebring. Judge Sebring was one of four American judges hearing the "Doctors Trial," and had been personally appointed to the tribunals by President Truman.

The case was *The United States of America v. Karl Brandt et al.* The top brass of the Nazi medical corps were adjudicated for crimes against humanity. The charges ranged from the outright genocide associated with Brandt's eugenics and the T4 Action euthanasia program, to atrocities committed against concentration camp prisoners in the course of conducting medical experiments on them in clinical trials.

These medical trials included infecting inmates with malaria, hepatitis and typhus; exposing prisoners to mustard gas; introducing lethal doses of poison into their food; and shooting them with poison bullets. Incendiary bomb experiments were conducted on inmates by applying burning phosphorus directly to the skin to then determine the most effective burn ointments.

Infections of the bone and muscle tissue were created by injecting patients with active pus and then treating it with an experimental sultanilamide drug—the fever associated with fighting infection often killed the subject before the actual infection did. Techniques for bone grafts were refined using healthy prisoners. Limb transplants were repeatedly attempted, and proved futile. Unnecessary amputations were also regularly performed, not only to advance surgical technique but to test the effectiveness of polygala, a blood coagulant.

The limits of human endurance were tested, and the potential survivability of airmen explored with a frozen pressure chamber that simulated 70,000 feet of altitude. Because airmen also bailed out over open water, tests were conducted with subjects being immersed in nearly freezing water for hours at a time. Many died, but some were brought to the very brink of death to then be revived. The objective was to determine the most successful techniques for dealing with hypothermia. Trials were also conducted with prisoners drinking sea water, both untreated and desalinized, over a period of days.

Phenol is a powerful poison with corrosive characteristics and closely related to carbolic acid, which is used as an antiseptic. Phenol was used to treat gangrene infections that were intentionally created to mimic battlefield conditions by cutting into healthy tissue and implanting staphylococci and streptococci cultures mixed with wood shavings. Phenol injections to the heart were also the preferred method of execution for these prisoners when the clinical trials ended and the postmortem examinations needed to begin.

Subjects used for these experiments started with what Brandt termed the "lives unworthy of life," or "useless eaters." Initially, these were Germans who were visibly diseased—the mentally retarded, simpleminded, senile, epileptic, emotionally unstable, blind and physically deformed, as well as social undesirables—alcoholics, drug addicts, homosexuals and criminals. As time passed, Jews, Gypsies, Slavs and, ultimately, captured Poles and Russians joined the ranks of those destined to undergo medical experimentation. Inmates were often promised preferential treatment and more food if they volunteered. Some were even promised a life-granting reprieve, but this particular promise was never kept, as no inmate ever survived more than four or five rounds of clinical trials before succumbing.

VI

never before had a defeated power been so harshly judged— their values, their morality, their very humanity questioned. Subsequently, many so-called refined, erudite human beings were judged and found utterly lacking. The war crimes of the Third Reich set a new standard for depravity and for those who lived through the period, it's hard to believe that any modern government could engineer and condone the wholesale murder of some six million people whose only crime was being of the wrong religious ethnicity, sexual persuasion or having a deformity. There were also the brave few who refused to remain silent in the face of genocide.

The Nuremberg doctors trial was an entirely American court proceeding—the other three Allied powers already had a full schedule of their own tribunals. Many doctors and health care workers were implicated, but few were prosecuted. Of the twenty defendants tried, nineteen were men and all except three were full-fledged doctors.

Nathan quickly made himself indispensable to Judge Sebring. Because he had witnessed the initial trial of Nazi leadership, he was well versed in the legal precedents set by that tribunal, and could quickly locate and condense these source materials. Sebring's chambers were in the grandiose Palace of Justice, and Nathan worked from a small annex there.

There was also a girl in Nuremberg—Astrid, a bombshell widow and unapologetic former Nazi, was the mother of two. Her dead husband had been an illustrious U-boat captain who had received the Knight's Cross of the Iron Cross with oak leaves, diamonds and swords—Germany's equivalent to the medal of honor for officers. Nathan begged her to marry him and move to the United States. He was in love for the first time in his life, and she dared to share this impossible dream right up until Nathan's train pulled out of the Hauptbahnhof without her.

Astrid remained on the platform wearing a stoic smile, resolutely perched upon her cardboard suitcase as her young son and daughter shared a bottle of Coke, each slurping away at their own individual straws. She was the human face of German defeat, broken but unbowed—a destitute but nonetheless arrogant beauty right to the end. She waved goodbye—four fingers bent at the knuckles. It was the farewell a mother gives her broken-hearted little boy who's off to summer camp. Her body language said it all.

Their love was stillborn. The romance was particular to a time and place and couldn't survive a change of scenery. She would remain in Germany to rebuild her life and homeland—a green shoot sprouting from the ashes of total war. She had made her bed with her larger-than-life husband all those years before and would continue to sleep in it now that he was gone.

VII

Upon returning stateside, Nathan took a job as an attorney for Packard Motors. War work had rewarded Packard handsomely, though it had been nearly impossible for even the worst-run companies not to thrive in such a demand-driven economy. In addition to creating and producing the Packard Liberty Marine engine—three of them were found in every single navy PT boat—Packard also produced over 55,500 supercharged V-12 Merlin aircraft engines, which powered the North American P-51 Mustang fighter for the Air Force, under license from Rolls Royce. A lot of new technology came out of the war, and the auto companies were eager to incorporate these advances into their new postwar designs. The problem was that many of the cutting-edge developments had been created in an environment of public governmental and private initiative joint-ventures, and determining just who held the rights to what technologies was a legal quagmire as intricate and time-consuming as untangling a barrel of string.

Historically, Packard was a manufacturer of low-volume, exclusive luxury automobiles, but it just wasn't the same car company after the war. Much of this was due to a lack of vision on the part of its management, who were blind to the urgency of introducing entirely new postwar models into the marketplace. Indeed, the first five years' worth of Packard's postwar production was rewarmed prewar derivatives with cosmetic makeovers. Packard was also a full five years behind Cadillac in introducing a

V-8 power plant.

Packard executives were astute enough to recognize the ongoing value of their war work, namely that the P-51 Mustang remained in widespread service. While it is true that jet propulsion quickly superseded propeller-driven aircraft, the Mustang was the most advanced piston-driven fighter ever developed, and it soldiered on as a frontline flying workhorse for the U.S. Air Force through the Korean War. Surplus Mustangs were also widely exported the rest of the world's burgeoning air forces.

The Merlin was the best aero engine to come out of the war, and it was widely anticipated that a detuned version would make its way into civil aviation. By the end of WWII, a P-51 Mustang cost $51,000, and the Merlin engine fully accounted for $40,000 of that price. Packard desperately wanted to continue to turn a profit on those revenues.

It was also equally anticipated that the Packard Liberty Marine engine would become the preeminent power plant in recreational yachting for decades to come. Income from both these products could act as a financial buffer—a kind of streaming annuity—giving Packard financial breathing room and time to fully develop their new line of passenger cars.

Nathan lead a delegation to London for face-to-face negotiations with Rolls Royce to extend their wartime license, but the keepers of the Flying Lady would have none of it. If anyone was going to produce an expensive lump for commercial aviation and the world's air forces, it was going to be the Brits themselves. If Packard wanted to produce the Merlin, Rolls Royce insisted on profit-sharing as equal partners. They also demanded to be awarded exclusive manufacturing rights to the Packard Liberty Marine engine for all of Europe, without a penny going to Detroit. Nathan's plans were dashed.

* * * * *

The Packard job had required relocating, and Mother never did gain a social foothold in Detroit. She whined endlessly about how they should have moved to Grosse Point instead of the city proper, and she never missed an opportunity to compare the Midwest unfavorably to life back in the County. Professionally defeated and personally exasperated, Nathan finally accepted a job at Pan American Airways overseeing their steady stream of accident-related litigation.

Air travel in those days continued to be outright dangerous. Many commercial aircraft were well-worn military surplus and quite unreliable. Any young lawyer doing even a short stint representing the airlines quickly learned his way around a courtroom, and Nathan even acted as the second chair co-counsel on several trials. Finally, he grew tired of legally defending mortal tragedy. Each case was essentially the same: Something happened—either a part of the plane broke or someone made a mistake—and he was tasked with negotiating the price tag on a planeload of dead people.

It was fate that placed Nathan at the same table as Senior at an outdoor afternoon wedding at the Little Kill Country Club one August day. Thankfully, Nathan had already spent enough time in the presence of another great man—the visionary founder and chief executive of Pan American Airways, Juan Trippe—so as not to be intimidated. The two spoke casually about the war and the North Atlantic convoys, the Nuremberg trials and product patents and liability, Nikita Khrushchev and the iron curtain. They discussed the opportunities of so much cheap military surplus floating around, and both noted the concentrated uptick in birthrates from returning soldiers. Fortunes would be made by catering to this swelling demographic that had yet to be labeled the "baby boom" generation.

It was the kind of casual conversation that Senior rarely ever experienced anymore but treasured all the same. Someone was sharing their take on the world and expected absolutely nothing from him in return. The eloquent young lawyer was fluent in a wide range of fields and was both unassuming and unpretentious.

He was straightforward and direct and seemed a man of principled integrity. Senior wanted executives like that working for him— men of high character and strong conviction, willing to share their unvarnished opinions and then tactfully defend their positions. Then Senior did something he never had done before: Right in the front foyer of the Little Kill Country Club, he dug a business card out of his wallet and handed it to Nathan.

"I've enjoyed our time together, young man. All I'm good for is shop talk, and in sheltering me from all those swells, you saved me from a fate worse than death."

Nathan shook hands warmly with the industrialist. "I've enjoyed it too, sir. I hope we'll have the chance to do it again sometime."

"I'd like you to come around and see me next week . . . about a job."

Nathan was taken aback by the abrupt advance, and momentarily struggled to gather his wits. "I'm flattered, Mr. Winston, I truly am, but I've already got the job I want with Mr. Trippe. He hired me personally"

"Juan's a good man—shrunk the globe singlehanded," Senior said, with a glimmer of admiration, but then caught himself. "But don't you go quoting me back to him; Trippe and I have battled more than once for the same chair at the head of the table. It's almost like we're gasping for the same breath of air. Juan Trippe *is* a great man and a great American—but Pan Am is empire and as long as he remains its Caesar, you'll never be more than a centurion. I ascribe to more of a round-table approach. My only objective is success; I don't care where the ideas come from 'cause I'll get credit for them in the end. With me, you'll never be king, but I can probably fix you up with a duchy on the wrong side of the tracks," he said, with a wink of his eye.

The look on Nathan's face led Senior to believe the lawyer was softening. "Besides," he continued, "unless Trippe's grooming you to run the entire Pan Am legal department, I think you can do better with me." Nathan's jaw fell open—he was flabbergasted.

"You've been schooled in patent law and product liability litigation. A quick study like you oughta be able to figure out the firearms angle."

Nathan remained dumbfounded. "I honestly don't know what to say to you, Mr. Winston."

"Say you'll come down to the plant so I can show you the corner office."

VIII

Only after he took the job in the Winston Firearms legal department did Nathan broach the subject of living separately from his mother. Through a torrent of tears on the heels of hysterical accusations that she was being kicked to the curb, Mother finally agreed to move into a posh penthouse residence apartment in the newest upscale hotel in downtown Bridgewater. It was conveniently located directly across the street from Nathan's spartan one-bedroom apartment. While this finally provided the relationship with some much needed breathing room, Mother did have a way of frequently popping over at inopportune times: More than once she plowed through a crack in the door at the break of dawn, breathless in her neuroses, wearing a dressing gown and slippers and begging a cup of sugar when she suspected he might have an overnight female guest. Everything was provided for in her hotel suite: A call to the front desk would produce a bellboy in under ten minutes whose sole purpose in life was to satisfy her every heart's desire, but Mother always—always—found a reason to pop over. This smothering relationship was much of the reason Nathan didn't marry earlier.

On the recommendation of her psychiatrist, both Nathan and his mother read and then reread *On the Children's Ward*. This was five years after the war ended, and the book had recently become an international bestseller. She had a serendipitous moment of true clarity and finally recognized the direness of her condition, which had only worsened over the years. The intervals of emotional stability were briefer, while the catatonic depressions became more pronounced and prolonged. Finally, she voluntarily underwent a series of electroshock treatments and made a miraculous and seemingly instantaneous recovery that lasted nearly a year. Her next slide into depression was quickly halted and reversed with further treatments. Ongoing therapy proved effective and Nathan's mother seemed cured, though he would later argue that more than a little of the twinkle in her eye and spring in her step went up in smoke with all those electrical jolts.

Nathan didn't shoot much or golf at all, but he was a social sort and was obsessively devoted to his sailing. He joined the Pequod Yacht Club in Southhold, which in addition to providing dock access to his moored sailboat was also engaged in sanctioned competitive dinghy racing against the other yacht clubs on the Sound.

* * * * *

Less than a year after his mother died suddenly from a cerebral hemorrhage, Nathan fell ass-over-teakettle in love with a girl half his age whom he met at the Pequod Yacht Club annual Fourth of July regatta. Brown-haired Kathy with a K and the blue, blue eyes and perfect bite came from an affluent family in the County and was a high-spirited young lady who preferred the company of men. Nathan fell hard and fast—the kind of puppy love he shouldn't have been susceptible to at his age. With his mother recently buried, Nathan seized the initiative and threw caution to the wind. Against his better judgment (and Senior's level-headed suggestion that they quietly shack up together) he married the young lady on a mutually rising tide of heavy emotion and bedroom acrobatics—and immediately regretted his impetuous decision. It was only the second time in his life he was having sex on a regular basis, and he had completely lost his head.

She was simply too young and immature. There was incessant tit-for-tat bickering. She chaffed under the constraints of being married to a respectable, middle-aged lawyer and loathed the staccato tempo with which her married name—Kathy Clarke—rolled off the tongue: It sounded like a candy bar or a stripper. There was also the intellectual disparity—she hadn't even managed to complete finishing school. There was plenty of sex, however, which steadily transitioned through the phases of decadent, daily, dutifully and then finally dearth.

What should have been nothing more than a May-December romance, Nathan naively mistook as true love of the more permanent variety. There was heated acrimony and recrimination, the adolescent rebellion and a trial separation (she moved back with her parents), the infidelity with another young member of the Yacht Club and finally, the inevitable abandonment.

She cavalierly headed south with her young sailor for the winter season in Palm Beach, leaving Nathan with a stack of divorce papers and her lawyer's bill. Heartbroken, Nathan was living proof of the well-worn maxim that there's no fool like an old fool, and this old fool was humiliated—emotionally disemboweled—in the way that only an age-inappropriate pairing all but guarantees.

Annulment allowed everyone to avoid culpability in their mutual *great mistake* and Nathan was entirely released from financial obligation to his formerly betrothed. He was once again a free man, much more cynical if not measurably wiser than he'd been before. He still had his job and his sailboat, and he cautiously stayed away from social events at the Yacht Club for a while to give all those nice people a chance to forget his great public humiliation.

Kathy had the good taste to stay away entirely. There were plenty of other yacht clubs in the County beside Pequod. It was now a simple matter of out-of-sight, out-of-mind as opposed to constantly picking at the scabs of social anxiety and emotional regret. Nathan never could quite forgive himself for his folly, though: He knew better and had simply deluded himself into believing the impossible. He was bitter and lonely—resigned to spend the rest of his life alone.

IX

The Concordia Company still exists for the sole purpose of maintaining the 102-sailboat fleet of its own design. The boatyard can work on just about any kind of wooden craft, but its bread-and-butter is the annual care and feeding of the magnificent—if maintenance intensive—39- and 41-foot-long, two-masted Concordia yawls. Every year, all the exposed mahogany bright-work, which is considerable on these boats, needs to be revarnished. Many boats still have their original hollow wooden masts that also need attention. Then there is the bottom below the waterline, which needs to be sanded and taped, and a fresh coat of anti-fouling paint reapplied annually. This paint impedes marine growth like barnacles and wood-boring worms that go to work on a wood hull just as carpenter ants would on a wood-frame house. These lengthy and expensive procedures are the bare minimum required each year to maintain one of these boats in good fettle.

The Concordia hull is made of African mahogany, steam-bent over oak timbers, the seams of which are then stuffed with cotton wadding and caulked over to create a watertight seam. These planks are attached to the timbers with bronze fasteners and the decks are covered over with canvas fabric applied with a kind of waterproof dope lacquer.

Wood rots. Oak ribs crack. Caulking fails. Doped canvas separates. Fasteners pop in high seas or simply weaken due to corrosion. In order to affect a proper repair, this complicated jigsaw puzzle needs to be disassembled to access the offending part, section-in the appropriate remedy and then reassemble the disparate pieces and make it watertight again.

Wooden shipwright skills were already a dying art by the 1980s. By then virtually all modern boats were being constructed of fiberglass or metal. The only new wood boats being produced were traditional work craft like fishing draggers and lobster boats. Cutting-edge racing sailboats were just beginning to use the new technology of a cold-molded epoxy system of glued wood veneers laid crosswise against each other to create a sandwich of wood composite that was both lightweight and strong.

By the early 1980s there were only two kinds of sailors who remained committed to wood boats: the bottom-feeder, deferred-maintenance cheapskates looking for a bargain, which was easy to come by as they were practically giving these traditional craft away, and the purists, sailors who didn't care what it cost to maintain—those graceful lines combined with organic sailing qualities all stylishly wrapped in maritime heritage made the prospect of Concordia ownership irresistible.

Nathan had no mother, no wife and no dependents. The fact that four years' worth of maintenance on his 39-foot *Halcyon* would have more than paid for a modern fiberglass sailboat was irrelevant: She was his one great indulgence, a luxury he regularly took for himself in a mostly solitary way. For six months each year, he spent his weekends racing dinghies out of the Pequod Yacht Club or cruising singlehanded up and down the coast. *Halcyon* was only the third Concordia Yawl ever launched (in 1946) and one of only four ever actually built in America at the Casey Boatbuilding Co. in Fairhaven, Massachusetts. The other 99 were built by the Abeking and Rasmusen Shipyard in Lernwerder, Germany. Every Easter, Nathan took a long weekend off from work and sailed *Halcyon* down from the Cape after rousting the yawl out of her winter slumber in the storage sheds of the Concordia Company. Every Thanksgiving he repeated the reverse course, sailing her back up on a reach tinged with autumn chill.

X

The first task Nathan undertook when he arrived at Winston Firearms was to review Senior's will and estate planning to come up with a strategy for how the company could pass to the next generation with a minimum tax liability. This was in the mid-1950s and the tax code was punitive: High earners paid a top marginal rate of 92 percent and the inheritance tax on the largest estates was a whopping 77 percent. There really wasn't much Nathan could do.

It wasn't until 1976 that the instrument of the irrevocable, generation-skipping trust became law. Senior already had grandchildren by then so the principal beneficiaries of those trusts became their descendants, Senior's great-grandchildren. This avoided multiple estate taxations and created a pathway for Winston Firearms to pass intact down through the generations. Nathan revised this trust when the law was rewritten in 1986. The only catch was that the company at least technically was no longer in the direct ownership of Senior or Double or even Connie. Winston Firearms, or more specifically the financial instrument that held the company's assets, was the future property of the principal beneficiaries, namely Connie's (and his cousin's) unborn children. Everyone else concerned was entitled to draw income from the asset, but the rights to principal rested entirely with the great-grandchildren. Future decisions regarding investments and income would be decided by two appointed trustees, Senior and Nathan. Nathan would later act as Double's trustee.

* * * * *

Upon Senior's death, Double's sister Marjorie, a divorced mother of two, engaged a new financial advisor who convinced her that a country swimming in military surplus weaponry left over from four large-scale conflicts as well as unpromising late-twentieth-century demographics—baby boomers for some reason didn't seem to enjoy shooting and hunting to the same degree their ancestors had—spelled an uncertain fate for the sporting firearms and ammunition business. This same advisor correctly predicted that the country was on the cusp of boom times in the equities markets and that all Marjorie needed to do to participate was to sell her stake in Winston Firearms and reinvest the proceeds.

The urgency of this prediction created a problem for Double: Winston Firearms was a privately held corporation entirely owned by a holding company controlled by the Winston family trusts. Marjorie couldn't just sell her shares into the public marketplace—there had never been a public offering of equity stock. The only way to pay out Marjorie was to either to take the company public by selling shares onto the open market through an initial public offering or to simply sell her interest—her holding-company shares representing half the total equity of Winston Firearms—to an outside firm.

The Orion Corporation was a global industrial conglomerate with holdings in gas and oil, sugar, chemicals and paints, mining and metal foundries. They also owned a mattress and bedding company, a financial services company, a record label and television studio, a book publisher, a sporting goods manufacturer, a chain of auto parts stores and even a motorcycle manufacturer.

Diversification was the watchword at Orion: The idea was that well-run, noncorrelated businesses could help each other ride out any short-term market turbulence. Orion liked large acquisitions: Before purchasing the Winston Firearms stake, it had considered purchasing a large position in the American Motors Company from French auto giant Renault. Ultimately, Lee Iacocca acquired the block of stock for Chrysler.

Orion was attracted to Winston because although the arms company wasn't nearly as flush as it had once been in its heyday, it still showed consistent profits and remained an industry bellwether. Winston was legendary to those who knew guns and shooting, and this was an opportunity for Orion to acquire a majority stake in one of only two household names still dominant in the industry. Winston also presented Orion with another opportunity to apply its winning business formula: Buy a large bloated company and then cut the fat to the bone.

Double certainly didn't welcome the prospect of partnering with Orion, but short of directly buying Marjorie out himself, a sale to Orion was the only way to satisfy her demands. He decided that in the interest of providing himself a financial anchor to windward, Orion would purchase Marjorie's share as was well as a small stake from Double, bringing the total Orion controlling interest in the company to 51 percent.

In an effort to shield his assets, Nathan Clarke advised Double to make a one-time, nontaxable gift between spouses of half of Double's share of Senior's not insubstantial stock portfolio to Francesca. Nathan was worried that one of any countless pending firearms liability cases might actually work its way up to Double, and he wanted to create a buffer. Once the gift was made, however, it was irrevocable: Excluding the trust assets invested in both Winston Firearms and Orion stock, Francesca Winston now legally owned half Double's personal wealth.

When the merger was complete, Orion celebrated by repurchasing the old Dogham plantation to use for its own corporate entertaining. Double was promised free run of the old place, newly renamed Onori. Little did they realize that quail shooting was the least desirable aspect of the plantation for him.

XI

On his eleventh birthday, Connie was a golden child of sorts. Impulsive, spoiled and occasionally selfish, he played well with others and was instilled early on with a fatalistic sense of having a big future. He could also be unhesitatingly generous, sharing food and giving away toys if he sensed that someone else needed it more than he. In an already affluent town, he knew his family was wealthier than nearly everyone else, and he felt the tug of charity early.

He was a wiry kid—slight but also energetic and athletic. He had a crew cut in summertime because his mother had entirely given up on getting him to pull a comb through his jet-black thicket, and the buzz cut eliminated this problem entirely. He had vibrant brown-amber eyes and a top front tooth slightly misaligned to the others—a casualty of some poolside roughhousing at Little Kill the previous Fourth of July.

Connie was adventurous and loved to climb trees, scale granite boulders and claw his way up stone chimneys, and he was a perpetual pollywog in summer, spending so much time in the water that swimmer's ear seemed a weekly occurrence. He was a happy kid who wore a smirk, born not of cynicism but rather genuine pleasure mixed with a healthy dose of self-confidence. The boy was game for life—be it child's play or a scrap. Connie enjoyed in equal measure flirting with and teasing young girls, in whom he showed an intermittent preoccupation. He was the apple of his father's eye; their relationship representing the chance for Double to grant his son all the time together his own father had denied him. Warmth and attention transcended a generation of separation and created a rapport that touched the four bases of love, mentorship, fun and respect. Conrad's mother was gleeful at how her "men" carried on, enchanted by two assertive males some thirty years removed from each other.

Connie ate oysters on the half shell because his father did. He also drank virgin Bloody Marys with celery, carrot and a hard-boiled egg at the bottom for exactly the same reason. Sunday brunch at Little Kill never varied for the two: freshly shucked Blue Points, Caesar salad—anchovies on the side—and spicy steak tartare finished with the dining room specialty, Grand Marnier soufflé. Connie's mother, who usually arrived dressed in her whites, straight off the royal tennis (or jeu de paume) courtyard, would order the crab or lobster cocktail and a salad with cottage cheese. She would then proceed to tease young Connie, pretending to abscond with one of his mollusks or a peak off his mountain of raw beef. Young Connie would respond with gnashed teeth and a theatrical growl that sounded curiously badgerlike.

Connie kept his pony at the Little Kill stable. Cosmi was a fourteen-hand-two-inch half-hackney-half-thoroughbred gelding that moved with all the grace of a hand-cranked egg beater and had cleared an oxer with the back rail set at four feet.

The pony had been a Christmas present when the boy was ten. Double had ridden bareback for two miles through snowy backyards and driveways from the stables at Little Kill over to Bailiwick. The pony was tied to a tree in the backyard when Connie climbed out of bed on Christmas morning. The moment he spied the animal, wearing a red bow, the boy, still dressed in his pajamas and slippers, slipped out of the house and climbed aboard. He and the pony disappeared onto the area bridle paths for nearly an hour. When he reappeared, frozen to the bone, Connie was beaming a smile as bright as the North Star.

Every boy would love to have a pony of his own, and while Connie didn't take to horses in quite the same compulsive way that Double had, he enjoyed riding and loved that pony, whom they named Cosmi for the obscure Italian maker of high-end semiautomatic shotguns. Father and son often trail-rode together with Double on Westley Richards, and they were even paired together in a costume class over fences at the local winter Gymkhana. Connie dressed as General Custer in union blue with a buckskin fringe jacket, and Double costumed as Chief Sitting Bull, wearing war paint and riding bareback. Westley had seagull feathers braided into his mane and a finger-paint circle surrounding one eye.

XII

All was well with the Winston family on the morning of Connie's eleventh birthday. Double was tan and fit and still quite athletic. He hardly ever drank more than two highballs in a sitting, and was still very much in love with his girlish bride. Francesca at thirty-nine was spellbinding in her feminine charms: Intelligent and refined, she had a wonderful aesthetic taste and was a doting mother to her charismatic son. Connie was the quintessential American kid, pulling at girls' pigtails, scaling the church façade and showing off his latest skinned knee, all in a single morning at Sunday-school class. They were a successful, happy and well-adjusted family—the envy of the County.

Connie's birthday present, the Winston Model-52 .22 rifle, was now a single shot. The five-round magazine had been replaced with a loading block, a fitted, machined, solid block of aluminum billet with a ramped grooved inlet to feed individual cartridges into the breach. The original ladder-sight and shrouded front blade remained—this was an instrument of accuracy, not a toy. A good strip-and-clean and re-oiling of the internals were all that were required to restore the rifle to pristine condition. The installation of a new adjustable canvas sling rounded out the package. Double hypothesized that given the weight of this heavy target rifle, the patience required to acquire an objective with the graduated aperture sight and the slow reloading time of a single shot, there was a limit to how carried away his son could get in a mock firefight.

Forty-eight hours after young Connie frantically tore into the colorfully wrapped package on the kitchen table, Double realized his error in judgment: It seemed that every other neighborhood mailbox, streetlight, sprinkler head, flagpole, flower box, weather vane and traffic sign had telltale punctures suggesting the source of those perforations originated from the breech of the birthday present. Then to the exasperation of their housekeeper, Connie lined up his game bag from The Great Backyard Safari: six chipmunks, two brace of mourning dove, a blue jay, a cardinal, a pileated woodpecker and every other disassembled specimen part of finch, sparrow and chickadee. The boy had also skinned and butchered four squirrels with the intent of having them fried for his dinner. Every saltshaker in the house was empty, and the squirrel hides were nailed to the workshop door.

Double immediately determined that the boy wasn't ready for his own rifle and, over a Shakespearean tragedy of objections, confiscated the Model-52. Double locked it away in a fireproof gun safe, the hiding place for the key which only he—and one other person, unbeknownst to him—knew. That other person was Connie, who had a sixth sense for when the coast was clear and it was safe to shoot his birthday present. He also knew to limit the number of trophies he took on his expeditions and then to properly dispose of all the evidence. Double was oblivious to all this, and even after several of the neighborhood cats went missing, it never occurred to him that his own progeny—now twelve years old—might be the neighborhood assassin.

* * * * *

O rion's timeworn model for maximizing profits with every new acquisition was to economize and trim the fat. Winston Firearms, which had long been synonymous with quality in the industry, quickly became known in its new incarnation as a nickel-and-dime outfit.

For Orion, each individual area of the business needed to justify its existence. The custom shop was immediately under threat, as it served only as a kind of prestige umbrella—a conspicuous image-builder for the entire product line, with highly skilled artisans turning out handmade shotguns and rifles to order for an elite clientele.

Orion was primarily a petrochemical company, and the concept of a halo marketing effect was completely lost on them. How the mere existence of the hand-built, custom-engraved Model-21 side by side could add cachet in the mind of the customer to the low-cost, mass-produced Model-23 struck Orion as marketing hokum. They especially felt this way about that colossal loss-leader, the Strattford Gun Club. Here, anyone coming in off the street could exchange five dollars and a driver's license for a box of shotgun shells and a loaner scattergun to go out and shoot a subsidized round of trap or skeet. Shooters bought at-cost ammunition and reloading supplies in bulk and, at the end of each season, the entire stable of loaner guns was sold off at fire-sale prices.

The Strattford facility consisted of a dozen combination skeet and trap fields laid out in a horseshoe shape around a twenty-acre waterfront peninsula overlooking the Sound. For over sixty years, trap and skeet shooters discharged thousands of tons of lead shot off this shoreline at a rate of 1⅛ oz. at a time, five days a week, twelve months out of the year. In addition to the high running costs of the club, expensive range personnel and exorbitant waterfront property taxes, there was also the steady legal cost of ongoing civil litigation over noise and environmental pollution in the form of lead shot and plastic-wad shot-collar contamination. It therefore came as no surprise when Orion surrendered completely to one of these nuisance lawsuits without ever even mounting a fight, volunteering both financial restitution as well as undertaking to clean up the shorefront by dredging all the lead from the sea bed.

* * * * *

Double was regularly called on the carpet by Orion internal auditors to justify his business expenses: There's an awful lot of entertaining that goes on in the gun business. Yes, Double regularly mixed business with pleasure, pushing the envelope on what qualified as legitimate business expenses—just as his own father had done. Why pay for something yourself, the rationale followed, when you could just as easily expense it to the company?

Double's problems finally came to a head when a Texas wildcatter cum corporate greenmailer by the name of T-Bone Sanders took a 14-percent stake in Orion. By Winston Firearms' own corporate bylaws, this entitled him to a seat on the board of directors. When Sanders demanded to exercise this right, Double simply dismissed it out of hand, going public with his decision via a press release: no convening of the board of directors, no discussion with Orion corporate and no official input from the Winston Firearms in-house counsel. In truth, Nathan Clarke had verbally advised Double to call Sander's bluff just to see if he could get away with it.

Sanders was so incensed that he made a public charge of embezzlement in the form of improper expensing—a frivolous and petty accusation at the level of chairman, especially as Double's corporate expenditures, while ill-advised, weren't nearly on a scale worthy of such serious allegation. Yes, Double used company credit cards for virtually everything under the sun, but he also regularly reimbursed Winston Firearms for his personal expenses.

Lavish corporate retreats were also a normal part of the business schedule. A handful of top Winston executives could look forward to two four-day getaways every year: once in July on Nantucket Island and the other in January at the five-star Breakers resort in Palm Beach. Meetings took up several hours each day in order to justify the trips, but the overall effect was to provide all-expense-paid vacations to the executive inner circle. Then there were the regular jaunts to Onori during quail-hunting season. These were boys-only affairs, and Double would typically only shoot for an hour or so in the morning. He would start drinking at lunch and then would while away the rest of the day on horseback, watching the dogs work and accompanying the other guests in the field.

For several years running, Double and Francesca flew round trip to London on the SST Concorde under the official guise of meeting with British Winston distributors. The first two days were spent in legitimate meetings, but the remaining three were spent riding to the hounds of the Bilsdale hunt, foxhunting in Yorkshire. And then there was the company car.

Double had always lusted after a real sports car, and the prospect of a paid corporate vehicle finally presented him with the opportunity to indulge this weakness. He drove to work each morning in his own BMW, a sensible, reliable executive sedan—exactly the sort of transport one would expect of an up-and-comer. Double, however, requested as his official company car a rare thoroughbred: a mid-engined, low-slung supercar—the two-seat, high-output, six-cylinder BMW M1. The design and mechanicals were courtesy of Munich, with styling by Giugiaro and fiberglass bodywork by Lamborghini. With its high build quality and breathtaking performance good to160 mph, this hand-built exotic was heralded as the most reliable performance car ever produced—an uncompromising supercar that could be enjoyed every day. The cramped vehicle was totally preposterous in the role of legitimate business transport, however.

It was also very, very expensive at initial purchase. When the two-year lease expired on his first white M1, Double got another—the latest iteration in red. All the bugs had been ironed out of the design when he took delivery of the last of the 1981 models, and when that lease expired, the M1 was out of production. Double purchased his last red M1 off lease for pennies on the dollar as a fully depreciated second-hand car.

T-Bone Sanders knew that in Double Winston he was regarding a coddled dilettante, a former athlete playing at a business career, who had no idea what things cost and couldn't be troubled to keep an accurate accounting of his own expenditures. It infuriated the self-made gas-and-oil tycoon that anyone in such a high position of corporate oversight should have the nerve to take such galling financial liberties. With a chairman of the board like that it was no wonder that Winston Firearms was a chronic underperformer.

Ultimately though, Sanders just wanted to be paid to go away, and in Double Winston, Sanders hit pay dirt. His allegations would be but the first salvo in a long battle campaign, and Double's ongoing undisciplined spending habits and sloppy record-keeping would keep him well supplied with ammunition. Clearly there was money to be made here and Orion, or more specifically Winston Firearms, was now under his magnifying glass.

In his defense, Double did try, but running his life by the book and to the penny didn't come easily, and he soon began to chafe under the yoke of his corporate masters.

* * * * *

The Orion merger had always been a shotgun wedding, and Double hoped that perhaps by finding a wealthy suitor, he might get the rocky marriage annulled.

A comprehensive solution to all Double's problems arrived in the person of his former business school roommate, who had risen to become the chief operating officer of Continental Distillers. Distillers was a huge amalgamation of international subsidiaries and, like Orion, was constantly on the lookout to acquire well-established business in unrelated industries. Double met his friend privately for drinks in the city to discuss general terms, and the stars seemed to align: Double's headaches, it appeared, were about to become a distant memory.

Distillers then formally approached Orion to acquire their majority interest in Winston Firearms. If the deal came off, Double would remain as Winston chairman. It appeared that fate would smile on the acquisition, and everyone began to grow optimistic as the deal moved forward. Then suddenly, Double's friend, a man not yet fifty, with two small children and in seeming perfect health, dropped dead of a heart attack on the ski slopes. The deal fell apart when his successor at Distillers reviewed the proposal and found it lacking. Continental Distillers took a pass on Winston Firearms and eventually acquired the Fotomat chain of drive-thru camera film dealers and developers instead.

In preparing Winston for the sale, Orion had combed the ledgers in search of value, and ultimately priced the company to perfection. What was immediately clear from even a cursory look at the books was that most of the bottom-line profit came from the ammunition division. Firearms production was both expensive and labor-intensive, requiring specialized skills and requisite high levels of training. There was also the looming problem of employing expensive union labor and their accompanying legacy costs.

Orion sent an emissary to Japan to approach the firm manufacturing the 101 series of over-under shotguns to enquire if they might consider purchasing the entire firearms division. Their reaction was positive but also conditional: The Japanese very much wanted to acquire the firearms division, but had no interest in any of the tooling, personnel or real estate. They simply wanted to purchase the designs, which they would then improve and put into production. If this new transaction came to fruition, the Winston Firearms division would cease production, its entire workforce sacked in one fell swoop. Yes, employees would be awarded severance packages based on length of service, but the hard fact was that thousands of livelihoods—the very skilled working-class bull-work that made up the economic foundation of Bridgewater and its outlying suburbs— would permanently disappear on a divine wind emanating from the East.

Orion now became fixated with spinning off the gun business, and Double suddenly felt cornered. From a financial perspective he recognized that Orion was correct: The country was awash in high-quality sporting arms which if properly maintained had an indefinite useful lifespan. He also realized that manufacturing in Bridgewater using expensive union labor was an outdated nineteenth-century business model and that the Japanese plan was the most viable long-term. He was conflicted however: These were his father's people—the workers who'd won two world wars, built a great manufacturing city and kept food on the Winston family table through the generations. You didn't just shoot a retired horse who'd given loyal service, and you certainly didn't fire nearly 2,500 employees simply because the shrewd business move was to relocate manufacturing to a lower-cost provider. To the MBA in him the issue was black and white, the solution obvious. To the human being who'd seen his father give his entire life over to this business and these people, he knew he couldn't live with himself if he didn't at least try to save the firearms division.

Nathan Clarke engineered the employee buyout, selling the firearms division over time to its own workers. Orion would finance the transaction, but with interest rates at nosebleed levels (the U.S. prime rate hit an all-time-high of 21.5% in December 1980), the financing would be both expensive and risky. Orion was surprisingly receptive to the idea: They could do without all the bad press that would surely accompany plant closings and mass layoffs, and this employee buyout, even if it ultimately failed and the entity reverted back to Orion by default, would entirely avoid that.

The executives leading the firearms division were longtime Winston employees who pinned their hopes on putting into production three cutting-edge designs that had languished in development for years.

There had long been an unwritten rule that handgun makers wouldn't manufacture sporting long guns and Winston Firearms would stay out of the pistol market entirely. The first firearm to skirt this convention and break precedent would be a single-shot, bolt-action, nylon-stocked handgun in rifle calibers like .223, 7mm and .308. This was a highly accurate handgun that could be used at long range for everything from varmints and silhouettes right up to big game. Their second idea was an adjustable rifle barrel, a kind of harmonics optimizer which would allow the shooter to custom-tune the pitch of a barrel's vibration to a particular load. The third was a heavy single-shot, low-recoil, bolt-action trap gun that was a radical departure from conventional target guns: It effectively reduced the 1⅛ oz., 12-gauge target load to the perceived recoil of a ¾ oz. 28-gauge.

These three designs showed such promise and created so much excitement that firearms division executives imagined the new products might even initiate a late-twentieth-century renaissance in sporting arms and create a new standard for the industry.

Added to this was the offer to license the Model-42 pump .410, a scaled-down version of the Model-12. Nicknamed "Everybody's Sweetheart," this diminutive shotgun had been the state-of-the-art for skeet guns before the engineers finally figured out how to make an autoloader cycle with such a reduced ballistic payload. With that advance, the Model-42 was immediately rendered obsolete and went out of production. There were still plenty of original Model-42s floating around, many repurposed into quail guns. Some were even starting to show up on the sporting clays course, and this renewed interest fueled demand and a subsequent run-up in price on the second-hand market.

As the Model-42 had been out of production since the 1960s, Winston management regarded it as a vestigial relic and was only too happy to sign a fifteen-year licensing agreement. They immediately realized their mistake when the stylish knockoffs began showing up all over the country as a favorite raffle-prize for charity events. Many shooters who would never dream of purchasing the lightweight pump became instant converts the moment they actually held one in their hands and could appreciate its nimble handling. Thus the Winston Firearms division missed out on the little-pump scattergun fad, collecting only a pittance in royalties per unit instead of the lion's share of profit.

Winston management was confident, however, that the fresh drawing-board designs, in conjunction with the Model-42 licensing deal and the wholesale elimination of costly low-volume product lines would return the firearms division to profitability.

XIII

The summer that Connie turned twelve, the Winstons spent the month of August at Sun-Up, the family's lakefront cabin at the Big Pine Club. Its proximity to the County made it imminently practical: If Double got a call in the morning, he could be back at his Bridgewater office in the afternoon.

The rustic family cabin had been built by the unlikely founder of Winston Firearms, Marion Davis Winston. Marion was the mass-marketing, mail-order haberdasher responsible for creating the first properly fitting made-to-measure suit. Your participating local tailor took the initial measurements and filled out a detailed order form in exchange for a fifteen-percent sales commission. This same tailor then also made any final alterations.

Marion had taken possession of the various components of the firearms company when he foreclosed on a nonperforming business loan. This narrowly predated the outbreak of the Spanish-American War, which although it lasted only ten weeks, initiated America's first foray onto the world stage as a global power.

Global powers require vast, well-equipped armies with accurate rifles and ammunition. Marion aggressively developed the lever-action repeating rifle into a reliable workhorse and then relentlessly pursued military contracts, motivating elected officials with lobbyists and hard cash. (The reason that no other Winston descendant was ever named for Marion was that silent-era movie actress Marion Davies, one of the motion picture industry's first mega-stars, was forever the image that popped into everyone's head whenever they heard the name Marion Davis Winston.)

* * * * *

The Big Pine shoreline was ringed with evergreens interspersed with sugar maples and hardwoods, and under this green canopy grew fiddlehead ferns and wild blackberries. The shoreline itself was mostly rocky, much of it unkempt, with snags of deadwood and tree stumps noting some long-ago flood high-water mark. Periodically the shore was broken up here and there by several sandy beaches made of low-quality gravel trucked in from a pit on club property.

A doll-sized island, Coney Island, sat not a hundred feet off this craggy shore, and although it was not even an acre in size, it was completely sheltered and isolated from the cabins of Big Pine. It constituted an entirely separate world in a young person's mind—a child's world. It had its own pebble-stone beach that faced the mainland, a fieldstone campfire and beside it, a wooden picnic table sheltered by a large tent fashioned from an oversized blue tarp lashed over a log that had been secured with lag bolts across the crotches of two big oaks.

Everything smelled like hemlock at Big Pine, and the water came out of the taps so cold Connie couldn't believe it remained liquid. At night, owls hooted and coyotes cried their haunting ballad, and all day long the children, from toddlers to teenagers, could be heard rejoicing at play: laughing, yelling, showing off and hacking off; walking, running, sailing, canoeing; swimming out to the dock and back, and launching themselves far out into the lake; flying high off a swing made from an old tractor tire. A kid went through three or four swimsuits a day trying to keep dry, and the smart ones simply resorted to wearing a fast-drying Speedo under their shorts.

The days were long and hot, and young Connie made friends with a regular gang of kids who also had cabins at the lake. He was active and constantly on the go from dusk till dawn. It was only the ringing of the cast-iron triangle on Sun-Up's front porch which signified that dinner was ready that finally drew these sundrenched days to a close.

Connie was Tom Sawyer, and a couple of cabins down the shoreline resided his Becky, a fresh-mouthed, sandy-haired little girl who liked to weave a colorful thread of yarn into one long thin braid of hair. She also wore a pukka-shell necklace that struck Connie as terribly tropical and exotic. Kimmy had the early beginnings of womanly curves and was a prime example of girls maturing faster than boys.

Her father, Kevin Conner, was the youngest of the three Conner sons to step into the family's swimming pool business. Kevin was the black sheep and the family's sole college dropout. He was also a prodigious drinker and offered the broken capillaries on his nose and cheeks as evidence. Conner Swimming Pools was the County's leading builder of premium in-ground pools, but his brothers were careful to keep Kevin out of the spotlight and away from the clientele. His professional duties were limited to opening and closing customer pools each spring and fall, and cleaning and servicing them throughout the season. He rode herd on his seasonal crews and hired on the extra summer help. His days began by sending the men out on their established rounds, immediately followed by a half-hour stop for a bracer at the only remaining dive bar on the Avenue. Kevin had at one time been an enthusiastic volunteer fireman, but its demands of temperance clashed with his lifestyle. Though he hadn't fought a fire in over a decade, he continued to don his navy blue uniform and march in the Memorial Day parade each year. He also kept a blue flashing light on his dashboard and a police scanner squawking away in his work truck.

Kevin was a legacy member at the Big Pine Club, otherwise he never would have made the cut with the membership committee. Whenever he was in residence at his lakefront cabin, Kevin could most often be found wasting away his afternoons luxuriating with his great pride and joy, a dormitory refrigerator with a cutout to accommodate a beer tap. Kevin would sit out on that porch in a battered wicker armchair wearing his Irish green derby regardless of the temperature, indulging himself with sickly sweet, aromatic cigars and glass after glass of frosty beer poured directly from the mouth of his refrigerated goddess. Any male passerby got a longwinded salutation and the offer of a frosty draft. If Kevin really liked you, he'd produce a bottle of Black Bush and join you in a snort of Irish whiskey.

Lacey Conner, Kevin's wife and the mother of his three girls, tolerated the intolerable that is day-to-day life with an alcoholic.

She abided him as a part of the unwritten social contract that was still in place during that era: He was a good provider from an influential family ensconced in the trades that enjoyed a fine reputation in the County. So he drinks too much—lots of people drink too much. The two hadn't slept in the same bedroom in years.

Kevin's youngest daughter, Kimmy, was cute, but aspired to be distractingly pretty like her two cheerleader sisters, Karen and Katie. As a result, Kimmy desperately tried to act older and more mature, which came off as condescending and snotty whenever she was interacting with someone her own age. Anyone looking at Connie and Kimmy together would note that although they were the same age, he was still a child and she was starting to become something more.

The human condition dictates that we want what we can't have, and Kimmy made it clear to Connie from the start that he held no interest whatsoever for her and that any attempts to win her favors would prove futile. Connie exhibited his commitment by vigilantly following her around and shyly attempting to engage the girl, but she avoided interacting with him. He was reduced to a silent, solitary presence hovering just outside her immediate sphere. He didn't stalk her per se, but he certainly did spy on her, of which she was quite aware.

Connie was heartsick over his sandy-haired little girl. Often in the mornings, he could be found patiently waiting on her cabin's front stoop, with his arm nonchalantly looped through one of the varnished hardwood branches fashioned into banister spindles which spelled out CONNER. She would descend that staircase, rushing past him without saying a word, leaving him frustrated and patiently awaiting another chance to break the ice. Kimmy could see that the boy had a crush on her, and when her older sisters teased her about it, explaining in detail all the things young Connie hoped to do to her, she was simultaneously revolted and mortified; the very idea that once he got started, Connie wouldn't be satisfied until she had a baby growing inside of her only increased those fears. She didn't like Connie—she didn't like any boy. She resolved to ignore him, and if that meant being rude and barging right past him without murmuring so much as a hello, so be it.

And so the barefoot girl would silently pad back up the porch stairs coming from day camp, and then go right back out again in her favorite blue and yellow Ms. Pac-Man one-piece bathing suit for a swim in the lake. As Connie finally screwed up the courage to deliver his overture to her, the little girl snapped at him in passing, "Late for swimming lessons." And then upon her return, bounding up the porch steps two at a time, she indignantly let fly, "Scat, feral boy—go home to your badger den!"

Once Connie even tried to maintain a solitary vigil on her front porch, but then Kevin Conner began his afternoon ritual. This resulted in the awkward scenario of Kevin half-drunkenly encouraging the boy with tasteless, slurred pontifications about what it is that women really want.

Hard up against this locked door, his heart crestfallen, Connie would wander back to his family's cabin and sulk. He was a good boy in his own way and had been led to believe that he was special and well liked. The sandy-haired little girl was the first time Connie ever tasted anything like rejection, and it was debilitating to his psyche. If she would only take the chance to get to know him: Sex was the furthest thing from his mind unless you count kissing with tongues as sex. A French kiss was his long-term goal for the entire summer, to be consummated ideally on or about Labor Day.

Connie's parents took notice of their lovesick son, who clearly wasn't himself, and tried to help him. What the boy needed, Double concluded, was a diversion to take his mind off his troubles, and nothing could redirect a boy's attention like a .22 rifle.

XIV

On an overnight trip home on business, Double unlocked the fireproof gun safe and liberated the rifle. He held it in his hands, admiring its design and workmanship. It truly was a marvel: Guns like this had trained an army of citizen soldiers and won a world war. Derivatives of the Model-52 had been at the vanguard of rifle accuracy for nearly fifty years, dominating competitive target shooting for generations. The rifle was a design his own father had helped develop, and it would now become the gateway to sport shooting for his own son. The gun was immaculate and sweetly fragrant from the G-96 brand gun treatment that had always been Senior's preferred lubricant. Connie was quite the perfectionist when it came to thoroughly cleaning and returning the rifle to its exact spot in the gun safe: To the naked eye, nothing ever looked out of order. *It was time enough*, Double finally decided. *The boy served his penance, and the time was right to give it back.* It was the only surefire way he could think of to put a smile back on Connie's face. Double zipped the gun into a soft case and placed it in the trunk of his BMW sedan. The brick of .22 long-rifle cartridges was already waiting.

XV

Most days when the sky was clear and a break in the afternoon heat seemed imminent, Kimmy Conner would don her Ms. Pac-Man swimsuit and paddle out to Coney Island on her blow-up rubber sea-serpent raft. She'd land on the pebble beach and wade around, skipping stones over the dark placid waters. More than once Connie had spied on her for long periods of time from the shore. He watched her theatrically recreate animated conversations with her sisters and even sing songs to herself as she paddled the inflatable craft to the island, its sea-monster head craning well above her sandy hair.

Several thoughts occurred to Connie all at once. First, the inflatable raft was only about three feet long and little more than a drugstore toy far more appropriate to lounging around the confined space of a swimming pool or backyard pond than the expansive waters of Big Pine Lake. Second, even though Coney Island sat just offshore not 100 feet from the mainland, if that polymer raft were ever to start leaking air, this sudden inconvenience might seem more like an outright emergency in the mind of a twelve-year-old. Third, Connie was confident in his marksmanship—very confident. The serpent's head towered over the girl when she was aboard that raft, and if he could just put one round through the monster's eye, he could then nonchalantly paddle his canoe out to the point, discover his damsel in distress and heroically save her.

Then, out of the blue, his rifle arrived from Bailiwick.

Connie scouted the shoreline for just the right vantage point, which was obvious: A low spot on the lakefront and the underbrush and scrub of the shallow hollow had already been gladed and thinned to open a small clearing. There were some immature trees not much bigger than saplings left to grow that would eventually create the next generation of shade trees. One in particular, an immature hemlock, could provide camouflage, and was situated directly in front of a boulder large enough to hide behind but not so tall that Connie couldn't easily shoot over the top of it. The tree had alternating branches on each side, several of which were the ideal height to use as a rest. Connie could select from any of these, depending on the given angle. Even though he would hate to have his gun come into contact with any of the evergreen's sap-laden limbs, he trimmed back the needles of several branches with the saw blade of his Swiss army knife in preparation.

Connie's judgment hadn't entirely taken leave of him, however. He realized there was some small element of risk involved in his plan and that the right gun for shooting accurately under 100 feet was really a high-powered air-rifle. The only air-rifle his family had at Big Pine was an underpowered .177 pellet gun which, if he actually managed to hit the serpent's head, he was afraid wouldn't be powerful enough to perforate its rubberized polymer.

The .22-caliber Model-52 was his only choice, but Connie soundly reasoned that between the long-rifle, rim-fire cartridges he'd be using and it being such a straightforward and close shot of 50 to 75 feet, he couldn't envision any scenario where he'd have trouble. He even reckoned that if there was an onshore breeze, the boulder in that hollow might muffle the rifle crack to the point that Kimmy wouldn't even hear it.

* * * * *

Sunday morning, immediately following a flapjack and sunnyside-egg breakfast, Connie made his preparations, dragging the green fiberglass canoe up on the rocky shore so it would be there at the ready in anticipation of his impending rescue. He also stowed the rifle, zipped into its soft case and wrapped in a gray wool blanket, underneath the fiberglass hull.

He had three .22 rounds scotch-taped to the custom loading block that fit into the magazine port of the rifle. Double had shown him something Winky Wagner taught him on their one day together: Take a knife and gently tap the blade into the soft head of the solid lead projectile, first bisecting and then quartering it. This creates a scoring effect which when the bullet hits its mark mushrooms the slug. The head opens into four distinct petals, exponentially increasing its lethality. Connie sat at the kitchen table meticulously tapping bullets with a ball-peen hammer, ruinously dulling Francesca's favorite kitchen knife until she finally made him stop. It was no surprise then that the three bullets taped to the Model-52 also displayed these telltale knife marks.

* * * * *

While everyone else at Big Pine watched the club tennis championship, made preparations for an afternoon barbeque or looked forward to the annual barn dance that evening, Double napped away a good portion of Sunday morning to recuperate from the exhaustive, fruitless negotiations with the Orion Corporation that had been simmering all summer.

Double was attempting to renegotiate the financing on the firearms division employee buyout. The initial spinoff had taken place in a historically high-interest-rate environment. Now that borrowing costs had come down in the booming Reagan economy, Double felt it was in the best interest of the shareholder-employees to refinance the debt at a lower rate. The problem was that the firearms division was currently only limping along, and even though one could argue that the rate being paid was exorbitant, Orion had no intention of lowering it.

So Double enticed the Orion board of directors with his last remaining plum—his trust fund stake in the ammunition division. He offered to sell Orion his part of the ammunition business in a staggered transaction culminating over some eight years in exchange for an immediate refinancing of the firearms division at an even rate of nine percent, amortized over twenty years. Assuming the gun company prospered, Orion would be repaid in full and Double's shares in the ammunition division held in escrow would eventually convert to Orion stock—a liquid asset he could then hold or sell. Should the firearms division fail in its debt obligation, the entire entity would revert back to Orion along with Double's ammunition-division-collateral stake.

He would resign as chairman of the ammunition division but remain as a nonexecutive member of the board of directors for the duration of the eight-year buyout. In short, he was offering a binding promise to get out of Orion's hair for good, and this was certain to waylay all pending litigation from T-Bone Sanders. As it was Double who was initiating the recapitalization, the firearms division board insisted he take the helm as its chief executive.

Double might have just as easily left the firearms division to its fate. He had already facilitated one stay of execution by initiating the original spinoff into employee ownership. One could argue that any obligation he had to these employees had long since been satisfied, but pensive guilt gnawed at him anyway. He didn't want to own any part of the firearms division; he wanted it to stand on its own two feet and walk away from the Winston family forever, relegating him to being nothing more than an Orion stockholder. But Double was also certain that he alone was their only potential savior. Only altruistic leadership and luck could safely guide the firearms division's ship of industry through the rocky shoals of modern commerce. Without a refinancing, the firearms division *would* fail—the terms of the initial purchase were just too dear. In order for its employees to have any kind of realistic future, Double Winston would have to throw in with them and ignore his own better judgment by laying his own personal fortune on the line.

* * * * *

athan Clarke managed to secure an agreement with the city of Bridgewater for incentives and tax abatements, which he believed would ultimately mean the difference between mere survival and true prosperity for the firearms division. Rumors had circulated for decades regarding a potential Bridgewater civic bankruptcy and, realizing the dire prospects for the city's vulnerable union manufacturers, the Democratic mayor—an old brass foundry worker himself—created enterprise districts in the city's blighted industrial areas. He also wooed casino operators with the idea of petitioning the state to relax gaming restrictions thereby allowing gambling in Bridgewater. The thrice-divorced, fifty-something-year-old bachelor was the city's first black mayor, and was notorious for his gambling junkets to Atlantic City as well as low-level graft, demanding tribute be paid in the form of gifts easily converted to cash.

The mayor cultivated his own unique style: In addition to having his hair straightened into a pompadour, he wore a tuxedo as his regular business attire, only switching to a white dinner jacket in summertime. He also had a connoisseur's palate for high-priced white call girls, and had only recently discovered the joys of freebasing cocaine.

Nathan arrived at City Hall, an ornate marble building, for their only face-to-face meeting carrying a cased commemorative rifle in each hand: a drop block, single-shot Sharps Carbine in .50 cal. and an 1894 lever-action in .30-30. These presentation rifles came from the firearms division company arsenal and had been issued to commemorate the 1969 Western *True Grit*, starring John Wayne and Glenn Campbell. Scotch-taped to the pistol grip of each gun was a Double-Eagle Liberty-Head $20 gold coin.

"We thought that inletting the coins right into the stocks might personalize them a bit for you, but some astute collectors such as yourself prefer not to mar the originality of such a fine rifle," Nathan said knowingly. "Drop by the plant anytime, should you want the inlays."

The mayor took a disinterested look into the satin-lined boxes and plucked the two gold pieces off the pistol grips like a wide-eyed child greedily snatching up chocolate coins. Then he had Nathan close up the cases and resign the rifles to his office closet.

It was a simple matter of a single stroke of the mayor's pen to designate the entire neighborhood surrounding the firearms division plant complex as an enterprise district. Once his recommendation was summarily approved by a pliant city council, civic and state funding would kick in and the firearms division would instantly become a protected member of the Bridgewater business community. While the mayor was generally regarded as a man of his word, especially when there were ongoing kickbacks in the offing, the firearms division's future and ultimately Double's personal fortune rested on nothing more than a promise and a handshake.

* * * * *

Double and Orion had been doing the corporate fan dance all summer long and there had been offers and counteroffers followed by feigned insult and outrage. Both sides knew they were close to a deal when Double and Nathan Clarke stormed out of the Winston Firearms board room in a fit of indignation at the latest counteroffer. It was late Friday afternoon leading into Labor Day weekend, and Nathan and Double wanted to give Orion the holiday to mull over the deal.

The truth was that Orion had been negotiating in good faith from the start. Nathan was swinging for the fences on the staggered Orion stock transaction, however, and Double knew they were walking a fine line, risking souring the entire deal over relatively meaningless minutiae. Brinksmanship aside, both men fully expected to shake hands with Orion's representatives on an agreement-in-principle the following week.

XVI

unchtime came and went at Big Pine, and the heat of the day climbed and then finally broke in the late afternoon. Connie sat on the front steps of Sun-Up, nonchalantly reading back issues of *Mad* magazine, drinking a cold glass of milk liberally spiked with Bosco syrup. His mousetrap was set to spring—all he needed was the girl.

Kimmy Conner's afternoon appearances were punctual enough to run the Swiss rail system by. She appeared as a junior miss bathing beauty in her blue and yellow Ms. Pac-Man swimsuit with a lone slender braid highlighted in purple yarn dangling from her hair. She dragged her blow-up raft and collapsible floating plastic-and-aluminum paddle out from under the porch and carried it down to the water's edge. She never even glanced in the direction of Connie's front steps, and only once did the boy self-consciously look up from his reading to take her in. As his sandy-haired girl waded out into the lake, Connie downed the last of his chocolate milk and left the sweating glass on the top step. After a brief moment inside Sun-Up, he exited through the front door with his father's expensive Zeiss binoculars hanging around his neck.

Connie patiently walked the trail that led out to the small peninsula on the shoreline and rehearsed in his mind just exactly what he'd say to Kimmy after he successfully made the shot and paddled out to save her. He was debating whether to call out "I'll save you!" from the canoe or to preface his heroic pronouncement with "Don't panic!" He was confident that she wouldn't see him launch the canoe, which sat just as he' d left it resting on the rocky shoreline along with its paddle, the rifle and two life preservers stowed underneath.

As he approached the point of the peninsula, Connie could see that Kimmy was making slow work of it, belting out the Go-Go's "Our Lips Are Sealed" off-key at the top of her lungs as she methodically churned the lake's surface with her paddle. What was most notable about her singing was that it faded in and out on intermittent gusts of wind. As so often happens in hill country, the heavy heat of the day was clashing with the cool air coming off the mountains creating brief, tempestuous squalls on the lake surface—a visible chop and all manner of wavelets. The high, thick canopy of foliage surrounding the clearing rustled every which way; leaves were thrashed from their branches, resulting in much of the greenery coming to rest on the forest floor like a cool carpet of oversized confetti. *The noise of the rifle might be a problem*, Connie thought to himself. He needed to be lucky in timing the shot.

He calmly retrieved the rifle from under the canoe and carried it, still inside its case wrapped in the blanket, across the peninsula to the hemlock he'd prepared behind the boulder. There, he would wait. "Don't panic!" That would be his opener. He'd just paddle out into open water and announce, "Don't panic! I'm coming for you." It was at once both authoritative and understated: simultaneously modest and valiant.

He laid the bundle on top of the boulder, unrolled the blanket, removed the gun from its case and opened the breach bolt. Then he wrapped his arm in the canvas sling for support and placed the unloaded rifle first on one of the alternating branches and then another. His work was not in vain: Both rests would provide adequate vantage points to shoot from. It was just a question of where and when the optimal opportunity would materialize. He closed the bolt and dry-fired the rifle several times to reacquaint himself with its trigger. Connie then carefully peeled back the scotch tape from the trigger guard and inspected the three .22 caliber rounds. They were all about the same, though one of them did seem to have its solid lead head cleaved just a bit more neatly than the others. He held the bullet up between his fingers, kissed it for luck and carefully chambered it into the rifle breach.

Connie was a patient boy and knew to come prepared for a long wait. Each of the back pockets of his Wrangler blue-jean cutoffs held a set of Wacky Packages, novelty trading decals. Modeled on baseball cards, Wacky Packages were comical advertising parodies of popular consumer products. Each came with six peel-and-stick decals and the same thin rectangle of pink bubble gum found in a pack of baseball cards.

He opened the first package and withdrew the brittle, slender wafer of chewing gum. He breathed in a bit of its powdered sugar before he started chewing and he seemed to taste it deep down inside his lungs. The stick cracked and crunched under his back teeth as it fractured and softened—*old pack*, Connie thought to himself, as he absentmindedly thumbed the cards. He had a Cram ham card spoofing Spam, a *Shorts Illustrated*, Mr. Mean cleanser, Irish Ring body soap—which promised to leave rings around the bath tub, and a Czechlets which contained overcoated midget Czechoslovakian citizens inside a Chicklets-like pack.

The bubble gum lost its flavor in no time and started to become hard to chew. Connie could now hear the girl defiling Madonna's "Borderline." He reached into his other back pocket, withdrew the other packet of decals and opened it. He inadvertently dropped one of the sticker cards on the ground as he removed the bubble gum from the wrapper and added it to the bland wad already in his mouth. He didn't notice this because he was paying ardent attention to the raft which Kimmy was hectically paddling toward Coney Island. He trained the field glasses on her, which was entirely unnecessary as she was so close to shore that the image through the reticule was grossly oversized and made her appear out of all perspective, like some kind of child giant.

A shot this close required the use of an open iron-sight, which made no allowance for yardage and shot absolutely dead flat. The hinged ladder-sight had a recessed, notched groove cut into it which, when laid flat against the barrel, served this purpose. Connie removed the bubble gum from his mouth and stuck it to the bark of the hemlock. Then he once again snaked his arm through the canvas sling, closed the rifle bolt and flicked on the safety.

Buck fever is a physiological phenomenon that happens when a hunter is about to attempt to take an animal. It can happen to a first-timer on an easy shot or it can happen to an experienced gun when the shot becomes challenging or it's the *animal of a lifetime*: The hunter becomes tense and tight, his heart rate rises uncontrollably, accompanied by a rush of adrenaline. It becomes very difficult to hold the gun steady and make the myriad meticulous adjustments required to achieve accurate sighting. No hunter wants to needlessly wound an animal if he can possibly avoid it. A clean kill is a testament to a man's character, and no one wants to take a chance on a bad shot.

Connie felt something akin to this last feeling, in that he knew he had to be careful. He flicked off the safety and placed the towering head of the blow-up serpent on the front blade of the rifle. He kept both eyes open—only rookies squint. Then he lined it up with the recessed notch of the iron-sight and began to gently squeeze the trigger. Suddenly, he lost his nerve and removed his finger entirely from the trigger. He reengaged the safety and wiped his eyes with his free hand. *It's now or never,* he thought to himself: Kimmy was beginning to turn away from him and toward Coney Island. If he didn't take the shot in the next five seconds or so, her back would be to him and the serpent's head inaccessible. Connie screwed up his courage. With his canvas sling and shooting off a rest, he floated the sight over the target and locked in tight. *It's an easy shot,* he thought. *Do it exactly like you do at home: Just line it up and squeeze it off.*

He flicked off the safety and aligned the sights. The green serpent's head of the raft was now quartering slightly away from him, making for an angled shot that actually brought his intended target into even closer proximity to the child. He held that sight picture for a moment and then thought, *now!* to himself. Just as he began to pull the trigger, the foliage above him churned abruptly and he could feel a sudden wind gust against his back. This caught the evergreen needles of the hemlock he was resting the rifle on, bending it forward and ever so slightly pulling him along with it— and that's all it took.

Connie felt the trigger break under his finger and the gun

discharged with a crack. At the last moment, Kimmy had turned slightly toward him, placing her full-on profile into the bullet's path. What Connie couldn't know however, was that the wind's brief effect on the tree top by bowing it slightly forward in an arc had made the rifle shoot low. That .22 solid projectile hit the surface of the lake and improbably skipped, freakishly ricocheting back up into the air, striking the girl directly in front of her left ear. She kept stroking in pantomime even after the paddle fell away from her hands.

He reached for the binoculars and instantly noted the raised red mark of the mushroomed bullet under the skin of her cheek. Blood began to trickle sporadically from the wound and it began to pulse, spurting a crimson flow into the lake with every beat of her heart. Kimmy Conner briefly slumped forward, her hair fell over her face and she became a truly macabre sight before flopping over the side and slipping silently beneath the dark waters of Big Pine Lake.

Connie couldn't believe his eyes and immediately covered them with his hands. He lowered his head until his nose was scraping against the boulder, which smelled of moss and impending rain. *Was she dead?* He opened his eyes and looked out at the lake again. *Why wasn't she floating?!* Even if she were dead, which was unlikely, she should at least be floating out there somewhere, but she wasn't. Connie tried to gather his wits: *Did he actually just do that or did he only imagine it?* He looked down at the rifle resting on the boulder, opened the breech a crack and smelled the whiff of burnt powder and suddenly felt flushed and light-headed. His knees buckled and he slid his body down the granite rock face until he was lying on green leaves and evergreen needles. The sky clouded over and the wind now ceased entirely. He could momentarily hear the songbirds chirping as rain as dense as gumdrops began to pelt the foliage and splatter the ground around him.

He was utterly alone in the world: No one else had seen or heard what happened. If he stood back up to look, would she still be out there paddling frantically in her raft trying to beat the storm to shore? He regained his vantage point only to watch the now capsized toy raft skim across the water on a gust of wind and onto Coney Island's shore and inland where it lodged itself against a bush.

The thing to do was save her, Connie thought as he closed the breech without shucking the empty hull and placed the rifle back in its soft case. He rewrapped it all in the wool blanket and headed for the canoe. What would he do if he somehow miraculously found her on the bottom and managed to pull her up? What could he do? He was just a kid, after all. Would he scream for help or try to breathe life back into her? He paddled out to where he thought she'd gone under, taking strained, mannish strokes all the way. He dropped the makeshift anchor cement coffee can off the stern of the canoe and stripped down to his Speedo. *All I can do is try*, he thought to himself and then he was underwater—cool and dark—diving deep just as far as he could go and never once touching bottom.

When his lungs felt as if they'd burst, he turned back for the surface and looked up toward light and life-giving air. When he was this deep, he could see through to the lake surface and that nothing was there: nothing suspended in the state of in-between waters of life and death. The rain was drumming the lake and now he was swimming in a downpour. He could hear thunder in the distance and knew that he'd need to retreat to shore soon. He remembered the wayward raft on Coney Island and felt compelled to retrieve it. He pulled the coffee can up by its clothesline and now his bare skin was being throttled by the downpour. He wiped the water from his brow, and in six or seven long strokes of his canoe paddle, he had retrieved Kimmy's floating paddle and was nosing the bow of the canoe up against the pebble-stone shore.

He crossed the island, cold and nearly naked, and after a brief frantic search found the raft dancing across the pebble-stone beach and headed back toward open water. He threw himself upon it and could feel the small oval river stones of the beach coming through its bottom. He tried to rip it open with his teeth to no avail, and then located the air valve. He popped the cap off and gathered up the inflated ring in his arms, hugging it to force the air out. He needed that raft—for what exactly he didn't know, but he couldn't just let it blow away. He wasn't thinking of anything in particular except that he wished the hard rain would let up.

Once the toy was deflated, Connie took shelter under the blue tarp spanning the two oaks. He sat on the picnic table under that tarp and wrapped himself in the deflated raft for warmth. He wanted to dive for her again but knew that with all the lightning about it would be too dangerous. He waited, traumatized by what he'd done, still not quite able to grasp that it was in fact all real and that he was the sole instrument of another child's death. He would find his father and tell him exactly what happened. His father couldn't change it, but at least he'd know what to do.

Connie rolled Kimmy's paddle into the deflated raft and paddled the canoe back to shore. The rain finally relented, replaced by a raw penetrating fog. Still in his swim trunks, the boy dragged the canoe onto the rocky shore; his body was growing stiff from the cold. He took the rolled paddle and added it to the rifle and wrapped them all up inside the wool blanket. He rolled up his own wet clothes separately and put the binoculars around his neck and then wandered the trail back toward Sun-Up in a daze. He needed to hide that rifle, not for all time but for temporary safekeeping. His father would probably want it later, but he couldn't very well bring it back to the house with him. He needed an out-of-the-way place to stash it for the time being.

Connie spied an uprooted tree near the trail. The root ball was huge, and the hole it left in the earth was large enough to swallow a draft horse. Connie jumped down in that pit and pulled the roll in after him. The soil inside was dark, moist and mixed with gravel. The tree stump just above him provided a kind of sheltered overhang. He jammed the rifle up into farthest nook of that hole, high up among the fine fingerlike roots where the earth was still soft but undisturbed. Then he stood briefly at the other end of the pit. He couldn't even see it—and he was standing right there next to it. No one walking past on the trail above ground would ever guess it was there.

He reached for the lip of the hole and started to pull himself back up, but the crumbly earth at the edge gave way and he fell backward. He landed on the soft loam, his head just inches from the tip of a deeply seated boulder. He lay on his back shivering and wet, fantasizing that he'd hit his head and that hole could now become his grave. If the hand of God could push that huge root ball back over on top of him, they'd never find his body. Not even the smell of his rotting flesh would give notice of his presence. He wanted to be dead, but he was very much alive and short of fishing that rifle back out of the dirt and turning it on himself, he would remain so. *Go home*, he thought as he finally pulled himself out of this dark netherworld and back out into light of the living. *Confess everything: Dad will know what to do.*

That's how Francesca found Connie, shivering uncontrollably at the front door with blue lips and chattering teeth to the point where he couldn't even get a single word out. As it wasn't even dinner time yet and virtually everyone at Big Pine had been caught in summer squalls out on the lake at one time or other, nothing seemed that unusual about his condition. Francesca wrapped him in blankets, drew a hot bath in the cast-iron ball-and-claw bathtub and poured him into it. Francesca sat on a stool next to the tub as her son thawed out and then Connie, in the first words he spoke to her, asked for his father.

Double was at the dining room table reviewing his notes on the Orion counterproposal.

"The polar explorer is asking for you," Francesca deadpanned from the top of the stairs.

When Double had appropriated the stool from his wife, Connie asked that they be alone. Francesca closed the door and Double looked down at his naked boy in the tub, still more child than man.

"There was an accident out on the lake," Connie said as he began crying. "And a kid got shot." Connie's hand went to his eyes to hide his tears. "I did it, Dad. I shot Kimmy Conner—I think I killed her." The child started to roll over in the tub as if to drown himself. Double reached in and grabbed his son violently by the hair.

"What?!" Double thundered. "You what?!" he repeated, as Francesca, who was obviously listening outside the door, now stepped inside.

"I was trying to pop the rubber raft, but I shot her by mistake. She fell in—I dove but I couldn't find her. She never back came up."

"I don't believe you." Double said. "How could you ever shoot in the direction of another child? I didn't teach you anything?!"

"What makes you think she's dead?" Francesca asked.

"I shot her in the head: I saw it—the blood. It was really windy and the tree I was leaning on moved. I was really close and saw right where it hit her."

"God help us," Francesca said as she began to weep.

"You're sure?" Double asked. "Maybe you made a mistake: Maybe she was only playacting—or you dreamed the whole thing like, a hallucination?"

Connie shook his head morosely.

"You know, once we call the police, there's no turning back. They will come for you—they'll arrest you tonight."

"There was blood coming out of her head, and I saw her go in the water. I'm pretty sure I killed her, Dad." Connie said, his voice withering under emotion. "She's down there somewhere . . . I'm really sorry."

XVII

Nathan Clarke was recovering from a day of dinghy racing at the annual Pequod Yacht Club Labor Day regatta and had fallen asleep in his lounger with his pipe in his mouth and a dog-eared anthology of O. Henry's short stories open on his chest. Southold sits nearly equidistant between town and Bridgewater, and the confirmed bachelor, now in his mid-sixties, had long since moved there to be closer to his sailing. He lived alone in a tidy two-bedroom apartment in a red brick building overlooking the harbor. The phone rang once and then twice. Nathan rarely ever got business calls at home, and never on weekends. He answered the phone with a sense of foreboding—whatever it was, it couldn't be good.

"There's been an accident, Nathan. It's just horrible," Double relayed. "Connie's killed another child—a twelve-year-old girl, Kimmy Conner. He shot toward her on the lake and hit her in the head by accident."

"Christ almighty . . ." Nathan whispered calmly into the phone and then, in a cold reflexive action, pushed aside the empty aluminum TV dinner tray from the kitchen table and reached for a yellow legal pad. He whetted the tip of a Blackfoot Indian pencil and started taking notes. "That's tragic—just terrible! Okay, what have we got—where are they holding him? Is it state or local police investigating?"

"Holding him? He's right here with us. There hasn't been an arrest: No one's investigating yet—no one's even been called. They haven't found her—I don't even think they know she's missing. Connie only just told us."

"Then the body's floating around somewhere out on the lake."

"I don't know. Connie said she never surfaced. I don't even see how that's possible?"

"It's possible—it's possible. No body . . ." Nathan noted clinically, as he underlined the words on his notepad. "Did anyone see it?"

"Connie says he was alone, but he's admitted everything. I think we need to contact the authorities and arrange his surrender."

"Have him give a full confession . . . are you kidding?" Nathan asked dispassionately as he laid the pencil on top of the legal pad.

"I think it's our only hope,"

"Our only hope for what?"

Nathan reached into his pants pocket and fished out his gold pocket watch. He opened the clamshell case and compared the watch face to the clock on the mantel, wound the stem and then closed the case and returned it to his pocket. The phone was silent throughout this procedure but Double knew the patterns and routines of the old lawyer and didn't need to be present to know that this elaborate ritual was taking place.

"Hold on a minute," Nathan said. "You don't have a homicide until you have a body. All you have is the story Connie told you—we don't really know anything. Currently, this is a potential missing person case, but even that won't apply for a couple of days. You've already got him confessing to a homicide, and you don't even know if a crime has been committed. Let's not get ahead of ourselves: If I put a call into the district attorney tonight, your family's on the front page of the *Times* tomorrow morning. You'll have a *60 Minutes* crew bivouacked at the end of your driveway till Thanksgiving. They'll say you should be held liable: *If the chairman of the board of Winston Firearms can't even keep his own son from killing another child, then firearms are just too dangerous and ought to be outlawed.*"

"What am I supposed to do?" Double asked. "Wait until the body pops up and then pretend I don't know anything about it?"

There was a long pause at the other end of the phone. Nathan's next words were pure, cool logic. "It'll be a charge of criminally negligent manslaughter, I expect." Then he changed his tone. "Think about what I'm saying here because you're not going to get another chance to get this right; we crank up the legal system now and there's no going back. The police and the media will hunt you to the ends of the earth. You're rich, and you run a gun company—they'll ruin you.

"I'm walking the fine line between providing legal counsel and acting as accessory after the fact; I could be disbarred."

Nathan exhaled into the receiver. "I suppose I can always wrestle with my conscience in retirement. Your father was a mentor to me, and I promised him I'd look out for you. You're a good man, Double. You're principled to a fault and I'm trying to stop you from making the mistake of your life. They'll make examples of you both. They'll demonize him and savage your family simply because of who you are. They'll prosecute him and then they'll litigate for the whole company—lock, stock and barrel.

"At present, you hold all the cards," Nathan continued. "Assuming you still have the gun, you control the physical evidence—the very facts of the case. If Nuremberg taught me anything, it's that an oven doesn't leave much for the prosecution." Nathan paused and let the implication resonate.

"Limit his exposure—decide when and where he's seen. Keep him out of the public eye and just let this thing play out a while—a couple of days. Let's see what turns up. Should you choose, Connie can always confess later without any physical evidence. The objective now is to keep our options open."

"You want me to destroy the rifle?"

"Of course not," Nathan replied. "Both the advice and the act would be illegal. But if they prosecute Connie, evidence tampering will be the least of your worries."

"Okay, I think we should proceed thusly," Nathan said as he read back the bullet points scratched onto his notepad. "Show yourself tonight so no one will say you acted strangely. Go out and do whatever it is that you normally do."

"We don't normally socialize in the evenings."

"Socialize tonight. See someone—anyone. Take a walk, borrow a cup of sugar. Go out and have a drink, but for Christ sake's be loud about it. Make damned sure people remember you and that you seemed like yourself. I need time to work through the next few moves on the chessboard. Slip out at dawn—I'll meet you all at Bailiwick in the morning."

"I can't do this, Nathan; I just don't think I could live with myself."

"What's the point of doing the right thing if it doesn't make any difference? Sacrificing your family and business isn't going to bring that girl back. A noble gesture—certainly—but also a pointless one; it'll only compound the tragedy."

"It's called accountability, Nathan. I still believe in doing the right thing."

"Spare me the sermon. There are German war criminals dying of old age every day who in a just world would have swung from the rafters on VE day. Atrocities go unpunished all the time—life is a filthy business." Nathan took a moment to recompose himself,

"For Connie's sake, I suggest we try to manage this situation for a while. If he's to come through, we'll have to play it just as slick-and-dirty as bilge water. To the media, you represent everything that's wrong with society: vast inherited wealth derived from a company that peddles in death. Your son surrenders to the authorities now, and what does that do to your employees? Those people rely on you for their very livelihoods. Are you really going to just hand over the keys to the kingdom and the heir to the throne?

"Besides," Nathan continued. "What do you think is going to happen once Orion discovers your son pulled a Lee Harvey Oswald with a Winston rifle? They'll shut down the refinancing—and just what kind of person do you think Connie would become after even a year in stir? He'd come out a bona fide criminal and probably queer—they all do at that age. His life will be ruined. Think: It's not just your conscience or mine at stake here. If she's dead, and that's by no means established, ruining the company and your only son's life isn't going to change it."

"Why would he make up such a story?" Double asked.

"They don't lie until they do, and I only pray that's the case here."

"I don't know . . ." Double added.

"Just meet me in the morning."

XVIII

That night they put Connie to bed with a mug of consommé liberally spiked with sherry to help the boy sleep, and Double did something he never did before: He played in the Big Pine poker game—seven card stud—and won nearly $500. It was a total fluke. He was there for an entirely different purpose and was aggressively laying bets in a foolhardy way. He even successfully once drew to an inside straight. His bluffs worked and when he was called, his cards held up. After little more than an hour, he finished two drinks and was clearing the table of his winnings against the other player's boisterous protests. Kevin Conner was wearing his green derby, with an unlit cigar clinched in his teeth, critiquing the beer on tap like he was some sort of half-assed sommelier. Kevin was also a lousy card player, prone to rambling chatter and off-color humor directed in an overly familiar manner toward people who no longer considered him a social peer and to whom he endlessly reminded that he remained *one of them.*

There was no talk of a missing child, as children came and went, slept over at each other's houses and were generally unaccounted for large stretches of time. If they could have cracked open Double's mind, out would have spilled the rudiments of a sinister plot, but instead, the men played a game of chance together and lost their money on a few exceptionally big pots. As the screen door slammed shut behind him, more than one guest noted that they had always regarded Double Winston as aloof and arrogant, but now that they'd played cards with him, they could see he was all right.

Connie was snoring deeply when Double and Francesca looked in on him later that night. Double then retreated to a small potting shed out back which Senior had repurposed into a workshop. There in the glow of the moonlight, Double placed the blade of the kitchen knife, the very knife he had seen Connie use to quarter the solid heads of dozens of bullets, into a heavy vise. He hammered the knife blade edge-on with a small sledge, ruining its cutting profile and forever destroying any link it had to Connie. Finally, he reset the knife and began snapping off sections of the hilt with swift, shallow blows from the hammer. When he was finished, he had a handful of battered, dull metal to go along with the wooden handle. He found a coffee can of loose nuts and bolts on the windowsill and emptied it out onto the work bench. He placed the pieces of the knife blade into it and replaced its plastic top. Double would be taking this home with him in the morning.

Then Double proceeded to drink several low-balls of Red Label Scotch. Finally, he sat silent at the kitchen table directly across from his wife, the square quart bottle and glass in front of him. There was nothing to say, but they spoke anyway.

"Do you think Nathan will . . ." she began.

"I don't know? We'll just have to wait."

"But it's not too late: We can still go to the police."

"It will be soon."

"Do you think we should?"

"I don't know, Franny—I honestly don't. Nathan *may* know exactly how to handle this, but that doesn't make it right. You make a mistake, you live with the consequences."

"It'll hover over him for the rest of his life," Francesca added.

"'Cowards die many times before their deaths; the valiant never taste of death but once.'"

XIX

Connie awoke from a terrifying nightmare at nearly four a.m. He was on the bottom of Big Pine Lake down amongst the weeds and bottom growth with the fresh-water eels and mud fish, and they were all nibbling at him, biting his fingers and toes. He was all tangled up in vegetation and drowning, and every time he tried to surface, the weeds would constrain and prevent him. Francesca came to his room to comfort him and sat on the edge of his bed. She held his hand in hopes that he might doze off again, but it was futile. He was soaked in sweat and had wet himself. As she comforted him, she also noticed that for the first time ever, she felt awkward touching her own son. Connie seemed different to her now, and she was different toward him because of it.

There was a ripe waxing moon bathing the night sky in pale light and at nearly five in the morning, Double announced to Connie that they should retrieve the rifle. This would be the first big risk they would ever take together. Everyone knew each other at the Big Pine Club, and if a child camping out under the stars, a paramour returning from a wayward bed or a drunk returning from a night on someone's sofa were to see father and son stealthily traversing the woods in the moonlight, there would be no plausible explanation for it.

Five a.m. isn't the same as three, where you might have a late night reveler making their way home. Nor is it the same as six, where one could expect the early risers of the world to throw open wide their windows and pull back the drapes to heartily greet another day with the good cheer and optimism that only a true morning person can muster. But neither type was afoot now, nor were there any children camping nearby. Indeed, the only stirrings in the woods were the wildlife, in particular the birds, which began their intermittent morning song.

After a brief search, Connie found his way back to the overturned tree, and momentarily the two peered down into the chasm of the root hole.

"Jump in and get it," Double commanded but Connie just stood there frozen. "It's about to be daylight. What the hell are you waiting for?"

"I'm scared," Connie admitted. "I don't wanna go back down there."

"Jesus," Double said, getting on his knees to peer down into the gaping hole. "A criminal conspiracy, and you're afraid of the dark." Double managed to get himself down into that pit and all the way to the back of the root ball when he suddenly heard the distant slam of a screen door. In an instant, Connie was down right alongside him, cowering in the soft, aromatic soil.

All that was apparent from outside the hole were two sets of blinking eyes straining against the weak light of daybreak, peering up from ground level. In a moment, they both heard the patter of feet, and the jogger passed by them on the trail not thirty feet from the hole. Hypervigilant in the last dawning twilight, Connie decisively reached up high, back into the root ball and withdrew the wool blanket roll with the rifle in it.

"Push me back up and I'll check that it's clear," he whispered nervously to his father.

XX

Double pulled his BMW sedan past the front gate of the Winston factory complex, and the security guard in the shack waved him through into the parking lot of the executive office building. It was unusual for Double to be at the office on a holiday weekend, but as chairman of the board of Winston Firearms with a prospective divestment in the works, weekend comings and goings were well within the realm of normal activity. It was six-thirty in the morning and other than a handful of security guards making their rounds, no one else was on site. Double parked the car and retrieved the blanket roll and coffee can, leaving a sleeping Connie on the back seat alongside his mother.

He crossed over the catwalk leading from his private office directly to the plant floor, his footsteps on the metal grating sounding a ghostly echo in the vast space. The morning sun was now luminous and full through the opaque glass windows, and while he could see well enough to navigate the huge open space of the massive factory floor, the dawning light left him with a spooky, lonely feeling. The great antique machines sat dormant like a static museum display of prehistoric creatures. Acres of large and small mechanical devices driven by current, steam, air and even pressurized oil were covered in a uniform silty layer of dusty grease that reminded Double of the Spanish moss–draped Live Oaks overhanging so much of Onori. The custom shop Heat Treatments and Forgings occupied a caged workshop in the corner of the building and required his private key for access.

The coal-fired forge with its electric bellows sat idle, with only a breath of air flowing through the system. Double opened the guillotine door of the oven, could feel the residual heat from its last firing days ago, and threw in a dozen shovelfuls of coal. He balled up a piece of newspaper, lit it with a loose Diamond Strike Anywhere match, carefully laid it in on the bed of coals and closed the gate again. He flipped the toggle switch to activate the electric bellows fan that stoked the fire, and the coals caught. He let the bellows run nearly half an hour. He put on a heavy suede apron and a set of insulated leather welder's gloves that went up to his elbows, and when the coals burned a bright orange, he arranged the hot bed evenly with the tip of the shovel. When he was satisfied, he laid the blanket roll on top of the work bench and opened it.

Inside the wet, gray wool blanket was the blow-up sea-serpent raft, and inside of that was the aluminum and plastic paddle and the soft case containing the rifle—the rifle from his own childhood. It represented all that he wasn't, his father's best efforts. It was now brown-orange with rust and still wet to the touch.

The rifle, the coffee can, the brick of ammunition and especially the loose rounds still scotch-taped to the trigger guard, were the only physical evidence directly linking his son to the crime. The rifling inside that barrel, which provided the slug with its unique "ballistic fingerprint" made it traceable directly back to that specific firearm. It was singular evidence that could hang a man. He worked the bolt and slid the breech open just enough to see that the spent brass shell casing left from the killing round remained. He closed the bolt again without ejecting the hull. Other than the round which struck Kimmy Conner, all the evidence relating to the homicide sat before him.

Double removed the clear plastic brick of .22 long rifle bullets. He wanted to look them over and slid the plastic rack out of the box, using too much force. The entire thing came out in one big jerk, sending dozens of remaining bullets flying individually, each one of the production lot a piece of incriminating evidence and all marred by the same telltale quartered solid head that Connie had so meticulously cleaved into them. The small, rim-fire cartridges were scattered all over the concrete shop floor like spilled coffee beans. Double was on his hands and knees, blind to the interior darkness, frantically scooping them up by the handful into the skirt of his leather apron: Any one of these could convict the boy. They could easily match these things up now—comparing the production lot and the blade-marks left by the kitchen knife with the bullet that killed the girl!

The concrete floor was strewn with cartridges, and those were just the ones he could see. Double carefully funneled his leather apron skirt into a large cast-iron frying pan big enough to handle an entire flank steak, which the custom shop employees often used for cooking their lunch over the hot coals of the forge. Then he got on his hands and knees and felt around the cool, hard floor, into corners and under work benches for any loose pieces that escaped his immediate view. Double wasn't feeling very satisfied or very confident that he'd found every single bullet from the brick. He even resorted to turning on a few lamps to illuminate the shop floor, but he couldn't be certain he'd gotten them all—it was a big space with lots of shady spots for small objects to hide in. *Besides*, he thought in an attempt to catch his imagination before it completely ran away with him, *the factory complex manufactures both arms and ammunition. The police would find thousands of rounds of loose ammunition lying around before they'd ever stumble onto an actual piece of evidence.*

The solution to his problem, Double realized in an epiphany, lay directly in front of him in the form of that frying pan. When he returned to work from the holiday weekend, he'd simply take a stroll down to Heat Treatments and Forgings with a beefsteak and baking potato and make use of that frying pan. While his steak was cooking, he'd casually poke around to make sure he'd gotten everything. Senior used to take his lunch regularly with the men down there, and while Double's presence might seem a bit unusual, the custom shop employees were already half-afraid of him anyway and would be certain to leave him alone.

His mind eased as he rolled the cased rifle and aluminum paddle back into the sea-serpent blow-up raft, and wrapped it all back into the wet blanket. He opened the door to the forge and the sudden burst of heat licked at his face and eyebrows. This was it: He was crossing the Rubicon into felony evidence tampering and obstruction of justice. Double knew it was wrong, knew that the killing of the Conner girl might even be regarded as a legitimate accident, but his own behavior in this moment was intentionally criminal.

Connie *had* shown poor judgment in his deliberate actions

and fully deserved to be punished. Nathan was correct though, the price for this justice was simply too high. This was the only hard evidence linking Connie to the missing child, and once they were destroyed, the crime would effectively become untraceable—all connections to the Winston family severed.

Double put on the insulated leather welding gloves and gently tossed the blanket roll onto the hot coals. Then he threw in the coffee can and finally took the frying pan with both hands by the handle and flung its contents like gravel into the forge. He closed the gate, and the flames engulfed the firearm. The bullets began to crack like popcorn, harmless without the compression a breech provides to make them lethal. His heart fluttered briefly and he felt faint: He too was now a criminal.

The wooden stock completely burned off the metal hardware of the rifle, and all that remained was the glowing, barreled action. Double turned on the belt drive to the industrial air compressor for the 2,500-pound pneumatic forging hammer—a drop hammer on a flat die—which was used to improve heated raw bar stock before it was worked into a finished product. He put on a set of earmuffs and safety goggles, and when the machine was up to pressure, he placed his foot on the treadle and activated the hammer's full length of stroke. The drop hammer made a deafening strike against the flat die. Double then opened the forge and fished out the remains of the rifle action with two sets of blacksmith tongs. He laid the rifle action on the die, floored the treadle and guided the metal under the ram with the thongs. Orange sparks exploded off the die as the pneumatic hammer rapidly pounded the steel again and again. Double then turned the steel on its side so that it could be worked again. Finally, he reheated what was now becoming a crude alloy bar.

When he was certain that nothing about the remaining lump of metal could discern it as the specific instrument of death, he removed it from the flat die and doused it in vat of water. The threat was gone, just a harmless lump of metal now—or was it? Science was forever inventing new ways to investigate a crime, and just because Double couldn't see any way for the crude forging to incriminate his son, he thought better of abandoning it to the scrap hopper.

The slag from the bullets and coffee can were unidentifiable, but what to do with the remains of the rifle?

The final method of disposal of the murder weapon was simple but effective: salt water and time. As Francesca drove south on the turnpike in the slow lane and with Connie asleep in the back seat, Double hand-cranked open the car's sunroof, crouched low on the passenger seat and then stood up through that hole as he lobbed the forging off the towering highway overpass and into Bridgewater Harbor far below.

XXI

The Winston family ate breakfast at the kitchen table in silence. Connie devoured his plateful of food and then helped himself to another serving of scrambled eggs and toast. Double forced down a few forkfuls; Francesca didn't touch a thing and drank only black coffee. Finally, a rap came on the window pane of the kitchen door and there was Nathan Clarke, briefcase in hand, graying hair under his brown fedora, unlit pipe upside down in his mouth, standing rail-thin against the morning drizzle.

"Send the boy upstairs," Nathan said cryptically as he sat down at the kitchen table. "The time for niceties is over, and I need to be frank with you both. Just know," he said, wagging his finger at Connie, "what a mess you've made. It'll be all I can do to keep you from spending the remainder of your adolescence behind bars."

Stunned by the indictment, Connie left the room, but only pretended to go upstairs and instead stood at the door to the dining room leading directly into the kitchen, eavesdropping on the conversation.

"As it stands," Nathan continued, "there's only one way I can think to the put the toothpaste back in the tube, and neither of you are going to like it . . ."

Double and Francesca both shifted uneasily in their chairs.

"Sooner or later, the police are going to bring Connie in for questioning, and when they do, he's sure to crack. Children generally can't handle a formal police interview. They've been conditioned to obey authority and if he tells what he knows, we're done for—all of us. I propose that you leave immediately—take him out of the country." Both parents began to object, but Nathan quelled their protests in short order. "If he's in Switzerland, it adds a layer of geography and red tape that could buy us valuable time."

"How's it going to look, him running off immediately after the ... incident?" Double noted. "It's suspicious as hell."

"You're married to a Swiss national. You might have a *perfectly good* reason for being there?"

"What?"

Nathan shifted forward in his chair, literally leaning into his argument. "Were you to accept the latest Orion offer—I have a contact over at the *Journal* and the announcement could run in tomorrow's paper. A man who's just agreed to divest himself from a major stock position has many millions of legitimate reasons to access the Swiss banking system—to go there in person even. In fact, he may need to spend quite a lot of time there and might want to bring his family along; perhaps put the boy in school—give him a language."

"My son is an American," Francesca objected.

"An American with a Swiss passport," Nathan noted dryly. "I told you we're chasing options here. Once we get him over, he can remain for a few years and then come back and try his luck with the authorities. The trail will have cooled, and his memory of the incident may have—shall we say *evolved*. Or he could choose to remain in Europe as an expatriate, finish his education and begin a whole new life there. You could visit him periodically and your parents could . . ."

"Raise my son? I think not, Mr. Clarke," Francesca stated bluntly. "Connie will remain in the United States with his parents."

"You could also . . ."

"What?" Double demanded.

Nathan reached for his attaché case, opened it, removed a dog-eared hardback copy of *On the Children's Ward* and opened it to a page notated in highlighter. "It's all right here: Your father chronicled the whole procedure for generating amnesia—the deliberate clouding of memory."

"My father didn't write that book," Francesca declared indignantly.

"We're not really going to play that game are we? Simon Wiesenthal and *The New York Times* say your father wrote *On the Children's Ward*. I was witness to the Nuremberg Doctor's trial, for Christ' sake! I reviewed his dossier—read the depositions. It's a wonder he wasn't in the dock with the rest of them."

Double looked on quietly, and then it suddenly dawned on him. "You're not suggesting . . ."

"Dr. Berger documented that experience doesn't fully catalogue into long-term memory for forty-eight hours. You land in Switzerland tonight, start the treatments right away and . . ." Nathan said snapping his fingers. "You might be able to bring him to a point where he could actually survive a full-on police interrogation."

"I won't allow it." Francesca said.

"Don't you think you should at least talk to him?"

"Jesus Christ, Nathan, why don't you just give him a lobotomy while you're at it?! We're not going to plug Connie into a wall socket like a lab rat!" Double snapped.

"If you've got a better idea, I'm all ears!" Nathan responded just as viciously. "We've only got a handful of viable options left to us, and this happens to be one of the best. Try it. If it works, he's back in school in a week and no one's the wiser. If it doesn't, he can always just stay abroad."

"And if your cover-up succeeds, it's sure to turn scandalous. We'll all be tainted by it," Francesca added.

"But you will come through it—Connie without a criminal record and you with the company as a going concern. I'm not saying you won't need a change of underwear, but you will survive it."

"There must be some other way," Double finally lamented.

"He can't be seen in public," Nathan continued. "I put two pilots on standby last night. A noon flight should give you just enough time to . . ."

"I can't take the company jet ocean-hopping on a lark; there are rules—corporate bylaws." Double said.

"There are—I wrote most of them myself. I say go."

"There must be some other way . . ." Francesca repeated.

"If there is, I can't think of it," Nathan said definitively as he finally leaned back in his chair, removed the tobacco pouch from his pants pocket and began to pack his pipe.

"This is insidious stuff, Nathan. Really sinister," Double noted.

"I'm not telling you what to do. The actions we take now may lead to all sorts of unforeseeable consequences—unfortunate outcomes for both the boy and us. May I?" he asked politely as he struck a match, and when granted permission, proceeded to light his pipe.

"What to do?" Double said, wringing his hands.

"'The fault, dear Brutus, is not in our stars but in ourselves.' Life is unfair, but this *was* an accident. Connie *is* a good boy and you *are* decent people—you don't deserve to have this thing destroy you."

Connie's eyes went wide with fear. *What were they going to do to him?* He didn't want to go to Europe for the rest of his life—and just what kind of treatments would they administer so he would forget what happened? None of it made any sense, but what could he do—run away from home?

"I guess we pack then," Double announced.

XXII

A transatlantic crossing by private plane is an elaborate proposition, with the route being dictated by the range of the aircraft. In this case the plane was a Learjet 24, a six-seat, second-generation executive jet with a total range of 1,700 miles. The corporate pilots had to route through Gander, Newfoundland; Reykjavik, Iceland; and Shannon, Ireland before finally clearing customs at Zurich and continuing on to the airfield at Agno near Lugano, Switzerland. Neither pilot—one older, one younger—had ever flown off the North American continent, and both men found the journey disorienting and the reasons for it mysterious. Stranger still was that after only a 24-hour layover in Agno, the empty jet initiated the return flight. It seemed a fabulous waste of fuel and wear-and-tear on the aircraft when a commercial flight was faster, more direct and less expensive by a factor of twenty.

The journey took seventeen hours, and it was noon when the Winston family finally checked into a suite at the five-star Hotel Splendide Royal, a former palace overlooking the lake a short stroll from the city center. They ordered room service—club sandwiches—and then went to bed. When they awoke, Francesca called her parents to announce that they were in town and wanted to have dinner with them.

*   *   *   *   *

The clinic had been an odd environment for Francesca to grow up in. The Berger family lived in a private apartment on the top floor of the villa above two stories of patient housing. One floor had six bedrooms and appointments on par with a deluxe pension, the other floor had a four-bed hospital infirmary with two additional padded rooms. There were several common rooms in the villa, a small library with books in four languages, a common television, and each room had its own radio. Normally there were no more than a half-dozen patients in residence at a given time.

Mature, neatly kept Cyprus trees overlooked the clinic's three acres of parklike grounds which had gravel paths so patients could walk for exercise. The compound also had terraced gardens with rose bushes and sitting areas for taking in the mountain air and lake views. The clinic had its own chef, and the staff and patients took their meals communally, albeit at separate tables. Only Dr. Heinrich Berger took his evening meal entirely separately in his quarters with his family. After the patients and staff had all been served, Dr. Berger would retire to his residence on the top floor, where a dumbwaiter would shuttle dinner directly up to the family's private dining room. The cuisine was exceptional, and Francesca became rather spoiled by it. Later in life, whenever she was served something she felt wasn't up to snuff, she would quip, "Back at the clinic, we wouldn't serve this to the cat."

There was an annex building which housed Dr. Berger's private office as well as the treatment center and all the ECT equipment. This building had Italianate frescoes adorning its vaulted ceilings, with live grapevines and fig plants climbing trellises on its outside walls. It also contained, as do all postwar buildings in Switzerland, a bomb shelter in the basement which served double duty as Dr. Berger's laboratory and storeroom.

As a child, Francesca was curious about her surroundings and sought to thoroughly explore the clinic complex from the stone retaining walls of the terraced lawns to the underground grotto that acted as cold storage for root vegetables and other foodstuffs. She poked around inside the villa and found a large cellar room still half-filled with coal and an accompanying furnace that was dormant, abandoned in place and no longer fired for heat. When she expressed interest in the treatment center, Dr. Berger took her through the building. He even showed her his private office and then his lab, but the accompanying store room remained locked and off-limits.

Francesca never saw what was inside that basement room that occupied half of the footprint of the entire building. What was the great mystery which Dr. Berger kept hidden behind the heavy vault door with its spinning-dial combination lock? His daughter suffered the anguish of overwhelming curiosity, but then Dr. Berger put an end to this by informing her that it was for her own protection that she should never know what was inside. They were things left over from the war and, yes, some of it *really was that horrible*. Eventually the doctor's wife was able to cool the burning inquisitiveness of her daughter; certain things in life one could never know, and everyone, her father included, had the right to privacy. Francesca would simply have to learn to live with the great mystery of the locked door.

*   *   *   *   *

D r. Berger had gained notoriety in the scientific community as the sinister stepfather of electroconvulsive therapy. In the postwar era he published some 70 peer-reviewed articles on ECT clinical trials, covering a wide range of areas. During the war, conventional clinical trials were conducted dealing with depression and manic-depression in conjunction with ECT, but experiments were also undertaken on adolescent female hormonal imbalances, arousal and a woman's ability to conceive, and clinical depression in pregnant women.

Unorthodox clinical trials were conducted on cognitive function and memory, investigating ECT's effect on the ability to learn, as well as the improvement, manipulation and intentional destruction of memory. From this starting point, Berger then explored the very outer limits of the therapy, experimenting with variable voltage and duration of electrostimulation to various isolated areas of the brain. There was also a trial where holes were bored into the subjects' skulls and electrodes attached directly onto the surface of the cerebral cortex. It was these trials which explored and later established the baseline thresholds which shut down the various areas of the brain's higher functions, deliberately inducing a permanent fugue state by destroying basic long- and short-term memory, as well as the very building blocks of personality, ultimately putting the subjects into a permanent vegetative state.

Comprehensive findings derived from these clinical trials were based on complex cognitive tests. These were followed up with detailed questionnaires in conjunction with scrupulous scientific observation. Finally, there was the comparative postmortem examination, always of healthy identical twins or triplets ranging in age from nine to seventeen; one sibling acted as the passive control subject.

XXIII

A soft, cooling breeze rolled down from the mountains, bringing welcome respite from the heat of the day. Rainclouds accompanied by occasional lightning bolts drifted over Monte Brè toward the lakefront. It was an awkward surprise meeting with Francesca's mother, Gerda, in the dining room of the Berger family apartment. The sudden visit could only mean something was awry. They didn't speak of it to Gerda just yet because they didn't want to have to explain it all over again when Dr. Berger appeared. So they all made anxious small talk until the dumbwaiter shuttled their meal up to them and Gerda laid the food on the table.

The apartment was comfortable, furnished with heavy pieces and artwork from Germany. As is so often the case with expatriates, they imported their own heritage, along with themselves, in the form of home furnishings.

At 7:30 sharp, Dr. Berger took his turn around the dinner table, first kissing his daughter on the forehead and then chucking his grandson behind the back of his neck. He clicked his heels smartly at *attention* to Double, took his place at the head of the table and began ladling out the consommé. His white lab coat hung on the back of his chair, and he wore gray flannel slacks, with black horse-bit loafers, a fitted pink shirt with a red, black and white striped bow tie—the color palette of the Nazi swastika flag.

He was baby faced, with a high forehead, jug ears and a thick head of straw-colored hair. He wore a Van Dyke beard that he meticulously maintained each morning with an antique straight razor. Other than the heavy black-framed glasses he required, he was a very young seventy. Dr. Berger was a man for whom many things came easily, especially languages. He spoke in the same clipped British accent as his daughter—a sort of refined mid-Atlantic hybrid which he articulated loquaciously and in grand flourishes. His oration was to speaking what calligraphy is to writing.

The doctor was obsessive about his weight and general fitness: How can a medical professional sell good health in all its forms when the prescribing doctor is himself unhealthy? For this reason, every day he walked three kilometers down the hill to the city square—the Piazza della Riforma—to buy his daily newspapers at the big Presse Internationale booth there. Then he climbed the long, steep stairs all the way back up to the clinic. Ticino partakes in the Latin tradition of the *siesta* with a two-hour lunch, so Dr. Berger dedicated a full hour each day to this sojourn.

Gerda Berger was sixty-five, small, dark and little bit spindly, with olive skin and short black hair exhibiting fine wisps of gray. That day she wore burgundy lipstick the hue of a ruby gemstone and an ornate, flower-print dress. Even in heels, she didn't stand five-feet tall.

Dr. Berger gave a brief thanks in German to the Almighty for the meal they were about to receive, and they all ate: soup, salad and spaghetti carbonara—the cream, egg yolk, pancetta and cheese specialty of the region.

As coffee and cookies were served, Dr. Berger finally addressed the elephant in the room. "Though I'm delighted to have my entire family together, what brings you to us without so much as a hint of warning?"

Double reached into Francesca's oversized purse, withdrew Nathan's marked-up copy of the *On the Children's Ward* and laid it squarely in front of the doctor.

XXIV

D r. Berger spun the dials on the combination lock to the vault of his laboratory storeroom. "You're the first person I've ever shown this to. There was plenty about the children's ward that I didn't chronicle: It's all right here, and I expect you to keep it confidential." He gave the vault handle a sharp turn and swung the heavy steel slab on its hinges. He reached in and flicked the switch activating the ceiling lights that illuminated the windowless room. The concrete floors were painted institutional green, and crude, rough-hewn wooden racks containing large specimen jars with ground-glass stoppers packed the space from floor to ceiling.

"Had I stayed in Germany, cooperated with the War Crimes Commission and testified accurately to the facts of my wartime activities, I certainly would have been executed. I chose this life instead.

"I don't make myself an easy target. I haven't stepped over the border in fifteen years. Swiss neutrality is the only thing keeping me alive. If I leave, Interpol will detain me or the Mossad will kidnap me. I've become a minor prize, and they *will* try for me—eventually. They started at the very top and have worked their way down to a little fish like me.

"My family was wealthy," Dr. Berger continued. "I had connections. The Vatican was sympathetic to my plight and arranged a visa to emigrate. For most, Switzerland was only the first stop on the way to South America, but I found myself unable to continue."

Awestruck, Double browsed the aisles of racks and studied the labels on the jars, which were all in German and marked with Nazi symbols.

"I knew this remained—irreplaceable tissues and accompanying data, enough to last a lifetime—entombed in Bavaria waiting to be rediscovered. Meggendorfer—Dr. Friedrich Meggendorfer—was a pioneer of electroconvulsive therapy. I interned under him in Hamburg. During the war they sent him to teach at the medical school at Erlangen-Nuremberg. When I was conscripted into the medical corps, he requested that I be assigned to him. I conducted all the clinical trials on the children's ward—unorthodox trials to test the extreme limits of electroconvulsive therapy. Dr. Meggendorfer had very high connections all the way up to Philipp Bouhler, who was administering Tiergartenstrasse 4, the German national euthanasia agenda, T4 Action.

"Early on, we were given German children from the state

mental hospital in Eichberg, the special children's ward at the psychiatric clinic at Heidelberg and the Brandenburg Euthanasia Center—mostly epileptics, but also some backward children and spastics. Later, Mengele sent us Jewish twins and triplets: perfectly normal, healthy children—nine- and ten-year-olds—from Auschwitz. Meggendorfer maintained strong ties with Hamburg, and the Neuengamme work camp there provided subjects as well." Double reached the far wall and noticed a series of carefully framed signed correspondences lining the wall: Viktor Brack, Dr. Brandt, Dr. Mengele and Kurt Blome.

"These men were my colleagues," Dr. Berger continued. "I was only too proud to be associated with them during the war. . . . I honor them now because although our actions in hindsight were obviously wicked, our intentions were altruistic—unproductive lives sacrificed on the altar of medical advancement."

Double was looking at hundreds of preserved brains—gray, immature, textured cerebrums—floating in hazy formaldehyde solution. He came upon another row of racks on which complete skulls were preserved. The skin had been removed, along with the lower jaw, lips, teeth, ears, eyelids, eyes and hair—all gone. But the human likeness of the diminutive skulls remained unmistakable. Clearly, they were children: nine- or ten-year-olds. Double stared deep into their ghostly visages for any sense of emotional expression.

"I awarded them sweets: That's how the orderlies knew which paperwork to prepare in advance of the postmortem. I gave candy to those unlucky children at the morning bed check; later in the day, I would administer an injection of phenol or chloroform directly into the ventricle of the heart. I felt the life pass from them with my own hands. It was humane, I suppose, but it was also murder. I euthanized most of these myself," he said, gesturing with a vague wave of his hand. "Monstrous times."

Double continued down the line of skulls, and suddenly he was into a series of perfectly preserved children's heads, with skin, lips and eyes, replete with waxen enigmatic expressions. A pair of twins was separated by glass jars just inches from each other, as intimate in death as they'd been in life.

"It's all true then—everything they said about you," Double noted.

"Much of it—yes. Many point to the period of the war—the prevailing culture of strident nationalism, anti-Semitism and the personal oath to the Führer as an excuse. I was a grown man—a fully-qualified physician—and should have been beyond such influences. I *could* have left—it wasn't easy, but some did. I had connections in New York, but I chose to stay. I *wanted* to be a part of it.

"Suddenly, I could do anything! Legally, these were no longer even citizens and were regarded as subhuman. I, Dr. Heinrich Berger, alone was going take this epochal leap forward in neuroscience. I had complete authority on the children's ward, and reported to only two superiors: Dr. Friedrich Meggendorfer and Dr. Karl Brandt, chief medical officer of the entire Reich. Life was cheap, and the subjects were far and away the easiest matter to arrange. I knew it was damnable, but I became intoxicated by it. There were no rules, and this vacuum of accountability made me delusional."

Finally, Double came across three special jars—the bifurcated heads of three pretty females, triplets, more women than girls.

"These three, I attempted to keep as pets," Berger said, peering at the statuesque faces inside the jars. "The Blankenese triplets, the sisters Lillianthal: Jewesses barely, from Neuengamme in Hamburg, the near embodiment of the Aryan ideal. Fair skinned, copper hair, hazel eyes." The faces were refined in structure and features, with high foreheads, cheekbones and narrow noses.

"They were quite fetching in life. The father was a prominent antiques dealer before the war, with substantial land holdings, and they were raised in the Blankenese suburb. Their mother was a music teacher, and each could play piano and harpsichord. In hindsight, I believe I hoped to prolong their lives long enough for them to actually survive the war. I used them first in the cognitive learning trials, then in the arousal and fertility study. They shared quarters, so their menstrual cycles were already synchronized.

When all eventually conceived, I used them in the depression study on pregnant women.

"Expansionist policy suggested that native Germans would resettle the newly conquered lands—exterminate the locals and repopulate with our own superior genetics. Obviously, to put this into practice would require a major increase in birthrates. Mengele was obsessed with twins and triplets because in perfecting the division of the zygote, we could repopulate new territories at ever increased forces of magnitude. The same holds for arousal and fertility: If we can arouse a frigid woman to sexual intercourse through ECT and generally increase her chances of conception, we can reproduce that much faster. If we can keep a crippling melancholy at bay throughout the entire gestation period, this is a good thing.

"Each of the Blankenese triplets engaged in sexual intercourse with the same three Russian boys every day for five days running. The trials proved inconclusive, however, and I eventually terminated fetuses in all three. In the end, it was all just so much wasted effort. Provincial bureaucrats conceived these preposterous theories— frigid women, depressed pregnancies. These were typical young girls with normal levels of sexual desire, nothing more. They were triplets; that's the only reason they were chosen. Trying to cure healthy subjects of nonexistent ailments was a waste of resources.

"Educated young ladies from a genteel society, forced to spread their legs like Reeperbahn streetwalkers—sick!" Dr. Berger now huffed slightly in sincere indignation. "Shy schoolgirls who should have been contemplating a first kiss instead of engaging in such perversions!

"There was a small medical gallery of clinical observers assigned to document these proceedings. The top political appointees: not scientists, mind you, simple laymen, but men of real influence just the same. They heard of the clinical galleries and demanded to observe these reproductive acts, and it became a kind of private show. Social hygiene policies forbade all sexual contact with Jews, but *this* they had to witness."

These specimens, which completely mesmerized Double, were unusual because only half their heads were present. They had been bisected—cut clean through bone and soft tissue. One had been halved horizontally, front-to-back, directly under the nose. The next was split vertically between the eyes and through the centerline of the nose, and the third was divided from behind the right ear through the left side of the jaw. These three cross-sectioned skulls of nearly identical triplets gave a unique anatomical perspective. Taken from just the right angles, they remained beautiful young woman, their wisps of copper hair, light as corn silk, drifting on microcurrents within the formaldehyde solution.

"My father died suddenly," Berger continued. "And I went home for the funeral. When I returned, this is how I found them. Word had got round about the spectator galleries, and Meggendorfer was humiliated. He could be quite prudish, and put an immediate end to it. Then he reviewed my files and realized how long these particular subjects had been lingering about. He preferred very young subjects for his trials anyway. They ate less and lacked the self-awareness to fully comprehend what was happening. These girls weren't even children anymore. There was to be a museum in Alsace—anatomy and skeletons at the Institute of Forensic Medicine at Strasbourg. The medical chief heading this program, Dr. August Hirt, was an SS man. He was undertaking to find attractive nearly identical subjects for a particular display, and I imagine the Lillianthal sisters just proved too appealing . . .

"Naturally, this result upset me. These girls looked like me, spoke like me with the same high dialect. I completed my medical training in Hamburg: They might well have been my sisters or perhaps even my daughters. How can one then say that these unique human beings have value only as tissue samples? From that day forward I could never reconcile my inner conflict, and became quite useless. The war ended before the Strasbourg exhibition ever opened."

A twisted, shocked expression lingered on the girl's tragic faces, an echo of emotion across the decades.

"At Erlangen, there was an orderly with a clubbed foot and a horse-faced wife—a childless couple. As the war was ending, I gave them twin infant boys to keep for their own and told them I might someday try to return for all this," Berger said, gazing about the space. "They looked after it in the years following the war. I sent them postcards from the resort Island of Sylt in the North Sea and the address of my Vatican contact. This was how they communicated with me. Each Christmas, I sent them a bit of money through Rome, and every August I was forwarded a postcard from the beach. *The weather is fine*, meant come along anytime. *It rained all week* meant the samples had been discovered and I should abandon my plan. I received regular correspondence of sunny weather for five years, but I couldn't figure how I could possibly retrieve the materials. I certainly couldn't return to Germany to live, and bringing it all back to Lugano would have required several moving trucks.

"So I waited patiently and followed the war crimes tribunals with great interest. Meggendorfer was very clever in not leaving a paper trail, as well as keeping his official distance from me. He was the head of the entire Psychiatric Department at Erlangen, but the children's ward fell under Pediatrics. Administratively, one couldn't easily connect us. My mandate was broad, and my instructions often verbal. I was in awe of Meggendorfer to the point of being naïve—and I showed initiative. It was my name, my signature, authorizing nearly everything. Later, he simply lied, disavowing the program and betraying me in the process. No one could prove otherwise. He was saving his own skin of course—that much I understand, but his prejudicial testimony made me *a person of interest* to the authorities.

"During this time, I gained fluency in Italian and was awarded my medical license in Switzerland. We purchased this villa and undertook to establish our clinic. I wrote *On the Children's Ward*, and was as surprised as anyone when it found a publisher and became successful. I also hoped that some miracle would materialize, allowing me to return to Erlangen.

"Then Francesca began taking horseback riding lessons and the light went on: A horse is a free license to move about with a lorry. I brought a second-hand horsebox over from England and had it modified, creating a false wall with a hidden compartment. After that, we only ever went to horseshows in Bavaria, and we always stopped at Erlangen on the way back. Toward the end of the war, the building which housed the children's ward had been partially bombed out, and all of this was consolidated inside the foundation. We hid it in the dry-goods pantry of the damaged commissary.

"We would stay overnight with the orderly and his family. I would slip out with him before dawn and load the horsebox while Francesca slept. We had to offload the horses to do it—and this was inside the city center, mind you. It was still blocks and blocks of bombed-out rubble, and it was certainly odd to see horses in such an environment. Only once, at the very beginning, did anyone ever investigate. It was the local constable, but the orderly knew him. I told him I had been a doctor at Erlangen during the war and was simply allowing my animals to stretch their legs. I gave him a package of cork-tipped cigarettes with a few Marks tucked inside for his trouble, and that became a regular routine. Once this pattern was established, he stopped caring about what we were doing and looked for his packet of Craven "A"s.

"We always crossed the Swiss border on the eastern shore of the Bodensee. It was an obscure passport control, and the guards became quite familiar with us. Perhaps a half-dozen times they poked their heads inside the horsebox, and only once were any of them brave enough to actually climb inside. Horses are intimidating even to an armed border guard, and they generally wanted nothing to do with us. Once they even threatened to unload the animals to make a proper inspection, but the supervisor put a stop to it.

"It went on like this for years. Each season going to and from horseshows in Bavaria and, gradually, I was able to transport the collection." Dr. Berger went to the end of one of the racks, reached down and withdrew a black metal ECT box. "That's what I'm after," he said, as he laid it on top of the stone laboratory countertop.

"If I want my grandson to flicker like a glowworm tomorrow, I need to rewire this box tonight," he quipped, as he wiped the dust off the box with a shop rag. "Seimans-Reiniger was located in Erlangen and made these units especially for us: sine-wave, variable voltage and duration—quite devastating. I haven't used one since the war, but it will be necessary. There is no other way."

"Forty years of mystery and you finally show all this to me now. Why?"

Dr. Berger was at work with a Phillips-head screwdriver, patiently removing the black metal housing of the device. "The truly momentous secrets we live with alone: That is the burden of *getting away with it*. Now that you're as compromised as I and have every bit as much to lose, I can share it with you. We have perfect leverage over each other."

Double was perplexed.

Dr. Berger removed the housing, took a photographer's lens brush with a pneumatic rubber bulb and began blowing the dust off the internals. "I don't know how much longer I'll live, but when you eventually go to sell the clinic, none of this can remain. My life's work," he said, broadly surveying the space. "What little reputation I enjoy—good or bad—is because of it. At such a late stage, I'll not have my medical achievements diminished by the sinister means required to achieve them.

"Incinerate it," he continued. "There is an abandoned furnace in the cellar of the villa which burns coal—there's still a half portion in store down there. Fire that oven, and I expect it could consume everything in a week's time. This sink connects directly to the sewer, so you can pour the formaldehyde solution down the drain—this will significantly lighten your load. Everything must go: subject files, every paper scrap, all the tissue samples and slides. The glass pieces must be crushed and buried."

"I'm not sure I can do that," Double said, looking around the room. "These were human beings once."

"Who are long dead: just a bit of meat suspended in solution now."

"I'm chairman of the board of an international brand. I can't have anything to do with this," Double reiterated flatly.

Dr. Berger laid the screwdriver on the stone countertop and wiped his hands on the rag.

"In that case, I'm not certain I'm willing to risk impairing my own grandson for you. *This* is the quid pro quo, you realize. Connie is a perfectly healthy adolescent. You want me to administer a severe therapy—to intentionally induce grand mal seizures, hoping not to cure him of any ailment but rather to incur a very specific side effect. You want me to manipulate his mind—to wipe clean the memory of a crime he committed. During the war, I was quite effective at eradicating entire windows of recall. Perhaps we get lucky and your problem disappears like magic. But make no mistake: We are in the bronze age of brain science. I *could* kill him—make him a vegetable. It's happened before, and I'd prefer not take the risk at all.

"I can try, but you owe me and I need you to take care of this for me when I'm gone. That's our arrangement. You shake my hand on this night and promise: No one can ever know, not the scientific community and not *this* community—certainly not my daughter. Remove everything and destroy it before the property is sold. Do you agree?" Dr. Berger held out his hand and waited for Double to place his within it. "Swear on it."

Double grasped the old man's hand—soft, warm and pink as a baby's. "I swear," Double said as he shook it.

XXV

The immediate changes to the boy were dramatic and acute. It was clear to Connie's parents that this core shift was fundamental to his basic personality. So desperate were they for a solution to their dilemma that in spite of these changes, they allowed the series of shock treatments to continue. For his part, Dr. Berger administered the electroconvulsive therapy twice daily and announced that the results, while not optimal, were quite typical and fell within the normal range.

Connie didn't smile much anymore—his perpetual smirk was gone. Nor was he playful or outgoing. He didn't initiate conversation, and then often slowly parroted back words or snippets of sentences others spoke. His eyes seemed inanimate and dead, his spark of life reduced to a smoldering ember. The side effects might seem devastating at first, Dr. Berger cautioned, but they were quite temporary and usually subsided entirely on their own. The boy seemed weary and withdrawn—detached and indifferent to the world around him. Both parents agonized over concerns they had made the biggest mistake of their lives, permanently impairing the boy.

The litmus test came when Dr. Berger gave Connie an exit interview, asking him several leading questions about the family's summer vacation at Big Pine Lake.

"Do you have many friends there?" Dr. Berger asked.

"Friends," Connie repeated in monotone. His cranium was mostly shorn clean of hair and only a small thin oval patch remained on top. He looked like a Marine recruit on his first day of boot camp.

"Other children with whom you enjoy playing and spending time."

"I like to play," Connie answered earnestly.

"Do you have any girlfriends?" the doctor inquired. Connie remained silent and evasive. "A girl you especially favor?"

"No," Connie replied. "No girls."

"Your parents said they thought you had a romantic affection for a particular girl. Is this correct?"

"Affection?" Connie repeated blankly.

"For a girl—for Kimmy Conner," Dr. Berger asked coyly.

Connie seemed perplexed for a moment; his entire intelligence had been short-circuited and was now in the process of rewiring itself. "Kimmy Conner . . ." the boy muttered blandly as he pondered the thought. "She doesn't like me," he finally said, definitively and without a hint of emotion.

It was unclear just what the boy *could* recall, and Dr. Berger didn't want to risk knocking something loose by delving further into the incident. This was a start, and so long as Connie never revisited the facts of the shooting to reestablish his memory of it, there was every reason to expect that the incident was permanently expunged from his catalogue of recollections.

On the morning they were to leave the clinic for home, Dr. Berger called Double and Francesca aside and gave them a set of forked, bilateral electrodes attached to an electrical cord.

"This was widely used during the war to administer therapy under primitive conditions when the proper equipment wasn't available. You'll need to install the correct plug when you get home." Dr. Berger said, snipping off the German Schuko-system plug and stripping the insulation off the copper leads with a set of wire cutters. "The dose only approximates what we normally administer, but I've seen it used quite effectively. On the morning of his interrogation when he first wakes and is still groggy in bed, coat the contacts with petroleum jelly for improved conductivity, and then place them here and here," the doctor said, indicating a point between the temples and the jaw hinge.

"Plug it in and unplug it as quickly as possible—this should easily meet the threshold for seizure. And then immobilize him. Before we started using sedation, patients were often injured by falls while convulsing, so hold him down. He will likely eliminate his bowels and come out of the seizure disoriented and dull, his memory clouded."

"Jesus," Double said. "You want us to literally plug him into a wall socket?!"

"I have done all I can," Dr. Berger continued. "This apparatus may prove useful later. At any rate, it's the only option you've left after you return home. Don't prompt him about the incident. Either the seeds of memory remain or they don't, and the only way you'll know with certainty is when the police question him."

XXVI

onnie missed the first week of school entirely, and after only the second week of the academic year, his homeroom teacher at the Country Day School called his parents in to meet with the principal in order to recommend that Connie be held back a year. Connie had lost an enormous amount of ground over the summer, she said: He seemed to have forgotten all his multiplication tables, as well as how to calculate both long and short division. Fractions were a total mystery. He struggled with vocabulary and spelling and seemed to have reverted back to what she regarded as a fifth-grade reading level. He couldn't even recall the basic plot and details of *Johnny Tremain*—the book about a colonial silversmith apprentice who becomes a patriot of the American Revolution—a story that Connie had particularly identified with only earlier that spring.

Clearly something about the boy was different this semester—a bit off. "Was it possible he was already experimenting with drugs?" she asked. The recommendation was for Connie to repeat the sixth grade, as well as to engage an academic tutor. Francesca was devastated and Double seethed. It wasn't supposed to be like this: The ECT side effects were only supposed to be temporary, and here Connie was already being held back a year in school.

XXVII

ouble's request was a simple one: The procurement of a beefsteak and a baking potato, but Mrs. Beeberstein couldn't help thinking, as she purchased the shell steak from the German butcher on her way to work, how odd and completely out of character it was for her boss to make such a request. Unlike his father, Double Winston took his lunch every day at an Italian restaurant several blocks away from the factory complex. The place was a holdover from better times in Bridgewater, and remained the last decent restaurant in the neighborhood. Double didn't particularly enjoy cooking, and always recoiled at the prospect of rubbing elbows with employees in general and line workers in particular. In the way that Senior had been most at home walking the factory floor and being among his employees—*his people* he called them—easily remembering their names and families and knowing the most minute and mundane details of their specific job, Double felt isolated and out of place. He loathed walking the plant floor and dreaded trying to remember the names attached to the multitudes of coarse-looking faces who worked for him. They were universally Bridgewater born and raised, and they all seemed to look and sound the same—a particular accent that sounded quite foreign to him.

A request is a request, though, and Mrs. Beeberstein delivered the shell steak and potato to her boss. Stranger still was when she found the parcel of meat untouched, still wrapped in its brown butcher paper with its red twine bow undisturbed and sitting on her desk after she returned from her own lunch, eaten out of a brown paper sack. "Forge was cold," read the note under the package. "So the steak dinner's on me," signed, Double Winston. Her boss then took his regular lunch at the Italian restaurant and did not return to work that afternoon.

*　*　*　*　*

The bullets had been right out in the open—two of them sitting inside an empty glass jar for instant coffee: a pair of .22 cartridges quartered by his son's own hand sitting right there on the center work bench waiting for him. Double could feel the heat coming off the glowing forge, and noted there wasn't a soul around. Heat Treatments and Forgings appeared to be completely abandoned, and he was certain at that moment that he was completely alone. He shook the contents of the jar directly into the small rubber change purse he carried inside his pants suit pocket. Then he made a final canvass of the floor for bullets and surveyed the general area. No one was watching or even seemed be in the general vicinity. Continuing the charade now seemed pointless—he possessed what he'd come for, so why hang around? He tucked the wrapped steak and baking potato under his arm and made his exit by way of the catwalk back up to the inner sanctum of his private office.

* * * * *

veryone's always on the lookout for that catwalk: You can see him coming across to the factory floor, and you got plenty of time to duck out and make yourself scarce. Now that forge is cooling down from an earlier firing, and it's just about right to cook on. I got some bacon grease I brought from home, and we're about to burn a flank steak so big it's spilling over the sides of that big pan, and here comes that pill—here comes smiley. Now, his old man was alright: He knew the work and always wanted to hear from you about it. He also had a sense of humor and didn't take himself too seriously. But this guy—Fancy-Prancy—is all superior in his attitudes. Doesn't know shit about the gun business, and talking to him reminds me of the time I had a boil lanced. I know he was supposed to go to the Olympics for horse jumping, but he can't even tell you which teams played in the World Series! I think if I saw him coming, I'd cut out one end of the plant and walk around the entire building—that's a whole city block—and come back inside from the other end just to avoid having to talk to that stiff. So, I seen him coming across with that package of meat under his arm, and I sound the alarm and the boys scatter like roaches. He steps down off that catwalk and the next thing you know he's stupefied by a couple of loose cartridges we found sweeping up. They're just a couple of .22 solids where someone notched the heads with a knife, but he's looking at 'em like he found a lost set of pearls or something. He unscrews the top of that jar and shakes 'em right out. Then he looks around all sneaky-like, checking to see that the coast is clear, and he just leaves. It was the damndest thing to watch. No steak and no conversation—and he just disappears back upstairs. I was relieved as hell at the time, but looking back on it now, it was all pretty peculiar to witness.

XXVIII

The Parsonage School is an upstate boarding school serving grades K through 9, with a reputation for success in dealing with problem children. The parklike campus runs to nearly 150 acres and has a trout stream meandering through the flinty, rolling green hills which, taken from afar, most closely resemble the rich landscape of Ireland. The student body, with a sprinkling of notable exceptions, seems as normal and well-adjusted as any other college-preparatory institution. Parsonage was not, however, Double's preferred choice, but at such a late date, beggars couldn't be choosers. It was clear to everyone over at Country Day that Connie had undergone some sort of dramatic change since the previous academic year, and the questions regarding his shift in personality trickled forth endlessly.

Kimmy Conner was still missing—no body had yet been found, though at this point it had only been a couple of weeks. What concerned Double and Francesca was what might happen when and if the body ever appeared: In the County, Connie would know of the discovery immediately, as many students at Country Day also summered at Big Pine. The last thing the Winstons needed was for Connie to experience some sort of flashback leading to an emotional breakdown in front of an audience well versed in the details of the case and who could potentially connect all the dots. Parsonage was a controlled environment removed from the County. Certainly there were several students attending from town, but it was never anyone's first choice of where they wanted to send their child: Your kid went to Parsonage because it was your last best option.

Parsonage worked its methods to bring a student through, or work around their particular difficulty, and while the institution provided a reasonable education with a lot of extra attention at an eye-watering cost, it also left behind a kind of permanent black mark on a student's record: For reasons unknown *this* particular pupil had taken an academic off-ramp onto this scholastic side road. To the trained in-County ear, the Parsonage School meant only one thing: The child in question was unquestionably screwed up.

* * * * *

A significant donation to the endowment allowed Connie's entire admission process to be completed over the span of a weekend, and the Monday of Connie's personal interview was also to be his first day of school. The boy and his parents experienced their awkward parting right in the admissions director's office.

"This isn't my school," Connie said, looking forlornly out the window. "This isn't where I go."

"This is your *new* school," Francesca said optimistically.

"You're going to stay with us and eat pizza and swim and fish for brook trout and play all sorts of sports with a whole bunch of new friends," the director of admissions, a portly bald-headed man with a handlebar mustache, pronounced enthusiastically. "You're going to sleep over with us in bunk beds, and it's going to be just like summer camp."

"It isn't forever," Double added bravely through a cracking voice. "Maybe just for a while."

"This is boarding school . . . and you're leaving me here?" Connie said unflinchingly to his parents. "What did I do wrong?" Both Double and Francesca were taken aback by his directness. "Tell me and I'll stop it—I promise! I'll be good, but please don't leave me here," he said as he began blubbering and hugging himself by the shoulders. The director of admissions walked around his desk to the boy and gently clapped Connie on the shoulder with a comforting if anesthetic hand. Connie now held his face as he cried, and the director waved the parents off, gesturing for them to make their exit. That's how, against a landscape overripe with September lushness, Double and Francesca Winston left their only son at the Parsonage School in the golden light of a fine Indian summer morning—both of them distraught and in tears.

XXIX

very prep school alumnus is haunted by the memory of the student who never went home—the hapless kid who remained on campus even when everyone else returned to their families for a holiday weekend—the de-facto orphan who spent his vacations as the awkward charge of a charitable faculty family. From the age of six, George "Red" Welles had been that kid.

As Connie tried his best to silently cry himself to sleep that first night on the top bunk in a cinder-block room that roughly shared the dimensions of a jail cell, Red finally threw in the towel, got out of bed and stood beside his new roommate. In the bright glow of the beaming harvest moon through the dormitory window, Red's port-wine-stain birthmark—the great liver-colored *nevus flammeus*, the tragic disfigurement that spread over large swaths of his forehead, cheek and nose completely overwhelming his right eye, seemed monochromatic and camouflaged in the twilight's lunar gray. This raised mark was textured and porous, leathery and slightly reminiscent of orange rind.

The rule at Parsonage was that all male haircuts had to clear the shirt collar, and any student skirting this standard was given the kind of haircut no one ever wanted to get again. This rule also applied equally to the sheepdog look of long hair hanging down into the face and eyes, with the single exception of Red Welles. His bangs cascaded down in a great wheaten sheaf nearly to the very tip of his nose when left untended, but the entire faculty seemed to acquiesce to the idea that whatever cover it might provide against his mark of Cain was welcome.

Red turned toward the window, and Connie could see crystallized the tragedy of his new roommate. Red was a fine student and athlete, spending each summer break in an extra academic session in England playing competitive-league soccer. As proof of how cruel children are the world over, in the UK his nickname was Tawny. His father was a jumbo-jet captain for British Airways, and his American mother had been a London department-store clothing model and then an airline stewardess—a woman keenly attuned to physical appearance and presentation.

Red's mother had been utterly repelled by the first sight of her newborn son and refused even to breastfeed him. In her eyes, his deformity was grotesque: His very lack of physical beauty precluded her from ever loving him, and this prejudice doomed the marriage. Red's father, who had come up through the ranks of the RAF and seen every kind of burn and disfigurement among the veteran fliers there, loved his son unconditionally and tried to stage-set a home life based on a penthouse apartment, paid nannies and globetrotting girlfriends. When the captain finally remarried and started a second family, it just seemed so much simpler to send the boy off to a boarding school where he would be safe and well cared for.

Red reached for the soccer ball on the desk next to the bunk bed and began to dribble it from one knee to the other in the moonlight. "First night away from home: always rough."

"I'm sorry," Connie blubbered.

"It's okay," Red said, snatching the ball out of the air and placing it on the bunk beside Connie's head. "Cry yourself out every night for a week and you'll get over it, I promise." Now he began to work the ball off the arches of his feet, effortlessly switching from one to the other.

Connie looked at Red. Backlit by the glowing moon through the window, he was a kind of golden boy, a superior specimen in all aspects, and in this peculiar light, even handsome. "You think?" Connie asked with his first hint of optimism.

"*I know it*: every first-timer—every time." Red put the soccer ball back into play, this time bouncing it against the cinder-block wall using only his head. "That's a retard haircut they gave you—it's coming in with white circles. I already heard some kids calling you *skunk*. I got some shoe polish we can try. For the next couple of weeks they're gonna ride you, though. Do you know how to fight?"

"You mean like boxing? No. Not really."

"I'll show you some wrestling moves that'll help," Red continued. "Get 'em on the ground and start workin' 'em, and they all wanna' quit." Red now swatted the air and slapped the ball back down on the desk. "Everything'll look better in the morning. It really isn't so bad here once you get used to it. Home is just another idea someone came up with: It isn't a real place or anything." With that depressing thought, Connie was finally able to close his eyes and drift off to sleep.

* * * * *

Connie did cry himself out every night for a week, after which he was finally able to function normally. The rooms were cramped and lacked proper doors, making due with hanging fabric curtains. The toilets stood in rows, one right next to the other, with no stalls and no privacy. Everyone dressed the same—a blue blazer with the school's gilded crest at the breast pocket, a collared shirt and necktie, khakis and oxblood loafers. Everyone ate the same starchy cafeteria food in the dining hall and then crapped it all out on the same institutional lavatories. Every male student showered communally each day following athletics—you pressed a metal button on the wall and it gave you about 45 seconds of lukewarm water that could neither be adjusted for flow nor temperature.

Connie's first fight came in the dormitory common room. His heart raced and the adrenaline flowed so freely, he was afraid he might collapse. His opponent, Randy Ryan, was a snotty Irish kid from the city and a notorious brawler. The two were well matched in size and weight, and when Randy went to put him in a headlock, Connie was able use Greco-Roman wrestling moves newly learned from his roommate to turn the tables and collapse his opponent onto the floor, where he then utilized a scissors maneuver. When the dorm master arrived to break it up, Connie was hammering the boy with the fleshy part of his clinched fist. A gallery of a half-dozen students was enthralled by the scene of the new kid's first fight, and when the teacher pulled Connie off him, Randy cursed a blue streak through a mouthful of blood.

The fight to a draw was an unsatisfying outcome, and Randy

took another shot at Connie the following week on the way into the locker room. Other altercations followed, and the two boys quickly became bitter enemies and archrivals. Randy seemed to genuinely relish revisiting this violent struggle every couple of weeks. His abrasive personality and Irish jaw seemed to demand it. Contrary to Red's prediction, there were no other comers. The consensus in the dormitory seemed to be that while anyone was free to pick a fight with the new kid with the funny haircut, this particular matchup was special—incomparable and exquisite to witness. Why not just enjoy this gift that kept on giving? The boys would fight at the drop of a hat—the setting was entirely irrelevant. They once brawled on the way into chapel for Sunday mass and then again on the way back out. Eventually Connie began to regard his existence at Parsonage, with its well-worn routines and even his biweekly brawl with Randy, as a new version of normal.

In October, Connie's teachers began to take notice of him, and the shy student who started the fall semester at the back of the classroom gradually began to reengage academically. First his English Literature teacher suggested to the department head that Connie sit in on seventh-grade classes. His teacher argued that he had already completed most of the sixth-grade reading list the prior academic year, could recall it in detail and was becoming bored at rereading the same works again. Then his Mathematics instructor expressed the identical sentiment—and then his American History teacher. Finally, several of these faculty members made a direct appeal to the academic dean: Why was this promising, if somewhat withdrawn, student repeating the sixth grade when he clearly had a proficient grasp of the curriculum?

The answer to that question is how Conrad Winston III came to spend the remainder of Thanksgiving weekend at the Parsonage School after only briefly visiting home and his parents. Connie and Red Welles took the train down to the County when school let out on Wednesday and spent the night at Bailiwick. They had their afternoon Thanksgiving celebration with Double and Francesca at the elaborate lunch buffet served in the formal dining room at the

Little Kill Country Club. Then they returned to school that evening so that Connie could spend the rest of the weekend reviewing the entire academic semester with his teachers. The stated objective was to ensure that Connie was current in the entire seventh-grade academic year and could therefore return to school after the Christmas break having jumped forward a year, transferring him back into the seventh grade at midyear.

XXX

Just as the Winstons and Red Welles were sitting down to their Thanksgiving meal at Little Kill, Michael King was slowly motoring his ancient fiberglass work boat across the placid waters of Big Pine Lake. Every autumn, King stopped shaving until he bagged a whitetail deer. The beard always came in two or three shades blonder than the brown hair on his head, and was now in its itchy phase. King had been a rare kind of cop for the County. While most of the town's police force had come from Bridgewater and other similar tough environs, Michael King was born and raised working-class right in town. He was a six-foot-three former male model who had been recruited directly onto the force after receiving his community college associate's degree. He had served in a junior constable's law-enforcement program in high school and managed to cement his career prospects back then.

Incomplete education aside, it had always been assumed that the sky was the limit for Michael King's law enforcement career in the County. He had chiseled movie-star looks, a calm welcoming demeanor and, most importantly, since he was a local he could navigate the social minefield required of a peace officer in a rich community of spoiled children and preening adults.

Everyone expected Michael King to retire as the town's chief of police, but he was no Machiavelli, and the game of political chess required to ascend to such heights was beyond him. He spent fifteen years in a patrol car and then another five as a junior-grade detective. He finally took early retirement at forty-one, after just twenty years on the job, to accept the position of general manager at the Big Pine Club. After he settled into this new position, he ran for town sheriff—and won. His jurisdiction in the part-time post included the expansive club grounds (some 5,000 acres in all) and the small village down the hill, which consisted of a diner, a post office and a gas station. He practically never wore a uniform, rarely carried a firearm or handcuffs, and the nearest jail cell was two towns away. He often went weeks without a law-enforcement-related phone call, and spent most of his free time moonlighting as a cabinetmaker, painstakingly repairing and restoring Early American furniture.

Back when he was still a cop in town, Michael and his wife, Rose, had put their two daughters through the excellent public school system there. Both girls were then able to secure partial scholarships to Cornell, four years apart—one right after the other. Rose was very smart and, before embarking on family life, had worked as a securities analyst for a large mutual fund. She was one of those women who, with age and happiness, gain a certain earthy appeal. By her late thirties, every male with blood pumping in his veins could see she undeniably had something.

* * * * *

One of the lakefront couples, the Wilsons, had been missing in action all summer long and were correctly rumored to be in divorce proceedings. Their cabin, Bough-Wow, was a relatively new construction by Big Pine standards; the rough-hewn knotty-pine ranch dated only from the 1950s, having passed down through her side of the family. It was isolated at the far end of the lake and tucked back into a remote stand of hemlocks. Michael King knew that the cabin had sat unused for the entire season from the moment he opened it up and launched their swim dock the week before Memorial Day, right up to this Thanksgiving morning.

He was putt-putting across the clear waters of Big Pine Lake in his thirteen-foot Boston Whaler. Its hull was painted bright orange and reconfigured with a four-by-four towing post anchored amidships. It also had a kind of flat wooden pram that was bolted directly to the boat's squared-off bow for the express purpose of pushing docks and swim floats around the lake. The expanse of water was calm this morning, its reflective surface bursting with nature's autumnal colors broken only by the trickling wake this odd craft left behind as it inched across the lake at idle.

This was the beginning of the quiet time at the club. Most of the cabins at Big Pine were uninsulated and already closed up for the winter. Pulling the Wilsons' swim dock was one of the last jobs on his long list of things to do to button up the club for the season. When King got the call that the Wilsons wouldn't be coming for Thanksgiving weekend, he got started immediately. His oldest daughter, a new Cornell graduate, had her college boyfriend—a newly minted stockbroker—along with her. King dragged the stiff young man along on this job to give Rose some time alone with the girls.

The breeze on the lake was only a whisper, but as every boater knows, you always want to approach a moored object from the leeward side, and as Michael made the wide turn upwind toward the swim float, the sickly sweet stench of rotting flesh overwhelmed them both.

The boyfriend gagged.

King already suspected the source of the stench, but pulled alongside and hopped onto the dock to confirm it. "Breathe out of your mouth and hang on to that cleat," he commanded. He took his flashlight and began shining it between the dark gaps of the wooden deck. He couldn't readily see anything down there, so he used a crowbar to pull up two long, central two-by-fours running the length of the dock. King stuck his head into the hole, exploring deep down with the flashlight, inspecting the large, dark gaps running parallel to each other, separating the great blocks of orange Styrofoam. There in the corner underneath a thin, slick coat of pea-green algae, was the unmistakable blue fabric and yellow graphic design of a Ms. Pac-Man one-piece bathing suit. He trained the flashlight deeper into the corner and it shone upon the sun-bleached anterior of a child's skull, now denuded of skin and flesh right down to the waterline. It was firmly wedged between two bricks of Styrofoam, and he could clearly see the exposed neck vertebrae, like a gray gelatinous chain loose within the rotted flesh at the base of the skull, fanning accordion-like on the tiny wavelets lapping at the dock.

Deep bodies of landlocked water like Big Pine Lake are fed by underwater springs which create mild current flows along the bottom. Obviously, the girl's body had been carried along the entire length of lake by those currents, finally arriving at this swim float. Decomposition and its expanding-gas by-product had raised it to the surface, where it had become trapped under the platform. As the body rotted and became more buoyant, parts of the body and skull impressed deep into the Styrofoam, becoming firmly lodged there.

The mystery was solved: After an exhaustive and ultimately fruitless weeks-long search, he now knew the Conner girl had died on the lake, and her body had remained trapped under that dock, decomposing, for nearly three months. Michael King crossed his fingers and hoped it might remain there, intact and undisturbed, for just a few more hours until he could eat his Thanksgiving supper and a state police diver could retrieve it.

King said grace over his Thanksgiving table and a separate prayer for the dead girl, and then broke bread with his own family and their invited guest. The day was wasting, and it was certain to be a long night. As soon as he could make a general identification that it was in fact a female child's body, Sheriff King would end his day by placing the heartbreaking phone call to Kevin and Lacey Conner to confirm the discovery of the their youngest daughter's corpse.

The sheriff had seen what was stuck to the underside of that swim float and recognized that if he telephoned the Conners now, they would want come out and see it for themselves. The by-the-book cop in him told him to call as soon as he tied up the boat. The father in him insisted he wait until what was left of the child was safely in transit to the morgue. He alone would decide the order in which this horrible day would unfold for the Conners. Right now he was celebrating the Thanksgiving holiday with his own family, but in a few hours he would grieve with another family sharing their personal loss over the telephone. *There but for the grace of God go any of us who have children*, he thought to himself.

The police diver was a paunchy, gray former navy frogman with a high tight crewcut and a passing likeness to W. C. Fields. He was already half in the bag from his own Thanksgiving dinner by the time he arrived. His expert opinion was that old decomposed floaters like this often had the disgusting tendency to disintegrate— "like tuna salad swirling down the privy"—when they're disturbed. At his suggestion, the swim platform was uncoupled from its mooring chain and the entire float was slowly pushed back to shore.

Then the police diver put on a small auxiliary aqualung with diving weights and stood underwater, his feet planted firmly on the paved boat launch, as he pried lose the remains of the little girl directly into a body bag. Her hands were gone entirely, and most of her facial features, nose, ears and eyes had been nibbled off. The facial skin was mostly gone and gray muscle underneath showed through. Her lower jaw was stripped almost entirely of muscle tissue, and the arched bone flapped loose and free on its hinge like a macabre articulated puppet. The police diver wore only swim trunks into the lake, and the stench of the rotted corpse now clung to his skin even after he toweled off. When Michael King asked the officer if he wanted a shower after his work, the diver enthusiastically accepted. He also welcomed both a first and second helping of turkey leftovers, as well as a water glass full of Michael's best bourbon as "a snort for the road."

King placed the call to the Conners at a bit past ten o'clock that night. Lacey was half asleep in bed when she answered the phone and was at first annoyed by the late hour. She said that Kevin was there too, but couldn't come to the phone just then. She expressed her relief at the sad news that had been so long in coming. At least now they knew with certainty that Kimmy was really gone. Michael didn't have any idea about the cause of death. He assumed she drowned, but the details would fill in after an autopsy. Lacey quietly whimpered into the telephone receiver, devastated. She would get off the line now to tell Kevin the awful news that realized all their worst fears. At least it brought them some closure, she said. They would come out the next morning to see Kimmy—to be in her physical presence again and to positively identify the remains of their child.

XXXI

From the start of the whole nightmarish ordeal, Double drank—alone, every night and far beyond where providence would suggest he stop. Franny and he were all alone now at Bailiwick, and their home life was haunted by the absence of their only child. In the short span of an autumn season, their lives had been reordered and turned upside down, their happy little family disbanded. Double couldn't talk to Francesca about any of it, and practically refused talk to her at all. They had made one decision which then led to another, compounding into a long, inadvertent chain which took them down this unexpected course finally landing them here—at the dead-end corner of WALK and DON'T WALK.

Neither of them could recall the exact moment they made the conscious decision to cover up a homicide. Both were now accessories to manslaughter after the fact, guilty of evidence tampering and obstruction of justice. Now, when Francesca needed the love and support of her husband the most, Double drank alone every night and withdrew into himself. Finally, one morning over breakfast she spoke up.

"I'd like to go to the city—see some shows and maybe stay at the Astor," she announced on the Tuesday after Thanksgiving.

Grizzled and unshaven, Double looked sluggish and saucer-eyed, like the image on a black-and-white television set with the picture slightly out of focus. "That's a fine idea. I'll take a day off and we can make a long weekend of it—really enjoy the city like we used to. Take in some culture and eat some of that Lobster Newburg. We haven't been back to the Astor since my last night at the Garden when I retired Westley. I remember thinking at the time that . . ."

"I want to go alone," she said interrupting. "I want some time to myself—to think."

"You want time to yourself?!" Double seethed, his voice rising right along with his temper as he realized what she was saying. "To think! *You* want to think? Just about what exactly?!"

She looked at him in disbelief. Finally she also lost her temper. "Are you really that daft, you blind fool?! Look at what this is doing to you—to us. You drink too much—every night! You're not the only one, Double: *It* bothers me too. I think about it all the time. What's the point if living with this if it destroys us?"

"I'm not having this conversation with you! It's just like you to get cold feet now that it's over with. All that's left to do is forget about it! He's no criminal, and we're not that kind of family. There's no evidence, no body, no weapon, no suspect. As far as I'm concerned, it never happened!"

"It happened. I was there—we both were," Francesca said. "We *are* that kind of family, and someday Connie is going wonder just what in God's name happened to him and to us. He may even begin to remember. What are you going to tell him then?"

"Me? You were right there with me. You should have said something *then*. It's too late now! Being an adult means you make a decision and live with it! You're not a child, Franny—there *is* no do-over!"

Francesca sat quietly in a chair at the kitchen table crying. Double suddenly realized his heartlessness; clearly he'd gone too far.

"I'm sorry, I didn't mean it. I know it's hard for you—it's hard for me too. I really don't even know what I was thinking back then. Nathan started selling me on this plan, and it all just sounded so . . . I thought we'd go back to being the way we were before—to being normal again; I didn't think it was going to be like this."

"Nor I," she said, looking up. "You don't talk to me. You're gone all day and then you come home and get drunk. You're always too busy and then later, you're just not yourself. I would say it's like being alone, but it's worse than that because I know who you used to be—who *he* used to be. He's clearly not the same person anymore, and neither are you. We've made a catastrophic mistake, and I'm finding it all extremely difficult to live with."

Double was quietly simmering again. The temptation to bring the conversation to its next logical plateau—*was she thinking of leaving him?*—was inviting, but even he could see how destructive continuing this whole line of questioning would be.

"Go to the city," Double finally relented. "Get yourself one of those nice junior suites at the Astor Towers. Go to the beauty parlor and take in a show. Think it all over—I want you to. You're unhappy; I understand that." Double was suddenly outside himself, maturely regarding the conversation almost like a casual observer hovering above the room, as he witnessed himself say the words with a pasted-on smile. "Take a break from me, and try to get the horse back under you. I'll do some thinking too: about how I can be better to you—easier on you."

She stood up and laid the dish towel on the kitchen table, crossed the floor to him and gave him a peck on the check. It was a platonic kiss, the sterile kind that sibling children give each other—a kiss of endearment but entirely lacking in passion. "Thank you," she said, as she climbed Bailiwick's back staircase to pack a bag.

XXII

The surest sign that a man has turned alcoholic is when he has an important reason to stay sober and finds that he is unable to. He is physically addicted to liquor, and interrupting the well-worn daily pattern produces the unpleasant feeling of withdrawal. His resolve weakens and then the door opens a crack—just one drink to take the edge off. The result is utter bewilderment at how the innocent suggestion of a single drink magically transports him to the ensuing hangover and its accompanying regret. Double had stayed overnight at his office, sleeping in the comfortable pocket bedchamber set into the stained-glass oriel window. He didn't want any distractions to preoccupy him or make him nervous, and the last thing he needed was to get stuck in traffic coming to work. What he had wanted was an Italian dinner, a good night's sleep and to not let his imagination run away with him, which was the entire reason why he stayed overnight in Bridgewater in the first place.

The heavy drapes were still drawn, but he could hear the tinkling of the empty glasses as Mrs. Beeberstein began making her eight o'clock rounds cleaning up after him. It had long been her habit to arrive at work early to organize first Senior's and now Double's busy schedule. Part of her duties as executive secretary was to protect her boss from public humiliation, and this currently included covering for Double's personal problems.

Now, as often as not, Mrs. Beeberstein's mornings began with disposing of the most recent physical evidence of Double's drinking problem. Double could hear her rinsing the lowball glasses in the bathroom sink, one for straight single-malt Scotch, the other for spring water. He listened to her put the empty whiskey bottle back in the hideaway bar—to be replenished again by the end of the business day. He heard the office door close again, and knew the next visit would be a hot cup of coffee and buttered toast. It was embarrassing being regularly awoken out of a stupor by her: She knew his dirty little secret—knew what a mess he was.

Double got out of bed and made his way to the bathroom. He felt that if the first time he spoke to her was after he had showered and shaved, that somehow it would make him seem all right. He was the conscientious business executive who often stayed overnight in order to be on the ball in the morning, charging hard right out of the gate; there was nothing wrong with taking a nightcap before bed. He knelt before the toilet now, concentrating hard, hoping that he might get something to come up before he took a shower. He finally stuck his finger all the way to the back of his throat and retched, vomiting up a bit of hangover bile. Then he threw up again, this time more substantially. Vomit, a hot shower and an Alka-Seltzer were now daily life for him. After he had coffee and something in his stomach, he'd really be right again and ready for the day. He stood in the bathroom shaving, clothed in his monogrammed bathrobe, as Mrs. Beeberstein opened the door a crack, handed him the cup of coffee and spoke.

"Mr. Clarke wants you as soon as you're available."

Double looked at his watch; it was twenty past eight. "A quarter to nine," he announced.

For many drinkers, the daily routine of coming back to life with a hangover can be surprisingly rapid—like a Labrador Retriever shaking the water from its coat. When Nathan Clarke arrived promptly at eight forty-five, Double had returned to the land of the living. The curtains were drawn, covering over the pocket bedchamber, and he was dressed in a fresh, neatly pressed gray flannel suit and on his way to finishing his third cup of coffee.

"We're conditioned to feel uncomfortable with awkward silences," Nathan Clarke said in opening. "Civility demands we fill a silent void, but please—unless it's a direct answer to a direct question, clam up—stay mum. And don't think out loud—this isn't any social call. The sheriff has a body. Now he's hunting for a suspect," Nathan warned, as he poured himself a cup of coffee. "He'll ask you the same questions several different times several different ways, looking for inconsistencies in your answers. Keep it short and just keep repeating yourself—verbatim if possible."

"I'll just defer to you."

"Try not to do that, either. It makes you look cagey. The objective is to politely answer all the questions but not give him anything extra. You're a prominent businessman—having legal counsel present for this interview is to be expected. A man of your stature would be a fool not to, but having me do all the talking makes you look guilty. Just remember—he's not expecting to find anything here, and basically he's intimidated by you. You're a big deal in this county, and he's just a blockhead beat cop, a retired detective who already owes you his job and livelihood. Use that.

"You already know him from town so start there: Ask about his family or Big Pine. When we're through, we want him to cross your family's name off his list. *Nothing here: Double Winston answered all the questions in full and even with his lawyer present, didn't seem uncooperative or guarded. He didn't incriminate himself, and doesn't act like a man who's hiding anything. Next!"*

XXIII

The call to Nathan Clarke came directly from the State Attorney General's office as a courtesy. There was a joint multistate inquiry into the death of Kimmy Conner, which had now officially been ruled a homicide. Based on autopsy results that produced a single mushroomed .22 caliber solid slug taken from just in front of the victim's left ear canal, Sheriff Michael King was now making the rounds in the County, interviewing select individuals on the membership roster of the Big Pine Club. While he was technically out of his legal jurisdiction, he had been granted local permission and temporary legal authority to conduct interviews with a state trooper present.

Finally, Mrs. Beeberstein entered the office with a fresh pot of coffee and a pitcher of water. Along with these items on the tray was a spray can of air freshener, which she now liberally dispersed about the room. "Smells like a speakeasy in here. Would you like a fire, Mr. Winston?" she asked, gesturing toward the hearth.

"No. That will be all, Mrs. Beeberstein," Nathan replied, curtly dismissing her and then adding, "Please buzz us when they arrive." Nathan picked up the chair he was sitting on and reoriented it adjacent to the two sofas flanking the fireplace. Double got up and did the same thing with the other. Then both men sat down on the leather davenports, facing each other. It was an awkward moment. Double finally spoke.

"How did we ever wind up here, Nathan? Trying to mislead a police inquiry?"

"Keep your cool."

"But this can't be right."

"Maybe, but here we are just the same," Nathan replied coldly, as the intercom buzzer sounded.

Mrs. Beeberstein led the two police officers into the office. Michael King was dressed in a brown corduroy suit with ankle-high suede desert boots and a black woolen knit tie over a red flannel woodsman's shirt. The state trooper was a large black woman with short, straightened hair and purple lipstick, eye shadow and blush. She sat down in one of the chairs, removed a stenographer's notepad and rollerball pen and wrote the date and Double's name at the top of the page.

"Judging by the whiskers on your chin, Sheriff, you haven't taken your buck yet this season," Double quipped cordially. "If you wait much longer, you won't be able to make it into the woods without tripping over your beard."

"Rose is always relieved when I finally bag one so I can shave it off. This year, though, I'm not sure it's ever coming off, what with an open homicide and all. Trooper Jackson here used to be a court stenographer—she'll be transcribing," King said, gesturing toward the state policewoman, who briefly looked up from her pad and smiled weakly in acknowledgement.

"I was led to believe this was an informal talk," Double said.

"That's alright," Nathan said calmly. "You're an important man and your time is valuable. Sheriff King only has this one opportunity to speak to you, and he wants to get all the details down so he can share them with his superiors; isn't that right?" Nathan asked as he pulled out his pipe and prepared to pack it with Virginia Burley tobacco. "Interesting choice they made, leaving you on this—a little odd, frankly. Really more of a job for the state police, don't you think?"

Sheriff King looked over at Nathan Clarke, who was playing with the bowl of his pipe. "A missing person case turned into a homicide—a cold case; I used to catch everything when I was a detective," King replied. "But I never got a homicide—we just didn't have any. I know the County and the entire Big Pine Club membership—lots of rich influential people. Business people, political people. That little girl was killed by a single bullet to the head, and it's a sure bet that either a member or a guest fired it. They left me on it because someone's gotta come down here and grill the membership for alibis. The governor knows half the membership personally, so it's basically a career-killer. They figure

I'm expendable."

"Conventional wisdom says it won't be solved—that the trail's gone cold and the evidence is too old," Nathan said. Now that he had gone to all the trouble of packing his pipe as a kind of conversational prop, there was nothing left to do but light it. By the time the fragrant tobacco smoke permeated the room and everyone seemed well satisfied with the state of Nathan's pipe, Michael King added, almost as an afterthought, "That may be, but the only way to really know is with shoe leather and interviews, so tell me please," he continued, "exactly where were you and your family over the Labor Day weekend, Mr. Winston?"

Nathan laid his pipe in the large cut glass ashtray on the table and let it smolder as he picked up a yellow legal pad, licked the tip of a Blackfoot Indian pencil and began scribbling. Double remained mute, and after a brief pause Nathan commanded, "You can go ahead and answer that," as if he were putting an obedience dog through its paces.

"My wife and I were at the cabin. You saw us there," Double said.

"It was the two of you alone?" Sheriff King asked.

"Alone? No, we weren't alone."

"You know very well that their son was with them, Sheriff," Nathan added impatiently.

King gave a flash of a smile, acknowledging the tactic, but also because he had just cracked the façade of the great steel door: These people were touchy, and he intended to keep poking them in the same spot.

"Young Conrad was there the entire weekend, then?" King reiterated.

"Yes."

"And how well did he know the Conner girl?"

"What are you are you getting at—in what way do you mean?" Nathan asked.

"Were they friends or just acquaintances? Did they play together regularly? Did they have any relationship outside of the club?"

"He knew her from the club only. They seemed quite friendly,"

Double answered.

"If you want a characterization of the relationship, ask the boy and not his father." Nathan said.

"All in good time. I know for a fact they knew each other very well because several times I observed Connie sitting on her front porch waiting for her—saw him with my own eyes. It was a bad case of puppy love—many members were aware of it."

"You don't need to respond to that," Nathan advised Double.

"A boy's first crush and she just ignored him; it was that way all summer."

Nathan was startled by just how well informed the sheriff was of the intimate details of the situation. "You're trying to paint the corners, and you can't even get the ball near the plate," Nathan charged. "Are you through constructing your own narrative of the events? Because if you can answer all your own questions, I'm not even sure you need us?!"

"No, I'm not finished," King said as he quietly collected his thoughts. When the state trooper stopped scribbling, the room went entirely silent. Nathan shifted uncomfortably in his seat. "When I first came on the force, police shows were the big fad," King began. "*Dragnet, Adam-12, The Mod Squad.* Everyone watched them, but they didn't do anything for me. It was like you go to work all day and then come home and watch it all over again on TV for entertainment? I didn't see any of them except for *Columbo.* You remember *Columbo* with Peter Falk?" Everyone in the room, including the state trooper, nodded.

"I guess it wasn't really a cop show in the regular sense that the others were," he continued. "It was pretty much just him investigating on his own. What was remarkable was he pretty much knew who the murderer was immediately. Every episode was just letting the case play out long enough for the suspect to incriminate themself. Columbo always gave them room to run, like he was feeding them the rope they were eventually gonna' hang themselves with. They always made the fatal mistake of underestimating him. They judged the book by its cover—how he dressed like a slob and acted like a fool."

When Michael King went to straighten the knot of his tie, in a dramatic flourish he popped off the clipped-on necktie entirely and stuffed it into his coat pocket. Then he casually unbuttoned the top button of his flannel shirt to make himself comfortable. "Columbo had his own brand of logic and never thought in a straight line. He'd put himself into the mind of the killer, and ask why they did this or that, and he never let himself get sidetracked by contradictory evidence. It was always the little overlooked detail—the tiny inconsistencies that tripped up the killer. I always remember that."

"What's your point?" Nathan snapped.

"My point, I guess, has three parts," the sheriff said, steeling himself. "Why does a man fly his family all the way to Switzerland on a small private jet? It's slow and cramped, and has to make all those extra refueling stops. It's also much more expensive than flying commercially. Why not spend less and go first class or even fly the *SST Concorde*? It's faster and a lot cushier. And once you're there, why do you then send the plane back empty? I got your flight plan from the FAA and spoke to the pilots. It costs the same whether the plane flies empty or full, and you only stayed in Europe for a total of six days. It just doesn't make any sense. It's as if you had a reason for flying over private, but not for coming back again.

"Secondly, why does a man pay expensive private school tuition only to send his kid to another school? Voluntary withdrawal in the first two weeks of a new semester results in only a sixty-percent tuition reimbursement; I confirmed it with the Country Day registrar. Now, I know you're a rich man, Mr. Winston, but both these points strike me as very poor business practices.

"Thirdly, what kind of parent allows their kid to skip the entire first week of school in a new year anyway? I wouldn't—my wife sure as hell wouldn't. Orion stock deal or not, none of it washes. The real puzzler, though, is if the boy was lacking enough scholastically to be held back, why didn't his teachers catch it last year?

"It was all a big mystery to me until I drove down to state

police headquarters. They got a machine there called a LexisNexis that's just fantastic! It's a computer that holds every newspaper and magazine article for the last twenty years. They started punching names into it—you're a celebrated man, Mr. Winston. Not exactly a household name like your father, but pretty famous in your own right. There were also a few snippets on your wife and son, but when they typed in your father-in-law's name, that computer lit up like a pinball machine.

"I didn't even think there were any of those guys still walking around. His book's out of print, but they managed to find me an old copy. I read *On the Children's Ward*, and right there in front of me's a pretty good working theory all laid out.

"Manipulate the boy's memory with electroshock. Eliminate his recall of a homicide so he can live with the crime and won't break under police interrogation. It accounts for the trip abroad, the private jet, the change of schools—everything. . . . Am I getting warm, Mr. Winston?"

Nathan Clarke suddenly banged out his smoldering pipe into the ashtray, fished his gold pocket watch out by its chain and opened its clamshell case. He compared it to Double's desk clock, briefly wound its stem, and then snapped it shut. He repocketed the watch and abruptly stood up. "I believe our little chat has concluded." he said, without a hint of warmth. Double followed Nathan's lead, and rose to his feet.

Michael King remained seated, and then an astonished grin overcame him. "A couple of pointed questions and *ppffft*?!" he whistled. "Out the door? You get all that?" he asked the state trooper.

"You did most of the talking but sure, I got it," she answered dryly. King stood up and held his out his hand to Nathan, who stared him down with ice-cold eyes.

"Out!" Nathan barked.

The sheriff looked knowingly to Double. "You strike me as a man with something to hide, Mr. Winston, and I've logged enough confessions to know."

Nathan crossed over to Double's desk and picked up the

telephone. "My next call is to the State's Attorney General. Do you want to see just what kind of a career-booster that is, missy?" Nathan asked the state trooper.

"I'm union rep for my barracks," she replied. "AG's come and go—the police union is forever."

"Let me leave you with this to chew over," the sheriff continued. "Conrad's a crack shot with a .22—your neighbors all attest to that. I found the spot he fired from: a sniper's nest with the branches trimmed back for a clear shot. There was still one of those jokey trading cards right where he dropped it, and a wad of chewed bubble gum with a partial molar imprint. I know kids grow like weeds at this age, but what do you bet that our guys can match the piece of gum to your boy?

"If this were an episode of *Columbo*," he continued, "we'd spend the rest of the show matching wits waiting for you to confess, but this isn't television. I have a lot of discretion over the way this is handled. Cooperate—really lay it all out, and I can help you . . . and him. The way these things dribble out to the press, the details of the crime, and of Connie. I can influence what they release and when, help you manage and maybe even minimize the impact. I can also eventually speak to sentencing.

"Suppose an indictment comes down and an ambitious prosecutor really sinks his teeth into this high-profile case with a society angle. The press just eats that right up. Mr. Clarke of all people should know from his experiences at Nuremberg—I punched in your name too, counselor," King said, gesturing to Nathan. "Something like that can really make a whole career."

"Kids play all around that lakeshore." Nathan said. "It doesn't mean anything."

"I can place you at the Bridgewater plant on Labor Day morning. The guard-shack log has you there for a little over two hours. Who goes to work on a national holiday? Don't fool yourself, Mr. Winston: We could prosecute him on what we've got right now. The next time you see me, it may be through one-way glass. Your boy'll be on the hot seat, and nobody's gonna' ride to his rescue—

not even you, counselor.

"Intimidation is a tactic of desperation," Nathan said. "Don't mind the sheriff, he was just leaving."

"It's not intimidation, Mr. Winston. We got this psychologist who consults for the state police. He can put you under in about two minutes. They say he does this act every year at the Christmas party where he has people flipping invisible pizzas and strutting around like flamingos. Now, he says memory is kinda' like a dandelion: You can run a mower over it, but there's still this whole root system alive underground. Just 'cause you can't see anything anymore doesn't mean it isn't all still under there. I think you and the old Nazi did your level best to yank out all the roots in the six days you had him over there, but I'm willing to bet that if this guy puts your boy under, it'll all sprout back up again. Once I get him, he'll be at my mercy. Kids from nice families in the County crack open like plastic Easter eggs. Then I won't need you anymore; I'll know everything he knows, and I'll just leave him to the system. And if I so much as get a whiff that you tampered with evidence or acted as accessories, I'll bring you and the missus up on obstruction-of-justice charges and make it my mission to see that your booking is well attended; I'll send out the press invitations personally. So if you have something to say to me, Mr. Winston, you better say it now."

"Alright! If you won't leave, we will," Nathan stammered, as he led Double by the arm to the door."

"We're going—we're going," King said. "But just ask yourself this last question: Even if you get away with it, what are you really getting away with? So you outsmarted me? Big deal! You'll always know what happened, and your wife will too. Maybe someday your son will recall enough so that he knows it too. Take a good look at Claus von Bülow, Mr. Winston. Do you really think he enjoys his life? It's not the notoriety of a crime or even the punishment that does a man in: It's the inner knowledge of having gotten away with it."

XXXIV

fter Sheriff King and the state trooper left, Double stared blankly at the office door for a moment and then made a mad dash for the hideaway liquor cabinet, frantically searching the bar for a bottle of Scotch whiskey. "You treat him like he's a low-grade moron, and he's already figured the whole thing out. Jesus Christ, Nathan!"

"Don't get hysterical; it's just a bluff."

Frustrated in his fruitless search, Double buzzed for Mrs. Beeberstein on the intercom.

"Yes, Mr. Winston?" she said as she appeared, closing Double's office door behind her for privacy.

"Isn't there any Scotch left?"

"That was a fresh quart as of yesterday's lunch!" she said, exasperated. "You go through it faster than I can replace it. I'll pick up two more bottles today, and hopefully that'll get you through tomorrow. I'm not your bartender—but for the record, in the nearly thirty years I worked for your father, I never once saw him take a drink during business hours!"

Mrs. Beeberstein left them, and Double continued his crazed search until he finally arrived at a reasonable alternative. "Cognac, thank Christ! You want one?" he asked.

"It's 10:15 in the morning," Nathan replied.

Double poured out a large snifter and took two liberal swigs to regain his wits and then sat down on the davenport again. "He's just gonna' let me stew until he's good and ready to . . ."

"Think about what he said," Nathan interrupted. "Not what you read into it, but what he actually said: *Why does a man do this? Why does a man do that?* Why does a part-time cop a step above crossing-guard tip his hand so obviously? Because he isn't holding any cards, that's why. He threw the old prosecutor's Hail Mary pass: Show your only face-card and let the witness on the stand fill in the hand. Get a rise out of them and at least you know you're on the right track. You seem to forget that he needs more than just words and a guilty-looking suspect: He needs actual physical evidence linking Connie to the crime scene, and currently he's got none. I certainly don't ever expect that rifle to resurface . . ." Nathan said, looking toward Double who shook his head morosely.

"What's he really got then?" Nathan continued. "He said so himself: He's got insufficient evidence based entirely on coincidence, all of which can be reasonably explained. Why does anyone do anything? It's certainly not with the expectation that it'll ever be put under a microscope or see the inside of a courtroom. Circumstantial evidence is weak by nature. There's a very real legal standard for an indictment, and this bozo isn't anywhere near it. And remember that with murder at least, you've got double jeopardy: If they prosecute a weak case and lose, Connie can never be tried for the same crime again.

"He wanted to rattle your cage, and he succeeded. Next, he'll try to interview Connie. He won't arrest him, but he'll play on your sense of duty to cooperate with law enforcement. Tell him he needs an order of extradition back to Big Pine, and call me immediately. Should he bring you in for questioning, demand legal representation and don't say another word—literally not one word. He'll exaggerate and lie about the facts of the case, hoping for a confession or at least that you'll incriminate yourself."

"What if you're wrong, Nathan?" Double asked. "What if he arrests Connie and interrogates the rest of us?"

"An arrest would mean formal charges," Nathan said optimistically. "He could arrest all of you. In theory, he could arrest Mrs. Beeberstein for bestiality, but I'd make one phone call to the D.A. and he'd release you. Unless there's some blockbuster new physical evidence I'm unaware of, he really doesn't have enough to charge any of you.

"Actually, it would probably be one of the best things that could happen at this point," Nathan continued. "Every prosecution stems from the initial arrest, and if it's a bad collar with improperly obtained statements it weakens the very foundation of the case. The new D.A. out there has ambitions that go well beyond the law, and he wants a winning record to propel him. He won't convene a grand jury unless he's certain he can win if it goes to trial. Add to that the sensitive nature of the whole thing, and it's a pretty high bar to clear."

"Yeah, but the media—it'll all come out."

"It's bound to come out anyway," Nathan said. "If it begins to look like you're going to get away with it, King will probably start leaking details of the crime out to the press to make things hot for you. It's a good thing your boy is away at boarding school—it might insulate him a bit when that time comes."

XXV

Michael King paid a call to Bailiwick on a slushy gray Saturday morning in early January. He had the local assistant county prosecutor with him, and the awkward exchange took all of two minutes. King wanted to bring Connie in for questioning during his midwinter break at the beginning of February. It would be a voluntary interview, and currently, at least, he wasn't being charged with anything.

Hungover and still in his bathrobe and slippers, Double felt himself at a distinct disadvantage. Francesca was wide awake and already put together, finishing her breakfast when the doorbell rang.

"This is a major decision," King said. "Make the wrong choice and you leave me no option but to work it by the book. I just want to talk to him informally—before this thing snowballs. I'm asking you to cooperate. Stonewall, and I play hardball from here on out."

"Connie isn't available, and he won't be cooperating," Double stated dryly. Nathan Clarke would handle all future inquiries.

XXVI

Memorial Day is a major community holiday in many parts of small-town America. Monday in late May saw the town draped in the Stars and Stripes and tricolor bunting. Beginning at 8:30 in the morning, the Avenue was closed off to traffic, and the adults slowly worked their way out onto the edges of the pavement with folding lawn chairs to man their viewing posts. Children wrapped the frames and handlebars of their bicycles in red, white and blue streamers, and showed off their patriotism by prowling slowly up and down the Avenue in eager anticipation of the chance to ride alongside the moving parade.

Smartly uniformed high school marching bands strutted in time to John Phillip Sousa, and teams of draft horses pulled wagons filled with children throwing penny candy to the spectators. Riders in brightly colored cowboy garb flanked the procession on horseback. Double had long ago been one of these riders. Connie had been an outrider on Cosmi only the previous year. This year the boy was still away at boarding school preparing for final exams, and it was unlikely that he'd be spending any more Memorial Days at home. Francesca, who was now in the city much of the time, was also absent.

The honorary Memorial Day parade marshal and a few local dignitaries gave the steady beauty-pageant wave from the back seats of antique convertibles, and the great red engines of the local fire companies led their legions of volunteers marching in lockstep, dressed in their navy blue uniforms. Every quarter mile or so, this procession would let loose their earsplitting sirens, thrilling some children and scaring others.

After a brief speech at the cemetery, usually by some local war hero or Medal of Honor winner, the dedication was made, a prayer recited and the honor guard played taps. Spectators often spent a half-hour or so perusing the various headstones, paying particular attention to the ones displaying the dime-store flags signifying a military grave. Children reading on the headstone the conflict these soldiers fought in would then strike up an impromptu game of battlefield until some somber-minded adult would disperse the group, reminding them of the respect owed every veteran: *They sacrificed their lives for your freedom*. The message was largely lost on all but the most mature and insightful child. Then the kids remounted their colorfully decorated bikes and made for the volunteer firehouse at the bottom of the Avenue. There a boy could gorge himself on hot dogs, cheeseburgers, baked beans and root beer until he was ready to bust. All the fire engines were on display right out front, and anyone could climb on them and maybe even run the siren.

Having been a national figure in the war effort, Senior always felt it his civic duty to be a part of this proud day. Those casualties—Winston Firearms employees and their children, teenage conscripts fresh out of high school and adult men in the fullness of life with families of their own who simply couldn't remain idle stateside—deserved to be remembered each year. These men, recognizing that the American way of life hung in the balance, stood and delivered for their fellow countrymen. Their names, starting with the Civil War and running through Vietnam, were all engraved on four bronze plaques forming the block base of the flagpole in the little park of the town center.

In the spring of 1946 Senior began participating in this parade. He had been a civil defense warden—essentially the air raid official for the entire Winston Firearms plant complex in Bridgewater, which was second on Germany's list of important industrial bombing targets. In air raid drills, company employees crowded into the basements and boiler rooms of the factory buildings, but everyone knew the futility of it: Any bomb that came through the ceiling was certain to kill anyone cowering deep in the bowels of these facilities.

Senior purchased a war-surplus jeep and had a disabled .50-caliber Browning heavy machine gun mounted on a turret installed in back. He also had a hitch welded to the vehicle and set it up to tow a decommissioned Howitzer gun. Every spring until he died, Senior exhibited this machine of war at the parade. Hand-painted white block letters running down both sides of the cannon spelled the words WINSTON FIREARMS HELPED WIN THE WAR.

It was in this patriotic spirit that Double now rode in the passenger seat of this same jeep idling down the Avenue, wearing his father's white civil defense warden's helmet and cloth armband over his own gray Prince-of-Wales check suit. The driver, Troy Roberts, was a big, black, bald-headed former Green Beret with deep crow's feet at his eyes and a beaming white smile. He was a personnel manager at Winston Firearms who jogged the perimeter of the factory complex each day in a gray hooded sweatsuit during his lunch hour. He was also a Vietnam War veteran and National

Guardsman who wore his own modern combat fatigues to the parade.

Each Memorial Day it was his duty to drive the jeep and Howitzer down from the Bridgewater plant for the parade. Double didn't like him for two reasons: The first was that working in personnel, this manager was well versed in dealing with employees with substance-abuse problems. The second reason was the manager was a rehabilitated ex-drinker himself.

Troy Roberts was indifferent to Double's plight: Anyone at the office with a nose could smell that the boss had become a drunk. The body odor coming off Double was sour smoke, the lingering result of too much Scotch whiskey. The scent of curdled charcoal only intensified as the day wore on, and the trace toxins worked their way out through the pores of his skin. For this reason, Double now made liberal use of aftershave lotion, as well as taking the liberty of a supplementary shower and a change into a fresh shirt every afternoon.

Troy had long since discovered that some drinkers came around in their own good time, and others never came around at all. Many would rather die from drink than have to fundamentally change their way of living, preferring to lose it all rather than have to reinvent themselves in a world without alcohol. If Double Winston insisted on pretending that the emperor was wearing a fine suit of invisible clothes, who was a lowly personnel manager to argue?

The pewter flask bulged prominently from Double's breast pocket, and the liver-colored bags under his eyes said it all: If Double were just another employee, the options would be simple and few—*clean up your act or get out*; volunteer for rehab or be summarily dismissed.

Double was like the monarch profoundly uncomfortable with the trappings of his own court. This parade was part of his job, just as it had been for his father, but where Senior loved the spectacle—the pomp—the ornate displays of patriotism and relished the society of his fellow man, Double took no pleasure in it. Everyone knew who he was and the world greeted him like an old friend, but Double Winston, who never spent a day in the local public school system, could never put a name to a face. At work, Mrs. Beeberstein was there to save him, always reminding him of each person and their particular background, but on Memorial Day he was entirely on his own. Double went through the motions every year, just as he continued to host the policeman's picnic on the lawns flanking the long front drive up to Bailiwick. Both were institutions which, left to his own devices, he never would have created or nurtured, but now were long-established traditions, and he regarded himself as their sole unwilling steward.

As Double sat in the passenger seat of the jeep waving disingenuously to no one in particular, with a stiff, pasted-on smile that was actually beginning to make his face sore, he imagined his own son reluctantly shepherding the same traditions. To Double, Memorial Day had always meant the big weeklong horseshow at Dorset; it had been the first stop on his season-long national schedule for twenty-five years. Before he retired as a rider, he hadn't attended the Memorial Day parade in town since his own childhood.

*　*　*　*　*

Following the graveyard ceremony and the official end to the parade, the driver dropped Double at his own parked car near the volunteer fire department at the bottom of the Avenue. There, Double would indulge in the free lunch of hotdogs and hamburgers. After he had something in his stomach, he would make his way to the back of the firehouse to the Chief's darkened office where there sat a keg of ice-cold beer on tap.

It was there in the dim corner amidst the deafening squawk of police scanners and radios, overlooking a wall lined with legions of framed photos of Little League teams the department had sponsored over the years, that Double stood, pouring himself two waxed cups of beer from the tap.

The words seemed to come right out of the ether. "You gotta tell me about it," the voice pleaded. "Man-to-man, I gotta know."

Double turned and there, in darkened silhouette against the lighted doorframe, was a figure in a fireman's dress-blue uniform. The man seemed almost spectral, and the voice was downright small. As Double shifted uncomfortably on his feet, he could see that Kevin Conner had undergone a profound physical change. His uniform now fit him like a tent: He'd shed perhaps 35 or 40 pounds and appeared diminished and defeated. His face was as pale as a bed sheet.

"Kevin," Double said, nervously acknowledging him. "I didn't see you."

"King says you know plenty—way more than you're sayin'." Conner stood there wheezing a bit. "Is that right?"

"I'm really not allowed to discuss it," Double said, as he started to move past the ashen-faced man. "The investigation is still ongoing."

"My wife threw me out—got herself a divorce lawyer. She says your kid's gonna to get away with it on account of who you are. *A real man would do something about it*, she says. *What do you want me to do, burn down his house?* I ask. *It's a start*, she says. The thing is, when your kid gets killed, you don't much feel like smitin' anyone: Your knees just kinda' buckle and stay that way."

"I really wouldn't know," Double said as he barged past the man.

Kevin Conner grabbed Double by the upper arm and stopped him firmly, slopping beer onto the floor in the process, "Can't you even say her name?" he blustered. "Kimmy—Kimberly: That was my little girl."

"Kimberly," Double finally repeated.

"She shined bright—my little Fourth-of-July sparkler," Kevin continued. "She was gonna be the prettiest of the three—but, man alive, could she run that mouth. When you lose a child and the police come up with nothin', a father's supposed to do something about it—he's supposed make something happen. What am I supposed to do, Winston? Tell me! I had my chair and my beer tap and my green hat and maybe I *was* a clown to a lot of you people, but at least I was happy. My life is total shit now."

"You've got the wrong idea," Double said as he started back through the doorframe. "I'm sorry for your loss, Kevin, but my family didn't have anything to do with it."

"I don't even like drinking beer anymore—makes me want to puke knowing I was poundin' 'em back and losing at cards when she was . . ." Kevin peered down at the puddle on the floor with a hangdog look. "You know what it is for a Catholic to cremate their dead? It's an affront to our Lord and Savior; I couldn't even hold her—my fingers went right through. When they tried to cut that swimsuit off, it was like cutting open a sack full of house paint. The only thing to do was burn her up."

Double nervously pried himself lose from the man's grip. "I'm sorry, Kevin, but I really can't help you."

Double dropped the two empty waxed cups into the corrugated metal trash can. His socks were soaked through with Schaefer and he was unnerved. When he got outside, he reached for the flask inside his suit pocket, unscrewed the cap and took a long pull. Then Double looked back toward the firehouse façade where Kevin Conner stood full of torment, pointing a finger directly at him. Kevin didn't say a word or do anything else until, finally, another fireman came over and gently laid a hand on his shoulder.

XXXVII

Several things happened in quick succession that spring to unravel Double's life, and it all began with the overwhelming feeling that his wife was having an affair in the city. They had ceased all sexual contact after Connie's incident, and now she spent every available weekend there. The Astor had always been *their* hotel, but now she preferred the Plaza. They were civil to each other—like considerate roommates—but even an outsider could see the marriage was on its last legs. All that was required now was the blunt admission of the futility in continuing, or perhaps picking a convenient opportunity to get caught in the affair.

Connie was fresh out of school, and it was decided that he would spend most of his summer vacation away at camp and then his final month at home.

* * * * *

The policeman's picnic fell on June 15th that year, and the large party tent just seemed to magically erect itself on Bailiwick's sprawling front lawn as it had every summer since Double was a child. Sunday arrived, and at one o'clock, Double strolled down the meandering drive of the estate under the towering elms. Cold beer flowed and steaks sputtered over hot coals. It was a sunny late spring morning—warm enough for Bermuda shorts but, as host, Double wore wool slacks. He stood in the center of the tent and raised his cup in a toast to the gathering of lawmen.

"The rule of law is the bedrock of Western civilization. Societies succeed or fail on their ability to apply equal treatment under the law. America ascended to become the greatest society in history because our legal system transcends all social strata. Civil law protects the individual in his private affairs, and criminal law protects the community at large. The courts ensure that violent predators don't roam freely and that the victims of crime aren't forgotten. Justice *is* served and, as law enforcement, you are the first line of defense: an honest man, deadly with a firearm, charged with upholding the law rushing to our aid. Your bravery, incorruptibility and sense of community ensure that order prevails and that anyone entering the legal system is treated fairly. Without this fundamental integrity we have bedlam. The law is the law and everyone must stand equal before it. The courts must remain impartial—all must be treated fairly regardless of economic circumstance or social status. These simple precepts were forgotten in Greece and then again in Rome, and those civilizations collapsed. Corruption of the law and courts is the primary corrosive that predates the decline of a civil society."

Double raised his cup of beer to the group and made a broad sweeping toast to the tent of more than 100 people. "When anyone in the County calls the police, they'll receive assistance in the form of an upright peace officer, steadfast in his duties. May the Lord bless you all and keep you safe." As the plastic cup came to his lips, Double's gaze finally came to rest on a now clean-shaven Sheriff Michael King, who looked directly at him.

Several guests came through a kind of impromptu receiving line to greet Double, and the entire time he was glad-handing them, he watched the sheriff. King, dressed in his khaki constable's uniform with his police shield tacked to his shirt pocket, made his way across the lawn to his own parked private vehicle, and drove away. What Double didn't know—couldn't know—was that in the course of attending the policeman's picnic, Michael King had managed to stray up the hill toward the main house and discover several objects exhibiting bullet holes.

Using a sharp, curved wood chisel and a long set of needle-nose pliers, he dug .22 long rifle slugs out of a birch tree, a wooden lamppost and a No Trespassing sign. He placed these projectiles in plastic sandwich bags, which he then knotted and tagged.

As Double began to walk back up to the main house, he watched Sheriff King roll down to the bottom of the drive and then turn in the opposite direction of the association-exit leading back to town. King drove a long circuitous route through the neighborhood. He knew that bullets taken from Bailiwick were inadmissible as evidence, as he had procured them without a search warrant. He just wanted to find something to compare against the bullet that came from the victim, to confirm he was on the right track. The purpose of this brief neighborhood tour was to locate other bullet holes and slugs in public places that he could take into evidence without a warrant.

He found one hiding behind the large orbital mirror at the bottom of a neighbor's driveway. Its dome-shaped glass had a small section missing, a narrow shard out of the very top of it. Someone had shot at it hoping to shatter the whole thing, but had only succeeded in taking a thin sliver out of the edge. King stood on the roof of his four-wheel-drive as he first removed the mirror from its mounting base and then located the small bullet hole behind it. This mushroomed slug went into a proper evidence bag and hopefully would provide a usable ballistic match.

XXXVIII

On Tuesday morning at nine a.m., Sheriff Michael King knocked on the front door of Bailiwick carrying a search warrant. He had a local police officer, a state trooper, a state police detective and a traffic cop accompanying him. The warrant stated they were searching for photos, correspondence and journals relating to Kimmy Conner, as well as any and all firearms, ammunition, spent rounds and shell casings chambered in .22 caliber.

Any lead slugs in the confiscated caliber could be compared to the round taken from the victim. Each production lot differs slightly from one to another, and a match would be a significant break in the case, particularly if the unfired round also exhibited the same telltale knife marks as the spent bullet. A firearm would provide definitive ballistic evidence in the form of rifling—peaks and valleys or lands and grooves, the twist inside a gun barrel which spins the projectile giving the slug stability in flight. Rifled barrels are differentiated from each other by minute imperfections in the cut rifled striations, which provide each firearm with its own unique fingerprint. Should the search warrant produce the actual firearm used in the killing, those barrel imperfections could easily be matched to the bullet retrieved from the body.

Double had just arrived at his office in Bridgewater when the warrant was served and, thankfully, Connie had just been dropped off at his first summer camp session—a month in the wilds of Maine—for full immersion in camp-craft and academics. Double immediately returned Francesca's urgent phone call and instructed her to cooperate with the police. Then he and Nathan Clarke drove down to Bailiwick together.

The search took most of the day and the presence of law

enforcement at the Winston home wasn't overlooked by the neighbors. A patrolman in a squad car blocked off the drive, but the neighbors gawked as they drove past the entrance. Pedestrians and joggers stopped to peer up the tree-lined drive, pondering just what could possibly have taken place up there.

It was a complicated legal web that provided Sheriff King with the authority for the search. Technically, he was investigating an out-of-state crime, and it was only with the cooperation and temporary authority granted him by state and local law enforcement that allowed him to continue with the case. The chief of police wanted the case to simply go away, and authorizing a fruitless search of such a prominent family—as unpalatable as it was—was the probably most expedient way.

King and the Chief had come up through the ranks of the department together and had managed to forge a reasonable working relationship, even though they had always jockeyed for the same promotions and commendations. When King was ultimately passed over for the top job, he knew it was because he wasn't crafty enough to play the big game of *who's who*. The political networking required for the senior position in such an affluent community was simply beyond his abilities. All these years later, those very same insider dynamics were coming back into play.

If Michael King was the embodiment of the fair-haired, white-toothed, all-American ideal, the Chief represented the down-and-dirty, practical side of life. Having survived a hardscrabble upbringing in a Polish-speaking household in the middle of a working-class, Mick-Irish neighborhood in Bridgewater, the first thing everyone noticed about the Chief were his acne scars and his mangled nose, which had the appearance of having been smeared across his face with a butter knife. At five-foot-nine, he was on the small side for a cop, but he was broad-shouldered, barrel-chested and had learned to box as a kid at the Police Athletic League. In intercity Golden Gloves bouts, he was known for being a classically defensive fighter with a natural instinct to deflect punches with the shoulder roll and then viciously counterpunch his opponents while they were still vulnerable. That and his relentless jab were the only useful weapons in his arsenal, but he applied them to great effect. His wins were all by decision and were achieved by continually tagging his opponents with pistonlike strikes as regular as a metronome and then counterattacking whenever he got hit. Over the years, the Chief's nose had been repeatedly broken and poorly reset and this disfigurement, along with his acne scars and high, tight crewcut, made him look war-torn and ferocious.

The Chief had raised his family in a drafty old Victorian house out on the Post Road and sent his children through the public schools in town. His oldest daughter, now in her twenties, had married all the way up to the Little Kill Country Club. Her husband was a young MBA who was now in the process of amassing a Reagan-gilded-era fortune as the creator and majority stockholder of the first really successful nationwide HMO. The Chief, who had spent his high school summers working as a soda jerk at the Little Kill beach club snack bar, now strolled through the main clubhouse lobby, his commanding son-in-law holding the front door for him.

It was the next best thing to actually being a member himself—better, if you consider no expensive club dues or initiation fees. A half-dozen or so times a year now, he enjoyed golf followed by a sauna, a rubdown and a poolside lunch. Fourth of July, he spent with his family at the beach club luau followed by a private fireworks display. Labor Day weekend he played in the annual Member-Guest golf tournament.

Now that he was on the inside, so to speak, the entire club membership was falling over itself to get to know him personally—you never know when being on a first-name basis with the chief of police might come in handy. And they all wanted to hear war stories—accounts of his time as a beat cop patrolling the vicious Bridgewater ghettos. Gruesome tales of slum life and inner-city carnage never failed to enthrall the pearl-and-cashmere set.

The Chief had come a long way from humble origins, and wasn't about to let an out-of-state cold case make things uncomfortable for him now. A search of the Winston household was the very limit of how far he was willing to let things go. Ballistic evidence taken from the neighborhood was sufficient for a magistrate to sign a search warrant, and that was good enough for the Chief. Unless something really damning turned up, however, like the murder weapon itself and the ammunition to go with it, his patience and jurisdictional cooperation were nearing their end.

King knew from his experience as a detective that the first 48 hours immediately following a crime are the most critical, and that the longer a case remains open, the less likely it will ever be solved. The Conner homicide was now nearly ten months old. Any lingering physical evidence had long since been destroyed either inadvertently or quite intentionally. King also knew that body language said everything about the potential culpability of a suspect. *Were they nervous and fidgety? Did they immediately lawyer up or were they calm and reserved, treating the inquiry as just another mildly unpleasant inconvenience—like jury duty or a tax audit?*

But these people were *too cool*—lounging out on the back patio enjoying a second breakfast of poached eggs over Scottish smoked salmon and toast with English marmalade. Francesca was dressed smartly in her riding boots and breeches, as it was she who routinely exercised Westley Richards at the now nearly defunct riding facilities at Little Kill. After they finished eating, she brought out a fresh a pot of coffee and three newspapers, and they proceeded to pass the various sections around the table. She wasn't exactly calm about the situation: It isn't every day that the police comb through your personal belongings in a homicide investigation, but she couldn't very well crowd them as they snooped. She also couldn't leave them alone—*what if they found something?*

It was awkward for the three of them not to discuss the case, which was now unfolding under their very noses. There was a nervy calm about the whole situation as the police riffled the house— almost as if there was an unspoken compact that everyone was going to keep their wits right to the bitter end. Nathan remained on a hair trigger, ready to spring into action should anything incriminating turn up. The whole thing had the sophisticated air of a British drawing-room drama, with everyone waiting for the clock to strike thirteen and the butler to confess. But for Double, the moment was surreal: How did he ever arrive at a place where his own son was the prime suspect in a homicide and he himself was an accessory after the fact, having already covered up the crime?

The incident still seemed quite immediate, and as Francesca scanned the table, it was undeniable that the stress of the conspiracy had taken its toll. Double, while not exactly fat, was now jowly, soft and overflowing his waistline—bloated in the way that heavy drinkers are prone to become. His eyes were perpetually bloodshot, and he had liverish bags under them, giving him a bloodhound look. He also had a perpetually sour odor about him which only intensified in the heat of the day. He was beginning to lose his hair—Francesca found loose strands on the brush head and in the sink bowl every time she entered his bath.

Francesca had actually lost weight, and now looked gaunt and haggard. She'd also gone entirely gray in what seemed a matter weeks following the incident and now dyed her hair black. Her friends all said that menopause hit her early and hard. It had easily aged her ten years in ten short months.

Only Nathan remained outwardly unchanged. Forever lanky and trim, he now seemed to be literally rotting from the inside out. His dentist, observing his bleeding gums and marked decline of tooth enamel, had told him so when Nathan came in for an emergency procedure when a molar simply crumbled under a crusty heel of bread. His gastroenterologist had finally arrived at a convoluted theory about alkalinity levels, electrical polarity and emotional stress. The reality was that his breath stank all the time, which necessitated his use of Binaca breath spray several times each hour.

He was also gassy from both ends, but occasionally when he expected only to pass wind something exponentially more repulsive emanated. As a result, Nathan now nursed a half-bottle of Phillips Milk of Magnesia daily, but even this couldn't prevent the occasional accident that required a change of underwear and pants. For this reason he'd taken to wearing a blue blazer and gray flannel slacks, specifically because he could dry clean the shit stains out of his pants, as opposed to having to run an entire suit through the cleaners. At its worst, Nathan was compelled to beg the use of Double's shower to properly clean himself. His doctor finally pronounced that the only surefire remedy was a colostomy bag, but Nathan couldn't face living the rest of his life that way. He prayed for a miracle and he did have his share of good days, but his normal daily existence was exquisitely torturous and debasing.

"Only one house was ever searched in Lugano," Francesca finally said glibly to the men. "A little bank clerk with glasses who lived all alone in a basement apartment. Every deposit he took for a month, he placed into his own account. He had the idea to run away to Cuba; he hung himself instead."

"Never underestimate the importance of timing," Double remarked, glancing at his watch. "It *is* nearly noon," he said as he removed the pewter flask from his breast pocket, dumped the remains of his water glass into the flower pot and poured himself a liberal measure of single-malt Scotch. They were the only ones on that patio—all the policemen were either engaged in the search or around the front of the house.

"You're never very far away from a drink anymore, are you?" Francesca asked. Double looked into his glass. "And you don't bother to ask anyone if they might like one."

Double screwed the cap back on the flask and replaced it in his breast pocket. "Happy?"

"No, I'm not happy," Francesca replied. "The police are in my home because they believe my son to be a murderer. How could I possibly be happy?!"

"Quiet down, dear," Nathan said soothingly. "It's only for a little while longer."

"It's for the rest of his life—you know it," she said sharply, "And my husband, the great industrialist poseur, now uses his time simply as a way to mark intervals between drinks."

"Jesus, Franny!" Double snapped.

"You were supposed to be his friend," she said to Nathan. "At some point you must have realized he was totally unsuited to this work, both in aptitude and temperament. Why didn't you tell him? He doesn't even like guns," she said, regarding Double. "Not even a passing interest—and it shows." Her hand went gently to Double's scarred cheek as she continued her indictment. "I married a successful man, an ambitious man of accomplishment who knew who he was. We had a wonderful life together in that world—if only we'd had the sense to stay there." She withdrew her hand and grew cold. "No one would have blamed you for selling out and walking away, but you never could quite forgive yourself for not being your father! I didn't marry your father, I married you. That's certainly proving a bitter disappointment."

"Shut up about my father," Double mumbled.

"Your father! Your father!" she taunted. "You are both such fools—but you in particular," she said, wagging a finger at Nathan. "The Ivy League solicitor—so clever. You knew all about my own father—his torments. Here we are again—history repeating itself! But I must be the even greater fool, because I *knew* and didn't speak out. European culture teaches girls to always defer to the men. I thought it was horrid—stupid and dangerous—giving a real gun to a child. Now he's ruined!"

Francesca folded her napkin, laid it on the glass tabletop and finished the last of her coffee. "I'm going to ride your horse," she said, rising. "And then I'm going into the city to see about an apartment. I'll call you when I've settled on something." She turned and began to walk away, but then stopped and spoke again. "I'll be at the Plaza should the police require me, but don't worry—I'll be right here when Connie returns from camp."

XXXIX

K ing and his men demanded that the fireproof steel gun safe be opened, and inside they found a small collection of firearms. There was a Model-12 pump trap gun, a 101 four-barrel over-under skeet set, a .30-06 Springfield 1903 bolt-action rifle, a Mauser-98 bolt-action rifle in .375 H&H, a Lee-Enfield bolt-action training rifle rechambered to .22 caliber and a Winston Model-21 reconfigured as a double rifle in .450 Nitro Express.

All these guns were presentation models with upgraded Turkish walnut and fleur-de-lis checkering, given as gifts to Senior by his employees. The rifles had been specially created for his first safari following World War II, in 1950, and made a point of utilizing the three dominant infantry rifle platforms used during the hostilities. Each firearm announced its allegiance in the conflict by way of a flag in yellow, white and pink gold relief on the trigger guard. The Mauser flew the Nazi swastika; the Lee-Enfield, the Union Jack; and the Springfield, the Stars and Stripes. The Model-21 enjoyed no such embellishment, having never seen use in the war. Instead this shotgun platform was converted into a heavy rifle specifically to be used on dangerous game. A large-caliber cartridge dedicated to each barrel means no reloading between shots. Those precious seconds could mean the difference between life and death for a hunter on foot in heavy cover trying to dispatch a furious wounded Cape buffalo or leopard.

The target shotguns were engraved in a Western-themed lariat scroll and were a gift from the plant workers when Senior first joined the Little Kill Country Club. When the state police detective announced the .22 caliber Lee-Enfield, King was on the telephone in the kitchen. His eyes immediately went to the big bay window and outside to the slate patio where at the glass-topped wrought-iron table, Double and Nathan Clarke still sat talking casually, entirely oblivious to the goings-on inside. King was certain, judging by their total nonchalance, that this rifle couldn't possibly be the murder weapon.

Late in the day when King and his men seemed to wrap things up, the afternoon light turned golden and radiated down through the elms surrounding the main house. Neither Double nor Nathan had any personal experience with a criminal search. It all came as somewhat of a surprise then, after King's men had spent so much time fussing over a bullet-riddled weather vane, a dented sundial and the pulpy birch stump in the yard, that an arrest wasn't forthcoming. The police exited down the long drive, and with their departure, the great neighborhood mystery only deepened. Rumors ran rampant, the favorite being that since the boy was away at summer camp, the belligerent alcoholic husband had been beating his wife. Another had her caught in flagrante with a tall, older, well-dressed gentleman when Double returned unexpectedly from the office. The truth was even whispered once—that the Winston boy had killed the Conner girl out at Big Pine Lake with the very same rifle he'd used to shoot up the neighborhood—but the more level-headed dismissed such a theory as irresponsible and bordering on outright slander; the Winston family was top-shelf and beyond reproach, and there was a big difference between a titillating scandal and scurrilous defamation.

It was all just matter of time then, and Nathan Clarke told Double as much. Either the police now possessed enough physical evidence for an arrest or they didn't. It would take a bit of time to test the gun and the spent slugs—perhaps a week—and then they would know for certain if the boy was facing a criminal prosecution for homicide.

XL

It was an odd time for Double, and along with it came all sorts of curious feelings. It wasn't simply that he was all alone now at Bailiwick—Francesca had been running off to the city regularly on weekends for months. He just couldn't imagine how he ever managed to arrive at this low point in his life; it wasn't all that long ago that he was being heralded as the conquering hero—the best show jumper in the country and certain to medal at the next Olympic Games. He'd been a big deal in his own right, wealthy and a major-league success, with a devoted wife and son who hung on his every word. Now his business had soured and whenever his family came together, they seemed content to ignore each other. The great dream he had lived had now devolved into a nightmare, and he didn't know how to make it stop.

The gun business was in a general industry-wide decline, and the interest payments on the Orion refinancing were starting to overwhelm whatever small profit the firearms division turned. Double drank all the time now. Several nights a week he started at the end of the work day in the privacy of his plush office, sending out for dinner to the Italian restaurant. As he settled into his cups, he would often handwrite letters to Kevin and Lacey Conner, confessing to the entire conspiracy. He would write out in excruciating detail the exact circumstances of the crime and the ensuing cover-up and just how remorsefully he now shared in their sorrow. Each morning when he awoke, Mrs. Beeberstein would have already burned the letter.

XLI

Double spent Saturday morning at the local tack shop purchasing a black hunt coat. It was a cheap garment: a shiny polyester blend with a tasteless embossed pattern that didn't have brass buttons or a velvet collar. It also didn't fit him very well and was already quite snug around his potbelly, but it was the largest they had in stock. That coat was something he never would have worn in the show ring, but it would do. He'd long since bought himself larger-sized britches to accommodate his girth, and he'd had the calves of his old show boots professionally stretched for the same reason. Then, alone on Saturday night, he screwed up all his self-discipline and rationed his drinking. He took only one drink—a large water glass full of Scotch right before retiring to bed. It was the first time he'd drifted off to sleep in months and not been blind drunk.

The Little Kill stables were entirely deserted that Sunday morning as Westley Richards, tied on crossties, dozed and Double went about the familiar chores of grooming and tacking up the now-nineteen-year-old retired jumper. He vigorously brushed the horse with a rubber curry-comb and then again with a leather body brush, occasionally brushing it back against the rubber comb to clean it. Finally he went to work with the hoof-pick, gently scraping out the bedding and odd stones from the recesses of the hooves. Then he saddled the horse and put on the bridle, careful to loop the reins over the horse's head so that he wouldn't lose control before he could place the bit in his mouth.

Double could remember when it seemed like these stables were an entire world unto themselves and he spent his every free moment riding, working and socializing there. Little Kill had made him into a horseman long before he ever became a successful rider and now, with less than a half-dozen horses remaining in residence, the stables were a mere shadow of their former self.

The sole remaining structure of the once pristine and sprawling complex had steadily fallen into disrepair and was in desperate need of repainting. In another era, eight o'clock on a Sunday morning would have presented an organized pandemonium of children taking riding lessons on over a dozen riding-school mounts, both in the indoor riding arena and the outdoor ring. Adults might have enjoyed a leisurely ride around the golf course and onto the neighboring network of trails, and a small army of grooms as well as two full-time riding instructors would have bustled about in their various professional duties. The indoor riding arena had long since been converted into a royal court tennis facility, and Double was entirely alone at what remained of the barn complex, working in solitary silence.

Little Kill had once been a reasonably successful show barn, its students making the rounds of the local County horse show circuit. That circuit had both shrunk and consolidated over the years and was now down to a half-dozen small-scale events for the entire year. The lower part of the County wasn't even very suitable horse country any longer. The open land required for a farm had grown too expensive and all the serious horse people had long since moved out.

The remaining horses in the barn were retired, and their owners no longer had need of riding instruction. Cosmi had been shipped off to summer camp along with Connie in the hopes that his diminished equestrian interest might somehow miraculously reignite, but Double seriously doubted his boy would ever sit on the pony again. Connie had abandoned all the things that had brought him pleasure before the incident and now he seemed only interested in watching television. Part of the reason he was off to camp was get to him away from the idiot box, as left to his own devices he'd spend his entire summer break indoors watching reruns of sitcoms and old movies. It was almost as if he were trying to relearn how to be a human being, and using television as his primary learning tool. His eyes, those windows to the soul, now seemed dead, and sometimes gave Double the impression that no one was home.

The barn, the horse and even the man were relics of another period—out of time and place. Double ascended the tree-trunk mounting block and stepped into the left stirrup-iron of his old close-contact jumping saddle, confident in the depressing thought that he and Francesca were in all likelihood the last two people who would ever ride a horse at Little Kill.

The pistol remained in the glove compartment of his BMW sedan. Even though he held a concealed carry permit, Double had never bothered to actually procure a handgun, so he took his father's old FP-45 Liberator pistol instead.

The weapon was a design curio: Senior had literally penned it on a cocktail napkin at a war-production convention in Detroit during the war, and it immediately went into production at the Guide Lamp Division of General Motors. Senior's idea for the Liberator was to create a rudimentary single-shot pistol that was extremely cheap to produce and could be airdropped by the tens of thousands to resistance fighters in the field. The .45-caliber smoothbore only had an effective range of 25 feet, but Senior's thinking was that it could be used by an Allied guerilla to surprise and overwhelm an Axis occupier. The resistance fighter could then appropriate the enemy's superior weaponry. The design was crude, and because it was made from metal stampings, it could be manufactured by a wide range of civilian industries. It was a triumph of simplicity, and even though it never saw the widespread use he hoped for, Senior was rightly proud of it.

Double had tried out the pistol in the breast pocket of his show coat, and even though its skeleton frame was designed to be lightweight, the gun was just too cumbersome not to bounce around uncomfortably at his breast. Besides, if the moment seemed right and despair suddenly overtook him, the razor blade in his wallet covered over with electrical tape and cardboard would do the job just as well.

So for one of the handful of times in his life, Double carried a wallet on horseback, with the short 14-carat stub of a pen resting in the fold inside his breast pocket. He balanced out the other side with a small pewter flask filled with single-malt Scotch—enough to get him through the day. He wore a starched white shirt with a formal white necktie, form-fitting beige britches and a new set of short spurs. He even polished his black high-top boots for the occasion. He had Westley going in a set of rubber bell or overreach boots, which covered and protected his hooves should the horse clip himself on the trail. In concert with these were leather jump boots covering the horse's front shins and rear fetlocks.

Anyone seeing Double's formal dress would assume he was trail riding to a local horse show. Double rode off, disappearing into wisps of early morning fog and onto the ever shrinking network of local trails, rising up and down in the saddle at a slow posting trot, keeping cadence with the horse's gait.

The mist quickly burned off, and the morning became a beautiful summer day. The woods surrounding the bridle paths were green and lush, the landscape alive in both sight and smell. Double picked up a canter and rode the line into two felled trees that had long served as a two-foot-high in-and-out. Westley practically stepped over the obstacles, and Double pulled him back to a trot. As they crossed Little Kill Creek, Double stopped and let the horse drink until Wes grew bored and started to claw at the water. It all looked as Double remembered it from his childhood, but through the thick foliage just a few feet off the trail were large, high-end homes in an endless tract of new constructions. When the leaves were down over the winter, Double had watched the progression of these formations—from foundation, to framing, to roofing, to finishing. Most of the new houses were already occupied.

Double didn't have a particular plan; he thought he'd just ride along for a while, perhaps out beyond the Parkway to be alone with his thoughts, but the farther he rode, the fainter the trail became. The problem was that although Double knew exactly where he was going, in some places the bridle path had become so overgrown that it seemed to disappear entirely. Twice he gingerly rode through residential backyards, and once Westley skittered past the gaping chasm of an unfinished swimming pool in order to regain the trail.

Finally, Westley stepped out of the woods and onto North Street at the bridge that crosses over the Parkway. The traffic seemed oblivious that there was a horse and rider just off the curb as it zoomed over the span at speeds approaching 50. Double dismounted and stood nervously with his horse. The bridge was a narrow two-lane overpass. He well remembered crossing over the Parkway en route to local horse shows as a kid; they often covered their horse's eyes and hand-walked them across. Double rolled up his stirrups and removed his hunt coat, carefully wedging his wallet and pewter flask into the waistband of his britches. Then he gently tucked the black hunt coat high up underneath the browband of the leather bridle, veiling Westley's eyes from the traffic running rapidly over four highway lanes some twenty-five-feet below. He waited until the coast was clear in both directions on the bridge, then stepped off the curb and started across.

Almost immediately, a low-slung, souped-up Japanese sports car—a silver Datsun with the vanity plate that read CSHIN IN—came barreling through and was suddenly upon them. Double and

Westley weren't even halfway across the span when the obnoxious driver stood on his horn, unsettling the already skittish horse. Westley started to panic and Double laid his hand reassuringly on the horse's neck. Now well beyond the point of no return on the bridge, Double decisively trotted Westley across the remaining span and back into the woods on the other side. The instant they were off the paved road the sports car sharply accelerated over the bridge and then screeched to a halt directly in front of them.

The driver, a surly man in his late forties with a bitter scowl and a high, tight crewcut, shouted something to the effect that that the faggot horsey set should really restrict themselves to the hunt club. Double thought he vaguely recognized the man—perhaps from Little Kill—but it didn't matter: There were no meaningful standards left in the world; why should the country-club set be any different?

Double removed his hunt coat from Westley's eyes and put it back on. He unrolled his stirrups, and when he went to put his foot into the left iron, his protruding potbelly prevented him from doing so. He tried several times, even holding his breath to suck in his gut, but it was futile: He could not mount his horse from the ground. The personal humiliation was palpable—this former would-be Olympian was so fat he couldn't even get on his horse without a mounting block.

Double took the reins over Westley's head and led him down the trail on foot for a while. They had come five or six miles from Little Kill, and the trail was now becoming more pronounced and established, as it was clear that these bridle paths continued to be used for horseback riding. Double found a tree stump and got back in the saddle. He dreaded the idea of recrossing that bridge on the return trip, as there was certain to be even more traffic on a late Sunday afternoon. They trotted along the trail at a brisk pace, Westley making countless small turns, constantly adjusting for the terrain and simply following the exposed, dark earth. Finally, Double brought his horse back to a walk, and then they stopped entirely.

The sound was faint—a noise he knew but couldn't quite put his finger on. They rode onward toward it. When Double could finally see open space and light at the end of the trail, he stopped, listened again and realized he knew exactly what the sound was— and that he and Westley were going home.

The trail opened up into an expansive field, the very bottom of the Great Lawn of the Meade estate, a sprawling stately home and former family seat. The estate had a large Cotswold manor house, stables and over 300 acres of grounds that the family had donated to the County for a park. The noise that Double heard was the bleating of a public address system, and as horse and rider stepped out of the woods into this great meadow, Double was looking out over the panorama of a horse show.

It was a modest weekend-long event with a spectator's tent, cook tent, announcer's trailer and a booth selling ice cream and fresh-squeezed lemonade. There were also three temporary show rings set up on the turf for equestrian competition—one for children, one for hunters and one for the equitation and show jumpers. It was the local Professional Horse Shows Association (PHA)–affiliated competition, an event Double had regularly ridden in as a child.

Westley sounded one low, guttural whinny and then another, acknowledging the familiar scene, sending a greeting to the other horses. Horse and rider crossed the large grassy parking area chockablock with horse trailers and vans, ponies and horses, riders of all ages coming and going to their respective classes.

No one recognized him as he rode through the center of this choreographed three-ring circus. The horse show world has a short memory, and there is an enormous amount of turnover that is directly correlated to the health of the overall economy: In good times new money will try to spend its way into the top ranks. In really lean years, perfectly serviceable jumpers, still able to compete in the Junior and Amateur divisions, are given away for free just to get out from under the rolling cost of stabling fees. America had been through a prolonged economic stagnation preceding the Reagan-era bull market, so it wasn't surprising that the young riders competing should fail to recognize the famous horse and rider.

It was all just as Double remembered it. He'd been gone a long time—ever since his final triumph at the Garden, but now this homecoming on a beautiful summer morning at a local horseshow felt as grand to him as a march at the Rose Bowl parade. Children played in between classes, the adolescent boys flirted with pretty girls. Horseshow mothers gossiped in a coffee-klatch that has been their natural state of being since mankind first saddled a horse and parents began comparing offspring.

Double rode past the warmup rings and listened to the coaches giving instruction. He finally arrived at the jumper ring, a wide-open space with several mature trees—red oaks and black birches —scattered throughout the course.

The jump crew was setting the course for the combined Junior Amateur-Owner jumper classic. It was a kind of minor-league grand prix, with smaller fences but no less complex course design, which would begin at one o'clock; he still had ninety minutes. There were three fences set in the warmup ring. A three-foot-six-inch vertical, a roll-top at three-foot-nine-inches and an oxer spread-fence with the high back rail set at four-foot even.

Westley was already fairly well warmed up from his trail ride, so Double stopped and raised his stirrups a hole to better get off the horse's back in the air over a fence. He made a large circle at a posting trot across the schooling ring, broke into a canter and then turned into the first low vertical. Westley's ears pricked up and his undivided attention and focus suddenly went to the fence. The pair cantered into the base of the jump, sailed over it easily and upon landing Wesley bucked and farted spontaneously. Double pulled up to a halt and backed Wesley up two steps to recompose him. They cantered down to the far end of the ring and turned back into the big oxer and comfortably cleared that too. Yes, Double, fat slob that he was, still rode with a light touch and finesse that made him appear surprisingly fluid in the saddle.

Double dismounted, rolled up his stirrups, unsaddled his

horse and leaned the saddle, pommel down, against the fencepost of the ring. He pulled the reins over Westley's head and walked him over to the temporary horse show office, in the announcer's trailer.

When he arrived, Double paused a moment to think. *What the hell am I doing?* He had nothing left to prove, and why would he want to physically overstress Westley at this late stage in his retirement? But then again, it would just be one class and the fences wouldn't exceed four feet in the first round. Westley had just shown that he was still both willing and able—enthusiastic even—at the prospect of reentering the show ring.

As Double stood on the stoop of the trailer with the reins in his hands contemplating just how he could get inside to retrieve an entry form, the door swung open and Lady Metcalf stepped out onto the stoop and literally into his arms.

She was taken aback, surprised by their close proximity, but once she realized it was him she held her ground and remained face to face—close enough to kiss him. She cracked a broad grin from beneath her baseball cap. "My, my," she commented on his appearance. "Look what the cat dragged in."

Double kissed her on the cheek. "Lady . . . Jesus, you're a sight for sore eyes. You look great . . . something's different though. You changed your hair?" he said, complementing her. She was no longer the kittenish manifestation of raw sex appeal. She was a mature woman now, still attractive, but the years had aged her in a way unique to horse people. She was lean and athletic and tan, but now also hollow-cheeked with a slightly weathered complexion—a side effect of a high energy lifestyle spent out of doors in all weather. Her shapely curves were still in fine form and wrapped in a tight pair of Calvin Klein jeans. She wore her honey-blonde hair braided into a long ponytail, a pink alligator shirt and a set of diamond stud earrings as big as jelly beans.

"I had a boob job; the doc took a biopsy and didn't like what he saw. Cancer killed my ma, so I said take 'em both and let's downsize while we're at it. Now the girl who couldn't get a straight man to look her in the eye since grade school has smaller tits than you do."

"Well, you look fine, Lady—terrific even. Might even take a shot at you myself."

"Seems to me the last time I saw you we came about that close to . . ." she said through a smirk, as she put on a set of wire-rimmed aviator sunglasses.

"Just about that close," he repeated.

"You haven't changed much. Except for that show coat fitting you like a sausage casing and having a profile like Humpty Dumpty, you're just about the same. I see old Wes's still keeping on," she said, extending her hand to the horse, whose lips now nibbled at her flatted palm. "You're both retired, but here you are all dressed up for a horse show," she said. "What gives?"

"I don't know," he replied.

"Homesick," Lady said. "You spend thirty years loving something and suddenly go cold turkey—you shouldn't be surprised."

"I heard about the Amateur-Owner classic, and thought we'd ride over and take another turn around the dance floor—just for fun."

"You really sure you wanna do that?" she asked skeptically. "Risking him like that? This old man has done his time in the salt mines—earned his pension," she said, stroking Westley's neck affectionately. "Why not just leave well enough alone?"

"It's four-foot, for Christ's sake! He just jumped two fences in the warmup ring like he was stepping off a curb. He still works three days a week—I think he's up to it."

"You want to sit on a jumper again, fine. Come over and I'll put you on something. You want to get back in the show ring? Pay up and maybe swallow a tapeworm and I'll find you a horse you can win on at the Garden this fall. But this? You obviously haven't thought it through. You're still a hero to a lot of people. You go in there looking like Ralph Kramden on your famous Nation's Cup horse and start knocking down all the fences, you're going to feel like an idiot." She softened, and her hand affectionately went to the hoofmark on his cheek as she looked him in the eye. "Amateur-Owner division ain't the bush leagues anymore. Plenty of good riders struggle out there. You left on a high note, and you're the only one I ever saw do that. Don't spoil it now; this is a mistake." Her hand finally fell away from him.

"I haven't lost my mind. I just forgot how much this all still means to me, and today is the first time I haven't felt out of place in years. Franny's . . . well, she's not really around much—we're not exactly *together* anymore—and the gun business? Let's just say *that* was a big mistake and I certainly never felt about it like I do about this. It was so important for me go out on top—pretty arrogant, I guess. Athletes continue beyond where they ought to stop because it's who they are and they still enjoy it. I never did anything with that business degree, and when my father died, I thought fate was beckoning me to some great career. When you've had success in one area you fool yourself into believing that you can do anything well. This was the only thing I was ever any good at. I'm a one-trick pony and I never should have left. This is who I am—who I remain. I want to ride in this stupid class for the hell of it: not to win, but just for fun. If neither of us can cut it, I'll just pull up."

"It's like talking to Baby Huey!" she finally said, exasperated. "I suppose you need me to pay your entry fee, too?"

"No," he replied, patting the wallet in his breast pocket. "Just hold my famous Nation's Cup horse." With an upbeat smile, he handed off the reins to her as he opened the door and entered the office.

XLII

Lady finally led horse and rider back to her horse van, a six animal setup. The Argentine brothers had continued on with Lady all these years, and the one who was working this show made a big fuss over Westley. He watered the horse and gave him several leaves of hay to tide him over, but the brief reunion between him and Double was awkward. Both remembered the glory days fondly, but the immediacy of that relationship had long since dissipated—the emotional connection severed. The groom left to retrieve Double's saddle, and Lady brought over two fresh-squeezed lemonades and some grilled cheese sandwiches from the cook tent. She dragged two camping chairs over to some shade trees away from the prying eyes of her students, who were now intrigued by the stranger and were trying to sneak a peek at the two of them as they ate lunch.

"Once I got set up at the farm the business just started flowing to me," Lady began. "I figured it would be a way to offset my own expenses, but suddenly these kids were all jumping ship, and none of them seemed to care about the cost. It was quite the shit-storm when they discovered all the skin work I'd done, but my students were winning and the herd mentality took over. Suddenly I was the only coach who could take them all the way to the big time. Then I had a couple of young adult girls break through into the grand prix. You're a high flier—you probably know their father: Down on Wall Street they call him 'Mr. Market.'"

Everyone with even a peripheral exposure to the investment community knew the name. Mr. Market had recently launched a computer-based marketplace that made use of a new-fangled real-time, interactive technology known as the Internet. The fledgling endeavor had shown breathtaking promise, and immediately became the preferred method for handling municipal bond auctions. That segment of the industry became entirely computerized in the short span of eighteen months, and Mr. Market, in partnership with CompuServe, essentially held a monopoly on the technology that made it all possible. He had recently announced his master plan to create a virtual equities marketplace and discount retail brokerage to the entire industry. His boastful prediction—that within five years the total daily trades on his Stockmarket.com would equal those of all of Merrill Lynch—landed him on the cover of *Newsweek* magazine. Dressed in a chalk-striped suit, he was frozen mid-swing as he was about to smash an old-fashioned glass-domed ticker-tape machine with a golf club. Tanned and charismatic, he was beaming gleefully behind his signature Cheshire Cat smile. The tag line read, "Is This the Future of Finance?". The article and the man were met with ridicule and scorn by the financial community, but within five years his bold prophecy would indeed come to pass.

"Deep pockets," was Double's only response.

"Bottomless," Lady agreed. "He's got the idea that one or both of his girls are going to the Olympics, and he wants me to home-grow some horses for him—take some green prospects off the racetrack and turn them into grand prix horses."

"Nice work if you can get it," Double noted with a hint of envy.

"He's setting up down in Palm Beach. He wants me to shut down the King Street farm and come down to run his show barn."

"Sounds like you've landed in a tub of butter. My advice is take the money and run."

"I won't," Lady declared. "This is my deal now—I made it myself. I didn't show my kitty cat to the whole world just to trade it all in on a meal ticket now. It never fails that when girls discover boys, the horses suddenly disappear. Sure, I'd like some of that money, but I'm not going to sacrifice everything I built just to get it. Besides, I don't have the chops to make horses from scratch anyway."

An expression of disbelief came over Double's face. "What are you talking about? Of course you do. Nobody thinks they can do it until they do it. Read two or three books; a little trial and error and you've got a winner."

"Yeah, well, you don't exactly learn on the job with Mr. Market: He expects results the first time out. Now if I had someone down in Florida training the horses for me and I could just fly back and forth with my students . . . Hell, he'd probably even pay you to show his jumpers until they were seasoned enough for his girls."

"Me?" Double replied. "That's a hell of a leap going from one leaky-roof horseshow to training at a show barn full-time. You don't even know if I can ride anymore."

"Sit on three or four horses a day, and I'm sure it'll all come back."

"I have a job, and it's not exactly the sort where you give two-weeks' notice and walk away with your coffee cup and fern."

"You already said it—this is where you belong. Pissing your life away on something you don't even care about is just plain stupid. You wanna spend the rest of your days sitting on your fat ass, or do you wanna come back outside and play with us?"

"You make all these sacrifices hoping to make someone else happy but in the end, you only wind up making yourself miserable," Double finally said, between bites of his sandwich.

"I swore I'd never come back to the County. I only ever lived here for my husband; he couldn't make it anywhere else. The County, and that silly Country Club and Big Pine were Austin's whole world. I never been shy about takin' what I want, but even I didn't have the heart to make him to move to Kentucky. So *I* made that sacrifice."

Double winced at the mention of Big Pine, and abruptly changed the subject. "Connie came home from school and went right off to camp. He'll pretty much be gone the entire summer. My little family has scattered to the winds. That big house is as quiet as an empty cathedral, and I only ever see people at the office. Would you like to have dinner with me sometime?"

"You askin' me on a date?" she asked coyly.

He balled up the remains of his sandwich wrappers. "We have to be careful, though. I'm pretty sure she has someone in the city, but that's still no reason to . . ."

"By all means," Lady kidded. "We'll follow all the rules of social etiquette. I just gotta laugh though: I got me a date with Double Winston, only now he's fat and old and wants to cheat on his wife with me! You really know how to make a girl feel special."

"Yeah, well—let's get together sometime," he said dryly, as he reached for his hunt coat and removed the pewter flask from its breast pocket. He screwed off the cap and said "digestif" humorlessly, taking two greedy pulls like a baby animal feeding from a bottle.

"You think that's a good idea right before going into the ring?" Lady asked.

"Only if you don't want to see my head come off," he answered matter-of-factly, screwing the cap back on. Lady suddenly looked on mortified. "What?!" Double finally snapped resentfully. "You think I got this way eating bonbons?"

"Daddy," she finally proclaimed.

XLIII

Double passed entirely unrecognized as he walked the course with Lady and one of her advanced students. He orchestrated his strategy, choreographing the ride in his mind to maximize the chances of a clear round. Just as he always had, Double rolled the rails in their shallow cups and decided just when and where he would take his one great calculated risk to try to win the class.

Then they walked the jump-off course. Lady followed Double, giving her junior student explicit, detailed instructions on how to approach each fence. When they finally paced off the last line off fences, Lady turned to Double and asked, "Any advice on jump offs from the master?"

Double thought a moment and responded. "Fast rounds don't necessarily look that quick. Gallop wide through every turn and you'll get beat. Moderation of pace is the key: Cover ground where you can, but keep him collected and maneuverable so you can cut the sharp turns. The shortest distance between two points is always a straight line."

Double paused to let his words sink in.

"My horse is a mare—she is *not* a he," the student said, correcting him in a tone dripping with adolescent resentment.

Double rolled his eyes in exasperation, and Lady cackled.

For a man who shouldn't feel the need to prove anything on horseback, he intended to give his all to try to win this class. It had been six years since he'd last been in the show ring, and even then he never rubbed elbows with small-time, local professionals. Even so, he was visibly changed—a cumbersome wreck of a man on a famous old horse now so gray at the muzzle that Westley also went unrecognized.

Cognizant of the fact that this long day was taking its toll and was now about to demand a maximum effort on the part of the old gelding, Double cantered once around the warmup ring and jumped exactly two fences—the three-foot-six vertical and then the oxer with the back rail set at four feet. All seemed in order: Both horse and rider appeared up to the task.

Double streaked into the show ring at a gallop and then pulled up. Then he trotted nonchalantly back across the ring past the entire course as Westley, ears pricked and full of enthusiasm, scanned all the obstacles. Horse and rider had been announced by nothing more than their competitor number, and more than one spectator remarked that whoever it was, that opening gallop was Double Winston's calling card. Several riders then inquisitively approached the rail to watch this slack, doughy equestrian ride his round.

Both man and beast were back in their element, undertaking the one single activity on the planet to which both where uniquely suited. Like a fat man ballroom dancing with surprising grace, Double seemed uncharacteristically athletic and limber, his residual form overcoming the handicap of his corpulence.

Westley also impressed as he worked through the course of fences, but he also clearly wasn't the same horse anymore. If asked, he probably could have jumped even higher for a single fence than the required four-foot maximum here, but this one-off round of more than a dozen fences, both technical and complex in design, came off as labored, with the old boy periodically grunting in his efforts. When Westley crossed the timers with a clear round, Double could feel in his old friend an aged weariness of the flesh, entirely overwhelming any remaining willingness of the spirit.

The applauding crowd at ringside had grown in the short span of his round, and many people now recognized him, even though none were bold enough to approach him.

"I honestly didn't think you could pull it off," Lady said through a beaming smile, as she held Westley while Double dismounted. "Go on bread and water till November, and I do believe you could make a convincing comeback at the Garden."

"That was a whole lot more work than it should have been,"

Double said, doubting himself.

"I told you it wasn't going to be any cakewalk, but you both looked fine out there, honest injun," Lady affirmed.

XLIV

As Double stood at the in-gate and watched several horses fail to go clear in the jump-off, he knew that victory was within his grasp. The riders were all making rookie mistakes or they were unwilling to take a chance to win. The horses were uniformly of two distinct varieties: half worn-out former grand prix horses with precious few miles left on the clock, or horses of narrow scope for whom four-foot-six-inches was the very limit.

Lady was right: It was the best sort of homecoming, as it rekindled his one true love. It was now obvious to him that this was what he should do with himself going forward. How could he have ever thought himself too old when he retired at thirty-nine? Here he was about to win this class, riding out of shape and as fat as a house, on a horse that could just as easily be dead and in the ground.

He felt like a winner again. He knew exactly what he needed to do, and the bit was set in his teeth. He turned to approach his horse to warm up—and then it all came crashing home. Westley was dozing at the rail, head low and bone tired, standing on three legs and half asleep. It suddenly dawned on him—this was all wrong, and that no matter how the jump-off turned out, he would come away dissatisfied.

Double and Westley had both been world-class competitors, and it shouldn't come as a surprise that even at this late stage they could mop up the floor with a bunch of mucksack children and housewives. He was still head-and-shoulders above the field, and proving it again today would prove nothing. Besides, he thought, this class *is* a big deal to these riders and could very well be the pinnacle of their entire equestrian lives. Why ruin it for them?

As he approached Westley and pulled down his stirrup, his plan began to take effect. When he was on deck, he picked up a canter and jumped a single vertical fence set at four feet. When the announcer called his number, he galloped across the show ring like a streaking comet and then pulled up. He looked around the rail, which was now packed with spectators. The cat was out of the bag—everyone knew him.

The last element of the course was a tricky in-and-out—an elaborate wishing well with a peaked roof and wooden buckets overflowing with colorful plastic flowers. The combination had very long striding between the two fences, and every horse that had made it clear to that point inevitably wound up dropping the rail on the second obstacle, a big oxer spread-fence. Double picked up a canter and crossed through the timers. He rode past the first fence of the jump-off course, took a big loping turn and came onto the last line directly into that in-and-out. Once Westley realized the objective, his ears pricked up. Double held him back until he read the correct striding, and then committed. The pair arrived perfectly at the first fence and cleared it easily, carrying a lot of speed. Double goosed the great horse onward with his calf and short spurs, and they accelerated through the combination. He made an audible cluck with his tongue and teeth, and the two left the gravitational bounds of the earth with Westley arching his neck and tucking his knees deeply into chest, his hind hooves tight together, as they tapped ever so slightly the back rail, leaving it rolling hither-and-yon in its shallow steel cups as the oxer remained standing.

There was a loud applause from the gallery as Double and Westley passed through the timers, and the announcer proclaimed that horse and rider by intentionally going off course signified they had voluntarily withdrawn from the class.

As he approached the in-gate, Lady stood at the ready to take the horse from him.

"Pretty classy. Finally decide to pick on someone your own size?" she asked through a smirk.

"Wesley's had enough—he doesn't need to show off," Double replied.

She gave the horse a pat on the neck and said, "A regular

Galahad."

"The very least I owe him."

XLV

That night Double stood at the kitchen counter at Bailiwick in his bathrobe and slippers, replaying the events of the day as he poured a full measure of Red Label, entirely filling a water glass. He would again attempt to screw up his self-discipline and try to hold himself down to this one drink—enough to take the edge off to sleep, but not enough to get him drunk.

He was going to pull himself together—lay off the sauce—and miraculously, things were going to change for the better. If this day had shown him anything, it was that he had made the mistake of his life in ever leaving the horse world. He was miscast in his role of corporate titan. It wasn't that he wasn't a businessman—he had the credentials of an Ivy League MBA and perfectly understood the theoretical principals of commerce. It was that he simply didn't have a passion for this particular enterprise. Francesca was right: He'd undertaken the endeavor out of some hazy sense of duty to his father, and now the whole industry seemed to be souring anyway.

In recent years, he'd envisioned himself as the lone bulwark protecting the employees—all two thousand of them: the helmsman lashed to the ship's wheel. The fortunes of Winston Firearms had continued to founder, and now, faced with the prospect of actually making a clean break and entirely abandoning the family legacy, his resolve was wavering. These employees were really his father's people—not his. Any obligation he had to them had long since been fulfilled. *Besides,* he thought, *business is business, and if the old production methods were simply no longer viable, well then, there really wasn't anything to be done about it.* The fraying union between Double and Francesca was now a marriage in name only, providing a façade for continued social respectability and nothing more. She seemed happy enough in her comings and goings, and Double was fairly confident she was in love with someone else. He couldn't blame her: He'd acknowledged his drinking problem and realized that being married to him couldn't have been much fun. She had lost all respect for him as he gradually lost respect for himself and, in light of this, he couldn't blame her for taking care of herself.

But now, suddenly, he could imagine a new future entirely separate from her: a life back in the show ring, riding and training horses—and winning. Maybe even taking another run at the Olympic Games, which was still two full years away. It was all within him, lying dormant, just waiting to be reactivated.

Things were going to change from that moment on! Little Kill was a depressing, dying place, and Westley had returned that night on Lady's horse van, back to the farm on King Street, a stable buzzing with activity. There, the great horse would be fussed over as a celebrity and receive the pampered attention he so deserved. This proactive decision alone made Double feel like he was turning some sort of corner. He'd woken up that morning with vaguely suicidal intentions, and now he was mentally running through a fresh set of appealing possibilities.

Could the mutual attraction with Lady go anywhere? She was an altogether different sort of woman. There certainly was chemistry between them, but he'd never really thought about what it might be like—not to just briefly bed her but to be in an ongoing relationship. It was a preposterous thought. The entire world had ogled her privates in living color. For all he knew, she might have even taken payment for sex. Austin Metcalf was an old fool who'd grown increasingly eccentric in middle age, to the point that his family had questioned his sanity. Could Double, a scion of the American arms industry, ever seriously consider falling in love with that kind of woman?

Lady was now his peer, a self-made success both as a trainer and grand prix rider, and she'd made it using the only assets available to her. There is some truth to the maxim that all women—from the streetwalker right up to the heiress—are playing the same game, the only difference is the form and frequency of payment. *Why not*, he thought, *who's he saving himself for? She's still beautiful, has plenty of street smarts, and he'd have to be a damned fool not to at least take this last best shot at a normal life with her.* She could also help him get started back up in the show ring and find him horses. Hell, he could re-launch his riding career training alongside her at his old farm on King Street.

A self-satisfied smirk came over him as the thought occurred that he'd probably sleep with Lady Metcalf before he'd ever make love to his own wife again. He downed the last of his Red Label and retired to the master bedroom suite and the king-sized bed in which he now slept alone each night. Even when Francesca was in residence she stayed in a separate guest room.

It had been a nice life with a nice wife and home. His son, who was still not much more than a boy, had been the apple of his eye until a brief lapse in judgment—a reckless and callow plan—unfolded tragically in the blink of an eye, inexorably altering the fate of the entire family.

Michael King's investigation was a waiting game now. Either an arrest or interrogation would ensue or it would not; only time would bring that matter to its eventual conclusion.

* * * * *

D ouble needed to stop drinking—and then he needed to stay stopped. He had to discover the trick to this whole thing, and it occurred to him to pay a confidential call on his Memorial Day parade driver, Troy Roberts, the black personnel manager. Then he pondered the thought that he *could* in fact ride at the Garden this coming autumn should he choose to; all it required was his own commitment and the king's ransom that purchasing such an already competitive horse would command.

The jigger of Scotch warmed his insides, and as the alcohol began to take hold, Double was overcome with thoughts of the day and more pleasant times ahead. Indeed, his mind began to race. One chapter in his life was closing, but another was opening up. It was a kind of dreamy dance of sugarplum fairies prancing through his head, and the thought of such limitless potential made him euphoric.

He tossed and turned in his bed both with and without the blankets. He went to the bathroom several times, and then finally relented and returned to the kitchen for another full glass of Red Label. When he returned to bed, he watched television. Just an hour later he returned to his water glass. As he grew more intoxicated, the glories of the day were replaced with the burning shame that, contrary to his intentions, he was once again blind drunk. The day had been a new beginning of sorts, and here he was backsliding in just a matter of hours. This self-loathing compelled him to continue drinking, and when he finally woke to the sound of the doorbell ringing at 6:15 a.m., it was with a world-class hangover. *Who the hell would come unannounced at that hour?*

The thought immediately occurred that it might be the police. He stumbled over to the window and caught sight of a navy blue Mercedes sports coupe parked in the driveway below. Cops don't drive German imports, he reminded himself, as he pulled on his robe and slippers. Unshaven, grizzled and slit-eyed, he descended the perilously long staircase in a state of total disorientation. When he heaved open the heavy set of double-doors, there on the front stoop before him stood Lady Metcalf, arms around herself, morose and staring at the doormat. "Wes died in the night," she said solemnly. "They went to feed at five and he was already cold—looks like he went in his sleep. I'm awful sorry," she said as she started to tear up.

"Dead?" Double echoed in his stupor. "Shit . . ."

"He seemed just fine when we unloaded him—wasn't even that stiff. I remember thinking to myself, *that's one spry nineteen-year-old.*"

"Jesus," Double said, and it briefly appeared as if his legs might buckle, so he stepped forward, and Lady helped him, as she would an invalid, to sit on the front stoop. As he did this, his genitals slipped out from under his robe and came into view. Embarrassed, Lady averted her eyes. Double hastily stuffed the front of his robe between his legs to cover himself.

"If I'd'a only known something was wrong . . ." she said.

"I'm floored."

"You don't think yesterday had anything to do with it?"

"Probably," Double said stoically. "Fragile creatures prone to injury and dropping dead without warning: What difference does it make?"

"I was gonna call in a backhoe. Just tell me where you want him."

"When I was a kid, they'd just rend the carcass—feed it to the fox hounds."

"That's gross," she said.

"That's practical. Back pasture down in the hollow: That's where we buried the others."

"He's still on his side just the way we found him if you want to . . ."

"No." Double said flatly. "I don't need to see him like that. Just pull his shoes and mark the grave."

"He didn't look distressed or anything," she said reassuringly.

"He's dead; that's all that matters."

"You're takin' this a whole lot different than I expected."

"It's not the first horse I had die on me. Sooner or later it's something, and histrionics don't change that." Suddenly he felt the chill of the morning air through his bathrobe, and stood up. "Come inside."

"I got a barn full of horses waiting," she said, turning for her car.

"Have a cup of coffee," he called.

She faced him again, and her expression turned pointed. "I *am* sorry about your horse, Double. It's a real shame, but you ain't exactly fit for company right now, are you? You're still kind of a mess. You stink. Your BO's gotta be eighty-proof! Why you gotta' drink like that? I didn't see anything yesterday to give a person reason to go off the deep-end, but one look at you today and I know that's what happened." Double felt cornered and self-conscious, and he acknowledged her suspicions with a simple shrug.

"I like you—more than a little, but it's just as easy to fall for a teetotaler as a souse. Daddy was a card player in Reno—drank himself to death on the casino's free well. You got everything you need to succeed, but you can't be a show jumper anymore if you can't function at six in the morning—every morning. You need to get shitfaced every night? Don't expect me to be a witness. You wanna come back and be someone again, get a grip and put a cork in the bottle. I don't need to land another big fish—I *got* all the money I'll ever want. And I don't need any more friends—I need a partner. One month bone-dry and we can talk. Until then, we got nothing to discuss." She turned to leave, but then stopped and muttered, "My condolences."

Double, unable to respond to her indictment, just stood there. She had him pegged right down to his toenails.

"I'll try," he called.

"Don't just try—do it!"

As she pulled round the circular drive he meekly waved goodbye. She didn't respond.

XLVI

All that week Double was able to ration himself to a single water glass of Scotch right before bed. Every night he'd go out to dinner alone and then to the movies afterward. Every morning he woke up at six feeling good and ready to take on the day.

In the middle of the week, he gathered all his courage and determination, and beckoned Troy Roberts to his office. Troy knew exactly what it was about—what else could it be about? Because of this he carried with him a copy of the Alcoholics Anonymous *Big Book* in a brown paper bag under his arm. Double could barely bring himself to open the conversation. First he inquired about the man's family and then they discussed the company jeep. Only after they had exhausted every other possible topic did Double finally touch on exactly how one went about stopping drinking.

As the two of them spoke, hierarchy and all natural law of the corporate environment were upended. Troy was instructing and mentoring his superior, while Double, still unable to quite bring himself to broach the subject directly, regarded it all from the distant perspective one might give a conversation about an acquaintance. Troy simply listened. When Double finally finished, Troy did the only thing he could do—the only thing he ever found to help an ailing alcoholic regain their senses and start on the road to recovery. He made a gift of the book, suggesting that Double read it, and then asked that they pray, kneel together on that Persian rug and ask God Almighty to grant them both the gift of sobriety—just for that day.

When they were through, Troy presented a much mimeographed, faded sheet listing all the AA meetings both in Bridgewater and in the County. He offered to take Double to a meeting that very night, but then suggested that if Double felt shy about it, he might find an out-of-town meeting where he was certain to go unrecognized. After Troy left, Double thumbed the pages of the book. He felt self-conscious and foolish genuflecting in prayer in the presence of another, but he brought the volume home with him anyway.

XLVII

Dr. Heinrich Berger had first witnessed the commercial-grade Robot-Coupe food processor at work when the clinic cook used it to create a foie gras mousse, beating cooked goose liver into chicken stock and cream until it was a peaked froth. The cook gave the doctor a demonstration of the various function settings on the machine and showed off the large stainless-steel bowls and accessory blades that came with it. Dr. Berger was intrigued.

Like many older people, Dr. Berger's thoughts increasingly turned to his own mortality. He was still in excellent health, continuing his daily hour-long constitutionals to town and back, but he was nagged by the thought that should he die suddenly, his affairs weren't really in order. His work now focused exclusively on the clinic; his career presenting neurological research papers was over. He had a bomb shelter full of Nazi concentration camp–era human tissues that was becoming an ever increasing liability, and Double Winston was the only other person in the world who knew about it. According to the letters from his daughter, her husband had descended into an alcoholic nightmare and was becoming increasingly unreliable. Without any further need for the biological materials, the smart thing to do was to preemptively begin the purge. He decided then and there to put that food processor to work liquefying and disposing of the soft human-tissue samples.

He purchased a new Robot-Coupe machine for the clinic kitchen and stole away to his store room with the old one. In an oilskin bib and rubber gloves up to his elbows, he began the Herculean task of pouring the contents of hundreds of large specimen jars into the commercial-grade food processor and blending the formaldehyde solution and tissues into a gray slurry of cerebral tissue, which he then poured down the drain.

He began his backbreaking work in earnest, pulling one jar after another down from the wooden racks, always careful to rinse them out with hot water and meticulously peel off their identifying labels that could connect him directly back to the children's ward at Erlangen-Nuremberg. It quickly became apparent to Dr. Berger that getting rid of the soft tissues was the easy part, and that the skulls were well beyond the capabilities of even this miracle machine.

It was the heavy specimen jars that measured more than a foot across, with their ground stoppered tops, that posed his biggest problem. The empties took up a lot of space and couldn't very well be put back onto the shelves empty alongside the full vessels, but there really wasn't any other place where they could be organized before disposal.

Against the animated protests of his wife, Dr. Berger began lining the walls immediately outside his laboratory and storeroom building with these containers. His thought was that once he arrived at a nice round number like two dozen, he would dig a shallow hole, pulverize the jars in the pit with a sledge hammer, and then fill it back in. Unfortunately, Dr. Berger had arrived at the state of mind in old age when a person is still extremely competent and functioning at a high level by all outward appearances, but has become less observant, more absent minded, and therefore prone to overlook small details. Peeling the labels off those jars was painstaking, exacting work, and a single omission could incriminate him as a war criminal.

These jars were artfully made and substantial; they could be reused to hold lose change or whole bean coffee, macaroni or even live goldfish. A passerby with larceny in their soul—say a tradesmen or gardener working on the clinic grounds—could easily abscond with one of the literally dozens of glass pieces left lying around. To a layman, it wasn't unreasonable to expect that the jars might have some substantial monetary value. If one could make off with a couple and do a little horse trading, the jars might even provide a steady income for a short period.

So when a half-dozen of the nearly thirty jars walked off, Dr. Berger didn't notice. As far as he was concerned, the materials were clean and untraceable—and therefore safe. Nothing could directly link him back to the children's ward at Erlangen-Nuremberg. He was remiss, however, not only in failing to notice the missing containers but also in failing to recognize his less-than-impeccable inspections of said containers.

XLVIII

Sheriff Michael King was back in the County after spending several weeks at Big Pine awaiting the ballistic results from the state police. They only confirmed his suspicions. It was obvious that many different guns had been shot at Bailiwick over the years, but dozens of .22 slugs taken from the property matched the bullet from the victim. The ballistic evidence was overwhelming, and the case was rapidly moving toward an arrest. The murder weapon could now be placed at the Winston property and the next obvious move was to bring the boy in for questioning.

Connie arrived home from camp on Saturday. Early Monday morning, Michael King gathered three patrolmen and requisitioned a police cruiser to go pick him up. Virtually no one knew of the plan except the policemen directly involved, but in a small town, the unseen hand influences outcomes across both time and space.

The chief of police had spent the weekend competing in a golf tournament at the Little Kill Country Club where, teamed with his son-in-law, they finished third overall. He was now sitting at his desk, in his white undershirt, in his second-story office at the red brick station-house just off the bottom of the Avenue. A double-breasted, navy serge dress tunic with brass buttons and his police shield were carefully draped over the back of his chair. He was admiring the modest trophy in front of him when the telephone rang. It was a reporter calling from a local news channel, who had been tipped off that Conrad Winston III was about to be brought in for questioning on the Big Pine killing, and wanted to know if an arrest was imminent. The Chief, still reveling in his weekend triumph, was tongue-tied. He awkwardly begged off the inquiry, citing that he couldn't comment on potential suspects in an open investigation and that the press would be kept abreast of any new developments.

King was already down at the motor pool signing out a squad car when the Chief paged him over the station-house intercom to report immediately. The Chief buttoned himself into his dress tunic. No modern cop dressed like that—his uniform, like himself, was a holdover from another era. The Chief had risen all the way up from a beat cop on nothing more than a high school education; he would be the last chief of police in town to do so.

When King entered his office, the Chief was hovering over a golf ball, putter in hand, lining up his stroke into the electric putting machine. Without saying a word, King went to sit, when the Chief snapped at him. "Did I invite you to sit down?! Hold at parade-rest, you simple son of a bitch!"

King stood at attention with his arms linked behind his back as the Chief putted. The office carpet broke left, and the ball missed its mark. The Chief laid the club on his desk and glared at the sheriff. "I got six years to go till my pension. My kids are grown and out of the house and I play to a 15 handicap. Come January, they're gonna make me an honorary member up at Little Kill. I own two gas stations in this town—that's the pumps and the ground underneath 'em. I figured you were outa my hair for good. It took me a long time to get where I am, and if you think for a second you're going to come stumbling back in here and make things hot for me, you're outa your mind!"

King smirked.

"I just got a call from a reporter telling me you're about to pick up the Winston boy. On whose authority are you doing that, 'cause your local cooperation just dried up?!"

King remained at attention, but his expression blanched.

The Chief slid open the top drawer of his desk, removed a revolver in a bridle-leather holster attached to an over-the-shoulder Sam-Brown belt and lovingly laid it on the desktop. "That's a Colt Python Custom .357 Mag., fancy grips and a slick trigger: the Cadillac of service revolvers and a gift from old man Winston— that's Senior to you," he said as he unsheathed the revolver and swung open the cylinder. The firearm was tastefully embellished with a single bold flourish of scroll engraved on the frame and the checkered walnut grips had cutouts for the individual fingers. "First class," he said, snapping shut the loaded cylinder and reholstering the gun.

"Double Winston's got a scar on his cheek. When he was a kid a horse kicked him in the face. Senior was racing back home when I pulled him over in Bridgewater headed onto the turnpike ramp doin' about 90. When he told me who he was and why he was speeding, I radioed ahead and we gave him a police escort—a straight shot all the way down.

"It all turned out okay, so a couple of weeks later he invites the whole bunch of us involved in the escort up to the factory to have lunch with him—roast beef with Yorkshire pudding, a five-course banquet in his private dining room. Wood paneling, waiters in white coats with real silverware—all just for us. Senior had a fairly unique mentality. He was a man of the people—a regular guy, but also some kind of genius. This town's one big pain in my ass. Everybody thinks they're John D. Rockefeller or Henry Ford, but

Senior was the real deal, a titan who got along with everyone. He didn't lord it over you, and I never felt funny interacting with him.

"When lunch was over, he takes us to this side room and on the table was a half-dozen of these pistols in velvet-lined presentation boxes. WITH EVERLASTING GRATITUDE, CONRAD WINSTON." That's what the cards inside 'em read. They were special order from Hartford, and then the Winston custom shop reworked 'em. At the time we were still carryin' .38 Police Positives in Bridgewater, but when I came on the force down here, the policy was any blued six-shot revolver with a four-inch-barrel. I carried this every day of my life ever since. That's the kind of man he was, and that's the kind of people they are. Good family—nice kid. You wanna' go poking this hornet's nest? Not as long as I'm on the job."

"The slug we pulled out of the dead girl leads directly to that good family—that nice kid. It's our duty to bring him in."

"Bullshit! It's our duty to send the whole mess to the ATF. Let them confirm the findings."

"Alcohol, Tobacco and Firearms? That's where they send evidence to lose it," King said incredulously. "I'm the investigating officer—I won't allow it!"

"I don't need your permission; the county prosecutor out there doesn't like you any better than I do. He told me to handle it as I see fit."

"This isn't some DUI you can ignore for an easy C-note—it's a homicide."

The Chief went to cuff King at the back of his head with a closed fist, as fighters are so apt to do in a clinch. Then he thought better of it and hooked King by the nose with his first two fingers up inside the nostrils and pressed forcibly on the tip with his thumb. The sheriff's knees buckled and he sunk to the floor in agony.

"Noses are funny things," the Chief calmly explained. "You can blow it, you can pick it, you can even have a party out of it, but you always just kind of expect it to be there. You wouldn't know it, but it doesn't take all that much for the nose to vacation separately from the face, and then no one's gonna' want to take your picture anymore —so show me a little consideration!"

The Chief let go of King, who kneeled holding his face almost as if bowing. "When I told people I was gunning for top-kick in this town, they all said I was crazy. *You* got the education and the pretty wife—you look like a fucking movie star! You grew up in this town, for Christ' sake! A lock on the job, they all said, but here I am—an ugly mug with the big office. It must have been like a dumb animal in a thunderstorm: Lightning strikes all around, and you still can't figure it out. It's real easy, dipshit: You just wet your finger and hold it to the breeze!" The Chief went to lick his finger tip to demonstrate, but then remembering where they'd just been, proceeded to wipe them contemptuously on King's khaki uniform.

"They hung this thing on you 'cause they don't want it solved— any fool can figure that. The Winstons are American royalty—the Conners are shanty Irish. That boy could become the president of the United States someday, and if the Conner girl lived to a hundred, she'd have still died a nobody."

"We're not even going to bother to talk to him?"

"I don't really give a shit, King—it's not on *my* books! Besides, it was an accident. A tragedy and a crying shame, but crucifying that family isn't going to change anything. You got shaky evidence, and damned little of it. Sprawling backyard with a bunch of Big Pine members right there in the neighborhood—any one of 'em could have fired that shot. To a jury, that's reasonable doubt. You already rousted the family once and came up craps—if youda just found something *inside* the house . . . but as things stand, you'll never make this case. I've seen enough and I'm not willing to let it go any further. That D.A. won't risk his reputation either by convening a grand jury that won't indict. You really wanna drive a stake through that tin star of yours? Talk the governor into signing a warrant to take the boy into custody, and then extradite him—but I wouldn't recommend it." The Chief went to the door and held it open for King to leave, then began unbuttoning his dress tunic again. "You want a high-profile collar to stick in this town, you need an open-and-shut case. *You* drew a busted flush—a cold case.

It's over, King."

XLIX

Who can ever trace the root of a perceived obligation or loyalty? With so many philanthropic commitments and educational scholarships awarded by Winston Firearms over the years (many of them restricted to law enforcement and their offspring,) it wasn't surprising that the Winston family had countless unknown allies in the community. When the phone call came into Bailiwick, Francesca was preparing breakfast and Double, feeling sober and well-rested in the early morning hours, was drinking his first cup of coffee and perusing the *Journal*. It was the silent routine the couple had engaged in all their married life, only now it was purely for show—for the sole benefit of their son. The phone rang, and Francesca answered it. The voice at the other end was short and gruff and didn't identify itself. *They were taking the boy in for questioning. The squad car would be there any minute.* When the mysterious caller hung up, Francesca held out the receiver, observing it like a foreign object.

"That's odd," she said inquisitively. "He said the police will be here any minute for Connie. Do you think it's a trick call?"

Double resolutely folded his newspaper on the kitchen table. "I don't know if it's for real or not, but we have a plan and we need to execute it now."

"But he's only just recovered," she protested. "Started to become himself again."

Double stood and took her by the shoulders. "Are you ready to bet the rest of your life on what he can or can't remember? You may be happy with your life in the city, but how long do you think it'll be before they start asking *you* the questions if he remembers what he did—what we did? They'll come for us all."

"I don't want to do this again," she said, starting to cry.

"It's the closest we can get to being certain—that's what your father said."

Double fished the forked electrodes out of the wall safe, and

Francesca retrieved a jar of Vaseline to coat the contacts. Both parents were in tears when they pushed open the crack in the door to Connie's bedroom and found him innocent in slumber. They looked at each other and in that brief moment, their life together flashed before them—the happy marriage, the championship riding career, the happy-go-lucky kid, the big house on the hill. It all came down to this craven moment when they would once again attempt to suppress the memory of a violent killing in their son's mind.

"Hey, buddy," Double said softly to his son. "We need to . . . we need you to hold still for something."

Connie opened his eyes and in the darkened space he could just make out his parents. "What?" he asked.

"There isn't time to explain, sweetie. Please cooperate," Francesca said through tears.

"This won't hurt—I promise. You won't feel anything. It'll be over in a second," Double pleaded.

Connie looked up and in the dim light saw the rabbit-ear electrodes and something in his mind made the connection.

"Is this about Kimmy Conner?" the boy asked.

"Yes," his mother whispered.

"She doesn't like me," Connie said as robotically as an automaton. Then he added, "Just give me a minute."

They carefully placed a wooden cook spoon in the boy's jaws and tied it in place around the back of his head with a shoelace to keep his airway free lest he suffocate or bite his tongue. Francesca held the contacts by their insulated fork while the boy lay in bed flat on his back. The electrodes were placed low, at the hinge of the jaw. Double knelt by the wall with the electrical plug just inches from the outlet and his hand began to shake uncontrollably. He tried to steady it by bracing himself, but it was no use. Eventually he and Francesca switched places and, on the count of three, the mother put the plug into the wall socket and then removed it as quickly as she could, initiating a grand mal seizure. As the boy thrashed about in an uncontrolled fit, she joined Double in the effort to prevent him from falling off the bed. Eventually Connie went entirely stiff and catatonic, and the immediate danger passed, although both parents continued to hold him as a precaution.

Connie finally let out a gurgling, primeval whimper that gradually transitioned into his familiar playful badger's growl which completely unnerved both parents. Finally the boy simply drooled foamy saliva. The scent of fecal matter was in the air. It was obvious he had soiled himself.

"We need to clean him," Double said.

"I'll do it. *We* never changed a single diaper when he was a baby—why start now?" she sniped as she began to strip Connie. "I'll confess to the police myself before I'll do that again. If we survive today, I want to send Connie out of the country—back to my parents."

"How's that going to look?"

"I don't really care any longer how it looks. We've destroyed our child in the name of what? To save your father's precious company?"

"Shut up about my father!" Double snarled.

"We've lost him and you're about to lose *it*; the company will fail entirely of its own accord. Our actions were for naught!"

The harsh truth landed on him like the lash of a whip across a horse's flanks, and before Double could muster a retort, rage overtook him and he impulsively struck out, hitting his wife with the back of his right hand. "Who the hell do you think you're talking to?!" he shouted.

The fold of sable hair covered her face and as she brushed it from her eyes, a veil of crimson descended from her upper bite from where her lip was cut.

Double recoiled at the sight of his wounded wife—a state for which he was entirely responsible. His remorse was followed close by resentment. It was the first time he'd ever hit a woman, and he knew that the sudden violent act spelled the end of all tenderness between them. "Serves you right," he said scornfully. "Jesus fucking Christ, Franny! We don't have enough to worry about, and you needle me about my father, now?! You wanted to get a rise out of me—well, you succeeded. Happy?!"

Francesca remained silent, took a tissue from the bedside table, dabbed at her mouth and then inspected the blood on it. "No, I'm not happy, and neither are you," she said dismissively. "I expect you need to talk to Nathan before the police arrive, so why don't you call him now?"

"Let me help you."

"Leave it," she snapped. "Call while there's time."

Double reached across the prostrate figure of his catatonic son and gently laid an open palm on his wife's shoulder. Francesca withdrew from the contact, and Double knew that his relationship with his family—the immediate emotional bonds that are essential to love and intimacy—were now irreparably severed. He was a heel on every front, and hated himself for it.

Connie still had a slight froth coming from the corner of his mouth, which his mother wiped away with her bloodstained tissue. Then she expertly stripped the boy, flipping him over to remove his pajama bottoms and clean the feces from him. Francesca noticed Double was still there observing her work, and shooed him out of the room with a wave of her hand. Slowly, Double descended the grand staircase of Bailiwick to call Nathan from the kitchen telephone.

L

Nathan Clarke stood inside the front door of the red brick police station just off the Avenue, with his attaché case between his feet. By periodically leaning forward, he could catch a glimpse of the sidewalk through the holes in the wire mesh embedded in the door's tempered-glass side windows. He wore his old brown snap-brim fedora and gray flannel slacks with a candy-stripe bowtie. His father's gold Elgin pocket watch was cradled in the handkerchief pocket of his double-breasted blue blazer. Nathan was now stooped and seemed elderly. His once effortless lanky stride had been replaced by a scurried shuffle, and he wore blue canvas boating sneakers to facilitate walking. He was gray both in his hair and complexion—the side effects of a restricted diet consisting entirely of baby food spooned from glass jars. Recently, several of his teeth had fallen out, and his dentist was pleading with him to pull the rest.

There was a smattering of media curbside—a few photographers and print reporters and one local television crew. Although the morning was warming up into a mild summer day, Nathan brought along his trench coat. If he had the chance and the attending patrolmen were amenable, he intended to throw the beige Burberry over Connie's head as he exited the squad car in order to obscure his face and wrists should they be handcuffed. Nathan expected this would be the last quiet moment any of them would have for a while—the last morning when Connie Winston's name wouldn't be inexorably linked to sensational tabloid notoriety.

There was a nervousness in the air. Something big was about to happen, and even though Nathan desperately wanted to dispel his jitters with a smoke of his pipe—the very last physical pleasure he was able to take—he made do gnawing at the pipe stem instead.

As Sheriff Michael King hurried down from the Chief's upstairs office, he saw Nathan standing in the doorway and immediately knew the Winston family had been tipped off. As he approached, Nathan was too preoccupied with the goings-on outside the building to notice King.

"What brings you out so early, counselor?" the sheriff asked.

Nathan looked at King, who was standing beside him at the door. A lifetime in the law had taught Nathan that regardless of how awkward it made a moment, sometimes the only shrewd tactic was to remain silent. It was sage advice he gave all his clients, which he now adopted himself. "Sheriff," Nathan said, curtly addressing the man.

"Just like a school of barracudas," King said, referencing the crowd, "Waiting for the first drop of blood to hit the water."

Nathan didn't respond, and just assumed that a squad constituted entirely of local law enforcement must have been sent to retrieve the boy.

"They're wasting their time," King said. "We aren't gonna pick him up—there isn't going to be any interrogation." Nathan removed the pipe from his mouth and turned to King.

"Your client's gonna skate today, and unless I get a new D.A. who's actually got some rocks in his jock, your boy's going to get away with murder," King finally said in distemper. "Go ahead. Have yourself a victory smoke; there won't be a story about him today or any day. You win—you beat me. You played a game of *who knows who* and turned a homicide investigation on social influence. Congratu—fucking—lations: You're rotten to the core!" King barged past the lawyer to the door leading out to the sidewalk, but then stopped. "You really got nothing to say to me, counselor?" he asked.

Nathan pocketed his pipe and removed the gold pocket watch from his handkerchief pocket. He opened its clamshell case, glanced at the clock on the wall behind the desk sergeant and compared it to his own. He wound the watch stem, closed the case and replaced it in his pocket.

"You're out of your jurisdiction," Nathan answered dryly, as he placed the pipe stem back in his mouth. Michael King pushed his way out the door and into the sunshine. The pool of waiting media paid him absolutely no attention.

LI

The only vehicle that pulled into Bailiwick that morning was that of Nathan Clarke. The Winston family sat at the kitchen table eating breakfast, just as they'd done on the morning after the killing, as well as the morning of the police search. According to Nathan, the nightmare was over—or could it simply be the closing of one chapter and the opening of another? The old lawyer ate two tiny jars of strained beef-liver baby food—disgusting in flavor, but his only nutritional defense against chronic anemia. Before Nathan Clarke left Bailiwick that morning, he announced his intention to retire in the autumn as Winston Firearms' general counsel. His health was failing, and he wanted to spend whatever time he had left sailing his Concordia Yawl.

Relieved that their trials finally seemed over, Double shook Nathan's hand warmly and agreed to the plan. Though Double had recently managed to successfully cut back his drinking, he was still as rotund as ever, with liverish bags under his eyes and bald patches on his crown. Francesca was pale, hollow-cheeked and haggard. Connie sat with dead eyes and a dishtowel tucked under his chin, shoveling oatmeal into his mouth like a halfwit.

LII

The Winston Firearms division took a big hit when it lost a large government contract for the XM-21 semiautomatic, long-range Designated Marksman's Rifle. Winston had been finishing extremely accurate, synthetic-stocked conversions of the semiautomatic, detachable-box-magazine National Match M-14 in .308 NATO. They had been turning out this highly-profitable sniper rifle to the tune of some 2,000 a year for nearly a decade. To add insult to injury, Winston then lost out in the design competition for a replacement weapon. The firearms division company ship was foundering, and the permanent loss of this cash cow only hastened its decline.

Many more hunters and recreational shooters were dying than being born. Occasionally someone would arrive at the Bridgewater plant with a station wagon full of guns—prized possessions of a deceased father, uncle or husband, objects for which the heirs had no use and wanted nothing to do with. They would plead with the plant manager to simply take the guns off their hands. The manager would cherry-pick the collection and place the remaining discarded firearms in a gun rack at the base of the steps to the elevated catwalk. Any employee was free to inspect the cache, and whoever wanted one could simply take it. With the services of the entire plant at their disposal, not even the basket-case firearms were beyond salvage. In this way, a few lucky employees were able to procure high-end rifles, shotguns and even a few handguns from the entire alphabet of national and international makers for the cost in favors to those doing the restoration work. Unclaimed junk guns were eventually thrown into the scrap hopper and melted.

LIII

Double Winston crossed the art deco lobby of the Astor House, with its deeply included, white-veined black marble interior, past the room's centerpiece, a large chiming four-faced clock on a pedestal. He was dressed in a blue suit with a white shirt and a burgundy necktie, and wanted lunch. The Astor had recently been acquired by an Asian hotel chain, and Double chose it because it was in midtown, just a short cab ride to the international airport. He had two Swissair tickets in his coat pocket, and carried a small suitcase with him. The restaurant was empty, and Double could see all the way through to another crowded dining room where a large oriental buffet was laid out. The maître d'hôtel, an Asian man, saw him waiting and finally came over.

"Where's Hugo?" Double asked.

"You wann lunch?" the man replied.

"I want the Lobster Newburg."

"No lobster," the steward said. "Off menu—you wann eat—you go buffet. Other hall."

"Hugo wouldn't put up with this—where is he?"

"No more Hugo—you go buffet. Other hall," the maître d' said, shooing Double along.

"Where's Hugo?" Double finally demanded, stopping in his tracks.

"Goes back in Europe and dies. You wann eat—you go buffet. Other hall," the Asian man said, leaving Double all alone in the cavernous room.

Victor Kralick soon joined Double; the way the old Hungarian was dressed perfectly represented his penniless nobility. He wore a moth-eaten black beret, and in place of his signature ascot was a swatch of blue satin ripped from a discarded pillowcase and tied into a cravat. The sleeves of his white shirt were too long, and the entire shirt cuff was continually popping out from inside his jacket sleeve, which he self-consciously kept tucking back in. His brown twill suit was the only one he owned, and had dark leather patches sewn to the elbows to mask wear. He had cap-toed brown paddock boots complete with spur rests—the closest thing he owned to dress shoes. His hair was shaggy and in need of a trim, and he already had a five o'clock shadow because he'd boarded the bus at six that morning to be in the city in time for lunch.

Victor's wife, a lifelong smoker, now suffered from chronic emphysema and congenital heart failure. Poor circulation made walking difficult, and she was always cold, regardless of the season. Victor speculated that a move to the warm climes of south Florida might give her a new lease on life, but his meager finances precluded it.

The years had been cruel to Victor. In a span of less than a decade he had gone from the keeper of the flame for the equestrian Olympic torch to being as redundant as a lamplighter. His was the old way of the mounted cavalry, of spit-and-polish, starched white collars and discipline above all else. The *way* you did something was as important as the result, and if you wanted a berth on the Olympic team, you did it his way or you went home. The Kralick method produced generations of competitive horsemen until the working model on which it was based—wealthy patrons loaning world-class horseflesh to the Olympic team on a gentleman's agreement—broke down and disappeared. Riders were now expected to furnish their own mounts, and if they couldn't afford to play the big-money game, someone else would.

These riders arrived fully formed with their own coaches in tow, and when Victor demanded they pay tribute to his methods by rotating through the team facility to train directly under him, one after another flatly refused. If they could win team-selection trials outright, they had neither the need of the team facility nor of Victor Kralick. He futilely tried to keep his hand in for a while, but modern times were against his ilk. Then he tried to make a living giving instructional clinics, but he was impatient with the limited caliber of the students. Finally he was regarded as an irrelevant anachronism: After all, what could a man who rode an Olympic course of fences in front of Adolph Hitler in1936 possibly have to teach a rider in the modern era of Madonna?

The two horsemen ate lunch at the Asian buffet, which was an amalgamation of Japanese, Korean and Chinese cuisines, and Victor stuffed himself like a man who wasn't eating regularly. Finally, over coffee, they discussed business.

"It's not really clear what happened," Double began. "He was attending a neurological conference in Geneva and always stayed at the Mövenpick there because he liked the food and could eat right in the hotel. They found him in the bathtub with an electric razor plugged into the wall! Tell me how it's possible that a man who took great pride in shaving with a straight razor every day of his life suddenly decides to switch to a plug-in shaver? And then to use it in the bathtub—totally implausible."

"The war finally caught up with him,"

"The Israelis, more likely. They ruled it an accident and won't be investigating—case closed. How's that for Swiss efficiency?! Anyway, there's a storeroom at the clinic filled with old records and medical samples—thousands of file folders and human tissues left over from the war: children, mostly Jewish. Preserved brains as well as compete skulls—hundreds of them. I promised I would destroy it so it wouldn't ruin his reputation after he was gone. Every night, we'll burn the biological samples and paper files in the furnace and then crush the glass jars and slides and bury them outside in the garden. Pretty simple, but there's a lot of it to get through. I don't really know just how legal any of this is since they've been dead so long, but I imagine jail time in Switzerland for something like that wouldn't be very unpleasant or last very long. Anyway, I made a promise and I need help keeping it."

"Ironic: after all this time—still the ovens," Victor said, blotting his mouth with the linen napkin and then fastidiously folding it. "I'm afraid you've misjudged me. I absolutely refuse to partake in this. I'm actually quite pleased that the fascist turd is dead, and would take a great satisfaction were the truth about him known to the entire world. There are certain moral principles which cannot be compromised, and this is one. That wicked degenerate got far better than he deserved—and a generation too late."

Double removed the weighty envelope filled with $100 bills from his breast pocket and nonchalantly tossed it alongside Victor's coffee service. It landed with a thud that rattled the silverware. "That's quite a lot of money to turn down. I thought it might make a difference to you . . . what with your wife being so sick. It's $10,000, half of what I was prepared to pay, but if you're really sure . . . Two-hundred dollars ought to more than cover your time and expenses and get you back home. Please help yourself."

The old Hungarian peeked inside the envelope and thumbed the currency like it was the telephone book. Principles *were* important, but $20,000 in Reagan-era money was a decent annual salary! One could certainly live a long time on it, and it was more than enough for everything he needed. Victor and his wife could move out of their cramped rental apartment and take a mortgage on a modest air-conditioned single-wide in a seniors' trailer park overlooking the beach in Florida. He knew of just such a place called Salty Sands, a few miles south of Palm Beach. They'd even have enough money left over to purchase a reliable second-hand automobile. With that and his pension, social security and Medicare, an inviting vision of a much more comfortable future for Victor and his invalid wife came into view. With a full three months of winter horseshows now well established, he could reasonably expect to find seasonal employment during the Florida circuit, perhaps as a judge or ground steward.

"It's in keeping that you should offer me compensation so substantial I can't possibly decline. You were the beginning of my problems, and you shall be the end of them."

Double raised his eyebrows inquisitively.

"Wholly unteachable from the start, and the first to succeed entirely out of channels," Victor began. "Others saw this and followed. That's the only reason I can be bought now. What puzzles me most is after all your hard work, the gaining of experience and awaiting the opportunity for a spot to open up on the Olympic team, you leave to go work in a factory like a common laborer. Had you simply purchased two or three top-level horses, you would have been unstoppable. We have many such complete riders now, but at that time there was only you: twenty-five years my junior and every bit my equal as a horseman. Most people can't conceive the commitment required to achieve excellence—to become exceptional at something. To them, sport is a child's contest they leave behind on the playground. You fulfilled the necessary requirements: You had the time, the money—the ability to be the best, and for a brief moment you *were* . . . and you intentionally let it go. My chance was taken from me by the war—you surrendered yours. This I do not understand."

"If only we could see present as clear as past, none of us would ever put a foot wrong."

"I'm afraid your obscene generosity has pricked my arrogance like a child's balloon, exposed me for the fool," Victor said matter-of-factly. "Obviously, principle and arrogance are luxuries I can no longer afford. I accept your arrangement, as the sum is just too great."

"No one can ever know about this, though—about him," Double said in a serious tone. "You can never talk about it to anyone."

Victor dismissed the words with a wave of his hand. "Clearly I retain no integrity whatever, but if it eases your mind, you have my word: I'll never speak of it."

LIV

Dr. Berger's private clinic was permanently shuttered, as he had been the sole medical practitioner on staff and had made no succession plan. Francesca and her mother spent the first part of the week in Geneva dealing with the body and its cremation—it was Dr. Berger's final wish that his ashes be spread over the clinic grounds. Both Victor Kralick and Double moved into the patient accommodations. For the first time on a visit to

Lugano, Double wasn't staying in the Berger private residence. He thought it entirely appropriate that as their marriage was all but over, he should give Francesca some breathing room and privacy in her childhood home. Neither Double nor Victor ever really adjusted to European time as they both slept away much of each day and then went to work every night for a full eight hours, beginning at ten o'clock.

The task was backbreaking. Simply lifting the heavy jars filled with formaldehyde solution wreaked havoc on the lower back and biceps as the full sample jars weighed twenty pounds. The industrial food processor remained by the laboratory sink right where Dr. Berger had left it, and they dug a hole out in the garden to accept the sample jars and microscopic slides. They pilfered two shopping carts from the local supermarket in order to shuttle the jars first from the lab, then to the furnace for the incineration of the contents and then finally out to the patio overlooking the garden. The final leg over the lawn was via wheelbarrow, and once the glass containers and slides were in the hole, they used a sledge hammer to pulverize it. In the first moments of this very long process, Double suddenly found himself balking at the repugnant task. He loaded the first shopping cart filled with the defleshed and denuded skulls of a half-dozen children, and stood there looking at it.

"I know I made him a promise, but I'm not sure I can do this."

The Hungarian was at the sink, wearing Dr. Berger's black, elbow-length rubber gloves and oilskin apron, pouring excess formaldehyde solution from a sample jar down the drain of the stone laboratory basin while delicately retaining the preserved, denuded skull within. He laid the jar down inside the sink and turned to Double.

"You vowed you would—of course you can. We do it together—we go home and you pay me my money," Victor said.

"These were people: That was somebody's child!" Double replied, referencing the juvenile head inside the glass.

Victor slowly removed his gloves. "They've been gone as long as you've been alive. The world they lived in and everyone they knew, long since vanished—up a different chimney. You never saw the war in any immediate way—of course it's upsetting. Live with the body of someone you knew for a day or two, and you'll know as I do—human remains are but a repository which holds the person while they are alive. The thing that made them who they were was eliminated long ago. We are simply destroying the vehicles they moved about in. The first body you handle is very much a person, the tenth—much less so. By tomorrow evening, you'll feel differently about all this." Victor tsk-ed three times at him sarcastically. "You Yanks, so willing to die for a cause, but the first moment you see death up close . . .

"I wanted to live," he continued. "I was going to be somebody. Therefore every opportunity that presented itself, I was selfish. It's nothing to be proud of now, especially as I wound up a nobody. I lived while many around me did not, and I now I enjoy the luxury of regret: I'll live with it. *This?*" Victor said, gesturing with a wave of his hand. "*This* is nothing: We are cleaning up the mess of a wicked man's life. *He* did this thing, not you."

Victor slowly donned the long gloves and turned back to his glass jar in the sink. "Keep your promise . . . and then pay me. Then if you prefer, we needn't ever speak to each other again. Perhaps you too can then be haunted by the luxury of regret."

LV

The endless lifting combined with the repeated swinging of the sledge hammer resembled the hard labor of a penal colony, and the work visibly took its toll on the men. It was only dogged perseverance, the judicious administration of aspirin and daily visits to the thermal spa in town that allowed them to remain fit for work.

Getting the villa's coal furnace fired required dragging the local boilermaker out of retirement, and the elderly tradesman couldn't understand why they wanted the redundant system brought back on line, particularly when the modern oil furnace beside it was working perfectly. He was also careful to point out in his best pidgin English that the remaining half-load of coal wouldn't last two weeks with the furnace operating at full tilt. Private retail purchases of coal, he explained, were now restricted and required a special permit. Double overpaid the man and sent him on his way.

On the fifth day, the shelves in the storeroom were nearly empty of specimen jars, and a shady patch of back lawn appeared to the uninformed to have been tilled and was awaiting the fresh planting of new landscaping. Victor and Double had been operating the furnace for the last several nights, stoking it to ever increasing temperatures to the point where it could consume complete skulls, many denuded of skin and facial features but others nearly complete right down to the eyelashes. All that remained from the prolonged firing was a fine bone ash.

Finally, they came to the last three specimen jars, those of the Blankenese triplets, the pretty girls whom Dr. Berger kept as his *pets*—the sisters Lillianthal. While each cranium had been cleanly bisected exposing its inner biology, their mortified far-off expressions remained for all time.

Victor stood by as Double drained one jar after the other into the laboratory sink, and then both men suddenly felt ashamed in disturbing them. The formaldehyde solution which had suspended the tissues provided a basic level of support. With the full force of gravity now at work, the copper hair on each head became matted, and all three, when taken from just the right angle, looked as if they'd been drowned. It was unsettling to witness as the jaw of one of them flopped open revealing a blue tongue. Finally the jars were shuttled over to the furnace, which raged like hellfire.

Double reached his gloved hand inside each jar, removed the bisected heads by the hair and then carefully placed them, one after the other, inside a waxed cardboard box until all three were together side by side. Then he produced a photostat of an English translation of the *Av HaRachamim*, the Jewish memorial prayer.

"I don't know what's right by their faith, but we should do something," Double said, and Victor nodded affirmatively as he mopped his sweaty brow in exhausted agreement. Double proceeded to read the first part of the prayer.

> *"The Father of Mercy who dwells on high*
> *In His great mercy*
> *Will remember with compassion*
> *The pious, upright and blameless,*
> *The holy communities, who laid down their lives*
> *For the sanctification of His name.*
> *They were loved and pleasant in their lives*
> *And in death they were not parted.*
> *They were swifter than eagles and stronger than lions*
> *To carry out the will of their Maker*
> *And the desire of their steadfast God.*
> *May our Lord remember them for good*
> *Together with the other righteous of the world."*

When he was finished, Double carefully folded the prayer sheet back up and placed it inside the box. He put on a pair of leather work gloves and took up the waxed container in his arms, hugging it to his chest. In a brief instant, the craniums shifted slightly and it seemed each girl was staring up at him blankly. Then he delicately balanced the box on the broad, oversized blade of the coal shovel. Victor opened the fire gate, and Double gently tossed the box onto the glowing coals. Immediately the wax coating on the cardboard melted and the container was engulfed in fire. Before Victor could close the gate, the copper hair, once so like strands of spun rose gold, burned off each head and the dermis underneath began to pop and curl like peeling house paint.

Victor let the gate slam shut, and the two men looked at each other, gratified that the job was finally done. All that was left to do was to smash and bury the remaining glass and burn through the rest of the coal as a precaution to ensure that no potentially incriminating solids remained.

It was ironic that Dr. Berger's final wish was to have his ashes spread over the grounds of the clinic, as it was also the identical fate of his victims: The ashes of the children he personally euthanized all those years before at the children's ward at Erlangen-Nuremberg also wound up mixed into the soil of the clinic gardens.

Francesca and Gerda walked the terraced lawns of the clinic compound together, spreading the doctor's ashes and speaking of the life they shared in hushed tones. Every once in a while, Francesca would reach into the urn and sprinkle a handful here or there, always commenting as to why that spot was special, sharing her rationale with an unseen spirit.

Obviously, the two women had some idea of the work Double and Victor had been engaged in. They could see the turned earth covering the shallow pit and the raging exhaust pouring forth from the previously dormant furnace. Finally, a policeman arrived to enquire about the smoke and to find out just what it was they were burning; the neighbors had complained about a peculiar smell and wanted to know when it would stop. Without any prompting, Gerda posited that the clinic's walk-in freezer had failed and they were disposing of rancid meat. The constable was assured that the incineration was complete and that the smell and the smoke would shortly cease.

The officer then took the liberty of a promenade through the gardens to admire the commanding view of the lake below. A man with a considerable green thumb in his own right, the constable admonished them as he examined the dark patch of tilled soil with the toe of his boot. The particular spot they'd selected didn't receive nearly enough sunlight in his opinion, and if the intention was to grow roses, they'd do well to select a sunnier location.

LVI

Gerda prepared the evening meal in the Berger private residence that night, a simple presentation of assorted cheeses and traditional Swiss air-dried meats along with a tricolor salad and a risotto cooked in veal stock with wild mushrooms. Throughout the meal they engaged in small talk, first about the weather and then about the current cinema. The local movie theater was showing Bernardo Bertolucci's epic film *The Last Emperor*, a sweeping twentieth-century biographical drama about China's child emperor. Gerda, who was rather conceited about her language skills, intended to see it in the original English.

The meal was an awkward conversational pirouette around the obvious half-dozen elephants in the room. Dr. Heinrich Berger had recently been murdered and the crime would never be investigated. Connie had killed another child and only narrowly averted being charged with homicide. Dr. Berger had used the clinic facilities to administer electroshock therapy to his own grandson for the express purpose of inducing amnesia in the boy to avoid implicating himself under the strain of a police interrogation. Finally, both Double and Victor had only recently arrived from America for reasons unbeknownst to both women in order to dispose of all evidence of Dr. Berger's criminal Nazi past. Now that their mysterious work was complete, the two men would leave, with neither mother nor daughter ever enquiring as to just what the visit was all about.

*   *   *   *   *

When the dining room was empty and all the dirty dishes cleared, Double pecked his wife goodnight on the cheek and started for the door, when she stopped him.

"He's asked me to marry him," she said.

The words resonated.

"Who's asked you to marry him?"

Francesca closed her eyes at the question. "What does it matter? You don't know him."

Double Winston suddenly felt himself outside his own body again, a specter hovering over the scene. He knew his next line and hated the inevitability of the act that was playing out. "I suppose it doesn't matter at all. Does Connie know?"

"He caught us coming out of a matinee together on a school trip to the city to see a production of *Julius Caesar*. He gazed at us long enough so that it was I who finally turned away. Connie most certainly knows."

"That's bad luck," Double said. "I'm sorry."

Francesca now set her jaw and said determinedly, "As am I, but Connie is nearly a man now and won't need his mother so much anymore. Besides I'm not leaving *him*: I just can't remain in that repressed town any longer—or be with you. Our life together was like Devonshire cream . . . but now it's all curdled, and I can't bear to be reminded of it. It is ironic: We committed a cowardly act and it has since consumed both of us—and your business will likely fail anyway. It's almost as if fate has already passed judgment and sentenced us both."

"Can he take care of you?"

"He doesn't need to: I have my own money and you'll be paying me for Bailiwick. I'm keeping the stocks you gave me, of course."

"Of course," Double conceded, repeating the forgone conclusion that now seemed obvious to both. "But *could* he provide for you? Does he work?"

"He's a surgeon—very successful."

"Another doctor. Well, I suppose it pays well enough," Double said acerbically. "I'll talk to Nathan when I get back."

"Thank you," she whispered through a weak smile as she patted his hand platonically. "Thank you, Double."

LVII

Upon returning home, Double suddenly felt unencumbered—lighthearted even. The divorce would take time and prove painful to both, but he no longer felt constrained by marital fidelity—it really was over. He was all alone at Bailiwick now, and it was immediately clear that the impending sale of the property was actually fortuitous. Like Winston Firearms, Bailiwick had simply been handed down to him, and while there was no denying its stately pretense, the estate was his father's dream home, not his. When Double's mother passed away she left Bailiwick and Sun-Up entirely to him; his sister Marjorie had been evenly compensated by inheriting a two-thirds majority of Conrad Senior's blue-chip investment portfolio. In the recent years Double lived at Bailiwick, he'd come to realize that the spartan lifestyle he enjoyed with his family back at their hardscrabble King Street horse farm in Port Easton had been a much better fit. He'd always regarded it as a kind of temporary exile until he could return to Bailiwick. This estate had never really been a conscious decision on his part. Like the bikini-clad blonde lounging poolside at the club who is supposed to be the kind of woman every red-blooded man wants to marry, Bailiwick was someone else's idea of the sort of home you were supposed to aspire to.

For one thing, the house was absurdly large for one person. For another, Double couldn't really afford it anymore. The ongoing cost of upkeep and high property taxes would impose a severe financial strain on top of an already expensive divorce settlement. The bad news was that his current income wasn't nearly what it had been back when the company was hemorrhaging dividends. Although he still had a modest investment portfolio of his own that was performing well enough, he rationalized that if he sold Bailiwick at a decent price, he could then split the proceeds with Francesca and invest his half in the great Reagan stock market.

LVIII

The invitation was for a weekend at the Astor House where Lady Metcalf and Double could take in as much or as little of the city as they wished. Unfortunately, Lady was unavailable as she was spending the later part of the week looking at prospective horse properties near the Palm Beach Polo Club in Florida. Mr. Market was still quite intent on hiring her away as exclusive riding coach for his daughters. He begged Lady to humor him, flew her down first class and put her up at the Breakers resort.

As an alternative, Double proposed the perfect antidote to all that pretentious over-the-top service: Upon completing the South Florida leg of her trip, might she deign to join him at Onori for the weekend? Onori was still closed up for the summer. Although brutally hot down in quail country, the saddle horses would still be available for trail riding in the cool mornings and evenings and a handful of the guest cabins were air-conditioned. At Onori the couple could enjoy some time alone away from prying eyes and take their first halting steps toward intimacy.

The elation that comes with a newfound sense of possibility was inspired by the charms of a new playmate. At that moment Double half-fooled himself into believing that he would return to the horse world in short order for another turn in the show ring. In his daydreams, Lady would be right there by his side.

He had some hazy idea of finally allowing the firearms division to sink or swim entirely on its own. He'd given enough of his life over to that losing proposition, and now he intended to do something selfish and entirely for himself. Francesca had moved on with her life—it was time for him to do the same.

It was with this entire life-change in mind that Double sat in his car at Onori's filigreed, wrought-iron front gates waiting for Lady to arrive. She insisted on her own rental car, maintaining her own independence should she suddenly choose to leave. The two were as different as the Viennese Waltz and the Bump-and-Grind, but their mutual self-interests now overlapped.

It was a lie, however, that anchored this new relationship. She agreed to the weekend on the explicit condition that Double didn't drink any more—not at all—not a single drop, and hadn't for at least three months. He nearly choked over the phone in his assertions of sobriety but what was he supposed to do? She wouldn't join him if she knew the truth, and he desperately wanted her company. Besides, he was so much better than he'd been: He was in fact very nearly sober, and that had to count for something.

So he arranged a subterfuge by placing two identical eight-ounce flasks in the water tank of the toilet in the en suite bathroom attached to one of the bedrooms in the guest cabin. The modest stash of Scotch whiskey was the absolute minimum ration required for him to function normally, and he would consume it at the end of each day, just before turning in for the night. Without it, he wouldn't be able to sleep. He had already contracted with the cook to bring over a pint bottle of Red Label the next day. With this scheme, he'd have just enough to sustain him overnight but not enough to get drunk on. As he consumed them, he'd fill the empties with water and replace them in the reservoir to hide them. His only problem was that once he filled the bottles and placed them back in the water, they were weightless, and every time he flushed the toilet they rattled around inside the tank making a noise like the soft beating of a kettle drum. Occasionally one of the flasks would block the rubber valve stopper entirely, allowing the water feeding the reservoir to run indefinitely. Odd sound effects aside, Double couldn't come up with an alternative to hiding his stash, and it seemed preferable to secreting them away in one of the rooms where Lady might stumble across them by accident.

The remaining plan was to truthfully confess to being an earsplitting snorer in hopes that it would earn Double a banishment to the other bedroom for sleeping. This would give him easy access to his fountain of sanity and the privacy in which to partake its soothing effects.

* * * * *

Lady wore a flowing light blue linen dress, bare-shouldered with a cutout at the sternum suspended by only a single thin spaghetti strap around her neck. In the heat of the morning, she looked as fresh as a blooming primrose. With her height advantage, their embrace was awkward and a little distant, but just as he pulled away she murmured, "Look what the cat dragged in," pulled him in closer and kissed him once, briefly, for real.

"Now we got that out of the way . . ." she announced.

They didn't talk much initially, and when they did, it was about the three different horse properties she'd just seen down in Florida. Each farm was different in size and price, but any one of them would suffice. The prospect was still just an idea—nothing had been agreed to, and the idea of Lady working exclusively with only two students and being directly employed by just one man still sat uneasily with her. She hadn't entirely abandoned her own ambitions as a rider, and the lofty offer for her to sublimate her own competitive career to maximize a potential payoff reminded her of the period in her life when the right number on the front of a check had her disrobing for the camera.

They drove along the white pea-pebble drives on a tour of the plantation, first to the antebellum main house and then to the stables to review the saddle horses. Other than a handful of caretakers—the skeleton-crew employed full-time by Orion—there was no one else. They were finally alone, and had nothing to hide.

Walking down the aisle of eight stalls to look at the plantation's Tennessee Walkers, Double told some yarns about riding on the plantation as a child. Lady held her outstretched hand with a flatted palm to the nose of each horse for it to nuzzle. He took her through the rest of the barn, the tack room and the wash stall. It was a relaxed moment in the muggy afternoon heat of a late Southern summer.

Their modest guest cabin was once slave quarters, which had been remodeled and added onto. It now had three bedrooms with air conditioning. He showed her the master bedroom, and then sheepishly confessed to his deafening snoring and pointed out another bedroom—his room. She asked if she might freshen up, as he went into the kitchen and poured them both glasses of iced tea.

She padded out of the bathroom in bare feet and a short, sheer, light blue baby-doll negligee and walked over to the kitchen table where Double was sitting. She wore her hair up in a bun, along with a vibrant purple velvet choker around her neck. She had on a little rouge and lipstick and while the overall effect was quite pleasing, its modesty also acknowledged her fleeting youth. This once great erotic beauty was now self-conscious enough to cover over her surgically altered breasts and entire midriff. She towered over him as she picked up the tall, sweating glass of tea, and took one long sip and then another. She set the empty glass back down on the table.

"Come on," she said, as she took him by the hand and led him back to her room.

LIX

Late that afternoon when the heat broke, Double and Lady took a trail ride down to the banks of The Branch, where they ate a picnic dinner of cold fried chicken and cornbread out of a saddlebag. The thought of skinny-dipping crossed their minds, but as both were still euphoric after their late-afternoon romp, they remained satiated as one would several hours after a heavy meal.

While Onori provided privacy away from the County, they weren't entirely alone. Even in the off season, there were always several employees floating about, engaged in the regular duties of minding the horses and maintaining the buildings, transportation fleet and four-thousand acres of quail habitat.

On Saturday afternoon, legendary exhibition shooter Winky Wagner and her assistant-husband, Walter, pulled in with their camper, a compact, varnished wooden tow-behind trailer pulled by a white half-truck, half-car Chevrolet El Camino sporting the Winston Firearms trademark royal blue W. The middle-aged couple was nearing the end of their professional career barnstorming around the country putting on exhibitions of trick and fancy shooting. As was their habit, they stopped at Onori en route back home to Bridgewater to take advantage of a cool overnight stay in one of the air-conditioned cabins.

It was a bit awkward, as the buildings faced each other across a small grass compound and both couples could plainly see each other. Winky soon discovered that the chairman of the board of the firearms division was currently in residence with his new girlfriend—a woman who'd bared it all in dirty magazines and had even been shown fornicating in a Hollywood movie. She and Walter were still under contract to both divisions of Winston Firearms and therefore indirectly employed by Double Winston, but the old couple found the arrangement both scandalous and brazen. Winky well remembered Double's birthday from all those years before, and judged the man who grew from the child to be a total disappointment. Walter and Winky both wondered aloud if a woman of such low character might be some sort of celebrity prostitute brought in to satisfy the perversions of a useless dilettante. The overlap only lasted a single night, and on Sunday morning the Wagners pulled out, heading north.

* * * * *

Lady Metcalf was a no-nonsense kind of girl who felt no need to fill pleasant silence with mindless chatter. She was also physically demonstrative and not shy about touching Double affectionately. They made love, and as they gradually became accustomed to each other, the physical awkwardness dissipated. Soon they were moving together as one, entwined physically and becoming indoctrinated to one another.

They talked for hours, still naked in her bed, and she told him about her storied career as a sex symbol—he was captivated. She was astute enough to recognize that her fifteen minutes of fame couldn't last and that the shrewd thing to do was capitalize— literally monetize the moment and create a nest egg. Her highlight had come as a Bond girl speaking all of two lines, not as the superspy's main love interest, but rather as the agent provocateur— the romantic diversion who's secretly in cahoots with the villain. In her celebrated scene, she was incognito as a skin-diving archeologist recovering amphora vessels. She slinked out of the Mediterranean wearing only a wet T-shirt. The sheer transparency of her wardrobe left nothing to the imagination (she was in fact covered from her hairline, which was dyed black for the role, right down to her toenails in castor oil). Every square inch of her erotic form was on display: her magnificent breasts and backside and her pubic mound, shorn clean and entirely void of hair right down to the very pink petals of her fair sex—the first ever to appear on film.

In the movie, she returned with 007 to his villa, where the wet T-shirt wound up on the bedroom floor and she was last seen straddling the secret agent on his turbulently undulating waterbed.

It was only by pure intuition that Lady insisted her agent aggressively negotiate for any residual royalties that might come from appearing in the film. The Bond franchise had never resulted in any meaningful merchandising revenues other than the regular appearance of children's action-figure dolls, novelty lunchboxes and the die-cast cars from Corgi Toys to commemorate each film. So when *the poster* first appeared, she was getting a piece of the action—albeit pennies—on every one sold. As the poster—and later the T-shirts—developed into a worldwide phenomenon, eventually totaling sales of more than 20 million units, those pennies ran to a small fortune.

This Lady managed to parlay into her most overexposed appearance yet—a five-page spread with an Austrian bodybuilder in the pages of *Oui* magazine, one of *Playboy*'s racier brethren and a direct competitor to *Penthouse*. The photo pairing was ludicrous, as the muscleman barely reached her collar bone, but creative camera work saved it.

She made a lot of money, but confessed to Double the shame she'd felt in the horse world at being stigmatized and shunned for what she'd done. She was a tenth-grade dropout who had made her way through life using the only assets available to her. Then there was the never-ending gauntlet of men of every stripe—married and single, old and young—who were willing to go to the earth's end to sample her charms. Now that she and Double were together, she was shy and almost girlish—self-conscious in the knowledge that she was no longer young, and that her once effortless sex appeal was diminished.

All she had become remained inexorably linked to Double Winston and that muggy, buggy week at Rotterdam where, at his suggestion, she changed the bit and bridle on her horse, borrowed his spurs and proceeded to exceed all expectations. Finishing sixth overall in the individual standings, she came away with a competitive record substantial enough to launch a teaching career. At Rotterdam she was the best she would ever be on horseback, and though she still regularly rode in the grand prix ring, there was no denying it had been her zenith.

They talked about his potential future as a rider. He had no horse and no prospects, but spoke in hopeful terms of leaving his failed business career and going back to the only successful endeavor he'd ever undertaken. It was an obscure, mirage-like vision verging on the cusp of reality.

He'd done everything he could for the firearms division and had tried his best to take care of the employees, but their initial financing had been especially unfavorable and now the sporting arms industry seemed to be winding down altogether. The cutting-edge designs management had placed such faith in had fallen flat; the conservative sporting arms market rejected the unorthodox designs. The firearms division probably wouldn't make it much longer without a bail-out, and most of Double's private fortune held in trust would be sacrificed in a default. He'd left his father's people in the care of their own conscientious management, who in hindsight had been overconfident in their abilities. That decision would come close to ruining Double Winston.

Firearms division management had made their bed and now they would all have to lie in it. Double had some money of his own—enough when you considered that Connie would eventually be taken care of out of an inheritance from Francesca consisting of her remaining portion of the Krupp fortune as well as her take from Bailiwick and Double's gift of stock. Double could walk away from this huge mess with enough to get by on—enough to restart his riding career, provided he made the horses himself.

His plan was vague, but he was certain as they wasted away the lazy afternoon in bed that Lady represented the loose thread which if pulled would unravel his old life. He would finally be free from playing the business role for which he had been completely miscast from the start.

LX

hankfully, Lady never tried to share Double's bed. She was reasonable and recognized that there were plenty of reasons why both of them might balk at such a close-quartered arrangement so early on. Lady had a tendency to nod off immediately after her head hit the pillow, which left Double plenty of time to indulge his hidden stash. It was a complex deception as he absolutely needed that nightcap to sleep, but he also knew beyond a doubt that he would entirely consume whatever alcohol was available to him. For this reason he rationed himself to a single pint of Red Label each night.

The dining at Onori was catered out to the best cook in the area—a black lay preacher with a gold front tooth and a razor-part cut right into his scalp. He ran the local barbeque joint out of his home—a combination gas station and liquor store. This man could cook all the Southern standards, as well as grill a chateaubriand to perfection and whip up the Hollandaise sauce from scratch to go with it. Double spoke to him about including a pint bottle of Red Label when he delivered some prepared meals on Saturday, but Sunday presented a problem. The cook preached from the pulpit on the Sabbath, and declined Double's request to come out to the plantation with a bottle. Double Winston was his de-facto employer, and the cook recognized the dicey predicament of this dependent soul. If Double could make it out to the gas station before Sunday services, the cook promised to bend his principles and the law by slipping a bottle out the door.

It was just a simple matter of Double fabricating a plausible excuse for leaving Onori entirely alone on Sunday. The red herring finally dawned on him in the form of the Krispy Kreme donut, which in this era was an entirely Southeastern delicacy. On Saturday evening when Double announced his intention to drive to the bakery at the crack of dawn the next morning to procure a box of the confections hot from the fryer, Lady Metcalf didn't show the least interest in accompanying him.

Double drank a cup of instant coffee the next morning and was hopeful, even optimistic of his future when he pulled out of the white pea-pebble drive in his rental car. He was about as sober as he could ever remember being, and things were progressing nicely with Lady. She was low maintenance, easy to please and fun to be around, and their simpatico chemistry worked equally well between the sheets.

The Krispy Kreme bakery was a full 35 minutes away, and as he rambled down the road with the windows rolled down, Double ran through all the myriad of possibilities. *Would he be back riding on the show circuit within a couple of months? Could he lose some weight and recapture his former championship form? Where would he live and with whom?* These questions and others paraded through his head like Christmas Eve sugarplums.

The line was already out the door when he arrived at the bakery, and as he waited his turn for the honor of purchasing a heavenly assortment, the promise of the future seemed tactile and there for the taking. He was about to make a leap of faith back into a world in which he'd known great success and into the arms of a woman he might just grow to love.

* * * * *

Double left the motor running as he walked to the glass front door of the gas station. The cook wore his purple vestments as he arranged the rows of folding metal chairs transforming his convenience store into a makeshift chapel. The pulpit—a lectern with the Marriot Hotel logo conspicuously emblazoned across it—was situated directly in front of the humming beer cooler. A large crucifix crudely fashioned from quarter-inch pine and spray-painted fleck-gold hung off some halfpenny nails in front of the glass refrigerator doors. When he saw Double, the cook took a pint bottle from under the counter and started for the glass door. Then he stopped at the coffee pot and picked up a paper cup with a lid on it. He unlocked the door for Double, who held out a ten dollar bill.

"Please come inside while I make change," the cook said, retreating with the bottle, the coffee and the currency.

"That really isn't necessary," Double pleaded. "Keep it for your trouble."

The minister laid the bottle on the counter top next to the cash register, too far away for Double to easily reach "No trouble at all, sir. I do believe you take yours white," the minister said, sliding the paper cup of coffee across the counter to him.

Double took a sip—the cook certainly had his way with coffee.

"Ain't my place to speak, but the calling demands it," the cook began. "I don't know nothing 'bout your pretty guest and why it's her visiting with us and not your wife, but I do know that any man what leaves *that* to go pick himself up a bottle before decent people have eaten breakfast can't be in a good way."

Double placed the cup on the countertop and made a fruitless grab for the bottle. "I really don't think it *is* any of your business," he said.

"My business is bread and fishes—and souls. I see a drowning man—heathen or holy—I try to help."

"Duly noted, but if you want to continue on at Onori, I'll have to ask you to please butt out. I'm doing just fine—thank you very much—and if I need your help, I'll ask for it."

The cook finally inched the pint across the counter to Double, who snatched it up and headed for the door.

"'He that covereth his sins shall not prosper: but those whoso confesseth and forsaketh them shall have mercy'–Proverbs 28:13," the lay preacher said. "Never sold a pint bottle so early to one what really didn't need it. Repent—get right with the Lord while there's still time."

LXI

Instead of being apprehensive or ashamed by his deception, Double was buoyed and elated. He had what he needed—and Lady was none the wiser. Now it was a simple matter of finding the right moment to install the new bottle into the toilet tank along with the empties. The finish line was coming into view—he would survive the weekend and Lady would come away believing he was dry.

He was quite bewildered then when he pulled up to their cabin and noticed Lady's rental car conspicuously absent. He called to her as he came through the front door, but nothing is as quiet or lonely as a love nest that's been recently vacated. He went into her room; the bed was neatly made. There wasn't a trace of her to be found anywhere—not a scrap of paper not a hair clip, only the hint of her scent lingering in the still air. Double began to panic. He went to his room and as he entered, he saw through the open door of his bathroom something scrawled on the mirror in soap. He walked toward it and discovered the empty pint bottle and two silver flasks perched on the washbasin.

I FIXED YOUR TOILET! the words read. There was also a round smiley face, only it was frowning and had tears rolling down its face. As a former Reno showgirl, Lady was fastidious in her personal grooming. She had intended to surprise Double by getting herself dolled up again. As she brushed her teeth, she remembered her need of dental floss and went to his bathroom in search of some. Once she completed her quest, she squatted on his toilet and when she went to flush, she heard the bottles bumping about softly inside the reservoir and chalked it up to substandard plumbing.

Then the toilet continued to run. Being a hands-on girl who'd done a lot of troubleshooting on her horse farm, she innocently removed the cover of the tank to investigate and found one of the flasks blocking the rubber stopper.

He'd blown it. She knew everything, and was gone for good. He sat at the kitchen table, opened the box of donuts and bit into a honey-glazed. Then he went out to the car and retrieved the pint bottle from the glove compartment. He poured himself three fingers and added some tap water—water from The Branch. There was no urgent attempt to catch her at the airport or to call her later once she arrived home. He harbored no illusion that she would never speak to him again.

There was also no reason for him to stay at Onori. He was mad at himself—not for his continued drinking or for sneaking it, but for getting caught. He ate another donut, finished a first drink and then a second and packed his bags.

Double drove himself to the regional airport to catch a flight home. Devastated, he made it as far as his connecting flight in Atlanta before checking himself into the airport Hilton. He bribed a bartender for a bottle of Red Label and started drinking alone in his room. Two nights and two mornings later, in a brief moment of clarity, he called into Mrs. Beeberstein for his messages.

She put him right through to Nathan Clarke who, even though he was in the process of winding down his career at Winston, was still very much involved in the day-to-day affairs of the legal department.

"The firearms division board announced this is likely the last quarter they can meet their debt obligation. They need another refinancing."

Double listened to the words and once again was outside himself, hovering over this inevitable scene which was playing out. He didn't want to respond—didn't want to say the words which would further the plot, simultaneously propelling his own fate. "I'll be back in the office tomorrow," he said. He ordered some coffee up to his hotel room and showered. Then he put on a fresh set of clothes and headed downstairs to the ticket counter.

LXII

Nathan Clarke and a now sober Double took the train into the city to meet in midtown with the Orion chief financial officer. The discussion was brief: The CFO, a former accountant, had his own general counsel attend, and announced that Orion had finally had enough. He personally disliked the gun and ammunition business and if he had his druthers, he'd flog them both and reinvest the proceeds into burgeoning industries with long-term potential like the disposable-camera business. He did concede that the ammunition division showed predictable revenues, which at least would make it attractive as a potential spinoff. The gun company, however, was a perennial basket case. Its sole redeeming quality was the nine percent interest payment it had been making to Orion. Now that they were approaching default, he had no qualms about calling in the loan, liquidating the assets and laying off the entire workforce.

The fat lady was warming up in the wings. Even if they somehow managed to secure emergency financing from another source, the long-term prospects for the firearms division would always be suspect—their continued operations, touch-and-go. Double's fortune was on the line, and it was one hell of an economic needle for some potential *white knight* savior to thread. The entire thing turned on luck, government incentives and tax abatements. What no one could have known at that moment was that the rug was about to be pulled out from under the firearms division—and the entire city of Bridgewater.

LXIII

After a year-long federal probe into the Mayor's Office of Bridgewater regarding widespread charges of bribery and graft, the Justice Department announced its findings. The smoking gun was videotape taken on an Atlantic City gambling junket showing the mayor freebasing cocaine while being orally pleasured by a white call girl. This was followed with more footage of him accepting large stacks of valuable casino chips from gaming executives. Criminal charges were filed, but the mayor remained unrepentant. As he walked out of his arraignment in his smart white dinner jacket before a scandalized press, he mugged that he was long known to be a man of appetites and prone to indulging his fondness for the sporting life.

There had gradually been a seismic shift in Bridgewater demographics and the black vote was such a reliable Democratic block that this convicted felon was able to recapture City Hall less than a decade later. In this chapter chronicling his nine lives, however, a thorough accounting was made of the city's finances, and the findings of that audit soon became front-page news: Bridgewater was insolvent and had been for years. The mayor's attempts to retain a manufacturing base through incentives and tax subsidies had entirely overwhelmed the city's unfunded liabilities. The federal government appointed a bankruptcy manager with broad administrative powers, who immediately eliminated the mayor's enterprise zone programs and took the city into municipal bankruptcy.

Services were slashed, public-sector union contracts deemed null and void, and benefits were retroactively clawed back. Police and fire department retirement packages were renegotiated after the fact by a civic compensation board, and former city workers— long since retired and living out of state—suddenly found their fixed incomes drastically reduced, with no possible recourse. A city income tax was instituted, and the once thriving industrial center quickly degenerated into a wasteland. The previously bleak situation was now deemed hopeless, and everyone with the means to get out did, often abandoning homes and businesses in the process.

The municipal bankruptcy spelled the death knell for the city of Bridgewater, and the previous steady trickle of business outflows turned into a gusher. Factories were shuttered, entire plant staffs laid off. A reduced tax base meant less funding for law enforcement, which indirectly resulted in more crime. Abandoned properties were quickly looted and vandalized in a free-for-all. The derelict cityscape soon degenerated into a war zone of crime. In the brief span of a few years, Bridgewater descended into the kind of no-go zone that white people only visit to engage in sin.

LXIV

When Connie began the new school year at Parsonage, he requested that Red Welles again be his roommate. The two schoolmates were now best friends, sharing the anguish of being largely forgotten by their parents, both being regarded as the kids who never went home. On the drive up to drop him off at school for the semester, Double and Francesca had *the talk*, announcing their intention to divorce, pleading the case that Connie had nothing to do with the decision. Red saw it coming a mile away, and had warned his friend to prepare himself. Now that he had no real home to return to, Connie consciously confined himself to a self-imposed exile on the bucolic campus, sharing this limited existence with his spectacularly disfigured friend.

Connie remained a quiet child, a middling student and an unremarkable athlete who shied away from adversarial sports and was most content whiling away the afternoons after classes with a fishing rod in his hand or in wintertime on the ski slopes alone. He used the shoe polish trick that Red taught him to cover over his own blemished façade, regularly dying the two white roundels of hair at his temples with boot paste.

Mostly though, Connie Winston tried not to stand out. He was a voracious reader who escaped into literature, but most of what he read was unassigned and unrelated to his schoolwork. He continued to watch a lot of television in the dormitory common room, taking in the mindless sitcoms and police dramas as a way to rediscover his emotional vocabulary—a piecemeal Rosetta Stone for the human condition. He rarely initiated conversation, holding back instead and averting his eyes, generally avoiding interaction as much as possible. He tried his best to be inconspicuous, and actively aspired to blend into the scenery.

Connie grew into a meek, rather stooped young man. His slouched posture and halting demeanor foretold a retiring disposition. The twinkle in his eye, usually the porthole to the animal spirits of young stock, registered in him as only a dull flicker. Nearly everyone who came into to contact with him came away noting that this kid wasn't jazzed about life and didn't seem to exhibit enthusiasm for anything.

The fist fights with Randy Ryan, his snotty arch-nemesis, became as predictable as the full moon or the change of seasons. The rivalry did manage to raise from deep inside him a passionate fury that seemed out of proportion to the conflict. Connie often felt that if the opportunity presented itself, he would like to kill the disagreeable bastard, but time and again whenever the coup de grâce presented itself, Connie abandoned his mortal advantage and their mighty struggle continued.

It was a strange dynamic between the two, as they were often able to coexist in each other's immediate company with complete indifference—there was a time and place for everything. They tended their grudge in the way that one tends a rose bush, nurturing with spite, coaxing with provocation, fertilizing with verbal slights and then harvesting in a spectacular brawl. It was an explosive rivalry that regularly flowered into a visceral rage like a blooming perennial.

As he passed into puberty and began to develop sexually, it became clear that for a boy who had grown up entirely in gentrified, lily-white affluence, Connie had a strong proclivity toward ethnic girls. While his male contemporaries visualized as grist for their sexual fantasies the potential of their fair female classmates possessing actual blonde pubic hair, Connie preferred to ejaculate to mental imagery of different-skinned womanhood, be they Hispanic, Asian or black.

Omnipresent throughout this period of Connie's adolescence was the tragic cloud of the misbegotten hovering over him—a sinister aura of doom. It was the elephant in the room every time he visited his parents, and he was vaguely aware of a perpetual whisper campaign of rumors circulating in town about his having been complicit in the shooting death of Kimmy Conner. This he dismissed out of hand because he had absolutely no memory of it. If he had killed another child, he certainly would have some recollection of it. Like someone who had survived a near-death experience and come away physically impaired, Connie gave the impression of being maimed without exhibiting any outward physical manifestation of injury. Everyone who knew him at Parsonage, including Red Welles, just assumed he had been through some big traumatic experience, but no one had ever been able to pry out of Connie exactly what it was.

Occasionally Connie would dream vividly about trivial details associated with the killing: whitecaps on open water, wind thrashing through the treetops, frantically searching for some unspecified thing under water in brackish green light, looking up toward the luminous surface and fighting the urge to take a full breath of water into his lungs. He once even expressed his concerns to his parents about these nightmares, suggesting that perhaps he needed to talk to someone—a school psychologist or therapist. His parents minimized his worries: All teenagers experience nightmares about all sorts of things. His they deemed perfectly normal, and both parents suggested he would eventually outgrow them.

LXV

Nathan Clarke walked out of the Winston executive offices for the last time on the day before Thanksgiving. Mrs. Beeberstein arranged a retirement party at which Double presented him with a rose-gold Patek Philippe quarter-repeater pocket watch. No expense was spared in acquiring the timepiece, but the moment Nathan opened the presentation box, everyone knew by his false enthusiasm that the retirement gift was all wrong. When Nathan compared it lovingly to the pedestrian instrument residing in his handkerchief pocket, Double realized that the new watch would probably never see any use.

On Nathan's last day of work, he simply slipped out at lunchtime and never returned. His desk had always been ordered and his office remained surprisingly impersonal after some 30-plus years of service. Indeed, the chamber held no lingering presence nor even hinted as to the personality of its recent occupant. It was only after the main switchboard operator transferred several calls to the now abandoned office that Nathan's secretary finally confirmed that nobody was home.

This chapter of Nathan's life, which had begun all those decades earlier with a chance meeting at the Little Kill Country Club, was now ending with Senior's and Nathan's life's work teetering on the brink. Nathan expected only a brief period to ensue following his departure before the firearms division collapsed into bankruptcy.

Everything had changed. The United States had gone from being the lone first-world power to come through two world wars with its entire production capacity unscathed and a global marketplace clamoring for Western goods, to being outmaneuvered on every front by an ascendant West Germany that produced superior designs and a Japan which through relentless automation manufactured its consumer goods far less expensively. Industrial America was seemingly under assault by the very Axis powers it defeated in total war only a generation earlier. Now the very infrastructure which created the great American postwar economic boom was proving to be its Achilles heel. Just as it had with the industrial revolution in England, outmoded business models and production methods stifled late-twentieth-century American economic viability.

The firearms division, which had once employed some 17,000 workers and, at the height of the Second World War, turned out 100,000 guns a month, was now staffed by fewer than 2,000, with a total annual production of 300,000 units. Several factory buildings from both divisions now lay shuttered, their entire production lines and tooling abandoned in place. The great Winston shot tower was one of them.

The derelict ten-story edifice had fallen victim to vandals, and every single opaque window in the building had been smashed. The American flag that once proudly flew from the rooftop was now faded and tattered—shredded by the elements—fluttering on a peeling, rotted flagpole. Attempts had been made to take it down, but every time a worker went aloft with this objective in mind, some inner-city would-be sniper took potshots at them, forcing a retreat before the flag could be retired.

Initially, mischief in the shot tower was limited to graffiti and throwing inanimate objects from its towering height, but as Bridgewater descended into drug-addled economic despair, the tower become the method of choice to commit suicide for despondent Bridgewater residents. Every morning it was the first job of plant security guards to inspect the tower for ongoing vandalism and then to check the base of the structure for bodies. One a month seemed to be the prevailing average.

LXVI

athan's physical plight had only continued to worsen—his recent health trials only grown more burdensome. He wore Depends adult diapers under his clothing and had to change himself several times a day. The teeth comprising his entire bottom bite had finally crumbled away to where he had a bridge fitted and the only time he didn't wear the false teeth was when he slept. A trip to Minnesota for a battery of weeklong tests at the Mayo Clinic proved inconclusive—it could be any number of things. The only surefire remedy, they suggested, was a colostomy bag and the removal of his remaining teeth.

Nathan recently thought back to his time in Germany during the war crimes tribunals and of Astrid. *What had become of her after all these years?* His curiosity finally overwhelmed him, and he called in a favor to the private investigator who'd handled all of Winston Firearms' workers-compensation fraud cases. The grim findings only took a few days: She'd died alongside her second husband in a rail tunnel fire in the Swiss Alps on a ski vacation in 1972.

Nathan Clarke was an old man living entirely alone, and his likely fate was written on the wall for all to see: His condition would continue to worsen and he would eventually die alone, literally shitting himself to death in a clinical surrounding, tended to by strangers.

LXVII

he young man skinned the knuckles of his right hand, dropped the wrench into the soupy black bilge and sucked at the greasy wound to stem the bleeding. He was freckled, sun-blond and slight. At just sixteen, he was in the process of trying to manhandle a copper fuel tank into the old wooden work scow tied to the dock of the Pequod Yacht Club. He'd spent the last summer fishing for lobsters with a friend from prep school aboard this old boat on his own commercial fishing license. His parents were well-to-do Yacht Club members who insisted he do something constructive with his long summer break. The idea of being out on the open water every day as captain of his own fishing boat sounded a hell of a lot better than pumping gas or painting houses. His parents hoped the physical labor might build him up, and the club agreed to let him use their docks off season for occasional maintenance and for moving his fishing gear in and out of the water.

Wooden boats have always required a lot of maintenance, and with the advent of fiberglass boatbuilding, commercial vessels steadily moved toward composite construction. By the 1980s, serviceable wooden fishing boats had gotten so cheap they were practically giving them away. The same was true of the oaken lathe wooden lobster traps which were now rapidly being replaced by their maintenance-free coated wire counterparts. The young man had borrowed the money from his parents to purchase this boat and 160 second-hand wooden traps, but right now he wished he'd picked up a paintbrush instead.

Old equipment is unreliable, and many of the mechanical components on the 24-foot boat had either required rebuilding or replacement altogether. This fuel tank was just the latest: a clogged fuel filter had invited further inspection of the quality of the gasoline within the rusty steel tank; it was tainted with sludgy sediment. The young man removed the tank, drained it and proceeded to sand and repaint the exterior, only to discover a pinprick leak after he reinstalled it. Now he was trying to retrofit a 25-gallon cylindrical copper unit he had purchased second-hand at a scrap yard. This demanded the fabrication of cushioned, curved bracing mounts, and then screwing them to the bulkheads of the cramped engine compartment.

After he dropped his wrench in the bilge, the young man withdrew from the claustrophobic confines of the engine compartment to take a breather and reconsider the task which was overwhelming his private-school woodshop skills. As he stood up to take in some fresh air, he saw Nathan Clarke aboard his 39-foot Concordia Yawl *Halcyon*—chaffing bumpers at the ready—heave to and approach the Yacht Club dock. When the young man saw the elegant white sailboat glide in, he hopped onto the dock, caught the coiled stern line Nathan threw to him and put a hitch on the cleat, halting the sailboat within just an arm's length of line. The rubber bumpers squealed in protest as they compressed hard and rolled against the yawl's bulbous freeboard. Before the sailboat could rebound off the dock and begin to drift, the young man secured the bow and Nathan put a spring line amidships.

"Much obliged," the retired lawyer said, offering his hand in appreciation.

The young man shook it and replied, "Anytime, Commodore," and went back to work.

It was curious that the boy had chosen to address Nathan as Commodore out of all other possible ranks: Every navy man knows the yacht-club Commodore to be a stuffed-shirt title. As a destroyer-escort executive officer, Nathan had once briefly been in command en route to the turnaround point off the Irish coast (the Royal Navy escorted convoys the rest of the way into England). His own skipper was stricken with flu, and the munitions ship charged with relaying destroyer-escort communiques to the rest of the convoy, and thus designated, the convoy "commodore" ship was torpedoed during his watch. She went up like a powder keg, and though he briefly made a fruitless attempt to engage the enemy and a rescue boat was dispatched to survey the flotsam, protocols were clear: The convoy wouldn't break formation or stop to look for survivors—a merchant ship's full complement of more than sixty souls, blown to smithereens and sent to the bottom.

The young man on the dock was preoccupied with his vexing task, and made the sorts of assumptions we all make when we see someone going about their business. He could see that Nathan was transferring equipment from the *Halcyon* onto the dock and suspected that it was to better organize the sailboat in preparation for a voyage—perhaps to deliver the boat back up to the Concordia yard for winter storage.

It was a crisp autumn day, sunny and certainly not unpleasant or cold. Nathan got by in a Shetland wool sweater and pair of Nantucket Reds, the eponymous salmon-colored pant that is a fashion staple of sailors. The chill on the breeze briefly put the rose into Nathan's cheeks and a spring back into his step. Yes, he remained a sick old man prone to fouling himself, but on this day more than any other, he felt like his old self again. At one point in the afternoon Nathan even asked the young man for a hand in transferring to the dock the Dyer-Dhow tender that was mounted to the yawl's cabin roof. This dinghy, which could be rowed, sailed or propelled by an outboard motor, was one of two lifeboats of last resort aboard the *Halcyon*. As Nathan most often paid a commercial marina for a berth or relied on yacht-club launches to access ports-of-call when he was cruising, the tender had remained permanently lashed to the cabin roof.

* * * * *

When the young man stepped out of his rusted pickup truck after returning from a local marine supply with a Dremel grinder attachment and a set of galvanized lag bolts, it didn't really register what he was witnessing.

The autumn afternoon kicked up an offshore breeze, and the young man saw the great Genoa sail abruptly unfurl off the reefing system as Nathan Clarke released the stern line holding the boat at its berth. Nathan gathered up the jib sheet, put a couple of wraps on the winch, trimmed that big sail taut and was off beating downwind for the Smith's Ledge lighthouse. The young man noticed the dock littered with gear and held his hands aloft, pantomiming his inquisitive exasperation to Nathan.

Nathan locked the helm of the sailboat, stood up and, with dramatic fanfare, placed a white-peaked dress hat on his head. Then he hopped up on the gunwale, looking majestic, dressed head-to-toe in his Navy-service dress-blue uniform with the gold sleeve insignia stripes of a lieutenant commander—his last active rank. Nathan snapped-to and gave the boy a smart salute. Then he gave a more pensive wave goodbye and returned to the helm of the vessel already underway.

The young man was generally insecure and often unsure of

himself. He ran and reran in his mind exactly what he'd witnessed, and finally came to the conclusion that he must have misunderstood the whole thing. He figured the eccentric old codger must get his kicks dressing up like Captain Crunch and had simply cast off to test something out under sail.

It was a four o'clock and dusk when the young man finally finished the installation of the fuel tank, primed the filter, screwed it back on and poured in five gallons of gasoline. When he went to fire the engine, the gold pocket watch and chain dangling from a dashboard toggle switch caught his eye, and he knew his instincts about what he'd seen were correct: Nathan's gold Elgin pocket watch and chain—the one he carried for his entire career as an attorney and the same one his own father carried before him—was flush against the instrument panel, holding down $200 in twenties. The boy briefly examined the watch and chain, and puzzled about the significance of the Phi Beta Kappa key, having never seen one before.

The young man successfully started his engine, and when he stepped onto the dock to take a closer look, his suspicions were further buttressed: Every piece of safety equipment, the life preservers, dingy, auto-inflate life raft, signal flares, VHF radio, radio-directional finder, Loran-C receiver and the emergency-position indicator radio beacon had all been left behind, exposed to the elements. The sun was down when he finished. He immediately went home and enlightened his parents as to the *Halcyon* and the peculiar behavior of its owner. They contacted the Yacht Club president, who alerted the coast guard, who had the police track down the club's dockmaster on a local barstool.

To this day, if you pull up Concordia's 102-boat registry, you'll note that the 39-foot *Halcyon*, only the third of four keels ever laid in Massachusetts, remains the only yawl ever lost at sea. Neither boat nor skipper were ever heard from again, and no note or clue of explanation was ever discovered. There were some theories as to what happened, but the Yacht Club dockmaster, an old-salt navy chief who had been cordial with Nathan, suspected that the infirm lawyer had simply sailed out to the tidal headwaters of the Sound and scuttled her.

Nathan Clarke had lived a spartan lifestyle his entire professional career, so it wasn't surprising that he left behind an estate that came to a tidy sum. What *was* surprising was that he placed it all in an irrevocable trust for the benefit of Conrad Winston III. Apparently Nathan felt eternal guilt in his culpability at what had befallen the poor boy and, recognizing the dire financial straits facing both the firearms division and the Winston family, sought atonement by aiding Connie from the grave.

LXVIII

Anyone who ever bet big in business and lost will tell you that timing and luck are two indispensable ingredients. Often a sound business idea comes before—or after—its time: Edison and Bell were early pioneers of electricity and radio, but it was Tesla and Marconi who profitably monetized those technologies.

The go-go1980s saw the continued decline of the gun culture. Renewed threats of gun control always goosed the market with a sales pop in handguns and M-16-rifle derivatives, but sporting arms—a quality target or field shotgun, or a highly accurate bolt-action hunting rifle—suffered a dearth of demand. Winston's designs were outdated, its quality control spotty and its products built to a down-market price.

The Bridgewater municipal bankruptcy effectively nailed the coffin lid shut on manufacturing in that once prosperous city. The handful of industries that remained now closed up shop for good. Business felt it was doing the city a favor by remaining there in the first place, but when Bridgewater reneged on all its incentives and tax abatements and instituted a city income tax to boot, there was really no reason to stay. The ammunition division immediately pulled up stakes, laying off some 600 workers, and moved its production to Arkansas.

The firearms division had been permitted to continue operations because only in its ultimate demise could Orion take possession of the collateralized-equity stake Double had used to secure its refinancing. When the firearms division inevitably missed the critical interest payment, they were in breach of contract, declared insolvent, and Orion took them into receivership.

All the employees were laid off and given inadequate ad-hoc severance packages. Most tragic of all was the revelation that a substantial portion of the firearms division's defined-benefit retirement portfolio had been invested in now worthless firearms division stock. The promise of a comfortable retirement would go unrealized for many former employees who had calculated their golden years based on a steady income and now found themselves entirely unable to afford their lifestyle. There was no recourse— the goose that laid the golden egg and made that promise was dead.

From Double Winston, they took everything—his personal fortune in company stock and all the tangible assets from the real estate and plant equipment. They even removed the Tiffany stained-glass ceiling from the executive office building and sold it at auction. Thankfully, Double's private office furnishings had been contractually off-limits and were spared. The realized value of Senior's art collection alone acted as somewhat of a balm against Double's injured pride and sudden impoverishment.

LXIX

When word got out at Little Kill that the Winstons were divorcing and that Bailiwick was going on the market, Sugar McCashin waged an all-out campaign for her husband to acquire the property. The dark-haired beauty had attended several functions at the luxurious home and swore that if the opportunity ever arose, she would go to the ends of the earth to make the estate her own. Now was the moment—put up or shut up.

As the leading car dealer in the County, representing three different Japanese brands, the self-made Douglas McCashin was a rich man who hated spending money. Even he recognized that Bailiwick was an altogether different sort of proposition, however.

It was an opportunity for the last piece of his in-County high-society jigsaw puzzle to fall into place. Comprising eight acres, Bailiwick was a classic stone Frasier Peters–designed complex of buildings, an estate property in a town that by the 1980s was already running out of real estate. And it had history, having been built by Conrad Winston Senior, the scion of the last great firearms dynasty in America.

The brash and acerbic Douglas McCashin did what came naturally to him in business: He drove over to Bailiwick, banged on the front door and proceeded to brazenly work the hard sell-in reverse on Double Winston. The battle-ax had long been McCashin's preferred negotiating tactic, and he became outright belligerent, arguing that by completing an off-market transaction, the Winstons could screw some parasite real estate broker out of their sales commission. McCashin wanted permission to have a fresh appraisal and survey done on the property to better inform his offer.

Hungover and crestfallen by his misfortune, Double Winston found the exchange both abrasive and presumptuous. He'd sold his Port Easton horse farm to Lady Metcalf without a broker for what he deemed a fair price, but that was business with a friend and future lover—not some pugnacious social climber. Double realized that he'd actually welcome less money after broker's commission, rather than to suffer the indignation of passing his family seat directly into the greedy hands of this callow upstart.

There was a booming real estate market working in tandem with a hard-charging stock market, so it should have been a simple matter—like a trick rider transferring from one galloping horse onto another—but everyone knows that nothing in life is ever that simple.

* * * * *

There is a statistical anomaly—a jarring hiccup on the graphic charts of the stock market averages—that showed up on Monday, October 19, 1987. On this day the Dow Jones Industrial Average fell nearly 23 percent in a single session—the largest one-day percentage decline in history. The sky was falling, and anyone with the misfortune to have stepped into equities with fresh money in the preceding months was a dead duck, instantly finding themselves in a cavernous hole it would take years to dig out of. In a case of freakishly bad luck, Double Winston found himself among these unfortunates.

The trick for retail investors was to remain patient and fully invested in the stock market: By 1993, a new and even more robust bull market was under way. Double had bet on stocks appreciating, thus affording him an adequate income from a growing stream of dividends. With the sudden market crash, many companies drastically paired back or even suspended dividend payments temporarily. As the indexes moved sideways, Double did the only thing he could: He survived by selling investment principal— eating his seed corn instead of sowing it for a future harvest.

Once again, Double Winston found himself stalled at the dead-end corner of WALK and DON'T WALK. Bailiwick had been sold through a local real estate broker and was now the property of Douglas McCashin. Sun-Up, the family cabin at the Big Pine Club, had also been unloaded fully furnished the previous summer. Proceeds from these sales were divided equally with his now ex-wife, Francesca. He was officially broke. Other than retaining a few significant family heirlooms from Bailiwick, Double left his marriage and home with little more than the clothes on his back.

Double drove his red BMW M1 south on the turnpike to deliver the sports car to the high-end midtown dealership charged with selling it. There were no more thoughts of restarting his riding career. He couldn't afford the cost of maintaining a show barn or bankrolling the necessary purchase of fresh young prospects off the racetrack to turn into show horses. He'd also been away from the game too long now for his name to hold any meaningful cachet with potential students.

LXX

At forty-eight-years-old, Double Winston moved into the city in hopes of reinventing himself by securing a business position that would provide him an adequate income. He still had plenty of horse show connections, and he worked the phone relentlessly, calling in every favor and IOU he could think of. While the old guard genuinely seemed happy to hear from him and many took him out for the proverbial three-martini lunch, no one suggested that a real job for real money was in the offing. He was a kind of middle-aged nowhere man, once rich but now poor, a man inexorably linked to a famous American brand that had only recently failed under his stewardship. He was neither fish nor fowl—certainly not a real manager, as his lone sojourn into industry had lasted less than a decade. Just as a show jumper he had seemed to have a blinking neon sign above him that read CAN'T MISS, he now seemed to suffer an exact reversal of fortune and the glowing script now announced CAN'T SUCCEED.

He finally met with a businessman, an old Jew who made his fortune in metropolitan-area real estate and who'd once bought a long-in-the-tooth jumper from Double for his daughter. Double had gone to the trouble of spending a long weekend at his farm showing the girl how to get the most out of the horse, and she proceeded to win virtually everything with him in the junior-jumper division for the next several seasons. This businessman was still ecstatic over the experience and regarded Double as a true gentleman—a man of great integrity and character. When Double queried him about career prospects, the old man gave him a kindly smile and patted his hand.

"I won't make the crown prince into my bag man," he said paternally. "It wouldn't be fair to either of us. Why don't you become a riding instructor instead?" This pretty much summed up the consensus Double encountered everywhere he went.

Just as Double Winston spent the first forty years of his life as a sporting gentleman of leisure, it was only fitting that his final chapter following the demise of his business career should come full circle and that he should close out his earthly existence in the same high style. His salvation came from a most unlikely quarter—his ex-wife.

Double holed up at the Astor Towers as a temporary stopgap until he could find a job and an apartment. When Francesca stopped by the hotel to pick up the semester's tuition check for Connie's boarding school, she had cake and coffee with him in the café of the hotel's marble-lined lobby. Double confided that in his current financial state, he simply couldn't afford the expense of the Parsonage School any longer and that either she would need to shoulder the entire burden or they should consider public school for Connie. Double even volunteered to return to the County and take a rental in town so that the boy could have access to the superior public schools there. *That*, he timidly declared, was the best he could do in his reduced circumstance. He was a pathetic figure at that moment—a ruined man. A lone tear of humiliation trickled from a heavy-liver eyelid down his cheek tinted by a rosacea particular to those who chronically overindulge.

Francesca was newly remarried—a wealthy woman in her own right who had wed a prosperous surgeon. She wore a nautical-themed, navy-blue-and-white-skirted Chanel outfit, a knee-length look that Nancy Reagan had recently showcased. Any man who's ever known unconditional love can attest to the tender mercy often hiding within the heart of a woman who has no reason to forgive. Double had been more than an adequate husband for most of their marriage and she'd only recently cleaned his clock in the divorce. She was a woman of means even before they married, but the gift of half his father's investment portfolio made her wealthy even by County standards.

Torture on the rack over a pittance now seemed to Francesca the very height of sadistic retribution. This was a fundamentally good man, a man whom she'd only recently respected and admired. Besides, her new life in the city held fresh promise. For Francesca, it was blue skies as far as the eye could see.

"It's difficult to see you like this," she said solemnly.

"Not half as difficult as living it."

"I've *taken* plenty—now I'm prepared to give: I'll provide your room and board."

"And just where, pray tell, shall I lay my head, on your alcove sofa?"

"Right here, of course—upstairs," she replied. "You were good to me once—good enough anyway. It's the least I can do for you now."

Through the largess of his ex-wife, Double Winston was able to remain a resident on half-board in a junior suite at the Astor Towers. Every day, he took his breakfast and dinner alone in the hotel dining room; lunch and other incidentals were his problem.

LXXI

The Mont-Claire Riding Academy once sat a block off Central Park South in a nineteenth-century Romanesque-revival building. In addition to providing exorbitantly priced boarding privileges for privately owned horses, Mont-Claire offered school horses for trail rides on the park's bridle paths and riding lessons in the indoor riding arena in a subterranean basement. In all the years Double attended the International Horse Show in the city, he had never once set foot inside Mont-Claire. It was to a competitive jumper rider what miniature golf is to a pro golfer: better than nothing, but not by much. Since opening its doors in 1892, many famous riders had started at Mont-Claire as children, but it wasn't the sort of place where a rider could fully develop into a real horseman. Double scouted the facility with an eye toward running instructional clinics there.

When he announced himself to the management practically no one had heard of him, which wasn't surprising as only a handful of the grooms had ever been to an actual horse show. They finally polled the entire barn clientele to establish that his claims of success at the International Horse Show nearly a decade earlier were legitimate. With his bona fides established, they offered him the job of over-fences riding instructor. His prospects in the position weren't promising, as 90 percent of academy students never progressed far enough to even step over a ground rail. Double accepted the position anyway, and when word got out that he was in residence at Mont-Claire, he managed to draw a smattering of competitive junior riders who would rent one of the surprisingly nice school horses for a private lesson just to pick his brain.

Double supplemented these meager wages with a weekend staple entirely of his own invention. There had long been the tradition of holiday trail rides through the park on Thanksgiving and Christmas, but Double Winston turned it into a weekly event. The Central Park Hunt Ride ran every Sunday morning from November through March, and Double Winston led a pack of several dozen riders dressed in proper English riding habits on a kind of simulated fox hunt through the wooded trails and meadows of Central Park. Double even managed to secure permission from the Park's department to construct eight permanent fences to add a little thrill to the mock chase.

This brisk ride was followed by a brunch banquet held at a leading restaurant in the southwest corner of the park. There Double would hold court late into the afternoon, telling tales of daring-do from his illustrious riding career. The Hunt Ride was a profitable package deal that quickly became the upscale playdate of choice for the city's poseur horsey set. Double Winston was smack in the middle of it, collecting a ten-percent commission on everything from the horse rental to the restaurant tab. The Central Park Hunt Ride became so popular that riders from the suburbs would actually transport their own horses into the city to partake.

Double bought himself a new scarlet hunt coat befitting his new role-play as Master of the Hunt. Only this particular coat was actually a burgundy velvet smoking jacket with a silk shawl collar that he purchased off the tailor's mannequin in the front window of a formalwear rental shop. As the garment was held closed with a sash-belt like on a bathrobe, week-to-week changes in his girth could easily be accommodated. To the untrained eye, he looked every bit the part of a former world-class grand prix rider, but to anyone who knew anything about foxhunting or show jumping, he looked like a pimp on horseback.

Double was especially mortified when in the course of his duties working the Hunt Ride, a ghost from his past—a Champagne-Charlie English viscount with whom he and Francesca had ridden to the Bilsdale Hounds —suddenly materialized before him on a chance stroll through the park.

"Good God, man—what's become of you?!" the viscount shrieked.

Double candidly explained to his former peer that the glory days were over and he was now a divorced, working stiff. Old acquaintances were fine, but times had changed and Double had clients to attend to. The viscount's eyes sparked when he enquired if it might be overly presumptuous to pay a social call on Francesca now that they were divorced and she was presumably fair game.

Peeved at the impertinence, Double gave a cluck to his lumbering eyesore of a piebald to move him along.

"Go to hell!" Double said bitterly.

*　*　*　*　*

Occasionally on those long dark afternoons, a female member of this mounted troop would take a particular fancy to Double. Often a divorced alcoholic with a child in boarding school like himself, the woman would wind up in his suite back at the Astor Towers. Sometimes when he was really in his cups and the spirit fired him, he would start to talk like his old self, revisiting past triumphs and projecting future possibilities. When his Rubenesque paramour, unlovely in all her post-coital splendor, would wax poetic about her own dreams and ambitions, he would realize by contrast just how asinine his own pontifications really were—like a former bantamweight shadowboxing a failed title shot every time he got a couple of drinks in him.

In an attempt to cling to the glories of his past, he undertook to write a book on show jumping, a kind of instructional philosophy borne by a lifetime of equestrian wisdom. There had been a lot of literature written on general horsemanship and hunter-seat equitation, but hardly anything had been published with the expert horseman in mind. Several articles he wrote as a teenager had run nationally, and he hoped to revive this natural aptitude for the written word.

Double's suite at the Astor had a small dining room, and he set himself up in there with his father's L. C. Smith manual typewriter and a ream of Crane's Corrasable Bond paper. Each morning for more than a year, he plugged away on "the book project," as he called it. It quickly became the justification for his entire existence—the only plausible explanation for the life he'd lived and his ruinous fall from grace. *Why else would fate have visited him so catastrophically, were it not that he was destined for more greatness?* He was going to finish this remarkable work and then find a publisher, but the hours of a day spill through the fingers of a confirmed drinker. Factor in the variables of a city that never sleeps and bars that only closed up long enough for a catnap, and Double Winston didn't have many sober hours to work with.

The manuscript was really quite good. For a writer completely out of practice, it was fluid, insightful and even humorous in spots. It was cerebral instruction for the master class and nothing quite like it had ever come before. *Contemplating Show Jumping* easily found a publisher and was received with no small degree of fanfare when it was published posthumously.

LXXII

They discovered Double when he failed to appear for the oversubscribed Thanksgiving Day Hunt Ride. There had been a dusting of snow overnight, and as the horses and riders congregated on a raw gray morning standing curbside in a small, soiled snowdrift in front of Mont-Claire, the riding academy management rang Double's suite repeatedly, without success. An underling finally led the Hunt Ride, and when the large group retired for afternoon brunch and still nothing been heard from Double, they called the concierge desk at the Astor Towers.

The Residents Manager discovered Double Winston naked between the sheets, his mouth and eyes wide open in an expression of shocked bewilderment. Cholesterol plaque, which had broken off creating a massive blockage in his coronary artery, had taken him in the night. He was fifty-two.

* * * * *

It was Francesca and Connie who cleared away Double's personal effects. With his father's passing, Connie—now a young man—henceforth preferred to be known as Conrad. The walls of the suite were decorated with original advertising art from Winston Firearms, iconic framed images that every American farm boy born before 1950 would immediately recognize. Double had moved some of his own furniture into the suite—family heirlooms directly out of Bailiwick. There was also his wardrobe of clothes: bespoke business suits and custom dress shirts. Connie tried some of them on; as expected the jacket bodies were too loose and the legs and sleeves too short. This beanpole of a boy took after his lanky grandfather and wouldn't be inheriting any hand-me-downs from his father.

On the bedside table there was a thermos carafe of water, an empty glass and the slender shards of a single broken spur from the short set Double used on Westley Richards—the same spur he'd snapped off in a taxicab door in front of this very hotel some twelve years earlier.

Double's body was cremated and the ashes were received in a simple tin. There was a memorial at the Episcopalian church in town on the Avenue, but Double Winston's remains were spread in the hollow out at the old King Street farm in Port Easton where Westley Richards was buried. Francesca and Lady Metcalf shared the honors on a foggy December morning.

"'The evil that men do lives after them; the good is oft interred with their bones.' – William Shakespeare," Francesca said.

Mildly puzzled, Lady Metcalf shook her fist at the ground and jeered, "Why'd you have to drink so much, dummy?!"

These were just a few of the words the women shared regarding Double Winston that morning. Connie was away at boarding school.

In a final act of love, Francesca spent the next year editing the overflowing manuscript down to size. As the new mother of a baby girl, she tackled the ambitious project in hopes of bringing Double's last dream to fruition, working on it whenever she could. She understood the intricate inner workings of Double's mind. He had often monologued to her on a wide range of equestrian topics. She was certainly intimate with his philosophy of horsemanship and could confidently reorder his thoughts and succinctly edit his words. These were changes he never would have agreed to in life, but they allowed the slender treatise to become both a critical and commercial success.

LXXIII

Rosalie folded mayonnaise in with a can of pink salmon. Her kinked hair was gathered under a blue bandana and her black eyes focused on the task at hand. Her apricot complexion glowed in the sunlight beaming through the kitchen window. The wool cardigan sweater she wore provided comfort against the autumn chill.

All Connie was willing to eat now was canned tuna fish, salmon, chicken or corned beef. His doctors prophesized that it wouldn't be the actual cancer that would kill him, but rather an intestinal blockage turned septic. The high temperatures involved in canning virtually eliminated the risk of food-borne illness. Rosalie's son, a four-year-old as black as tar, teetered unstably as he carried the platter of Ritz crackers with salmon spread out to the porch and set it down on the tabletop next to Connie.

Conrad Winston III sat quietly in his wheelchair on the porch overlooking the lake. Sun-Up, the Winston family's former cabin at Big Pine Lake, had been sold off long ago, but Connie rented it for this mid-November week to take in the brilliant autumn foliage for the last time in his life. The house had been properly maintained through the years and was largely unchanged from his childhood, right down to the Adirondack-style log furnishings. These familiar objects provided him solace and emotional comfort.

Connie was dying—an emaciated invalid wearing a woolen bathrobe with a blanket swaddling his withered legs. He was gaunt, hollow-eyed and cancer-ridden: a living skeleton. His hair had fallen out in patchy clumps, especially at the temples. The spots where the electrodes had been repeatedly placed all those years before were perfect roundels of bare white flesh. He was the mirror image of what Senior had been when he was dying of the same variety of cancer. *Peritoneal carcinoma* was the clinical name for it—the very definition of a death sentence. Connie's teeth were pronounced, his visage birdlike. When he spoke, it seemed exhausting to project the words beyond this toothy awkwardness.

Connie feebly cleared the tabletop, removing the slim hardback copy of his father's book of riding instruction and the stub of a gold ballpoint pen that Double Winston had so long carried in the fold of his wallet. Then he plucked the two pieces of broken spur—the same spur Double sheared off in a taxicab door outside the Astor House all those years before. Connie absentmindedly spun the broken object by its neck. The incomplete fork beat the air like the wings of a flying insect.

"Why do we always have to do this?" he asked, examining the shattered pieces as if for the first time. "You know you'll just wind up hooking up a bag."

"Because the human body is intended to take nutrition orally. You can't maintain a decent weight otherwise," Rosalie said through the open kitchen window that looked directly out onto the porch.

With a bit of assistance, the boy climbed onto Connie's lap and started eating from the platter. "What difference does it make?" Connie grizzled. "I'll be dead in a week—if they don't arrest me."

She looked out the window and spied the boy with a mouthful of salmon and another cracker at the ready. "Topi!" she scolded.

"You wait till your Uncle Conrad's done and then ask him if you want some, you hear?"

The boy swallowed hard and sheepishly asked through lips caked with crumbs, "Can I have it?"

"Go on," Connie said, and the young boy wiggled down, snatched the platter off the table and sat quietly on the porch steps devouring the rest.

"You'll be dead in a week if they don't arrest you and you don't chicken out," Rosalie added as she stepped outside onto the porch.

"I'm a coward. As my father used to say, this is one horse I don't need to ride into the ground—I won't chicken out"

"Well, you're my Thanksgiving turkey, and we Pendergasts don't do no scrawny birds, so please eat something. Don't make me feel guilty."

"Later . . . maybe," he said dismissively.

"Try . . . for me?" she asked, gently kissing his forehead the way that a mother kisses a sick child.

"What I really need now is a lollipop."

Rosalie wept quietly as she retreated to the kitchen and opened the door of the refrigerator. Some ten years after she first met Connie at the snack bar of the pigeon rings at Onori, he was in the final stages of his life and she was still an exotic beauty not yet thirty-five. Her tears streamed from joyless black eyes down her high cheekbones and butterfly lips, and she finally wiped them from her chin with the protruding cuff of her tartan flannel shirt.

"Damned dirty white boy," she sniffed.

Connie wasn't at peace with his imminent death, as he hadn't been at peace with his life. He was leaving this world long before he was ready, having never made his mark.

Rosalie retrieved a silicone intravenous bag of clear liquid— parenteral nutrition good for 2500 calories a dose. It was taken directly into the bloodstream via a plastic catheter port installed into Connie's neck. She kneaded the cold stiff bag to soften it and then left it on the kitchen counter to warm. Then she reached into the egg compartment and withdrew the sealed package containing an opioid fentanyl lollipop—a powerful synthetic morphine taken orally in a piece of candy.

He was wasting away in front of her—all ribs and joints and sharp angles. As a registered nurse she had tended plenty of hospice patients to their deaths, but it was different with Connie: They had lived together as a couple four years now, and she had expected to spend the rest of her life with him—perhaps even bear his child. Instead, they had been married by the local justice of the peace only five days prior, standing together with Red Welles in the golden hue of a mild autumn afternoon overlooking Big Pine Lake. She very much doubted that Connie could even stand on his own now. Their feeble union remained unconsummated, as the physical act of love on their wedding day and every day afterword had proved humiliatingly beyond his capacities.

That day had been the first and last time Rosalie would ever meet Connie's grown daughters. Connie's ex-wife even made a brief appearance; bygones would be bygones, as this was a permanent goodbye to the man she'd once loved.

* * * * *

Connie and Rosalie would return to their Port Easton home that evening. They'd settled there because it was the only community near the County where an interracial couple could make a go of it. They would spend one last night in their own bed in the tumbledown gabled Queen Anne on the Post Road that cozied right up to the County line. Come the next evening they would board a night flight to Switzerland. After landing in Zurich they would continue south over the Alps to the semitropical climes of Lugano, the small lakefront city where Connie's mother grew up.

Several states in America had recently legalized physician-assisted suicide, but Switzerland had long since perfected it. Connie had the use of a studio apartment for exactly one day—the next day was reserved for someone else. A Swiss physician would prescribe a lethal dose of the sedative sodium pentobarbital. It would then only be down to the decisive act of Connie drinking a glass of this liquid to end his life.

He had made the appointment on the same day his diagnosis was downgraded to *terminal*. No treatment had ever successfully beaten back his cancer; none of the various chemotherapies had slowed its aggressive growth or provided remission in his malignancies. Soon he would make the journey back to where his own personal metamorphoses began, back to where his memory of a violent act was scrubbed clean and to where he stopped being one person and started becoming another.

The three of them would check into a specially appointed suite at the lakefront Splendide Royale, still the best hotel in Lugano. On this final journey, money was no object. Since his mother died, Conrad Winston III was a rich man. The hotel suite would be furnished as a hospital room, and he would spend his last hours in seclusion with the woman he loved and the little boy who had become like a son to him, waiting for an arbitrary date on the calendar to arrive when he would intentionally cross over from this world to the next.

* * * * *

Ingesting the lollipop made him sleepy, and Rosalie wheeled Connie back inside Sun-Up and laid him out on the day bed in the great room. It was heartbreaking that she could lift him from his wheelchair and lay him out unassisted, arranging his slack body like a marionette in repose. She covered his ravaged frame with a down comforter, drew the curtains and watched him nod off into an opium stupor, to sleep the slumber of the innocent.

LXXIV

Michael King had long since retired from both law enforcement and as manager of the Big Pine Club. His daughters had scattered south and west, and his own Rose had succumbed to cancer only four years earlier. They made him an honorary member of the club and now he spent much of his time socializing there, even taking his meals communally in the great dining hall on the crowded holiday weekends. King still oversaw the spring opening and autumn closing of most the lakefront cabins, and continued to work at his antique furniture repair and restoration, putting in six-hour days in the workshop. National Public Radio blared on the shop stereo—classical music in the mornings and *All Things Considered* in the afternoons. Keeping busy with this painstaking, exacting work was the only way he knew to cope.

Michael King was seventy-six years old now, and his hair was entirely white. The beard he used to grow in honor of his opening day whitetail buck was a permanent fixture; he hadn't been deer hunting in years. The beard grew in its typical shade of sandy blonde and looked preposterous contrasted with all the silver above.

He kept his own house, cooked his own meals and tried to carry on living a version of his old life. His daughters urged him to start dating—to find someone else to share his life with, but he just couldn't bring himself to do it. By all outward appearances he was a well-kept man in that old bachelor sort of way, but internally he was biding his time, waiting for fate to catch up with him.

The former detective continued to be haunted by his inability to resolve the Conner homicide. All these years later, it continued to wake him with a start in the night like a forgotten pot left on the stove. He maintained a set of duplicate files on the case and referred back to them occasionally, hoping to knock something lose in his mind. For the most part though, he never really made peace with the fact that he had completely failed in his pivotal role on the case. Sure, the full resources of the state police had never really been brought to bear and clearly he had been the wrong person to conduct the investigation, but the circumstantial evidence surrounding the homicide remained unchanged, as did his hunch about its perpetrator.

For a man as plugged into the Big Pine Club as he was, the handwritten envelope that materialized in his mailbox without postage one day came as a total surprise. Conrad Winston III was renting his family's old cabin down on the lakefront and requested that King stop by. Enclosed along with the invitation was the business card of an attorney—one George Welles.

LXXV

Michael King didn't know what to expect that golden afternoon as he approached the front door of Sun-Up, but he knew it must be something big and the anticipation made him nervous. Most of us dream our silly dreams, safe in the knowledge that what we wish for—be it success, accomplishment, fame or fortune—are but a kind of delusional mirage well beyond our immediate reach, a Walter Mitty pipedream that will elude us to the grave. *Answered prayers cause more tears than those that remain unanswered*, so the adage goes. Few of us will ever directly confront our dreams come to life, or have our prayers answered quite so directly as Michael King did on that November day. He knocked on the frame of the screen door and waited.

A figure appeared through the darkened mesh. "You're King?" the man asked.

Michael nodded.

"I want to speak with you privately before we begin." The man pulled the screen door open and Michael King noticed the disfigurement on his face. George "Red" Welles continued to live with a prominent port-wine stain, but modern medicine had managed to shrink the unsightly birthmark. Through a combination of plastic surgery, a pulsed-dye laser and creative tattooing, the deformity had successfully been reduced and camouflaged to the point where in the shadowy corners of the darkened study at Sun-Up, it wasn't so very prominent.

Red Welles sat behind the desk and motioned for King to sit down.

"In addition to being a client, Conrad Winston is my best friend—my oldest friend. I advised him against this, but he considers it a point of honor—unfinished business between you two." Welles tossed a set of rubber dishwashing gloves across the desk to him. "You probably don't want to leave your fingerprints on that," he said as he slid the manila file folder across.

King put the gloves on. "What is it?"

"Answers—an explanation of sorts. Call it a confession." There were only two sheets of paper in the folder. The first was a Xeroxed copy of a handwritten letter from Connie's mother, Francesca, dated 1988. In it she detailed the slaying of Kimmy Conner and how Connie had a crush on the little girl and had only intended to deflate the blow-up raft she was floating on so he could paddle out and save her. She wrote of spiriting her son out of the country to evade any pending investigation and then described the destruction and disposal of the rifle and ammunition. She spelled out the number and severity of electroshock treatments administered by her own father, Dr. Heinrich Berger. Finally, she accepted direct blame for the unfortunate outcome: Connie had been an innocent child who had shown a brief instant of catastrophically poor judgment. In the name of protecting Winston Firearms, the family name and her only child she, Double Winston and Nathan Clarke had initiated a cover-up. She accepted her half of the blame—she knew it was wrong, but went along with it anyway. She loved her son, and living with her deceit had become the bane of her existence.

"When the widower died, they found that in the safe-deposit box."

King flipped the page.

"It's a sworn affidavit from Conrad stating that to the best of his knowledge, his mother's statement is true and that he did in fact kill Kimmy Conner with a single shot to the head from .22 rifle at or about 5 p.m. Sunday, September 1st, 1985. He wants to talk to you first, and then he's gonna sign it—I'll send it on later."

"I'll be damned," King said under his breath.

"You're aware he's sick," Red said as he stood up.

"No."

"Cancer. He's terminal, so be prepared."

"I know what it looks like," King said unflinchingly.

"And don't upset him—I won't stand for it. I'm willing to remove you by force if necessary . . ."

King gave him a cold-blooded glance. "Move on me, and I'll

paste the wall with you."

"Just know that I'm prepared to do whatever's necessary."

"Alright, tough guy," King said, shoving the file folder back across the desk. "Let's get this over with."

LXXVI

Red Welles led Michael King down the hall to a closed door and knocked softly with a single knuckle. The door slowly opened and Rosalie stood before them.

"He just woke up," she whispered.

Connie sat in his wheelchair in the corner of the great room, silently staring out the big picture window at the lake. An intravenous bag hung off a metal rack, and liquid nutrition flowed into the port in his neck. There was an untouched cup of tea sitting on the table next to him. He turned from the window to glimpse King, and then returned to the view. Red lugged two upholstered chairs over, and he and King sat down.

"I made tea—Constant Comment. Would you like some?" Rosalie asked.

"Please," King replied.

The three men sat together and stared out the window, taking in the panorama of autumnal burnt oranges and blood reds, and the paddling ducks and loons. Finally Connie broke the silence.

"My grandfather died in this very room—same time of year, same cancer."

"My wife died in a hospice facility—I don't recommend that."

"Then you know . . ."

"I do," King said.

"I wanted to speak with you personally—tell you myself that I honestly didn't know. All those years, I didn't remember anything about it or *of course* I would have come forward," Connie said without turning from his gaze. "I had little flashes here and there but never anything very concrete. It really felt more like déjà vu than anything—I thought it was all just my imagination. People always talked about me in connection with this, and you live with the cloud of something like that hanging over you long enough. . . . Well, I just never even had a single memory of it."

The tea arrived. King took a sip and held the mug, warming his hands, breathing in the fragrant spiced aroma. "I found her on a day like today—Thanksgiving day. Whenever November rolls around it's all I think about."

"I can't imagine what I was thinking."

"Probably that it would be just like on TV."

"What kind of parents give a gun to a twelve-year-old?

"The kind that own gun companies."

"There should to be laws against that."

"There are."

"That's enough. Don't start with him . . ." Red warned.

"What?!" King responded. "I had my own .22 when I was a kid—lots of people did."

"It's alright," Connie chortled, with fatigued humor. "The sheriff is entitled to a little righteous indignation."

"Forgive me if I'm a little slow on the uptake," King began. "But your client finally comes clean and announces *never mind, I guess it really was me after all*—well whoopdee shit! What am I supposed to do with that?! I was the last voice that girl was ever gonna have, and it was my job to nail someone's hide to the barn door! I spend thirty years staring up at the Great Wall of China and now this? I knew it was you . . . couldn't have been anyone but you."

"Well, I didn't," Connie said defensively.

"You're not the victim here—Kimmy Conner is."

"She doesn't like me," Connie said automatically, and then upon further reflection added, "I'm dying; that must be worth a pound of flesh."

"Everybody's gotta' die of something."

"What do you want from me, Sheriff?"

"I want justice—I want you in that box on the hot seat answering for all this. I want you brought before a judge, sentenced and incarcerated for gunning down an innocent child. I want the whole world to know about it and I want your parents to pay the price. . . . But I want all that back then when it still mattered."

"My parents are dead. So is Uncle Nathan. The company's long gone. The Bridgewater plant is a vacant lot. I'm the last link to any of it, and I'm about to be gone too."

"I don't care if they're all dead. Your parents were accessories in a criminal conspiracy: textbook obstruction of justice."

"In five days, if all goes to plan, a doctor will help end my life in Switzerland."

"Most shooters just turn the gun on themselves when they get to this point."

"I'm not a shooter," Connie said unequivocally.

"Well, you sure didn't have any problem pulling the trigger that day! A lovesick brat who never learned to take no for an answer. You got away with murder—manslaughter minimum. No matter what you're suffering now, it sure as hell doesn't fit that crime. You *had* your life, and now you want me to grant you some sort of hall pass so you can sneak off and die in private like a sick dog. I won't do it—and I don't feel a bit sorry for you."

"You know how many lives you ruined?" King counted off his fingers. "Kimmy Conner. Lacey, the mother—botched suicide: overdosed and died in a home. Kevin, the father—pancaked into a bridge abutment driving drunk. Both sisters are all fucked up, and neither can stay sober or married. *Your own* father died an alcoholic all alone up in that fancy hotel. One look at the letter your mother wrote and I can add her to the list. And then there's you—little Mr. Wonderful, God's gift to the County. That makes eight!"

"'For want of a nail, the kingdom was lost,'" Connie croaked.

"Leaving the country so you can go kill yourself on your own terms doesn't strike me as exactly fair—almost like you're getting away with it all over again."

"Dead is dead—you ought to know that, Sheriff. The only distinction is in the *how*."

"I once told your father, it's not the notoriety of a crime or even the punishment that does a man in. It's the inner knowledge of having gotten away with it. How'd it work out for you? Think you might have been better off facing the music back then? It would have been one hell of a mess, but at least it would have been over."

Connie smiled aloofly, "When I get to the place where all the questions are answered, I'll be sure to ask that one. I'm afraid our conversation is somewhat constrained by the time," Connie said, fishing the gold stub of a ballpoint pen out of his woolen bathrobe pocket. "We have a plane to catch tomorrow, so I'll just sign this for you so we can go home—that's assuming you'll let me go home?"

"I'm not a lawman anymore—I have no authority," King said, as Connie signed the paper.

"That doesn't mean you won't have him arrested," Red Welles said. "You've got a signed confession to a notorious homicide there."

"Gee, that could make my whole career," King scoffed. "An arrest would be pointless—there's bugs flyin' around outside that window that'll live longer than you."

"This hasn't been very easy or pleasant for me; I said goodbye to my daughters only this morning. I'm begging you—allow me my dignity. I know it's late, but for what it's worth I *am* trying to do the right thing."

"It isn't worth anything: *It's too late!* What difference does it make *now*?

"It ends it. I did this—now you know it too." The words hung in the air and the room was silent for a good while. "Don't make me die like *that*. I'm leaving—permanently, if you let me."

"I had a lot of dreams about this over the years, dreams about you copping to the whole thing, but it never went like this. There isn't any satisfaction in this." King pondered his control over the situation, and then finally relented. "Fuck it—go. Dead *is* dead. No one else gives a shit about this anymore, why should I? They wanted it buried deep, and I'm sure they'd just as soon it stayed under now. They'll only be too happy to finally close the books on this dead-letter without actually having to spring for the cost of a prosecution."

"I'll send it on once he's gone—you have my word," Red Welles announced.

"*Your* word is meaningless," King said.

"It'll be taken care of," Connie added, holding out his hand, as emaciated as chicken's foot. "I *am* sorry, Sheriff."

King looked contemptuously at the shriveled appendage and then finally took it, lifeless and brittle as a handful of dry twigs.

"So am I," the old lawman lamented. "So am I."

LXXVII

The following spring on the Friday of Memorial Day weekend, Michael King returned to Sun-Up to inspect the cabin for spring opening. The sheets were off the furniture and the house had been cleaned, vacuumed and dusted from top to bottom. All appeared shipshape and ready for another season at Big Pine. He conscientiously went through each room of the house, and when he finally arrived at the great room, he came upon the spot in front of the big picture window where Connie had sat the previous November. There on the table next to the chair was the thin copy of Double Winston's treatise on horseback riding, the two pieces of fractured spur and the short gold pen that Connie had signed his confession with.

King picked up the book and briefly thumbed it. There were diagrams of jumper courses and illustrations of equine conformation as well as images of show jumpers soaring over fences. It was all Greek to Michael King. He closed the cover and there on the back of the dust jacket in black and white was Double Winston in all his glory, his athletic instrument still in its prime, aboard Westley Richards in England. The young bay gelding was back on his haunches, skidding down the legendary ten-foot-high earthen bank on their championship round at the Hickstead Derby.

King picked up the pieces of spur and pieced them together. *This means something*, he thought to himself. Conrad Winston III was dead, having ended his life in Lugano with the help of a Swiss physician the previous November. Why the condemned man chose to leave these items behind at Sun-Up was unclear.

King could try to contact Winston's daughters in Florida to pass on these heirlooms, or he could track down the mulatto widow in Port Easton. The fractured pieces came apart in his hands. These symbolic relics had meaning to only a handful of people—all of whom were dead.

King snatched the gold pen off the table. Red Welles had been good to his word and sent the documents to the local district attorney immediately following Connie's medically induced suicide. The case had since broken wide open in the media, and a former detective on the O. J. Simpson case was already at work on a true-crime book on the Kimmy Conner homicide. A cable network drama was also in preproduction. They all rang up Sheriff Michael King for his unique insights and came away disappointed by the lack of dramatic arc to his story. Of course, he never revealed to them that he was present when Connie admitted to the killing and signed his own confession

It was all finally over, and these token symbols were just so much junk now. King pocketed the 14-carat ballpoint stub as a hard-won souvenir of his endless pursuit of the case, and then carried the book and spur shards out to the kitchen. There was a sealed garbage bag full of soiled rags and used cleaning supplies awaiting disposal, and King opened it, placed the objects inside and resealed it. Then he took the garbage out and heaved it into bed of his pickup truck. It was a beautiful day at the Big Pine Club, the first long weekend of another summer season.

THE END

DISCLAIMER
& BIOGRAPHY

everal historical figures appear in "The Ricochet," and all of them are accurately portrayed, their individual histories plausibly dovetailing with their fictional portrayal, with one notable exception. Dr. Friedrich Meggendorfer was an actual pioneer of electroconvulsive therapy, initially working at the Friedrichsberg Psychiatric Hospital in Hamburg. From 1934 to 1945 he was the director of the psychiatric department at the University of Erlangen-Nuremberg. While he clearly ingratiated himself with the wartime leadership, I could find no hint as to what kind of work he did during this period. I have hung my sinister plotlines on him simply because he was in the right places at the right times. Meggendorfer remains a highly regarded neurologist who made significant contributions in the development of a successful therapy for a wide range of depressive disorders. The only thing Friedrich Meggendorfer is guilty of was working as a hospital administrator and psychiatrist in Nazi Germany. If in writing this tall tale I have inadvertently tarnished a sterling reputation, I sincerely apologize.

* * * * *

lark Stoneridge is a pen name. The author is a lifelong clay-shooter, upland bird hunter and onetime horseman. He lives in the Northeast in a house in the woods with his wife and son. This is his first work of fiction.

47847450R00272

Made in the USA
Middletown, DE
10 June 2019